To all the artist and dreamers

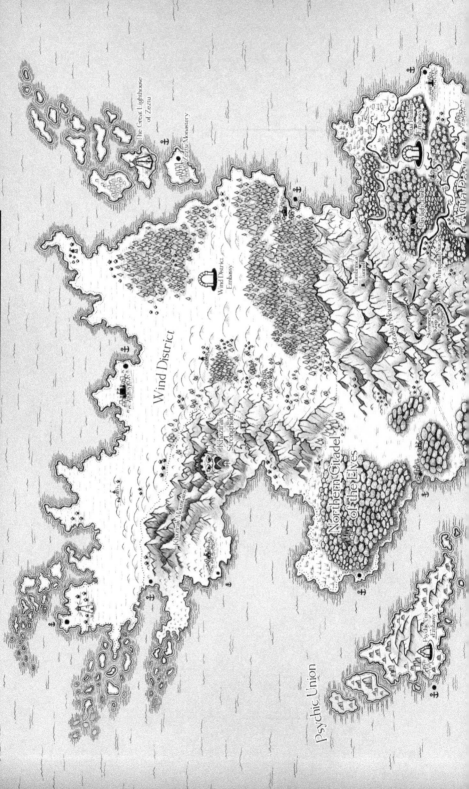

CHRYSANTHOS

The Great Lighthouse
of Zezu

Zezu Monastery

Wind District
Embassy

Wind District

Khazrak
Stronghold

Northern Citadel
of the Elves

Psychic Union

The Floating Isles of the Sound Federation

Sound Federation Embassy

Southern Kingdom of the Elves

Temple of Saldheri

Aimsul Port City

The Cerulean Sea

Karanmasi Port City

The Red Giants

Terra Nation Embassy

Terra Nation

Jiia

Merkabah City

Atakchini Mountains

Sanctuary Mountain Ranges

Igmi Territory

Igmi Embassy

Kia Ora

N

CONTENTS

PROLOGUE

THE WINDS THAT HOWLED THROUGH THE RED DESERT WERE DIFFERENT tonight. There was a bite to the air like static shock—if anyone were around to feel it. In the sky hung a red ring of fire as the solar eclipse moved into place. A solid black disk covered the burning sun.

Along a dried riverbed, a black fissure wormed its way through the layers of clay and stone. At first, it looked to be a craggy shadow, one of hundreds in the bedrock.

It continued to grow.

Spanning long and thin like a twisting black ribbon. Its high-pitch keening, like the screaming of someone in excruciating pain, was lost on the fierce winds. From the blackness, a shining silver light appeared, a curved surface emerging from the center. The object came, oozing into the world, and deposited like a foul seed onto the ground.

The orb dropped and rolled into the hollowed creek bed. The sphere was a solid mass of silver and looked perfectly smooth. It sat there like a glimmering pearl upon the dusty earth.

Behind the sphere, the black ribbon shrank, sucking in stray pebbles as it disappeared. The winds died down and the static energy dissipated. The keening screams faded into a ghostly whisper until quiet hovered over the scene.

Strange, red symbols shifted and faded on the surface of the sphere. A spell undulating, silently reaching.

PART I

THE CALL

VAYLIN

TAP, TAP, TAP CAME THE CLICK OF A BEAK AGAINST THE GLASS.

Vaylin Carina lifted her tired eyes from the endless paperwork she'd been poring over to see a brightly colored macaw sitting on the wooden ledge of her office window. Strange. Most messenger birds used in the Aqua Realm were usually kingfishers of a sort. She checked her Comm Crystal—a small, transparent square of clear quartz surrounded by metal—to see if she had missed any alerts from the embassy or Panthea Central.

There was nothing.

She dropped her pen and brushed loose strands of dark brown hair behind a pointed ear. Hours had passed while she worked on these aqueduct zoning forms, and she had forgotten to stop for dinner. Her stomach growled, confirming its anger at being ignored and demanding food now that it was finally being acknowledged.

Tap, tap, tap came the macaw again. The beady black eye of the bird stared at her through the textured glass, tilting its head. It clicked its beak a few times and made a high-pitched squeal before continuing its tapping, clearly agitated.

"All right, all right, keep your feathers down." Vaylin pushed away from the desk and stretched before striding across the room. The ghostly reflection of herself grew, green eyes and tall body distorting oddly in the glass and eerily lit by the rays of the setting sun. Unlatching the window, she tugged it open.

A whirl of feathers rushed inside, wing tips brushing against her skin and bringing with it the rich smells of earth and ozone of the surrounding jungles.

Immediately, the fog of tedium blew from her mind as she leaned against the window frame and sighed gratefully, relaxing her back and massaging the old ache in her shoulders. Sunlight, fresh air, and the feel of nature around her had always been a balm to her soul. Something she could instantly connect to and couldn't live without. She wasn't sure if that love of nature came from her fey heritage or was simply the result of spending most of her life exploring the vast wilderness of Chrysanthos, training herself in the elemental arts. Mastery of the elements and more was expected from an Elite Guardian of Panthea.

Vaylin proudly called herself one after succeeding her mentor, Jessamine Solance, in the position three moon cycles ago. She was now the one who oversaw the protection of the Aqua Realm Embassy, its inhabitants, and the ancient portal that sat at its heart, leading to Panthea Central, the capital city of Chrysanthos.

The macaw cawed again, loud, and startled Vaylin out of her revery. It had landed on her desk and paced across the zoning forms, ruffling its wings, and kicking various items off her desktop as it went.

"Stop that," she hissed, summoning a draft of air to keep an alchemical globe from shattering on the floor, its soft yellow aura twinkling as it halted midair. She guided it back to the desk on a current of air and cautiously approached the bird.

Its black eyes widened when she placed a gentle hand along its back. Her heart swelled with the bird's fear and urgency. What little fey magick she did possess allowed her to communicate and influence common animals.

"Shh, brave one. You are safe now." Her stomach knotted as she soothed the bird, reassuring the animal by emitting her fey magick in subtle vibrations from her palms.

The bird calmed noticeably, feathers deflating like a punctured kelp pod and standing still enough that she could finally remove the rolled papayra leaf from the sleek leather casing tied around its foot. The bird must have flown here from a remote region of the Aqua Realm to require such a large animal to deliver a message. Her Comm Crystal—an invention from Fabien Prince, the Elite Guardian of the Igni Territory—only worked within Panthea Central and its six embassies stationed in each country. If anyone wanted a CC to use within Panthea or its embassies, they had to register a new crystal into the grid network. Fabien wasn't her favorite of the Elite Guardians, but his invention five years ago had revolutionized Panthea and reaffirmed its longstanding reputation as a powerhouse of magick to those who whispered about its crumbling influence in the world. Considering CC antennas and signaling devices were being installed in cities around Chrysanthos, the influence of Panthea was thriving and as stable as ever.

A flattened disk of red clay with shining bits of mica sealed the papayra message. Prying it off with a long fingernail, she unrolled the scroll and read.

Then reread.

Vaylin's hand shook as a heady rush of adrenaline pumped through her system.

There was a threat in the Aqua Realm.

An actual threat. She would finally have the chance to get out and do something more than sign zoning forms.

Her heart beat loud in her ears as excitement and apprehension rose inside her. If she could handle this task smoothly, it would be her first unofficial rite of passage as a guardian. She was determined to do a good job. Looking between the bird and the letter, Vaylin dropped the message on her desk and grabbed for her CC, tapping on the clear screen until she found the right contact and dialed.

In the dim light of the alchemical globe, the auburn ink of the message stood out boldly against the faded tan of the papayra:

"A stone of starlight has come to Mingalla. It brings with it creatures of darkness. Our shaman protects the stone. We protect him. The creatures do not stop. They must not get the stone. They come at night, killing us. We cannot stop them. Help."

2

FAUX-CATION

VAYLIN

VAYLIN HELD HER CC TO HER POINTED EAR AND WAITED.

"Yeah, what's up, V?" asked the cool voice of Sloane Kintore, Vaylin's second in command at the Aqua Embassy. Sloane was two heads shorter than Vaylin and looked more like the average fey than Vaylin ever would, who stood nearly six feet tall with long, muscular limbs. Her hair was short, black, and cut on a sharp asymmetrical angle that covered her dark blue eyes. Sloane's skill in the elemental arts were on par with Vaylin's, but she had less experience with the higher levels of magick like vibration control and transmuting psychic energy to create lightning and energy shields. Nevertheless, she was a fierce opponent who blended earth and water magicks in deadly ways.

"Where are you?" Vaylin tried to inject a note of calm into her voice as she walked to the open window and peered over the grounds. Alchemical globes flicked on to illuminate the walkways and manicured lawns of the embassy.

"Having second helpings of dinner. Something you should be doing if you're this cranky when calling me," Sloane said in a drawing voice.

"I'm not cranky," Vaylin snapped.

Sloane laughed smugly and crunched over the CC. Vaylin's gaze traveled in the direction of the eatery, a collection of various food stalls that made staple dishes from all around Chrysanthos. Vaylin ground her teeth as her stomach grumbled audibly. She covered it with a freckled hand, trying to muffle the sound.

"Was that your stomach I just heard, or are you actually growling at me?"

"I'm not growling at you."

"Then that *was* your stomach, and you should really get your ass down here so we can talk and eat instead," Sloane said as if it were the most obvious thing in the world.

"I can't come down. I got a message from a nuca on the outskirts of the Yinara region. There is something happening out there, and people need our help," Vaylin said.

"Wait, what? Back up a sec and tell me everything." The crunching stopped, and Sloane's voice changed from lazy to serious. "The Yinara region? That's at the base of the Chazakül Mountains in the west. It'll take four days of trekking through jungle to get there, assuming we don't have any interference from the fey."

"I realize that, which is why we need to leave tomorrow, or tonight if possible. The smaller the group, the better. I think you and I could manage fine, but just to be certain, we should bring a few paladins with us, ones skilled in speed and stealth."

The paladins were an ancient order created to serve and protect the portal network, which they believed was a sacred place of energetic ley lines and cardinal magick. Vaylin always saw them as divine soldiers whose lives were forever bound to Panthea once their oaths were taken. They aided all the Elite Guardians and the gatekeeper in various tasks, and there was an active guard always stationed at Panthea Central.

"Tonight?" Sloane said in a flat voice. "You're joking, right? We are not leaving until we have an actual plan in place. Have you even contacted anyone from Panthea Central about this yet?"

Vaylin flushed. "Nothing about this case violates the jurisdiction laws of the Aqua Realm or surrounding countries. I don't need to contact them every time something minor happens within my own realm. That's the whole point of being a guardian now, isn't it?"

"I'd say it's about not being an idiot."

"Well, that's why I have you by my side."

"It's going to be that bad?"

"I don't know." Vaylin rolled her eyes. "There aren't many things that would be able to withstand the two of us to start with, let alone a squad of paladins at our backs."

"True," Sloane conceded. "Did this message hint at what type of creature was attacking them?" Her curiosity sounded piqued for the first time.

"No. It only mentions something about a stone of starlight and dark creatures following it."

"Read it to me."

Vaylin read the message. Sloane didn't say anything.

"It sounds worse when read out loud," Vaylin admitted.

"Uh, yeah. I'd say so."

A flicker of doubt ignited in Vaylin for the first time since receiving the message. "I can contact Panthea Central and let them know what I'm dealing with. But this is my first *real* mission within the Aqua Realm. It's the first opportunity I have to make the calls without Jessamine or Hearthfire watching over me. I want to prove my strength to the others. To myself."

Still no answer. Vaylin imagined Sloane's eyebrows raised in speculation and knew she was contemplating it.

"The paladins will be overkill, and if you're with me, we'll hardly break a sweat. Try to imagine this as a two-week vacation instead of a mission," Vaylin wheedled.

"Vacations don't entail trekking through jungles, sneaking around aggressive fey territories, and dealing with whatever the eternal elements have to throw at us."

"I beg to differ. To the right person, what you described is a perfect getaway."

"You are insane. Might I add that not all of us were born in the jungle. It's different for you. The forest bends to your will."

Vaylin grinned. "There are some good things that came from being part Elder."

The Elder race were the offspring of the great Sun Warrior and

Moon Maiden eons ago. This included the races of high elves, fey folk, faeries, pixies, goblins, gremlins, and a menagerie of wild and mystical animals scattered throughout Galindi, the world they all inhabited.

Sloane groaned. "Fine. I'll go. But you're not going anywhere until I see this message for myself and we contact Aldwin Hearthfire and tell him what's going on."

Aldwin was the Gatekeeper of Panthea Central and protector of the portal nexus. This magickal network of portals was created a thousand years ago during the birth of Panthea and those given the title of Gatekeeper were responsible for its protection and ensuring it's magickal integrity. Portal magick was very finicky and could collapse entirely if tampered with.

"Deal." Vaylin's grin widened. Shuffling noises in the background meant Sloane was making her way over. Vaylin loved Sloane, and her loyalty as a friend was exactly why she'd chosen her to be her second. "I knew you'd agree. One more thing before you head to my office."

"Yeah?"

"Can you *please* bring me some food?" Vaylin crossed her fingers, hoping she didn't sound too desperate. She should really keep a small pantry in her office for times like these.

Sloane snorted. "I'm way ahead of you on that. Your hanger is worse than anything we're about to deal with."

"You're the best. See you soon."

3

THE DAYLIGHT DASH

VAYLIN

Days into the Numinbah jungle, Vaylin led Sloane and the paladins through the most dangerous part of the Yinara region. This section of the border touched upon the fey territory for a fifty-kilometer stretch called the Daylight Dash. The Daylight Dash could be managed in a single day with a steady pace.

Woe to anyone near the demarcation line after nightfall, as the fey folk slept during the day and could see clearly in the dark. They were all mischievous and clever, ensnaring anyone who unwittingly crossed their path with traps or riddles, often ending in some type of debauchery or death. Fey had unpredictable temperaments.

There was an alternative, safer route toward the south, but the detour would add five days to the trip.

Five days they didn't have.

Vaylin was willing to risk the shorter route, trusting the fey would be sleeping all day and her party would be swift enough to avoid unwanted detection. The journey had gone according to plan so far, making steady progress west across the Numinbah jungle to where the Mingalla nuca was.

A stone of starlight has come to Mingalla. It brings with it creatures of darkness.

She had read the message so often she had it memorized, repeating the sentences like a prayer. *A stone of starlight.* What did that mean?

Some crystals like Danburite and Celestite were connected to angelic realms, allowing the user to communicate to higher beings or channel angelic power like wind, rain, and fiery brimstone. Human magick was a neutral magickal source, meaning it could adapt and blend with almost any other type of magick in the world. With a little effort, most humans could use any element that spoke to them. More advanced magick users learned how to access realms of angelic or nature magick, which vibrated at different frequencies that were accessible to humans with practice. Human magick could pull from these sources, using it to amplify their own power or as a component for complex spells and enchantments.

The creatures do not stop. They must not get the stone.

Were these creatures protecting it? If they'd arrived with it, they might think the people in the nuca were a threat and that was why it was attacking them. Especially if there was a shaman involved, whose magick was different from Vaylin's and, therefore, unfamiliar and more complicated to control. He might have cast protection wards or defenses to stop these creatures. She might not be able to aid or undo his enchantments if it required a lot of nature magick.

Shamans went through an initiation right called a walkabout, where they consciously entered the world of Dreamtime, a strange land that connected to Galindi and paradoxically existed outside it too. Only Shamans could access it. Dreamtime was the source of raw nature magick—the magick of water currents, erupting volcanoes, and shifting tectonic plates. During the shaman's walkabout, their human magick underwent permanent fusion with raw nature magick, blocking his access to all other sources and granting him enormous wells of nature magick. It was said to be painfully transformative. Not everyone survived the merging.

Vaylin could access nature magick for short periods of time, but it drained her magick and her body took a magickal beating afterwards. The key was to focus any accessed magick through oneself, becoming a conduit of sorts and not allowing the accessed power to remain in the body to inevitably destroy it.

Flesh and bone could not contain the might or will of nature.

They come at night, killing us. We cannot stop them. Help.

Did this mean the shaman's power wasn't working? Was the stone sent to Chrysanthos to get away from these creatures? A stone of starlight... Perhaps it came from the skies. If so, these creatures must have been powerful enough to follow the stone through space and time to get it.

That was absurd.

She hadn't read a single report of comets or falling stars in the Aqua Realm. Astrological events were always witnessed and reported on. She paid close attention to the movements of the cosmos for many reasons, the main one being that many of the healing herbs and plants in her apothecary relied on planetary alignment or moonlight for blooming, pollinating, and other medicinal remedies.

They must not get the stone.

Vaylin felt the pressure of the message on her heart.

She could do this. She had trained with Jessamine under every type of weather until she could switch from element to element seamlessly. She had proven herself in the guardian trials, where she'd finished first and placed top scores in the grueling obstacle course that spanned a week through the arid deserts of the Igni Territory and rocky canyons of the Terra Nation. The strategy scenarios she had to solve were perhaps her favorite part of the guardian trials, set in the Wind District and presided over by the monks of the Zeztu Monastery. She was particularly gratified in seeing Oberion Watson, the Elite Guardian of the Wind District, watching over her trial and looking impressed against his will while he examined her solution to the scenario conundrum.

She could do this.

They entered the Daylight Dash at first light and jogged the first quarter of it before slowing to a walk. At this rate, they would clear this stretch of border well before nightfall. The expedition had a run in with a tree nymph halfway through when they stopped for a break. A paladin unknowingly strayed too close to the nymph's twig hatchings while sneaking off to go to the bathroom. Vaylin heard the commotion and shot toward the fallen paladin, whose robes were tangled in twisting roots, before anyone else knew what was happening.

She approached the nymph confidently, using her Eucalypta staff as a walking stick instead of a deadly magickal tool of elemental wielding. The boulder opal atop was the size of a chimera's egg and gleamed with fiery rainbows of color, streaks of dark ironwood mixed between the crystal lattices.

The nymph seethed in primal fury, before recognizing Vaylin as kin and one of Elder lineage. She tilted her head, assessing Vaylin for a tense moment before releasing her hold on the paladin and withdrawing into her den of trees.

Vaylin bowed to the vanishing creature and focused on the magickal essences of the plants around her, encouraging them to grow. Delicate little flowers in shades of pastel pink, white, and yellow blossomed around the nymphs' den, and Vaylin knew the creature would allow them a swift retreat.

"I told you," Sloane muttered a few minutes later as they hurriedly walked away. "The forest bends to your will. I could have summoned those same flowers, and I would have been attacked the moment the nymph sensed my magick, assuming I'm a threat."

Vaylin laughed, ignoring the way Sloane shook her head in disbelief.

Vaylin's magick was unique, of course. She had the neutral energy of human magick and Elder blood. Her mother was human and had died shortly after childbirth and there was no father to raise her in the nuca she was born in. Her pointed ears and other parts of her body were distinctly Elder, giving her some clue to her potential abilities. Something about her mixed heritage enhanced her magick beyond most humans, making it bigger, brighter, more alive than what she could sense in others, even Sloane.

"You *are* a threat. You would have attacked first and maybe asked questions later. Most living creatures don't want to fight. They want to be left alone and live without our interference."

"Pfft, I'll offer the next thing trying to bite my head off a bunch of flowers and see how far that gets me."

"If it's the hangry version of me, that might just work." Vaylin nudged her second in the ribs.

"Oh right, you vegetarians eat flowers, don't you?" Sloane placed her hands on the hilts her dual swords as they walked on, several paladins trailing behind them.

"I believe in sustainable living. Plenty of things eat flowers. It's not that uncommon."

"You're impossible," Sloane said, resigned. "I guess you wouldn't have become the herbalist you are without eating all those plants and flowers."

"Is that actually a compliment?"

"Don't get used to it. You're only getting one because I'm on va-ca-tion." She spoke the last few syllables deliberately.

Vaylin smiled and sent a prayer of thanks to the eternal elements for a friend she could be herself with. She and Sloane had met when they were both ten and entering the Aqua Academy of Magick, instantly forming a bond that had remained unbreakable after twenty years of friendship. Her recently acquired status of Elite Guardian had changed how people treated her, and it got tiring, wearing the mask of diplomacy for everyone all the time.

With Sloane, deep in the jungle, Vaylin felt like she could free herself. She let the self-imposed restraints of control loosen around her and gave in to her Elder nature, connecting and assimilating with the forest in a way humans never could.

It felt like exercising a muscle seldom used. Tight and constraining at first, but as Vaylin's consciousness expanded and wrapped around the environment, she felt flares of magick where life was and sensed the plants stretching toward the sunlight. From the snakes looping around branching high above to the scurrying of rodents through the detritus of leaves, she heard everything. Felt everything.

A twinge of unease.

A shift from safety to danger happened instantly.

"Look out!" Vaylin gasped at the same time she heard the tightening of bow strings all around.

Instinct had her dropping into her elemental powers and forming a shield of yellow flame woven with a matrix of psychic energy around the expedition. Her shield was so precise it hovered like an aura around each person, protecting them and flexing with their movements.

An arrow whizzed toward her forehead, and Vaylin watched, chin raised, as it disintegrated upon contact.

4

WARNINGS

VAYLIN

"MOVE, AND WE SHOOT," SAID A RASPY VOICE TO VAYLIN'S RIGHT.

A group of fey emerged from the shadows, perfectly camouflaged against the jungle foliage with mottled skin in different shades of brown, green, and blue. Some had animal-like features like little horns or antennae, while others had wings like dragonflies' sprouting from their backs. The bows and blades they carried were hewed from obsidian and rough-cut wood, clawed fingertips gently caressing the weapons as they pointed them toward the expedition.

"Isn't it past your bedtime?" Vaylin asked in a bored voice. "I thought we had at least six hours of daylight." Raising a hand to her eyes, she looked up, where the sun was directly overhead. She used this moment to surreptitiously count twelve of them, outnumbering her eight, but not by much.

"Tricksy human." A female fey with clouds of white hair and skin the color of a clear, blue sky sneered. She had dragonfly wings and pulled another arrow from her quiver, notching it to the bow. "Thinks she can tiptoe through the woods without us noticing?"

That one shot first. Vaylin directed her gaze toward her.

"Sneakin', stinkin', filth." A wild-looking male perched on a tree branch. His black goat horns curled from a nest of hair full of twigs and leaves. "Smelled you from a mile off."

Vaylin frowned and sniffed her armpit, pulling a face. "My apologies. The luxuries of a bath house aren't an option out here. I promise our hygiene routine is normally quite thorough. Let us be on our way so we may freshen up a trifle and smell less appalling to those upturned noses of yours."

The insult of her words mixed with the polite manner in which she delivered the sentence. A few of the fey grinned at the jest. Good. They thought she was amusing, which made them less likely to fight. Fey liked their games, and Vaylin didn't mind playing if it meant getting out of here sooner.

"Don't push them," Sloane muttered next to Vaylin. Her twin daggers of Mithralite flashed in the light as she stood in a defensive position. "If we attack, they will have a hoard on us by the time we reach Mingalla, and we'll have to divert into the mountains."

"Clever words from a clever human," said the blue-skinned female with the bow. "She knows this is our jungle, not yours."

"No one will be attacking anyone today." Vaylin's voice carried. "This jungle belongs to all the free folk in these lands, including us."

"We are the ones who live in this forest, not you." An angry-looking male held a javelin of carved wood, similar in length to Vaylin's own staff. "You should leave."

"I am Vaylin Carina, Elite Guardian of the Aqua Realm. The law of the land decrees that the forest belongs to all," Vaylin repeated in a commanding tone. "Let us be on our way. We do not interfere in your affairs. I ask for the same courtesy in return."

The blue-skinned female lowered her bow, wings drooping slightly. "What is your purpose for being here?"

"We have come at the distress of a nuca in the western region of Yinara. We hope to find what is ailing this nuca and banish it henceforth," Vaylin said calmly.

A murmur went through the fey.

. . .

"Don't listen to them, Cloudspun," the horned male growled. "Why should we believe you? Humans are liars. There is something lurking in the jungle, and they are the only strangers we've seen in three turns of the sun."

Fey could not lie, an attribute Vaylin always found intriguing and often exploited when interacting with them. Maybe the fey knew what they were coming up against in Mingalla and could give her more information.

"Has something been attacking you?" she asked cautiously. *They come at night, killing us. We cannot stop them.*

"Not attacking, no," Cloudspun said. "We sense shadows moving through the lands, causing imbalance westwards. But we do not finds it."

"An imbalance?" Vaylin thought fast. "If you knew there was an imbalance, why have you not helped? Are you not caretakers of the forest?"

"We do not meddle in the affairs of humans," Cloudspun said. "This imbalance is from a human nuca. It is a human problem, not fey."

Vaylin should have known better than to ask, having evoked that right moments ago. "Do you think this shadow is the cause of the imbalance?"

"The result or cause of, we do not know," Cloudspun said with a small shrug.

Sloane cast Vaylin a weary look. Things like wraiths and ghosts existed in Chrysanthos. They had their own little magicks and could sometimes cause disturbances. But fey knew how to deal with spirits better than most humans. It didn't make sense for a spirit to be haunting the forest if it caused the fey to go on such high alert.

"Can you tell us anything about this shadow?" Vaylin was desperate for anything helpful.

"One moment we are tracking it, smelling its rank odor and nearly on top of it. The next, it vanishes, and we see not hide nor tail of anything. Not even the cold imprint of a spirit apparition." Cloudspun's wings went perfectly still.

A chill went through the circle of fey, and Vaylin nearly shivered herself, her mind turning over the types of creatures that fit the description. Spirits didn't usually smell, meaning it must be a corporal creature that had the ability to shift or change its appearance at will, maybe even its substance. Vaylin couldn't think of anything off the top of her head, and it was too late to go back and search the library for answers. They had to go forward.

"But you're fey," Sloane said, confused. "You see better in the dark than any of us combined. How could you not have found it yet?"

The fey grumbled and hissed at Sloane, insulted at the unkind reminder that something was roaming free in their territory and they couldn't find it. Vaylin checked that her shield was still in place in case one of the fey decided to shoot an arrow at Sloane for her rudeness.

"There are many places for shadows to hide, girly," the horned male cooed. "Why don't you show us how it's done with your fancy embassy tricks and capital training."

"Enough, Buckthorn." Cloudspun's skin morphed from light blue to the dark shade of midnight, and her wings rustled, making the clicking of a cicada. "We do not want to incur the wrath of Panthea, especially when they might rid us of this shadow once and for all."

She unnotched her arrow and returned it to her quiver. Most intelligent life in the forest knew who the Aqua Embassy was and what they were capable of. Most intelligent life also knew it benefited them to be on good terms with the embassy, despite their pride.

"Go," Cloudspun said coldly. She stood on her branch and gestured to the other fey to lower their weapons and move on.

They did so, and Vaylin nodded silently toward the paladins, who repeated the gesture.

"Be warned, daughter of the Aqua Realm. The imbalance in the west is a strange magick. Tread carefully. We will await your return for news."

"Thank you." Vaylin bowed.

Cloudspun bowed in returned and, in a flutter of wings, vanished into the canopy. The other fey withdrew quickly. All but Buckthorn, who gave Sloane a wicked, mischievous grin before disappearing silently amongst the branches.

Sloane's expression was stone cold and unamused. She stood in a fighting stance and her magick was thrumming down the Mithralite daggers, ready to burst into flames at Sloane's will.

Vaylin nudged her a little, trying to get her to loosen up so they could be on their way. "Come on, we need to keep moving."

Sloane reluctantly sheathed her daggers, and Vaylin dispelled the shield around them in a sweeping gesture, not at all reassured by what they'd just learned.

5

VAYLIN STRIKES

VAYLIN

Something was terribly wrong. Vaylin's apprehension grew as the small expedition neared the Mingalla nuca. It was far too quiet for the Numinbah jungle. No birds, no screeching animals from the treetops or rustling underfoot. The vibrant color of the wilderness had leeched to dull gray. Trees had turned to withered, black husks, and plants dissolved to dust when brushed. The temperature had dropped, and for an impossible moment, Vaylin thought the falling ash on their clothes was snow. Her mind and body were on high alert as they approached Mingalla and the silence pressed like a physical weight upon her.

No wonder the fey hadn't come to help. It looked as though the land was dying, and Vaylin's heart ached at the destruction around her.

They approached the edge of the nuca, waiting and watching for threats before entering.

It was devoid of movement.

No bustle of daily life or livestock grazing. Only a subtle keening that caused the hairs on Vaylin's arm to stand up.

"What do you think?" Sloane whispered.

Vaylin's eyes were closed, and she was throwing her magick into the earth and toward Mingalla, trying to sense life forces.

"We need to get closer to find out more. I can't see anything beyond the huts, I think everyone is in the center of town. Can you hear that noise?" Vaylin, with her pointed ears, wasn't sure if only she could hear it.

"Yeah. I doubt any animal or human can make that sound."

"I agree." Vaylin pulled her magick back and motioned for the others to follow her.

Each turn in the road felt like a sick surprise, knowing and not knowing what they were about to see. The keening became louder with every step toward the center of the nuca. Blood splatters bloomed across the path like red flowers next to severed and exsanguinated human limbs. Some were still attached to shields or the broken halts of spears.

"That's sick." Sloane's daggers had a thin edge of fire running down the blade.

Vaylin nodded grimly.

"Keep an eye out for any remains that aren't human," Vaylin called to the paladins. They looked tired but ready, standing there in mud-stained robes tied with blue sashes. She should have brought more than six of them. At least Hearthfire knew she was here, and she was grateful she'd listened to Sloane and sent him a message.

They crept their way through the nuca, the keening getting louder. It hurt her ears and effectively distracted her from her surroundings. The noise had reached such a pitch it made her eyes water. When she turned the corner and scrambled backwards at what she saw.

Before her were the dead bodies of every person in the nuca. They all wore similar clothing and sat in a circle, hands clasped and crusted with flaking brown blood. Empty eye sockets stared upwards, mouths frozen in silence screams. Their pale skin was stretched tight over protruding bones, like they had been sucked dry.

Gorge rose in Vaylin's throat as she struggled to comprehend what she was seeing. And not seeing.

Beyond the circle of dead villagers was a jagged black crack in the earth. It had its own gravitational pull and sucked on the air. The life of this place. Its gaping void was hypnotic. Fathomless. The noise was deafening, and Vaylin felt off balance. Tilting toward that darkness. How could a magickal chasm like this form here? It didn't make sense, and the magick of the thing felt wrong. Terribly wrong.

Hands grabbed Vaylin from behind, forcing her away from the crack. The pull of the thing. She was so stunned by the noise, disoriented by the bodies of those poor people, hardly noticing where they were going until they reached the edge of the nuca.

Dead forest around them instead of dead people.

It was her fault.

The ringing noise of the crack faded with every ragged breath.

Vaylin willed herself to stay calm and figure out a plan. She'd thought they would get here in time. She'd thought there would be people to save.

"We were too late," Sloane said, defeated.

"What was that thing?" A younger paladin looked like he might be sick.

"Never felt anything like it," another said. They all breathed heavily and looked to Vaylin for answers.

Her mind was a jumble of thoughts as she stuttered to speech. "We-we need to find out more about what happened here. Did anyone find or see something to explain the blood or the body parts?"

There was awkward silence as the paladins looked between one another.

"Er—no I didn't find anything," the younger paladin admitted.

"Nor I," said another in a small voice.

"Right," Vaylin said. "Understandably, we are not going anywhere near the center of the nuca again. Let's pair up and search the perimeter for clues about what the hell is going on. The message I received from Mingalla said creatures were here and attacking. Find evidence and meet back here in thirty minutes. Go slow and be careful. We aren't staying anywhere near this place after nightfall. I don't care if we have to camp at the edge of the Daylight Dash and risk our necks with the fey again. I'll take them over whatever this is."

They all nodded and paired off. Sloane predictably stood next to Vaylin as they entered Mingalla once more.

. . .

"There." Sloane quietly pointed to a winding path that led away from the nuca, mostly hidden with undergrowth. A trail marker stood there with strange markings on it.

"A shaman's place." Vaylin pushed the foliage aside and followed the path, the cold increasing with every step. Charms hung around the doorway and low-slung tree branches that surrounded the cabin. "Wait here."

"Are you crazy? You can't go in there alone."

"I will be fine," Vaylin said. "Cover my back and wait for me."

"But—" Sloane tried to protest.

Vaylin raised a hand for silence, flashing a warning look. "Now isn't the time. We need to figure out what the hell happened to all the villagers before the same thing happens to us."

Sloane looked pissed off and worried at the same time. "I'll be right outside the door. If I hear anything, *anything*, I'm coming in after you."

Vaylin nodded and entered.

A shaman sat in the center of the room. He appeared old, heavily tattooed with tribal markings, and white dreadlocks stained red and yellow wrapped around his head like a beehive. He was deep in his enchantment, eyes completely obscured by black. Thousands of tiny, pink crystals made a circle drawn around him. Rose quartz.

Vaylin's eyes fell upon another stone, directly in front of the shaman, outside the circle.

It was a clear crystal, double terminated with little, red stones across the surface. It looked to be made of quartz, but it couldn't have been. The energy signature coming off it was immense, like nothing she had ever felt from a quartz before. Her focus intensified on the crystal, and she was overcome with the urge to reach out and touch it.

Her magick flared defensively, and she was jolted back.

Avoiding looking at the stone, she made her way to the circle of crystal and peered at the shaman. Vaylin held her palms up, feeling the air in front of him, trying to decipher his magick.

He was muttering, and there were deep cuts in his arms from elbow to wrist. Blood slowly pooled at his knuckles, mixing with a darkness coiling up from the ground. His fingers looked like as if they were dipped in black ink that dripped upward.

Fear bubbled in her chest as the shadows wormed their way into the shaman's skin.

Wrong. Wrong. Wrong.

She could feel the magick here, sense the essence of nature leaking from the shaman—mixed with something full of malice and unending hunger.

A dark, twisting magick flickered toward her and moved with razor-sharp edges. It cut her magick when she tried assessing it, causing her to recoil. She silently contemplated what to do, her anxiety ticking up a notch. The urgency of the situation pressed on her as she realized her only living source of information was bleeding out in front of her.

She had to do something. Even if it was only one person she saved, she had to act.

A plan came to her, born on a reckless thought as she assessed the not-quartz and the shaman. If things went wrong, she would never hear the end of it from Sloane. What other choice did she have? She was an Elite Guardian, and it was her responsibility to protect these lands and the people within them.

Vaylin took a long breath, harnessing her magick and readying. Power emanated in her core, a steady force waiting and eager to do her bidding.

She was Vaylin Carina of the Aqua Realm, and she was here to protect *her* people. This precious land.

"Get ready," Vaylin said through the door, not giving Sloane a chance to stop her.

"Ready for what?"

Vaylin didn't answer as she brushed a minuscule area of pink crystals away from the circle with the tip of her boot.

The enchantment broke violently. A rush of air hit her from behind and brought with it wooden bowls, charms, and debris from the shelves. She lost her footing and summoned her own counter-gust of wind to avoid falling on the shaman and that black magick.

Gasping like a man saved from drowning, the shaman came out of his trance and peered wildly about, confused at the sudden change. Clearly terrified, he stared between Vaylin and his hands, the darkness below them now growing at an accelerated rate. The blood flow from his arms increased, and the blackness creeped up his fingers, snaking thick tendrils up his wrists and forearms, anchoring him to the spot with an unyielding force. The shaman grew paler, skin hanging in wrinkled folds as he somehow aged and diminished with each second.

Shit. The shaman had been casting an enhancement of containment, with himself as the object to bind the darkness.

And she had just set it free.

Vaylin tried to pull him free using another air current. He didn't budge. Maybe she needed a solid element—earth—to move him. She grounded her magick beneath her and called on the earth to crumble, part, or turn to sand. Anything to free him. When her magick got close to him, it was cut apart by that razor darkness, undoing all the magick she wove.

"You have come," the shaman said haltingly, "too late." He gasped in pain as the blackness crawled up his elbows. "Death. Is. Here."

Vaylin stayed close to him but dared not cross into the circle. Time was short. Her heart pounded.

Stay calm and think straight. Remember your training.

"How do we stop this?" she said, loud and clear. "How can I help?"

The shaman continued gasping in pain. "Take it. The world is breaking."

"Take what? Please, tell me how to stop this." She tried to focus over the rushing, sucking noise of the darkness but couldn't. It was born of the same energy of the crack in the center of town.

The shaman screamed in pain and gritted his teeth. She growled in frustration as he was pulled forward, his arms sinking into that strange nothingness.

"Take it," he gasped, muscles straining in his neck.

His bones cracked as he fought against the force binding him.

The blackness reached for that strange crystal with a black tentacle, and she felt an irresistible desire to protect the stone. She pulled on the air again, the not-quartz flew toward her, and she caught it with one hand.

The world slowed.

The stone pulsed. Ice and fire surged into her bones, nerves, and every filament of her being.

This was power. A raw magick she had never felt in all her years of magick. Moving and shaping her own magick.

Heat bloomed in her palm as the stone in her hand shone like a star.

Vaylin looked at it, wondering in a dreamy way. She was in control of herself—and not. Transported enough she could fly and yet anchored deeper into the earth than her magick ever reached.

She moved into a warrior's stance, raised her arms, and pointed the stone at the shaman. One command echoing in her mind.

Protect.

Threads of silver light shot from the crystal in both directions, molded itself around her arm. The sensation tickled slightly as this alien power channeled through her and twined around her own magick. Every cell in her body felt alive.

The winds picked up around her with the speed of a tornado, and the walls of the hut exploded outward, collapsing in clouds of dust.

Sloane covered her face and ducked as the doorway blew over her. Dried plants, jars of herbs, wooden sticks, collected animal skins, feathers, bones, and unknowable treasures scattered in every direction. Some of the items got sucked into the black mass, vanishing as it made contact.

"Vaylin?" Sloan said, a desperate urgency in her voice.

Vaylin wanted to answer and reassure her second but couldn't make her mouth move.

A white light erupted from the crystal point and washed over the shaman. The black ropes started to disintegrate, and he relaxed fractionally. The skin underneath looked withered and dead.

Sloane stood slack-jawed as Vaylin wielded the stone.

Vaylin focused the light over the shaman's chest and toward the ground at his hands, imagining covering up that darkness permanently. There was a shuddering in the earth, and a bolt of black energy barreled toward her through the opening in the circle.

She rolled away from the attack, rising into an effortless crouch. The light from the crystal flickered, and her concentration broke.

The shaman screamed, and in those few seconds, more black tendrils reattached themselves. The sinuous darkness that had reached for Vaylin retreated into itself and toward the shaman, ready to consume its captor.

Vaylin raised the crystal again, preparing to try, but her arm was impossibly heavy. Her vision filled with spots, and for a terrible moment, she thought she was going to retch. The shaman was now up to his shoulders in what looked like black quicksand. The pain across his face was too much for Vaylin to bear.

She knew in the look he gave her that there was no hope for him.

He knew it too.

"I welcome death," he croaked.

From behind her came the sound of string tightening and an arrow releasing. Sloane's aim was true as the arrow hit in the center of his forehead.

The shaman stopped struggling, and the blackness finally swallowed him whole. Vaylin had enough sense to pocket the not-quartz and push the scattered pink crystals in the dirt along the line of the circle. There was a flash of pink light as it was resealed. Nothing was left but a small, black pucker on the ground, in the exact spot where the shaman had sat a moment ago.

"Vaylin?" Sloan asked. "What the hell was that?"

Vaylin sat there, eyes fixed on the black scar in the earth. Anger and grief warred inside her. They had failed this nuca.

She had failed this nuca.

Fighting against the urge to cry, she composed herself enough to say, "I don't know," and hated herself for giving that answer.

6

PLANS

VAYLIN

VAYLIN SAT IN THE OFFICE OF THE GATEKEEPER OF PANTHEA, GAZING AT the faces of two men as she finished her tale.

"Do you think the circle will hold?" asked Aldwin Hearthfire, Gatekeeper of Panthea, protector of the portal nexus, and leader of the guardians. He was three quarters of a century old but didn't look it. Vaylin had never seen him looking this serious before. His pale purple eyes were sad, and the furrow between his eyebrows seemed to deepen. His head was freshly shaven and there were faint wrinkles around his face.

"You believe me?" she asked tentatively.

"Yes. I believe you," he said calmly. "In all the years I have known you, you have never been one to lie or seek unwanted attention."

Vaylin sighed in relief and relaxed minutely in her chair. Her failure in the jungle was a fresh wound, and she'd worried he would reprimand her somehow for what had happened. Or worse—dismiss her from the Elite Guard.

"Do you think the circle will hold?" he repeated.

"For now." She sat up a little straighter. "I left Sloane Kuro to monitor the area with a group of paladins. If something happens, they will send word immediately."

"Excellent. I'm sure the paladin guard will suffice for protection while we focus on the task at hand. Oberion, your thoughts?"

Oberion Watson had been in the office when she had requested the meeting with Aldwin. As the Elite Guardian of the Wind District, he was bound to find out about this sooner or later. Vaylin would have hoped for later, as he always scrutinized her to the point of being uncomfortable.

"We have had no reports about a similar occurrence like this happing in the Wind District," he said simply. His blue-gray eyes were skeptical. He was older than her with wavy brown hair and trimmed facial hair around his jawline. "Are you sure it was a true shaman you found?"

"He had the sacred tribal tattoos on his body that every shaman is given when they begin their walkabout into the spirit realms." Her words were steady as she spoke even though she trembled slightly. "I have witnessed the ancient ritual in the Numinbah forest, but I have never seen or *felt* anything like I did in Mingalla. I could feel his magick, holding the darkness back and resisting it. The magick stung and was able to cut through my own like nothing. It was an unnatural power that does not belong in our world."

Oberion stared at her curiously, eyebrows raised as if there was a lie in her story and he was determined to discover it. Even though she was worried about her own skin, it annoyed her that he looked at her that way—so full of doubt and contempt.

"How likely is it that *he* was the one who caused this crack to begin with?" Oberion asked. "Was it some sort of spirit magick that he was channeling? Perhaps something that *you* would be unfamiliar with?"

"Oberion," Aldwin warned gently.

Vaylin spoke before she could think, her voice full of venom. "Spirit magick requires precise timing and planet alignment, along with other cosmic events occurring in conjunction with the spell or summoning itself. The shaman cast a containment spell with himself as the source of binding. He wasn't trying to summon magick from the underworlds or some other hellish realm."

"With the cost of this protection being his life?" Oberion asked.

"He chose to do what was best with the time given to him. We are facing something unknown and dangerous. None of the elements had any effect on this darkness, and that whole area of the forest is dead. If there was a threat of that darkness spreading, I understand why he risked his life," Vaylin said quietly.

All three of them were still.

"Is it likely that the entire nuca would sacrifice themselves?" Oberion asked.

Typical. The people who lived in the jungles were connected to the land in ways that many city-dwellers—like Oberion—weren't. He would never grasp the true tragedy of seeing the forest dying. Or if he did, maybe it only mattered if it was happening in his district.

"That's exactly what they did." Vaylin could imagine the desperation and pain the Mingalla people felt in those last days. "I think they tried to fight the darkness and couldn't. Rather than fleeing, they stayed behind to hold the enchantment in place. The shaman did what he did for the people, the land, and the life of the forest. He died for *his* home."

She held Oberion's gaze, remaining silent as she gave him a stern look. He assessed her, that cunning mind of his turning over and examining every word, every detail.

"I agree with Vaylin," Aldwin said. "They have given us precious time and a warning to heed. We must not take it for granted. Let us see the crystal the shaman was using to hold the enchantment."

Looking away from Oberion, Vaylin rummaged in a leather pocket on her belt and pulled out an indigo velvet pouch. She opened the bag gingerly and placed the stone on the desk. "I've been calling it the Mingalla stone, since I don't know what it is exactly."

It was the size of her hand and, in this light, such a light pink it almost looked clear. Smaller bits of rounded red crystal were dusted across the surface, glittering in the light of the alchemical globes that hung from the ceiling. The stone emitted a soft radiance that glowed slightly in the darkened room.

Aldwin and Oberion's intake of breath was audible.

"I've never seen a crystal look this way without someone directing magick through it." Eyes wide, Oberion reached out a hand for it.

Vaylin felt an odd, possessive sensation in the pit of her stomach when he picked up the crystal to examine it. "At first I thought it was a quartz with some sort of garnet formation on it. It looks similar but doesn't match the energy signatures of either stone. It's a strange specimen. It feels...alive, sort of. If you watch it long enough, a light, or pulse, moves within the stone. Almost like a—"

"Heartbeat." Oberion finished her sentence. He turned the stone over in his hands, and a flash of light moved within the crystal.

"Precisely," she said. The stone in Oberion's hand twinkled. "It looks like its trapped underwater, and yet, it is not an enhydro stone. I cannot sense any water within it." She watched closely as Oberion passed the stone to Aldwin. "I don't know where the shaman got it. The message I received said it came to them. But how? There are no records of quartz veins, mountains, or deposits in that area, and it's remote enough that the nuca didn't rely on trade for its resources."

Aldwin weighed the stone in his palm experimentally. With a small tap behind his ear, a monocle flicked into place. He ran long fingers down the termination points and held the crystal inches away from his eye. Vaylin watched him apprehensively, not sure what his magick was sensing. After a moment, he sighed heavily and returned the stone to the table, tapping his monocle that vanished smoothly behind his ear.

"What are you thinking?" Oberion asked.

"I do not know what this stone is or where it came from. Why can it attract or eradicate this dark energy? Did this darkness occur naturally or by other means?" Aldwin steepled his fingers. "Whatever this stone is, it is connected to the anomaly in Mingalla somehow. We need more information and to seek out anyone who may be able to help us solve this problem. We also need to figure out if these ruptures are spreading across every region in Chrysanthos."

Vaylin cast a weary look in Aldwin's direction. She felt like he could sense her unspoken fear. "That darkness is sentient and came after me once I used the stone. Our elements did nothing, and only by summoning this stone's magick were we able to escape. Many people will easily fall victim to this power if it spreads."

Aldwin contemplated the Mingalla crystal again. "I think there is a solution to every problem if one can open their mind to see all possibilities. Put aside your fears, Vaylin, and focus on your actions. We do have magick that can combat this darkness, but that does not mean we should use this stone recklessly. If this stone has the energy to effect the cracks, logic dictates that it might also have the ability to seal them."

Vaylin mulled it over. She had been so absorbed by the attack and her failure in her first mission as an Elite that she hadn't considered this anomaly might be spreading.

"What if we approach the dwarves about this stone? They might know something about it and be willing to help," Oberion proposed.

"The dwarves?" Vaylin knew there were several dwarven strongholds but had never interacted with them. The Aqua Realm jungles were full of wood elves, fey, faeries, and sprites. All of which she had much more experience with than grubby old dwarves.

"Yes. The dwarves," Oberion repeated flatly. "Charming folk, most of them. I am acquainted with the northern Stronghold of Khazirak and have met the khan several times. They are a private lot who keep to themselves and were very hospitable during my visits. You wouldn't believe the treasures they dig up regularly. Of course, they find their fair share of gemstones and ore, but sometimes they unearth fossilized shells or water-dwelling leviathans with vertebrae the size of this desk. They could help us identify the Mingalla stone and maybe give us an idea of its origin and what it does."

Aldwin's eyebrows were raised, and he nodded at the potential of this idea.

"You do realize that any dwarf may not be very hospitable toward me, right?" She gestured toward her pointed ears.

"The elf-dwarf contention is something I never understood." Aldwin's purple eyes fixed on hers, and there was a kind reassurance there. "I trust that you've had sufficient practice in diplomacy over the years and have enough skill to peacefully negotiate this situation."

"Yes, sir." She hated that Oberion was witnessing this and lifted her chin a little higher.

"Good. Try to see this as a chance to create a different relationship than the ones your ancestors created for you," Aldwin said optimistically.

Oberion looked smug.

Vaylin gaped at him. Was she just supposed to walk into a dwarven stronghold with a basket of muffins on her arm and ask nicely to see their khan, hoping he would believe her story and take this anomaly situation seriously? All the diplomacy in the world wouldn't be enough to prepare her for that.

"Oberion's suggestion has merit," Aldwin continued. "Our libraries here at Panthea Central are extensive, and it will take time to conduct research for this specimen. Especially since you will be taking it with you."

"Right. And what can I possibly say to the dwarves to convince them to help?" she asked.

"I'm sure you will figure something out," Aldwin said.

"The dwarves might be more open to negotiation than you realize," Oberion offered. "They delight in the idea of glory and notoriety. They crave bragging rights, and facing dangerous deeds serve to bolster their name and reputation with each other. Pitch it to them that way, and I guarantee they will say yes."

She squinted at him suspiciously, not sure if his advice was worth heeding.

"Hmm," Aldwin said quietly. "If this is a naturally occurring anomaly, it might affect them too. We would be arming them with knowledge and a way to protect themselves, should they fall victim to one of these cracks."

Vaylin sat there, listening, exhausted, and dreading the prospect of what lay ahead. She ran a hand over her eyes at the thought of being underground. Not being able to feel the sun on her skin or the wind through her hair would be torture. The last thing she wanted to do was to go to the Northern Stronghold of Khazirak, by herself, and ask an unknown dwarf khan for help. This was going to be a nightmare.

As if sensing her apprehension, Aldwin said, "Oberion is well versed in dwarven etiquette and will be there to help you along the way."

He offered the Mingalla stone to Vaylin, who sat there, stunned.

Like hell she wanted Oberion's help.

"Err—" she stammered, trying to think of a polite way to dismiss his offer. It was bad enough that she was leaving the Aqua Realm to deal with dwarves, darkness, and discovering the truth behind an unknown crystal.

But to do it with Oberion watching her every step?

"What?" Oberion asked. Until now, he'd hung back and watched Vaylin squirm. Now that Aldwin wanted to rope him into this, he didn't seem too keen on his own idea.

"I—I can handle this by myself, Aldwin," Vaylin said. "Maybe I can pull Sloane from Mingalla and have her join me instead. Oberion can send me whatever information he has through the CC, and I'll have the whole journey to read it."

Aldwin's expression was almost pitying, and she was sure he saw through her feeble attempt. When he spoke next, his words were gentle but stern.

"Vaylin, his experience with the dwarves will benefit this cause greatly. The cost for our country is not always what we expect. This is an opportunity for you to grow into your power and position with grace. Do not waste it." He faced Oberion, who sat with his arms crossed. "You are the perfect liaison for this mission. Under your guidance, I trust that the dwarves can be persuaded to aid us and, given the chance, can accept Vaylin for her Elder blood. This is a chance to strengthen the bonds of friendship on all sides and between one another. Even you, Oberion, can benefit from this if you open your mind and loosen your judgements." Aldwin's pale purple eyes never left Oberion's. "The pair of you will go together and represent Panthea as a united front. I will, of course, oversee and handle any issues that might arise in the Aqua Realm or Wind District while you are both gone. I am tasking both of you with the responsibility of this."

Oberion gave a resounding sigh and lowered his shoulders. "Fine."

"It's decided, then. You and Oberion will leave tomorrow morning from the Wind District Embassy and head to the Khazirak Stronghold together," Aldwin said with finality. "Time is of the essence, and we need to find answers. As always, the portals of Panthea are open to you, but they will be little help once on the road."

Vaylin's throat was tight despite herself, and she nodded once at his words. There was no way out of this, and she had to keep it together. She could do this. For the people of Mingalla, she could do this.

"Excellent," Aldwin said brightly and clapped once. "I will make the necessary correspondences with the other Elite members about what has happened and where you two are going and why. I can also alert Khan Kharak to your arrival. That will give me time to touch base with the wanderer too. Perhaps he has seen these ruptures and will have some information for us. Have either of you received any word of Marshall's whereabouts lately?"

"Henrietta Scyth of the Sound Federation last saw him along the coast of the Floating Islands," Oberion said with a shrug. "No one has seen him since."

"Our wanderer has a knack for showing up exactly when he needs to," Aldwin said.

7

TO WANDER TOO FAR

MARSHALL

A ROAR WENT UP THROUGH THE CROWD AS TWO MEN WRESTLED IN THE middle of a dirt arena. Actually, it was one giant man and one giant elf. The man—Baxter Marshall—looked like a grizzly bear with thick, tan arms covered in coarse, black hair. Avon, the elf, was similar in size, all lithe muscle and skin the color of black coffee. Each wore a pair of rough-spun trousers and had no weapons. This match was about strength, not magick.

The crowd was on their feet as they cheered and jeered the fighters.

"Get him!"

"Come on now. He's only human!"

"Pin his arms, Marshall!"

"I've got gold on this, Avon! If you lose, you owe me!"

"Squirmy bastard! Get 'em!"

The banter continued from the circle of onlookers. The man and the elf grunted and kicked up dust around them.

Marshall lunged for Avon's knees, and Avon spun out of reach, quick as a snake. The elf used his momentum to pivot and grab Marshall from behind, pinning both arms to his side. He strained to break Avon's grip but couldn't. Avon pulled the man off his feet and slammed him into the ground.

The crowd roared and groaned in equal measure.

It knocked the breath from Marshall, and he gasped as Avon's full weight fell onto him, arm wrapped around his windpipe. Eyes streaming with dust and dirt, his whole head pulsed in time with his heartbeat as he strained to fill his lungs with oxygen.

There was no referee here to call the shots. The match ended when one yielded or knocked the opponent unconsciousness.

The southern elves worshiped the god called the Sun Warrior, who delighted in displays of physical prowess. Most of the southern elves had the strength of twenty men to a single elf, unlike their northern cousins who were less brawny and more brainy.

"Get up, Marshall! You can't stop now!"

"Almost there, Avon! Hold him! *Hold him!*"

With a tremendous lurch, Marshall dropped one knee and jolted to the left, breaking Avon's grip. He grabbed the elf's arm and flung him over his shoulder, pinning Avon to the ground and twisting his arm backward. Marshall kept pulling until there was a loud pop and Avon screamed as his shoulder ripped from the socket. Dirt plastered Avon, and little pebbles were stuck to his skin from being pressed into the ground. Marshall had Avon's one arm behind his back, the other tight to his side.

"Yield," growled Marshall in his pointed ear.

His breath was hot against Avon's skin, and sweat dripped off his face as the southern sun beat down on the ring, heat radiating up from the dry-packed earth. He was so close to winning, he could feel it.

"No!" Avon struggled to break free, but between Marshalls weight and his damaged shoulder, it wasn't successful.

Marshall closed his arm around the elf's throat and squeezed.

The struggle was going out of Avon little by little.

Marshall spoke again. "Do you yield?"

Avon squirmed feebly, practically turning blue before choking out, "Yi— yield."

The man released his hold and rolled off sideways. Marshall lay on the ground panting hard and distantly hearing the cheers of the onlookers. He couldn't believe it. He'd only agreed to take on the elf when he was good and thoroughly drunk the night before. Someone in the bar had called for a match to test his human strength against the elves. He remembered thinking that it wouldn't be too difficult and after shouting a bold statement of confidence and drinking enthusiastically to his impending victory. Considering the ground was still tilting by the time the match started, it brought a weak sense of pride that he managed to win.

Avon rolled away from him, gingerly holding his arm to his chest as a medic elf rushed to his side. He looked at Marshall as the medic fussed over the elf's shoulder.

"Good match," Marshall said to his opponent. He felt dizzy and needed water, but that was no reason not to acknowledge a worthy opponent.

"Get it over with." Avon's eyes were golden slits as he looked upwards, focusing on the blazing sun.

The medic elf adjusted his arm into position and, in one fluid gesture, slid the arm back into place. Avon sat perfectly still the whole time. No sound escaped his lips. Only a grimace of pain crossed his features as he adjusted his posture.

"You fought well," Marshall said again.

The crowd milled around, collecting money from bets won or grumbling softly at bets lost, forfeiting their coins.

"As did you." Avon's voice was as smooth as his skin, and his eyes assessed keenly. He reminded Marshall of a hawk. "I never thought I'd lose to a human. It would be a great honor to fight alongside you in battle."

He bowed a little after his declaration.

"Well—er, thanks." Marshall didn't know what else to say. He was taken by surprise by this notion. He considered this match to be nothing more than the consequence of a drunken promise. Not an actual test of valor. He couldn't imagine a scenario where the two would fight alongside each other. There hadn't been a war in Chrysanthos for over three hundred years. "Sorry, about your arm."

"Don't be. I'm guessing you don't get to exercise your true strength with most humans."

Marshall chuckled at that. It was true. He fought to survive his whole life in Merkabah, the second largest city in Chrysanthos, and quickly learned the limits of human bones. He had felt it right before he'd dislocated Avon's shoulder and didn't stop himself like he usually did. It felt good not to hold back the reins of his strength.

"Are you coming back to the citadel tonight?" Avon seemed to be taking his defeat in good stride.

Marshall hesitated. He had been on the island of the southern elves for weeks now and needed to make his way back to the mainland. Sending regular correspondences to Panthea Central was something he frequently forgot to do. He meant to leave yesterday and stopped at a pub for one drink before hitting the road. One drink led to several and, thus, landed him in this current affair.

There was something ambiguous about the title Wanderer and what exactly that entailed. He never knew where he would end up in Chrysanthos and what he would do once he got there. Which was the point. He just kept moving and helping people along the way. Gathering information and watching for threats rising in the lands.

Although, this little wrestling match had the likelihood of drawing unwanted attention to him. Not that he usually worried about his actions, but he technically wasn't supposed to partake in competitions, illegal or otherwise. His title and skills as wanderer gave him an unfair advantage in those types of events for common folk with simple magicks. His skills were on par with those of the Elite, hardly fair for anyone not trained in the capital. Not only that, his association with Panthea also meant he shouldn't be caught doing illegal activities and risk getting the politicians involved in his actions as wanderer. Marshall cherished his freedom and ambiguity above all other things.

That internal clock was ringing. It was time to get moving again.

"No, I'm hitting the road by tonight and heading back into the Terra Nation on a midnight ship out of here. I should've left days ago," Marshall said wistfully.

"You are a strange human." Avon gave him an appraising look. "But one I can respect. Until we meet again, Baxter Marshall."

"Err—you too." Marshall held out his hand to grasp Avon's in the typical human fashion.

The elf, however, bypassed the hand and grasped his forearm below the elbow. It was odd and strangely comforting. It felt more genuine somehow, and after nodding once, the two broke apart, walked away in opposite directions.

Marshall walked along the road at twilight. The time where shadows stirred from slumber and stretched across the land like a rising tide. He was heading west to the Amsu Port, and from there, he would make his way to the embassy within the Terra Nation. He always felt a sense of peace and deep reflection when he left somewhere. Like being exhausted and completely rejuvenated at the same moment.

The southern elves were a friendly people, and Marshall felt at home here. They laughed easily and enjoyed feasts, fighting, and healthy competition. The horses bred on their island were the envy of all mainlanders, and the blacksmiths were masters at the forge, rivaling any dwarven weapon or piece of armor. The southern elves spent most of their time in the training grounds and were steadfast warriors trained in the arts of war and strategy. They were wild in their own ways and would intimidate anyone with half a brain if faced in battle.

The northern elves were not unskilled nor unfriendly. They were quieter by nature and had an austere disposition that made them appear *loftier than thou*. The Northern Citadel and its people favored the healing arts, stealth, archery, and the subtle arts of alchemy and poisons. Many northern elves were known for their psychic abilities and cosmic connections that came from their goddess, The Moon Maiden.

There was an old tale about the Sun Warrior and the Moon Maiden being the first of the Elder race. Did the Moon Maiden run from her betrothed? Or did they love each other in secret and run away? Didn't the Sun Warrior mortally wound her and the Maiden cursed him?

He couldn't remember the specifics, and what did it matter anyway? He was human after all, and Elder tales were always too fanciful for his liking.

The one thing he made sure to remember was that the two cities were often at loggerheads with each another and the relationship between the two had deteriorated over the centuries.

The world was still tonight, and Marshall was deep in thought about the Elder races and ancient feuds. Red and tan cliffs rose around him, and thickets of dry grasses rustled in the light wind. The stars were bright against a darkening sky, and bands of clouds rippled sickly yellow around a half moon.

A tumbling of stones rolled down the cliff far off.

Marshall spun around, eyes probing the environment around him, trying to discern the source of the noise. It sounded like the trickle of stones naturally falling and resettling, which was perfectly normal.

Still, the hair on his arms rose, and he didn't trust the sudden darkness.

The rockslide had alerted him to his surroundings. He was in the gully between two walls of boulders and cliffs, forming a small canyon with him at the bottom. He'd come through here weeks ago, under the blazing sun without a care in the world.

Tonight, the place felt ominous. His gaze traveled up the rock walls. Ledges jutted out here and there, casting darker patches of shadows along its surface. He could double back now and find a way around. Or magick himself up and over the ledge if he really wanted too. Neither seemed desirable, and he felt a pang of annoyance at himself for considering changing his plan. This hesitation was silly, and his imagination was getting the better of him. He had faced countless trolls and hags in the mountains, fought saber cats, and hunted the Alizarik Bison across the plains of the Terra Nation.

He would keep going.

He debated conjuring some fire, which was unwise. Light would only blind him to the night, and flame would mark his location to any prey. Sometimes it was better to become one with the shadows.

There is nothing out here, Marshall. Get a grip on yourself.

Nonetheless, a wanderer didn't travel the world and not listen to their gut if something felt off. No matter how hard he tried to shake this feeling of being hunted, he couldn't.

Maybe some elves sought retribution for the match earlier? That was plausible. He summoned some magick to amplify his hearing. He'd learned long ago how to notice the subtle vibrations of living creatures and the tells that gave away their movements. Sound magick was one of his favorite subjects of study at Panthea Academy, and he was a natural at it.

There was something nearby all right, but it kept shifting in and out of focus. An animal of some sort then?

Marshall ran through a mental list of creatures on this island and which ones posed a threat to him. Mountain cats could be a problem, especially the saber-toothed ones. His mind flashed to a southern elf he saw in the city who wore those long, curved teeth gauged through his earlobes. The idea of fangs like that piercing him sent chills creeping over his skin. But those beasts usually lurked further inland toward the mountains, not along main roads like this one that led to the coast.

He lengthened his strides and was nearly halfway through this stretch of canyon. Once he was on the other side, he would feel much better. It was a struggle controlling his pace, wanting to run but not give way to a chase if something was stalking him.

Tapping into his sound magick again, he probed the surroundings as best as he could.

A pitch throughout the air muted all else.

Creatures of higher magicks emitted complex vibrations. If he was dealing with a minotaur or sphinx, things were about to get messy very quickly.

Another shifting of rocks, closer this time, caused Marshall to shed his rucksack entirely and, in one swift motion, pull a battle axe from his back. Heart pounding, he turned this way and that, unable to see anything moving toward him but certain there was another presence here.

From above on the cliff edge, a shadow unfurled itself from the skies. It was of a denser darkness than the night around him, and Marshall's feet felt slow and clumsy as he got them beneath him.

"Burning hells," he said aloud.

He thought he was seeing a dragon. A real, live, dragon.

Fear and elation thundered in his chest as he stood there. He had never seen a dragon in the wild. In all his imaginings, he'd never envisioned himself as the prey in this scenario.

And yet, something was off.

The creature in the sky was no dragon, not even a wyvern. This thing was distinctly smaller and looked grotesquely human.

Its wings were membranous and leathery, talons protruding from points along the wing joint like sinister scythes and silhouetted by moonlight. Its body was skeletally thin. Its arms and legs hung below as it flew circles over Marshall. It landed on a canyon ledge nimbly, claws digging into the stone as it peered down at him.

Marshall stared into the face of the monster.

Pointed bat-like ears stuck out of spikey fur, and its mouth was full of thin, pointed teeth. The thing tilted its head sideways, and red eyes considered him, sniffing the air as tendrils of drool dripped from its mouth.

It raised its head and screeched into the night.

The pitch was so deafening that Marshall dropped his axe and grabbed his head at the assault on his eardrums, his sound magick still amplified.

He barely had time to register his mistake when he felt a rush of air and dodged awkwardly in a random direction. The murderous creature slammed into the wall, claws gouging out foot-wide craters of rock. It recovered quickly and crawled up the canyon using hands, feet, and talons on its wings like a spider.

This was going to be difficult.

Marshall ignored the pain in his ears—it was second to survival—and he was upright with both hands on his axe again. Summoning fire, he opened his mouth and belched a glowing ball of flame at the predator.

Bright tongues of gold danced into the night, and the creature recoiled from the light and heat, crawling back over the lip of the canyon.

Marshall lost sight of it, and the fire he'd used had temporarily blinded him. He would have to rely on his other senses to aid him.

A tremor in the earth alerted him to the monster's new approach.

It ran on all fours with its wings pulled over its back and head, talons facing forward like spears. Its mouth gaped open and shrieked into the night, but Marshall could not hear it. He roared more fire in return, and the monster turned its head in discomfort but kept true to its course.

He swung his axe seconds before the beast collided with him. The two went down in a tangle of embers, blood, and claws.

Pain slashed across his forearms and chest as he landed backwards, the monster pinning him and biting the axe shaft. Its jaws yawned above him, a thousand teeth glinting in his face as he forced the thing away from him. A cold, sticky feeling coated his hands, and he wanted to retch from the putrid smell of its gore. He forced the beast behind him with a current of air and psychic magick.

The wounds across his chest and ribs burned.

The creature twitched, trying to skuttle around with one spectral wing hanging off its body in bloody tatters, severed at the shoulder blade. He laughed wildly, and in that split second where he thought danger had abided, the creature lunged unexpectedly.

Marshall tried to kick backward and screamed in pain as his ankle twisted and the beast sunk its teeth into his calf. His vision blurred, and all the heat left his body in a *woosh*, accompanied by sucking and slurping noises.

It was drinking his blood. He felt weak, dizzy, and paralyzed.

He tried conjuring fire. Nothing happened. No magick came to him.

Marshall vaguely registered that its wing was knitting back together as it used his life force to regenerate its limbs.

With one last effort, he tried to squirm backward, foot useless underneath him, numb arms slipping in sand. For the first time tonight, panic seized him at the failure of his own body.

How could he let this happen when he was so close to defeating this thing?

He realized then, with awful clarity, that he couldn't stop it. This was how he was going to die.

The beast continued sucking, and death was swiftly coming for him.

There was brilliant flash of white light, and a feeling of lightness spread throughout his body before darkness swallowed him whole.

THE BROTHERS ARGUE

ALDWIN

ALDWIN APPRECIATED THE SPECTACULAR VIEW FROM HIS APARTMENT'S balcony while he waited for Abraxas to arrive. The gatekeeper's tower was in the northern part of the grounds, high above the rest of the capital and a perfect lookout over the Vale of Panthea. Mists cast by the waterfall in the west glittered, alluding to the raw magick that floated in the air here. Two giant, wooden water wheels circled endlessly, supplying hydroelectric power to the capital from the waterway that ran under the city. For all the metal and rock that formed Panthea and its buildings, it lacked no grace in its architecture and uniqueness of character. After the portals were constructed ages ago, people from around Chrysanthos coalesced here to learn magick. The place grew into a landscape of influences, adding bits and pieces from the different cultures to the buildings and the various neighborhoods. A patchwork city had formed around Panthea Central, separated from the grounds and portal nexus by a thick stone wall protected with paladins day and night.

The domed glass building in the middle of the grounds held his attention, metal beams connected and spread like delicate spiderwebs across the open-air ceiling, glittering with multicolored panels in the early dawn. It was the portal nexus, filled with the six archways of

Panthea Central. Beautiful stone monoliths with carved geometric patterns and a variety of crystals inlaid into the columns, creating elegant designs that glowed and pulsed with the natural energy flowing and powering the portals. A low hum permeated the air, the steady heartbeat of the capital.

Nothing in their world had the ability to do this. It was what made the portals so unique.

Aldwin's mind wondered over the space around him, the space he'd sworn his life to protect. He had nothing but respect for these magickal wonders, wanting to be the steward of this place, not master.

His adopted father would have called him a fool.

Aldwin didn't enjoy this thought, but he couldn't help it. Today was the anniversary of their adopted father's death and it always brought about unpleasant memories. He hated how his brother Abraxas insisted they celebrate it year after year. Aldwin had only conceded since he knew how important it was to Abraxas and it was one of the few times a year that they saw each other. Aldwin hoped his younger brother wouldn't fixate on the past too much and felt naive for considering the possibility. Even in recent years, Abraxas had a hard time believing the truths Aldwin tried to lay before him about the man who'd adopted them. That he was abusive and Mundas had purposefully driven a wedge between them, hammering at it bit by bit to manipulate and control them. Abraxas refused to listen, choosing to blame Aldwin for Mundas' death.

He wouldn't be wrong in that assumption.

The past was the past, and Aldwin couldn't go back and change it. Not that he wanted to either. He only wanted to mend the tenuous bond between him and his brother. Too many years apart had let the bitter silence between them fester. Aldwin had missed his brother and decided to bridge the gap between them. Mundas was not going to ruin anything else in his life.

There was a knock at his door, and Aldwin crossed the living room to open it.

Two men stood there. One was the captain of the paladins, Rowland Blackwell, a broad-shouldered man who reminded Aldwin of an old lion. He was a respected gentleman with salt-and-pepper hair who always carried himself with honor and dignity.

The other was Abraxas Mundas. He was equal in height to Aldwin, black hair hanging loose around his shoulders and posture relaxed. He could be handsome and something about his looks reminded Aldwin of the well-known musicians in the sound federation with their metal piercings and tight black leathers. While Aldwin had pale purple eyes, Abraxas's were a dark amethyst. There was a hollowed look in his face, and a thin scar across the side of his neck poked up from his collar. The sight of it sent a chill through Aldwin as the memory of that night tried to surface. Aldwin pushed down, down, down.

"Brother. And Captain Blackwell, this is a surprise." Aldwin embraced Abraxas, who stiffened under his brother's touch and reached up to pat his back unenthusiastically. A poor attempt but still an attempt. "Don't act too excited, Brax, or the captain might not believe we are brothers."

The captain stood there in amused silence, watching the lackluster exchange.

"That wounds me, brother. Just because I don't respond in such an exuberant manner doesn't mean I don't enjoy my visits here. Today is a somber day after all, made none the better for your captain's insistence on following me here. Not that I'm ungrateful for his company, but the stoic silence the entire way was a bit dramatic." Sarcasm dripped from Abraxas's words.

"As Captain of the Paladins, I have every right to escort or follow those who appear on these grounds." The captain cast a scornful look at Abraxas. The man had expressed dislike for him after previous visits.

"Oh? What an honor it is that you unexpectedly *escorted* me here then. I didn't realize how important I am to warrant such attention from the infamous Captain Blackwell." Abraxas had a glint of mischief in his eyes. "I guess being the brother of the gatekeeper does have some perks to it."

"Enough," Aldwin warned.

Captain Blackwell stood there, glaring, as Abraxas smiled wolfishly.

"I'll be down the hall, sir, should you need me." The captain squared his shoulders and cast a disgusted look at Aldwin before leaving.

The door clicked shut behind him, and Aldwin's eyes locked onto his brothers'. Abraxas held the gaze unflinchingly.

"Glad to see we've started on such good terms," Aldwin said pointedly, leading his brother into the sitting room that adjoined the balcony lookout. It was full of plush chairs, bookcases, and the floor was dark, polished wood. The mantel above the fireplace was carved from green marble, with fresh logs poised in the center waiting to be lit. On a sideboard sat an assortment of liquors, decanters, and crystal glassware.

"Did you know he was going to follow me here?" Abraxas accused.

"No, I did not. I had told him you were scheduled for a visit here today but did not instruct him to do anything further," Aldwin answered.

Abraxas huffed.

"Something to drink?" Aldwin walked toward the bottles, hoping to distract.

"Of course." Abraxas crossed the room and walked out onto the balcony, observing the capital imperiously. "If Captain Blackwell is that easy to offend, maybe you ought to find someone else for the position."

"Rowland Blackwell is one of the most respected Captains of the Paladins that this age has ever known. He has been at Panthea Central for over fifty years and has never once failed in his duties to protect these grounds and the surrounding city." Aldwin approached Abraxas with two glasses of golden liquid. "A mead from the Fall Region of the Floating Isles. Would you like yours chilled?"

"If that's your recommendation, yes," Abraxas replied.

Aldwin squeezed the glass slightly, and in an instant, frost flashed over surface of the drink, effectively chilling the liquid inside. "Personally, I find a small splash of water does wonders to this spirit too."

"Since when did you become such a connoisseur in alcohol?" said Abraxas swirling the contents of his glass.

"It's hard not to pay attention to the things you eat and drink. I like knowing where it comes from and who the people are that harvest from the lands to our homes. It's a fascinating process, and the knowledge is worth more than gold, if you ask me."

"How very perceptive of you."

"To family." Aldwin raised his glass to Brax's.

"To Maximus Mundas," Abraxas answered.

Aldwin hesitated before clinking his glass to Abraxas's. He had meant the cheer for them, not Mundas. He didn't want to raise a glass to the man who had routinely beat and threatened them.

"You think it would get easier, and it never does," mused Abraxas. "I know he wasn't the best to us, but he inspired my love for technology. It's hard not to think about him most days when I'm tinkering on something."

Aldwin was sympathetic toward his brother's emotions, even though he didn't feel this way. As tragic as it was losing the only adult in their lives, Mundas had been an aggressive and demanding man, oscillating between creative calm and fury at his failures. Aldwin often felt it was a blessing when he died, not a sorrow.

Now wasn't the time to say that.

Abraxas's eyes were trained on him, observing his posture and expressions. "Dad always said your silence was equal to your intelligence and that I should learn from you."

"Did he now?" Aldwin highly doubted Mundas had ever said anything like that about him. "I was under the impression he hated my silence and was convinced I was plotting against him and ruining his experiments on purpose."

"Nonsense." Abraxas waved a hand in dismissal at the apparently ridiculous notion. "He was always eager for your help. Those were some of my happiest memories, you know. When all three of us were working together on a piece of machinery. I loved when he asked me to grab him tools or crystals. It feels silly now."

Aldwin didn't say anything, letting his brother reminisce.

"What's your favorite memory of Dad?"

Abraxas had a way of scrutinizing Aldwin and made him feel like he was being unjustly interrogated. He hated this game and had more and more difficulty answering these questions as they got older. Not wanting to fight with him, Aldwin decided to be polite and answer.

"Umm." Aldwin cast his mind about. "When we would scavenge for parts and scraps in Merkabah's junk yards."

Abraxas grinned sheepishly. "Your favorite memories are of us rummaging around in the trash?"

"We were young. It always felt like we were looking for buried treasure. I didn't understand half the stuff Mundas talked about, and finding odd junk got us exploring and away from him," Aldwin said defensively. "Can you blame a kid for having fun?"

Abraxas gave him an appraising look. "I suppose not. We did know the city better than he did."

"Yes." Aldwin took another sip of mead. "And he used it to his advantage when he needed us to steal something dangerous for him."

They were silent for a moment. Aldwin detected an undercurrent of distain in his brother's posture that made him wary and wished he would have kept his mouth shut.

"Why do you never call him Dad?"

"Why do you?" Aldwin shot back.

Why did his brother want to rehash this topic? It nearly always led to them arguing, and Aldwin didn't have the energy for it. He was tired of fighting and only wanted peace.

"Brax," he said tentatively, "he wasn't our real father. Nor was he a father figure *to me* in any way, shape, or form. He hurt and nearly killed us on several occasions. I can never forgive him for that."

Abraxas's mouth tightened as he stared at Aldwin, pain and frustration on his features. "He got us out of Merkabah, Al. That's something. We would have died there or have been stuck on the streets for the rest of our lives if he hadn't rescued us."

"You don't know that. We could have left on our own, gone to Panthea like I wanted us to and done anything from there. Instead, we got stuck with him. I was the one who found us food when he forgot to feed us or stole clothes when ours turned to rags. He used us and forced us to help him build those damn archways without really caring about us. No parent in their right mind would have treated their children the way he treated us. We were nothing more than free labor."

"I don't think he meant for anything to happen the way it did. He loved his work and got a bit lost in it, you know? I don't think he meant for you to take on as much responsibility as you did and he was teaching us what he knew," Abraxas said defensively.

"It was never a problem for me to look after you, even before he adopted us," Aldwin said. "When mom left us at the orphanage, she made me promise to always look out for you. I did. You're my little brother, Brax. I would never give up on you."

"If that's truly how you feel than tell me what happened the night he died?"

"Why? What does that have to do with anything?" Aldwin asked cautiously.

Abraxas wore a mask of calm, but there was a hunger in his eyes Aldwin knew all to well. "It has to do with my research, a theory I'm working on about portals. I need to know what happened to Mundas and his research. All you've ever told me was his portal failed and it killed him."

"It's the truth." Aldwin walked into the sitting room and set his glass on the mantel. He stared into the grate, avoiding Abraxas and doing his best to hold back the flood of unpleasant memories. Fists, fury, and flame. "What are you even doing researching portals? It's a banned subject of magick and anyone who studies it winds up dead, including Mundas. Shouldn't that be enough to dissuade you?"

Abraxas followed into the room and moved beside Aldwin. "I'm on the precipice of discovering a potential new source of magick, Al. One that others have attempted to tap into but never have. It could change our world! Everything about Mundas's research has to do with it. If I knew exactly what happened the night he died, it might give me a clue to the last part of his formula and what he was trying to do. I'm so close to discovering the answer. We could be the first ones to discover a new source of magick through the portals."

"How do you know that's what this formula does? It could vaporize you on contact or scatter your atoms across the ether of time and space. This isn't something to mess around with."

Red blotches rose on Abraxas's cheeks. "I—er—well I don't have complete proof but my calculations are flawless. I know they are. I need this, Al. Could you do me the courtesy of listening to what I have to say or is my older brother, the gatekeeper, too important to help the only living family member he's got left?"

The remark hit Aldwin like a dagger to the heart.

For all the pain Maximus Mundas had put them through, Aldwin would never abandon his brother. Not now and certainly not after all these years of hardship. If he was heading down this path, then Aldwin was the only person who could protect Abraxas.

Aldwin resigned himself to the worst. "Very well. Let's hear it."

ABRAXAS' THEORY

ALDWIN

ABRAXAS PAUSED, GATHERING HIS THOUGHTS BEFORE BEGINNING. "LATELY, I've been feeling like something has been missing from my life. I couldn't explain it, not even to myself. I was stuck in this lost and aimless feeling about everything and everyone. One day I thought I should go back to the root of it all and then maybe, I'd find some relief. I learned more about the past. *Our* past."

"How'd that go?" Aldwin asked, inwardly impressed Abraxas took the initiative to even question Mundas and try to find some peace after a chaotic and destructive childhood.

"It was interesting," Abraxas said tentatively, not willing to offer more.

"And…" He could tell Abraxas was eager to share what happened by the way his eyes got round and gleamed slightly.

"I know this is going to sound crazy, but I think the portal Mundas built was successful and that he has been trying to show us how to use it."

"What?" Of all the things he was expecting Abraxas to say, this wasn't one of them.

"I know, Al. I swear, I understand this sounds nuts, but it has to be him. He survived that night he went through his portal and has been sending us messages ever since. I got one when I finally found the collapsed barn."

Aldwin moved to the couch as the world tipped sideways. He was appalled by every word spoken by his brother, but desperate to hear more. "How did you find it?"

"I knew it was somewhere south of Merkabah, took me ages to find the exact spot. I asked around the local towns and villages to see if anyone remembered something like that happening twenty years ago. Well, it turns out that the one place did, the town of Jita in the Sound Federation. It was big news for an isolated town, and the older folks were fond of retelling the tale when gossip was sparce. Apparently, paladins arrived at the scene two days after some sort of magick anomaly triggered an investigation. They cleaned and cleared the collapsed barn, went on their way, and never found the two little boys people claimed to see traveling with their father."

Aldwin groaned and leaned back into the cushions.

It did nothing to deter Abraxas. "When I got there something happened." His voice went up an octave, brimming with excitement. "I don't know if my presence triggered it or what, but there was a rippling like water in the stone foundation of the barn, and this page flew out of it."

"A page?" Aldwin asked.

"Yes. It was covered with strange markings, and I had no idea what the language was. I spent weeks researching it and breaking the code. It turned out to be coordinates for a place up north. I went to that location and found another one of these pages. What's crazier is I think I remembered some of these places from when we were kids. He's not dead, Mundas can't be, and I think he's trying to tell us something important."

"If that is even remotely possible, why would you want to help the man that used and abused us for years?" Heat flushed through his body. This couldn't be happening. He wanted to wake up from this nightmare but knew he couldn't, that he was already awake, and this was real.

"He was on to something big, and I think he was trying to teach us what he knows. That's why he adopted us in the first place," Abraxas said. "He needed protégées, especially after he successfully tapped into this magick source. Now he is showing us how to do it too. It must be Mundas reaching out to us from the other side and not as a ghost or spirit. These pages have real, current information on them. Nothing else makes sense."

Please don't say what I think you're going to say.

"Aldwin, I think he built a successful portal that night and found Nimrothag, that place he was always telling us about."

"So now it's a world, not a magick source? Which is it, Brax?"

"A new world *is* a new source of magick."

"You're a fool. He manipulated you into doing his dirty work by lying to you. He fed me that same story, and I believed it too. Then I realized he was mad and there was no Nimrothag. No escaping from this reality into a fantasy land for us to go to and become kings. By the skies, Brax, he was a dangerous man then and if these messages are from him now, they will lead to despair. The night of his death, that portal shattered and the shrapnel sliced your neck open. He did that to us. And now—what?—you want to go on a rescue mission for him? It's insanity and treason to even be discussing this with me of all people. I'm the bloody gatekeeper!" Aldwin stood up and walked to the windows for some air, rubbing his burning eyes while his back was to Abraxas.

"He wasn't lying to us," Abraxas said. "I get it. He wasn't the best. But I can't deny that his research is nothing short of genius. If this portal worked, look at what he created. He's the first person to do that in nearly a thousand years. He's giving us that knowledge. He wants us to know the truth. I would imagine that is information that the Gatekeeper would want very much."

"Anything you accept from him will be poison. Or a clever trap you're walking into blindly. You don't even have proof that this is truly him or his work. A few coincidences aren't enough."

"It has to be him. Who else would be capable of this?"

"Be that as it may, you still can't prove it's him. You need to drop this, Brax."

"I can't prove anything yet. But I will soon. I just need more time. There is an object that keeps being referenced in these notes called

Ebenosite. It's used as the main navigation component and power source for the constructed portal it can—"

"Stop." Aldwin raised his voice for the first time. "This is nonsense, Abraxas. I have entertained your affections for Mundas these last few years as a courtesy, but this is where I draw the line. He was not a man of honor, and it's not worth your life to try to save him, should your claims be true. Whatever these pages are, they are giving instructions for something dangerous and far more complicated than you realize. As gatekeeper, it is my right to confiscate anything that would compromise the safety and integrity of Panthea and imprison those involved. Give me those pages, now, and we can be done with this. No one else needs to know." Abraxas retreated from Aldwin, holding his arms up to keep distance. "Do you think I would be so stupid as to bring them here for you to take?"

"You're acting pretty stupid now. If you're determined to keep this to yourself, then why involve me in any of this?"

"Aldwin, I need your help." Abraxas' purple eyes were pleading. "If this is a trap or whatever you believe— then help me. I feel like this is important and you're a part of it somehow. I came to you first. I—*we* —should try to understand them."

Was Aldwin really considering this? If he agreed to this insanity, he could try to take the pages and destroy them. Knowing Abraxas however, he probably had it completely memorized and hid copies of it far from his reach. What good would it do to destroy the pages if it proved to Abraxas couldn't trust him?

If Aldwin handled this diplomatically, he would be able to assess these notes himself and see if there was something more sinister happening. Panthea's interests were now tied into whatever Abraxas had unearthed and Aldwin did have a reluctant knack for understanding Mundas' theories. It was his duty as gatekeeper to watch for these sorts of threats. It was also his duty as a brother to protect Abraxas.

Warning bells went off in his head as he thought of the consequences, and his gut twisted with unease. He shouldn't trust this, especially if it had anything to do with Maximus Mundas.

"All right," he said with forced calm. "I will agree to examine these collected pages and give you my conclusions from there. I want the original documents, no duplicates, and to keep them here, under the protection of Panthea. If you try anything funny, the deal's off. I won't tell the authorities about this, but that's the extent of the brotherly protection I'm willing to give you."

Abraxas looked at him incredulously. "What guarantee do I have that you won't lie to me? To take my information and run? You'd be left with all the cards in your hand, brother, whilst I have nothing."

Aldwin paused. "Why would I lie to you?"

Abraxas looked pointedly around the room, gesturing wildly at the space. "Your loyalties are to Panthea, are they not?"

"You're still my brother," Aldwin said.

"I'm glad to hear that. We are family, after all. We should be looking out for one another."

Aldwin narrowed his eyes. "Agreed. While we are working on this, I want you to stay on Panthea grounds. I will have guards set around your residence for your protection, just in case something were to happen while we work with these pages. I wouldn't want you to come to any harm. Let it be known, brother, that if I catch one whiff of treachery, I will not hesitate to have the most skilled Paladins escort you off the premises."

"Of course. But you won't. You're just as curious as I am to see if Mundas is dead or alive. If he is dead and this is beyond my research, I will back out entirely and yield control of these pages to you and Panthea Central. I don't want anything to do with it if it doesn't involve Mundas."

"And if we find out Maximus Mundas is alive, then what?" Aldwin ground his teeth. "I don't want to bring that man back to this world, or this time, for any reason whatsoever. Got it?"

"Fine. I just need to know what actually happened to him. Once this matter is done, I promise I will try to move on. No matter what we discover."

Something isn't right about this. His gut clenched again, and his mouth went dry.

Abraxas held out his hand, waiting for Aldwin to shake on it.

Even though this whole thing made him uneasy, the best thing to do was keep Abraxas close. "Before I shake on it, if I find out this is some plot to take advantage of me, I will do everything in my power to keep Panthea safe, and neither I nor Panthea will suffer for your stupidity and recklessness. This is my first and only warning. Is that clear?"

"Deal." Abraxas kept his hand out, and his deep purple eyes never left Aldwin's.

Aldwin thought he could see a genuine desire for comradery when he reached forward to shake on the agreement. As soon as their hands touched, however, Aldwin thought he saw triumph flash in Abraxas' features, quickly replaced by a languid smile. His uneasiness increased as the evening went on, feeling as though he was playing a dangerous game with his brother. One where the secrets of their past were best left hidden and exposing them might ruin more than themselves.

THE NORTH

VAYLIN

VAYLIN AND OBERION RODE SILENTLY ON HORSEBACK, REFLECTING THE quiet nature of their surroundings. There was nothing but iron gray skies above them and a steely stiffness between them. The air was crisp and the open, rolling green hills gave the wind a speed and sharpness vastly different from the heavy, damp air of the jungles. It was early fall in the northern hemispheres of Chrysanthos, which meant the snows in the mountains were still manageable, according to Oberion.

Vaylin savored the days until they reached the Khazirak Stronghold. Her imagination was in overdrive as she dwelled on the cold darkness of the underground hold and shivered at the thought, hating her claustrophobia. She forced a breath of fresh air into her lungs and remained calm, showing no sign of stress in front of Oberion.

How could she admit her fear to him? Would he judge her for it? It would only make their mission harder if she had a panic attack while meeting the khan.

She had to try and explain her fear to Oberion if they were ever going to trust each other. They were supposed to be working together, and she would heed Aldwin's advice if Oberion wouldn't.

"So...typical fall weather for the Wind District?" she said pathetically. *The weather, really? That's what you're going to talk about?*

Oberion raised an eyebrow at her and then toward the skies. "Yes," he answered in a bored voice. "Overcast clouds are hallmarks of the north. If we make it to Adavale without getting rained on, it will be a miracle."

"I don't mind a bit of rain. It's always wet in the jungles."

He snorted. "These are northern rains. Capable of freezing you to your bones and cause hypothermia in minutes. Quite different from those warm, tropical storms that barely last before the sun is out again."

"Have you ever been in a hurricane? Not just read about it?" She hated when someone made her feel like her own experience was invalid. "Water rushes inland at top speeds like a solid wall of force capable of destroying everything in its path. The aftermath looks like a stampede of wild elephants and the rain cuts like a thousand knives. Nothing makes you realize the limits of your own power like facing off with Mother Nature herself."

Oberion gave her an appraising glance, and if she wasn't mistaken, he looked like he wanted to agree with her. "Well then, I expect no complaining with any inclement weather we might be up against since you're so resilient."

She scowled at him. It sounded like a compliment, but she sensed the insult in the comment. "That's not what I said."

"Isn't it though? Talking about withstanding hurricanes sounds like a clever way to stroke your own ego."

Vaylin's jaw dropped open. "My ego?"

"Yes, your ego. Isn't that what you're trying to prove to me? That you're some new hotshot Elite who can handle her own?" His wavy brown hair was wind tousled, and his jaw was set.

"If I could do this by myself, I wouldn't have you next to me, now would I?" she said. Was he always this much of a jerk, or was he just treating her this way because she was "new" to the Elite? Either way, it wasn't okay, and her patience was running thin.

To her surprise, Oberion chuckled. "At least you're honest," he remarked. "Fabien told me you were a bit of a wild card."

Her face flushed. Far ahead, a herd of deer crossed the plains, some with antlers noticeable even from this distance. "What else did the darling Fabien Prince say about me?"

The Elite Guardian of the Igni Territory had shown a keen interest in her guardian trials and pestered her with questions about life in the Aqua Realm while expounding greatly on his latest technological inventions. If anyone had ego, that man did.

Oberion was reluctant to answer. "He said that your skills in medicine and understanding of alchemy is far superior to most in the Medi-Center of Panthea."

"Really?" she asked doubtfully.

"Err—no, actually." He cracked a smile. "He said that your genius was on par with his own."

"That sounds more like Fabien." She smiled herself. "That man has the most ridiculous hair."

"The flaming mohawk does suit his personality though."

They laughed together, and the shared moment shifted the energy. Oberion was still acting like a watchful parent, but his shoulders relaxed slightly. The silence between them was not as taut as before.

"How long have you studied alchemy?" he asked.

Vaylin glanced at his eyes, blue-gray like the skies above, and found that he was being serious. "As long as I can remember. Those born in the Numinbah jungle must be as familiar with the plants around them as their own home. The first thing I learned from my Nestor was foraging for plants and learning which ones were edible and which ones were poisonous."

"Nestor?"

"Like a tribal grandmother," she offered. Not everyone was familiar with the nuances and names tribal people used. "I was raised by one after my mother died. Turns out I had a real knack for it and started apprenticing with nuca healers when I was six."

Oberion opened his mouth to say something when a baying screech echoed across the land and stopped him. It was the unmistakable sound of an animal in distress, and Vaylin perked up, sensing flaring as she heard what was happening. The horses nickered and tossed their heads uncomfortably. The noise had her triggered. The black crack was swallowing the shaman again and she tried to shut off the images but couldn't.

Something about this felt like Mingalla.

Oberion's features hardened, and he raised a hand cautiously, listening intently. "Something attacked a deer. Maybe a bear or pack of wolves. I doubt a troll managed to catch one. They are dumber than a sack of potatoes and typically stay closer to the mountains."

He listed the possibilities one after the other in an unphased, calculated cadence. Vaylin nodded, not disputing his assessment.

"We need to see what happened."

"What? There's no way we are going near that kill. We aren't the only things out here that heard that. These hills will be crawling with predators by nightfall, which is a few hours away, at best. We need to avoid the scene area entirely and move on."

"No," she said. "We can't. That wasn't a normal animal sound."

"That was the sound of a deer dying. It's part of nature, and we shouldn't interfere."

"Yes, I know that, but there was something else too. It reminds me of what I saw and heard in the Mingalla nuca. What if an animal strayed into one of those cracks?"

"You can't be serious."

"Oberion, I've already lost a nuca's worth of people to one of these things. What if the same thing is happening in the Wind District? I swear if it's not one of those cracks, then we leave immediately."

"That gives us less than an hour to ride to the site and get away before night falls."

"We have no other choice."

"Follow behind me and keep up." He kicked the horse in its hind quarters and galloped away.

They reached the rough location of the noise and tied the horses off to a tree. As a precaution, Oberion raised a thick, earthen wall around them, creating a pen of sorts.

Together, they set off on foot.

It was simple to pick out the hoof prints in the mud and slight trail through the heather, leading to a patch of gnarled pine trees. *Tracking animals in the north is much easier than tracking through the jungle.*

"The herd split from here," Oberion whispered.

"Whatever it is, I haven't seen any other tracks but the deer's," Vaylin said.

Oberion nodded solemnly and motioned to keep moving. They were getting close now, the hoof prints making an erratic pattern, trying to dodge whatever was chasing it. A patch of dark red appeared on the path, shining near the base of a tree.

"We're not dealing with wolves or bears here," Vaylin muttered. "Is there anything in the Wind District that can take down a deer from the skies?"

"King eagles could, but their nests are in the east."

A shadow flitted between two trees ahead, and she grabbed Oberion by the collar. Choking him slightly, she pulled them behind a tree, bodies pressed together to hide their bulk from sight.

"Bleeding hells," he hissed, rubbing his throat. "What are you doing?"

"There's something ahead," she whispered, peeking around the trunk.

"Are you certain?"

"Yes, I'm sure. Do you always have to question me?"

"Wonderful. Then we're leaving." He ignored her question.

"What? We're not leaving."

"Yes, we are. If you saw something, it could be one of a dozen different things, none of which are pleasant to deal with. This confirms it's not one of those cracks, so we're leaving."

"I'm not going anywhere. We never found the creatures that killed those people, and this could be one of them," she said. "I need to examine the deer to see if the injuries are the same."

"It would have had to cross the entire Chazakül Mountain Range in a half a moon cycle. It's impossible. Do you even hear yourself?"

"We need to be sure about this. I heard what I heard, and I need you to trust me. Part of being the Elite, right?" she said with all the confidence she could muster while keeping her voice down.

Oberion looked like he was grinding his teeth in frustration and nodded once, like she guessed he would. "Fine. I'll cover the skies, and you cover the ground. We follow the trail of blood until we get to the body. You have five minutes, and then we leave."

"Deal. Now, shut it so I can focus. We'll be lucky if that thing didn't hear us."

Not sparing him another moment, she closed her eyes and focused on the woods around them. It was no different from the jungles—except it was marginally less chaotic, making it easier to intuit her surroundings. They were the only life force she could detect for a thirty-meter radius. Even the birds had left the area. An ominous sign.

"Let's move," she said.

Oberion jumped swiftly, aided by a current of air he directed, and landed on a branch high in the tree. He moved and Vaylin ran as swiftly as she could beneath him, using her own air magick to streamline her through the forest. She didn't make a sound, her Elder blood showing her the precise path to take and giving her lightning speed. The patches of blood were getting bigger. Tuffs of the creature's hair were caught in the brambles, and Vaylin sensed what remained of the poor thing ahead. Slowing her pace, she came right next to the creature and knelt.

A doe lay on the ground, its body twisted in a grotesque way that made it obvious that this was not the same creature that attacked the people in Mingalla. Stripes of skin were ripped away from the doe in swirling patterns, reminding her of the tracks earth worms made under rocks. It lay in a puddle of blood. The people in Mingalla had been exsanguinated, and this deer looked like it was killed for no reason. A wound to the neck was the death blow, severed cleanly by a beak or talon.

Vaylin hung her head in silent prayer, beseeching the spirit of the doe to move on and find peace. At her words, the heaviness of the scene lifted.

"Vaylin." Oberion was probably wondering what she was doing. "What's going on?"

She didn't move at first, ear twitching at a sound nearby, like a cross between bubbles popping and a foot sinking into mud. Gesturing silently, she motioned for Oberion to retreat westward, away from the doe and the popping noise.

He obliged.

Her mind whirled as they headed toward the perimeter of the barren forest, keeping her Elder senses alert for any other presence that might be nearby. Her skin prickled, gut warning her something was here and watching them.

Why couldn't she sense it? Every life force gave off an energy signal.

They reached the clearing where they'd left the horses. Oberion swung down from the upper branches of the canopy and landed besides her softly.

"Well? Was that worth it, or was it a complete waste of time?" he asked moodily.

Vaylin sighed and crossed her arms. "Whatever killed that doe was not the same thing in the Mingalla nuca."

"That's something. At least it wasn't one of those cracks."

"Yeah, sure. Did you hear that noise back there?"

"What noise?"

"I dunno, like some sort of popping or the suction of a boot in mud."

"I think you need your ears checked. I haven't heard half of what you're hearing."

"And why would you?" Vaylin flicked one of her ears. Everyone knew that those with Elder blood had superior hearing and sight to most humans.

He glowered with all the appearance of someone wanting to argue and struggling not to. "Come on. We need to ride if we're going to get to Adavale before midnight."

He made a sweeping gesture with his hands, and the earthen walls that enclosed the horses receded into the ground, leaving the vaguest outline in the dirt and pine needles. Vaylin mounted her horse and trotted after him, turning to watch the forest as they went. A thrill of horror went through her as she thought she saw a shadowy shape peer around a tree and watch them go.

MARSHALL WAKES

MARSHALL

EVERYTHING WAS HEAVY. HIS BODY BOTH NONEXISTENT AND ALL AROUND him at the same time. Was this what death felt like? The world grew brighter behind his eyelids, and warmth built across his face. Maybe this was the heavens? He wanted to laugh at the idea but couldn't. He twitched his fingers and toes, and a dull pain emanated up his right leg.

If this was death, why was he still in pain? Distantly, he registered muffled voices around him and a soft rustling of clothes nearby. Shadows passed over his closed eyelids.

Dark wings. A gaping maul dripping with blood.

His blood.

With a sudden jolt, Marshall opened his eyes and sat up. The sunlight pouring through the window blinded him, and he raised his arms in defense, falling backward into his pillows at the pain in his eyes and foot.

Sturdy hands grabbed him and held steady.

He flinched, thinking of claws before realizing the feeling on his shoulders were hands. Human hands not claws. Panic subsided as the words these people spoke to him became clearer, finally entering his brain enough to make sense of it all.

"Marshall. Marshall, can you hear us?" a calming male voice said. "You are safe, Marshall. We need you to relax and keep that leg still, all right?"

Safe.

The word echoed hollowly in his ears, which felt full of cotton. The last thing he remembered was that ghastly beast sucking the blood from his leg. Nausea swept through him, and he looked down the length of his body, sagging with relief. He had legs and feet. His right leg was slightly elevated and bandaged from the knee down. He wiggled his toes, and they moved, accompanied by splinters of pain.

"Don't you move that foot," a different voice said. "The poultice is covered with a salve actively fighting the infection. We've healed all your broken bones, but the area is still tender, swollen from whatever was on that beast's fangs. We were able to collect some from your wounds and made an antidote. It's a fascinating chemical composure. I've never seen anything like it. A paralysis agent of some kind that strengthens the longer it feeds and…"

The words assaulted him one by one as he tried to understand. It made his head spin. Groaning, he laid one arm across his face and steadied his breathing.

"That's better," the calm male voice said. "You survived one hell of an attack."

"Yeah?" Marshall croaked. His head pounded, and he felt like he was swaying on the deck of a ship. "Where am I?"

"You are in The Healing Temple of Sakhet in the Southern Kingdom of Elves," the stern voice said again. Female. "It's a damn good thing you are too. You weren't long for this world when Avon brought you here."

"Avon? The elf?"

"Yes. Avon Nehym," she repeated. "The elven warrior who saved your human hide from that wicked creature of Nimrothag."

"How long have I been here?"

"You've been here for two days."

"Days?" Marshall was shocked.

"Yes. My name is Dr. Nour, and I have been overseeing your healing. I was also the one who developed the antidote to that bite in your leg, thank you very much. There will be some nasty scars but luckily no permanent damage. All thanks to the Sisters of the Temple."

Marshall had no words. The doctor prattled on about his condition and all the healing he received since arriving. The elves had obviously fixed his eardrums, since he could hear again. He cracked his eyes open, giving them time to adjust to the blinding brightness.

"Where is Avon?" he asked. The fact that the elf had saved his life was just as disorientating as waking up after his attack. He had thought death had finally claimed him, yet he was here, very much alive.

"Avon is with King Darius of the Southern Elves and the other nobles of the court. He will likely return here when the meeting is over."

Marshall glanced to the elf who kept a light hand on his shoulder, a preventative measure to make sure he wasn't going to go berserk and damage himself, or the others, further.

"I promise I won't move," Marshall said toward the male nurse, who looked at Dr. Nour and received a nod of consent before letting go. "When can I leave?"

Dr. Nour peered over at him over her spectacles, lips tight with disapproval. "You can be up and walking by tomorrow. You are welcome to leave then, but I strongly recommend you do not travel alone. Or at the very least, don't travel after dark. It's not safe if more of these creatures are prowling the countryside."

"A few more strikes, and I would have sent that creature back to the burning pits of hell." Marshall flexed his toes and grimaced at the stiffness in his joints.

"Don't do that," Dr. Nour snapped. "The poultice needs another hour to allow the chemical structure of the medicine to bind with the wounds."

"Listen, I need to be leaving here as soon as possible. I'm the Wanderer of Chrysanthos, and the Gatekeeper of Panthea is expecting me."

She tutted in response and continued with her ministrations. "You will need at least twelve more hours before your bones are completely set and mended. I haven't even mentioned the muscular reconstruction we've done on top of that. If you are determined to leave this instant, a limp is sure to develop. If you are so careless as to start walking before I give you permission to leave, then by all means, enjoy hobbling around with a cane for the rest of your life. Those are your choices."

"Wonderful," Marshall said sarcastically. "I guess I'm stuck here."

"I'm glad you're finally seeing sense. We can send word to Panthea for you, if you are so determined. I'm sure the Aldwin Hearthfire would like to know what has happened here and how the elves have saved you. Panthea should be most grateful we didn't let their wanderer die on our lands."

"Fine, send him whatever you like. Let him know I'm on my way back to the Terra Nation Embassy as soon as we're done here."

"It will be done," Dr. Nour said with a short nod.

As Marshall's mind adjusted to consciousness and cognitive thought, he dissected what he could remember. That creature, whatever it was, was not from this world. He knew that. He had a thorough knowledge of the all the creatures that roamed Chrysanthos. Trolls, ogres, and goblins were meddlesome but nothing of this caliber. Dragons were rare and legendary creatures, but they are very reclusive and hard to find. This was no dragon or draconid hybird. Was it possible there were more of these things? If so, how had they come to be here?

The door to the hospital swung open and interrupted his wonderings.

A tall, Black elf strode in, golden eyes glinting in the sunlight and reflecting several dermal piercings along his cheekbones and upper eyebrows. They too were golden and glowed like mini stars upon his skin in the midday sunlight.

Marshall was entranced, blinking rapidly, mouth slightly ajar and stunned into silence.

It was Avon, the image of an immortal warrior dressed in courtly raiment of red and gold, the colors of the Southern Kingdom. He strode in, spine straight and dual swords gleaming at his side. He hadn't worn his piercings the day of the fight but had re-adorned them now, and by the gods—

Marshall had to pick his jaw up off the sheets. His breath caught as they locked eyes and he stiffened at Avon's approach. Why did he feel so apprehensive? Was he feeling the effects of some drug they had him on?

"Hello, Avon Nehym," Dr. Nour said. "You have quite impeccable timing. Marshall has barely been conscious for five minutes and was already asking about you."

Marshall wondered why Avon was following him that night. Was it a more sinister reason? Revenge for the match? Had he set the creature on Marshall?

"Was he, now? When one meets as fine a warrior as Baxter Marshall, it's hard not to get invested," Avon responded coolly. "I'm glad to see you up and well."

"What are you doing here?" Marshall asked. He wasn't trying to be rude, but Avon's presence unnerved for him. An elf he hardly knew and defeated in a relatively illicit wresting match saved him in the dead of night from an unknown creature and was now here checking after him? None of it made sense.

"You're welcome," Avon said pointedly, not waiting for Marshall's apology or gratitude.

"Why?"

"Why, what?"

"Why were you following me? Why did you save me? I was supposed to be leaving here, and now I'm back," Marshall pressed. There was silence in the room as all four people stood still. "Are you trying to keep me here?"

"Marshall," Dr. Nour said, placating. "Avon rescued you from something—"

Marshall cut the doctor off. "Please, leave us."

Dr. Nour pinched her lips tight and gave the two men a stern look. He didn't care. He needed to have a private conversation with Avon without all the elves in this temple watching him.

"I'll be back in a half hour to check on your leg." She walked out of the room, followed by her assistant.

Once they were gone, Avon cleared his throat. "You certainly know how to be charming."

Marshall glowered at him.

"Perhaps," Avon said hesitantly, "my meaning was not clear when we parted ways after that match. Southern elves have a certain... attraction to the warrior spirit. Those who are blessed with the powers of the warrior are held in high regard."

"I am not elf kind," Marshall said.

Avon closed his eyes for a moment. "I felt a pull toward you that night that I cannot explain. I couldn't let you go—alone. The Sun Warrior urged me to protect you. You do not know the dangers that have been seen in our lands, so I asked where you were heading and followed from a distance. I could hear that terrible creature shrieking in the night and you fighting it. I saw flashes of fire, and by the time I turned the corner, you were under the beast, and I charged. You were a pretty good distraction, I might add," Avon said. "The chiro didn't even notice me until I was running my blades through it."

"You were following me on a hunch from your god?" Marshall said with as little emotion as possible. "How do I know you weren't trying to kill me instead for winning that match?"

"If I wanted you dead, I would have left you to that infernal beast." There was venom in Avon's voice as he spoke, insulted by the accusation.

Marshall couldn't deny the simplicity of that plan. Avon would've only had to stay back and make a quiet exit. No need to get his hands dirty while the beast killed him. He sat there, hesitant to trust Avon, but his feelings of suspicions were ebbing away. There was no denying Avon had saved his life, and his instinct about the man being decent still felt true.

"How did you kill that beast?" Marshall asked.

"Beheading," responded Avon casually. "With blades blessed with fire and sunlight."

"And you know what that creature was?"

"It's called a chiro."

"A chiro? I've never heard of such a thing." Marshall turned the word over in his mind.

"I don't doubt that. That knowledge has long been lost to men. I brought the head back with me as proof of the attack. Our scholars identified it immediately. The Great Library of Xanthus in our citadel holds over a thousand years of Chrysanthos's history. This creature belongs to a race of dark beings called the Underlings from a world called Nimrothag. They are deadly and dangerous, having plagued our world in the past."

"That's great news," Marshall muttered sarcastically.

"Isn't it?" Avon raised his eyebrow.

"How is this a good thing?" Marshall's mind still felt sluggish, and he doubted the gatekeeper would be thrilled to hear about this.

"Strictly speaking, it isn't. But we have identified the threat in our lands, which gives us full authority to launch an investigation into the matter. We have the best trained horses and militia of the south, and our numbers are vast. We can easily deal with this but we are none the wiser to the reason why these beasts have returned to our lands. I believe King Darius will send out a few legions, if he hasn't already, on a search and destroy mission for these chiros."

"Have there been any other reports of similar attacks?"

"Not on humans. Wildlife has turned up dead with injuries that match your own. Until you were attacked, none of knew what was happening. You've helped us quite a bit."

"Glad to be of assistance," Marshall mocked. "Does your king find it a bit excessive to send out entire legions of his army to look for more of these things? If they are rare and you already killed this one, what are the chances that they will find more?"

Avon sighed and ran his hand over his shaved head. "We elves have long memories and do not forget the past as easily as humans do, meaning no offense. It was agreed to deal with this situation thoroughly before more damage can be done."

Marshall considered everything. The elves had knowledge about the Underlings. Their immortal lifespan and libraries to match were the most reliable source of information. The elves did save him, and what Avon said made sense. It still didn't explain the sudden appearance of the chiro. Marshall had traveled the main road out of here a dozen times over the last two decades and never once heard or saw anything like what he had just experienced. Maybe a rune site or collapsed cave allowed these things to escape.

"If your king discovers more information, will he send it to

Panthea?" Marshall had to make himself useful somehow if he was going to be stuck here for a few days. It was the least he could do for Panthea and fulfill his obligations as wanderer.

"King Darius will send his correspondences to me," Avon said.

"Okay," Marshall said slowly. "Can he also send correspondence to *me* or Hearthfire at Panthea?"

"I'll be at Panthea."

It took Marshall a moment to figure out what Avon had said. "No you won't."

"Yes, I will. It was agreed upon at our council that the elves will involve themselves in this matter. We are not leaving this to chance and are offering our aid to Panthea Central. I have volunteered to go back with you and bring several ancient and informative volumes with me. It will adequately inform the gatekeeper of the issue at hand and show the loyalties of Southern Kingdom to the capital."

"Like hell you're going to come back to Panthea with me," Marshall protested.

Avon crossed his arms and stared him down. "I believe you don't have a choice in the matter. You'd have to change the king's mind, and I doubt you'll have the ability to do that."

"I'm leaving here without you, and that's final." Marshall abhorred the idea. He didn't need a babysitter to watch his back, let alone an elven warrior from the Southern Kingdom tagging along—he might as well have bannerman flanking him, proclaiming his path and destination. He always preferred to keep a low profile, especially when traveling. It made everything easier when there weren't extra eyes watching.

"That's the stupidest thing I ever heard," Avon said. "Once the king decides something, it's final. They are already preparing us for our journey, and you'd do well to accept our generosity. I also just saved your life."

Marshall gaped at him. "You don't need to uproot your life because I beat you in a stupid wrestling match. You owe me no allegiance."

"I can do what I want with my life," Avon countered, and Marshall's stomach clenched. "By the laws of the southern elves, you technically owe me a life debt."

Marshall wondered if his eardrums were still ruptured. "What did you say?"

"A life debt. The elves take these things very seriously, you see—"

"As I have said," Marshall interrupted, "I. Am. Not. An. Elf. Your laws have no bearing on what I do, and my position as Wanderer of Chrysanthos grants me immunity from your politics."

"Be that as it may, it still happened. You can either agree to let me come with you as a companion, or I can follow you every step of the way until we reach Panthea. Then you can explain your poor behavior and reluctance to aid a representative of the Southern Kingdom to the gatekeeper yourself."

"I never asked you to save my life. You can't force something like that onto somebody."

"I am not forcing anything on you. I have had days to consider my options, and the plans are in motion. The pull I felt toward you the day of that match is still present. The Sun Warrior has led me to you twice now. I don't find it a coincidence that the drunk who beat me in a wrestling match also happens to be the Wanderer of Chrysanthos, of all things. I don't know what will happen next, but I am choosing to stand by you and you would be wise to accept my help. Not only for your own sake but for Panthea too."

The conviction Avon spoke with hit Marshall square in the chest. Damn him for using Panthea against him like this. Avon was right, of course. Marshall's gut was telling him this issue with the chiro was not over, and Panthea was the best hope any of them had to solving this problem. He had been out of touch for weeks now, and who knew what was happening elsewhere. Maybe the chiros weren't only on this island. The Southern Kingdom of Elves could be a powerful ally, and he didn't want to jeopardize the position with them.

Strictly speaking, there weren't any rules stating that the wanderer had to wander alone. He simply wasn't used to company while traveling, since he naturally outpaced those around him. Avon was an elf, bigger and faster than most other humans. Marshall could only guess at the number of years and training he had to hone his skills.

Would Marshall be able to keep up with him on the road? Especially after his injury. He remembered the solid feel of Avon's muscles as they wrestled and knew he would be a useful ally. Hadn't he proven that already by saving Marshall's life?

"All right." Marshall sighed. "You win."

Avon smiled triumphally. "Ask me."

"Ask you what?"

"Ask me officially to come with you."

"Seriously? I already agreed to your ridiculous idea. Isn't that enough?"

Avon shook his head, dermal piercings glittering. "Nope. I want to hear you say it."

Immortal asshole. Avon was toying with him and knew he couldn't refuse.

"Will you accompany me to Panthea as a representative of the Southern Kingdom of Elves?" he said as officially as possible. Really, he had to give Avon some credit for his cunning.

"It would be my honor," Avon held out his hand in the same gesture they'd ended their wrestling match with.

Marshall reached forward, and they grasped each other's forearms. He couldn't help but feel a swoop of excitement at the prospect. This might not be a bad idea after all.

THE HEALING ARTS

MARSHALL

THE HEALING TEMPLE OF SAKHET WAS COMFORTABLE, DESPITE HAVING many people around him at all hours. The single tower was made of warm, red brick and surrounded by airy walkways of long, curving buttresses. Gardens scattered around the grounds burst with herbs, flowers, and honey bees collecting pollen from the petals. Tropical trees that bore bright colored fruits hung over walkways, creating shady patches as a respite from the sun. Healers milled about, collecting ingredients in wicker baskets or tending to the plants. An ingenious aqueduct system ran along the buildings and supplied water to the citadel and its many fountains.

For all the time Marshall had spent in the Southern Kingdom, he'd never once stepped foot in this temple. He had heard about it, saw the tower standing tall in the city, and never felt the inclination to visit. He supposed it was a bit arrogant of himself, considering how many people he had sent to infirmaries over the years. After what Marshall had endured, he realized how talented these elves truly were. He doubted anyone at Panthea could have saved his leg, except perhaps for Vaylin Carina, the newest member of the Elite. She was quite skilled in healing, and Marshall liked her immediately when they first met.

It took a lot to best him, and that creature had. He was not used to being defeated like that, let alone to be on the verge of death so suddenly and so completely. That was the thing about death. It always seemed so far away until the moment it wasn't.

He now had a ring of puckered, black scars around his foot and ankle where the chiro had bitten him. The healers who visited him to repair the last of his muscle and nerve damage analyzed the scars every time. Marshall had overheard a few talking about whether those scars held remnants of venom or not. The nurses fretted over his injury, and he was ready to be rid of them.

Avon was also a constant presence that he wasn't used to. He turned up when Marshall least expected him too and seemed to think Marshall might try to slip off in the dead of night without him. The thought did cross his mind, but he wouldn't get far with his foot. He understood why Avon was to accompany him, even though he couldn't grasp why the elf would be so attached to him.

His occupation as wanderer wasn't as glamorous as it sounded. More often than not, his deeds went unnoticed except by the people or places who directly benefited from his aid. That was what he loved about being the wanderer and the freedom it allowed. There was an inescapable feeling of possibility when the world spread before him—anything could happen on the road, and he embraced it. Yet, there were moments when the absence of home and the familiar struck hard and a wave of loneliness washed over him. It was his duty, of course, but some days pushed him to do something stupid and reckless just to feel alive. Like losing himself in drink in a foreign kingdom and brawling with elves for others' entertainment. Maybe it would be good for him to have someone watching his back.

Footsteps sounded behind Marshall, and he whirled, shifting into a defensive position and reveling in the strength of his newly healed ankle.

"Copper for your thoughts?" It was Avon, dressed in a simple, midnight blue tunic and white harem pants. His dark skin soaked up the sunlight, and thin gold lines were painted elegantly around his temples and the tips of his pointed ears. The dermal piercings along his cheekbones twinkled, and he stood at full height, the epitome of grace. "Are you always expecting an attack?"

Marshall's face went hot, and he awkwardly relaxed his posture. "Not typically." The elf was a stranger to him even though he'd saved his life. "I—er—didn't hear you approaching."

"I have been trained in the arts of stealth and have the uncanny ability to sneak up on people. It's part of my vast skillset," Avon stated confidently. "I also have an advantage on you."

"Let me guess, you've had centuries to hone yourself to perfection? Big deal." Unamused, Marshall leaned onto the railing that surrounded a lavender garden. If Avon only came here to make him feel worse, he wasn't going to stand here and take it.

"For your information, I'm only a hundred and five years old." Avon crossed his arms and stared at him.

"Only? That sounds pretty old to me." Marshall was forty-six and one hundred and five was young in elven terms.

"There is no real indication of our age beyond what we tell you. I can hardly blame you for not knowing."

Marshall was at a loss of words. He had never imagined a *young* elf and wasn't sure if he had insulted him or not. "I'm sorry."

"There is no need to be. Age is an abstract concept at best anyway." Avon shrugged and leaned against the railing too. "So, where did your mind *wander* off too?"

The corner of Marshall's mouth quirked. He said flatly, "Ha. Ha."

Avon, to his surprise, flashed a smile at his bad joke.

Damn, even his teeth are perfect.

"Oh, traveling with you is going to be amusing, isn't it? Speaking of, you'll be pleased to know the king has provided us with horses, supplies, and a ship from one of his private collections. We leave at first light tomorrow and should be at the Terra Nation in seven turns of the sun."

"Your king doesn't want to meet with me—or us, I guess—to discuss the events of the last week?" His position as wanderer granted him authority regarding the safety of Panthea equal to that of the Elite Guard and gatekeeper. He was certain the king would want to question him about the chiro attack personally.

"I gave him a full report of what happened. The elves have already set their course of action regarding this incident."

"Seriously?" Marshall wasn't sure why, but the refusal to see him felt like an insult. "Is this some stupid 'elves only' rule?"

"Something like that. You were also unconscious. Not particularly useful when discussing the fate of a kingdom and its people."

Marshall squared his shoulders. Were the elves always this serious or just pointlessly dramatic? Things surely got boring over the centuries, and they had to keep themselves entertained. He still questioned Avon's motives and what he stood to gain from all of this.

"Who exactly are you to the king? A spy? You said you were trained in stealth," Marshall asked. What if he was a high courtesan or even a royal? If Avon were part of the Southern Kingdom's court, Marshall couldn't get mixed up in all that nonsense. The wanderer was forbidden to interfere with politics of any race or region, and he didn't want any accusations coming his way.

"I am no spy," Avon replied. "I am, however, a knight in the Southern Kingdom."

Of course he was a knight. "You're telling me that a knight followed me on noble intuition and just so happened to save me from a terrible fate?" It sounded like a fairy tale, and Marshall's cheeks burned at the thought that he was the one in need of rescuing. Baxter Marshall, the wanderer, saved by an elven knight. "Oh, that's rich."

Avon's eyes burned, and his young, beautiful, face went stiff. His sudden resemblance to a hawk was alarming. "I do not serve the king in the way your human hierarchies would dictate. All elves serve the citadel and the kingdom. Whether you are born in the north or south, we live to ensure the continuation of our race, our knowledge, and our civilization. I have made no oaths to King Darius, nor am I bound to him through any bloodlines or marriage."

"How do I know you are not lying to me?" Marshall pressed.

"The king has a private guard. I am not one of them, nor am I qualified enough to be so. Ask anyone in this temple or the court if you don't believe me. My loyalties are to my country, and I am too young to be taken seriously by the elders of my court. They call me inexperienced. So tell me, Wanderer, how else does one get experience besides making his own?"

Marshall cringed. Young people were inexperienced, and the injustice they faced for it was unfair. Having someone believe in you can change a life. He thought of Vaylin and the extra effort she put forth to just prove herself. Who knew where she would have ended up if Jessamine had never given her the chance to be more?

"Fine. I believe you." Marshall paused, filling his voice with malice. "But if I find out you are lying to me or betraying me in any way, I'll leave you with nothing more than a gash across your throat. Understood?"

"Understood," Avon said. "You are different from most mainlanders."

Marshall shrugged. "And?"

"It's refreshing. What of your parentage?"

"Dunno. Grew up on the streets of Merkabah. Don't really remember Mum—can't have been a good one if she left me though. I was big and hard to feed. I fought to scrape by a measly existence until I was old enough to join Panthea academy. I didn't want to fight or hurt people to survive. I wanted to live a life free of pain." Marshall's voice had gone soft when speaking.

Avon raised an eyebrow, the golden disks above them flashing in the sun.

"It doesn't matter." Marshall tried to change the subject. He didn't like talking about his past if he could help it and didn't know why he volunteered that information in the first place.

"This is why I chose to follow you," Avon said. "You are an honorable man. It is indicative of a true warrior spirit. Not to use our strength to conquer our enemies but to use our strength to protect the innocent. That is why there is such a strong connection between us. Can't you feel it? We both fight for truth, above all else."

Marshall felt the corner of his lips twitch upwards. If he was being honest with himself, he swore he could feel that connection Avon described and wondered if the words were making an impression on him or the elf himself.

. . .

From port to port, their journey across the cerulean sea was filled with spin drift and salty air. Avon joined Marshall for daily training routine the first day on the ship. Marshall protested at first then soon realized the benefit in having a training partner. He was weaker since the chiro attack, and each day they practiced, he found strength and rhythm in his movement once more.

Avon wielded dual short swords like deadly extensions of his arms. Marshall favored a two-handed battle axe during battles and his hatchets and a dagger for close combat.

There wasn't much else to do on a ship besides eat, sleep, and train. Marshall was reluctant to speak openly around the ship's crew, not wanting to get close to any of them. King Darius had ordered Avon to keep him up to date on any news they might receive while making the trip westward across the desert. They were due to land at the Katoomba Port on the eastern coast of the Terra Nation today.

The city of Katoomba was the biggest port in the southern continent and stretched for miles up the coastline. It was ideally placed for sailors and was known across the seas as a city where everyone was welcome and anything could be found, especially dubious magickal objects. The ports were impressive, surrounded by two bays of white-sand beaches with an island rising upward in the middle. Atop the coastal mountain sat a colossal statue of a tentacled kraken sinking a magnificent ship. The entire thing was barnacled, weather-beaten stone and represented the battles fought, and won, at the sea to reach this port. The main ship mast also functioned as a lighthouse for all who wished to find safety in Katoomba. It was an iconic sight for any traveler.

Marshall felt elation as he stared at the approaching monument, which was easy to spot from a distance. He could tolerate being in open waters or, on very rare occasions, the skies, but he preferred to keep his feet on the ground whenever possible. Movement felt easier for him when his feet were connected to the earth.

They reached the docks, and Marshall was slightly disappointed they weren't going into Katoomba. The king had provided them with enough supplies and equipment to make a trip into the city unnecessary. Their top priority was reaching Panthea Central quickly by traveling through the terra embassy portal.

They left the gleaming port city for the tropical forests and dry heat of the red desert. The landscape was full of flying insects, raucous monkeys, lizards basking on rocks, and a riot of flowers displaying a kaleidoscope of color. The air was hot and sticky, making their skin damp with sweat. He hated humidity.

Marshall felt as though he was swimming through the air.

"Do you always plan your adventures for the hottest times of the year?" Avon asked sarcastically. The heat of summer was beginning in this half of the world, and the sun was relentless. The only reprieve they got were the shaded patches of forest they walked under.

"I didn't think an elf from the south would be one to complain about the heat." Marshall smirked.

Avon raised his eyebrows, dermal piercings glinting. "I am not complaining about the heat. But *our* journey nearly synchronizes with the summer equinox. It's peculiar. Wouldn't you agree?"

"No," Marshall said, unamused. "What do equinoxes have to do with us?" He had never been one to set much faith in the stars or the cosmos. Divination and astrology were connected to the physic branch of elemental magick, and he was never interested by the subject. The terrors he had seen in the world were wrought by the hands of people or monsters. Not planets.

"When the seasons pass and planets transition, it effects the energy here on earth, whether you believe it or not. It heralds times of change. If one can sense it, it can be used to one's advantage," Avon started. "We bear dark tidings with us. A creature that hasn't been seen in an age has attacked one of the most prominent members of Panthea. It has the potential to set in motion events beyond our control, and our movements align with one of the most powerful solar conjunctions of the year. Aren't you the least bit concerned by that?"

Marshall was taken aback and didn't say anything, letting the words settle into him. Avon's ideas were strange, curious even. Marshall had never considered that energy might be coming from giant floating planets in space and affecting how things happened on this earth. Against his better judgement, he asked, "What type of energy are we in the midst of now?"

"The cataclysmic type."

Marshall wasn't sure if it was a joke or not and said nothing.

"Eclipses inspire change, good or bad. They challenge us, demanding answers to difficult questions that affect our soul. Do we face our demons, or do we hide from them? If we do not face our demons, they will surely find us. Isn't it better to seek them out first? Would you rather be aware or blindsided?"

Eclipses and equinoxes. Creatures and legends. A grotesque image of the chiro surfaced in Marshall's mind, and he paused, thinking about sharp fangs and the spreading of leathery wings. Were the monsters he had read about his whole life fictitious or based on something more? Something real? Were the tales of history and myth one and the same?

He shook his head, trying to get rid of the thoughts. How important were eclipses, really? It was unquantifiable. It meant nothing that certain stars and planets aligned the way they did. He had managed fine in life without worrying about the heavens. He didn't want to start now.

"It's something to consider," Marshall finally said noncommittally.

Avon snorted. "You shouldn't close yourself to new ideas because they challenge old ones. What is evolution, if not becoming greater than that which came before?"

Marshall felt a pang of annoyance and looked directly at Avon. "Did the stars tell you that, or did you come up with it on your own?" His words came out harsher than intended. "My instincts have kept me alive my entire life, long before I took my position as wanderer and long before I had giving me divine warnings. No planet ever whispered in my ear, warning me of danger."

Avon didn't lower his chin an inch. "Human arrogance. You might not hear the planets or stars, but they are always speaking for those who know how to listen. Do not talk to me as if *I* understand nothing. I can see well enough that you don't want anyone close to you and have isolated yourself so thoroughly that no one bothers. Dead to the world in the one way that matters most."

Marshall recoiled and shot back, "How dare you. I never asked for your opinion and I don't see how my life is a substantial concern to you."

This was exactly why he didn't like traveling with people. Too much talk and divulging of personal information—too much potential for awkward situations to be stuck in for the duration of a journey.

"Isn't it?" Avon challenged. "We are working together to achieve the same end result, aren't we? I can't help but notice the tangled state of your energy and how it landed you in the temple to being with. Forgive me for caring. If that idea is abhorrent to you, then you're in a worse state than I realized."

The words fell into the hollow chasm of Marshall's heart and made him instantly defensive. Who was Avon to judge and tell him these things? How could he know those feelings locked deep within Marshall's soul?

"What exactly am I to you, a game? A problem to fix?" It was all Marshall could do to keep his voice even.

"I am the mirror you don't want to face," Avon said calmly. "I bet you haven't been close to anyone for ages and I'm the first person who's even bothered to try."

"Then why are you?" Marshall's ears roared with anger and perhaps a touch of fear at the truth in Avon's words. Why did it matter if he had no friends? It was his job, his duty to never be in one place too long. He had no home besides Panthea, no partner or family who cared about him. It was a sacrifice he was willing to make when younger, and he had never regretted it. Had he?

"It's disconcerting to me when my only ally on this journey has been recently wounded, energetically off balance, and probably sober for the first time in who knows when. Not only that, I sense there is worse to come, and I can't help but question your judgement or reaction in a potentially life-threatening situation."

"I'm not off balance!" The words felt wrong on his lips, and he knew Avon could hear the lie in them. *Damn him and this whole situation.*

"Then why are you so determined to push people away?" Avon's face, which was usually unruffled and full of immortal grace, turned wicked. Golden eyes narrowed like a bird of prey, and the sharp lines of his cheeks were accented by his piercings, making him look deadly. "Tell me, do you isolate yourself under the shield of duty to avoid facing yourself, as well as others?"

Marshall went hot and numb all over. He wanted to punch Avon, or better yet, to throttle him. Anything to stop that voice from piercing his soul in all the weak points of his emotional armor. "You have no idea the things I have done to stay alive. What do you know about struggle when you have spent your life under the protection of a kingdom far removed from any danger or poverty?"

His words hit their mark.

Avon was still for a long moment. "I may not be a senior of my race, but that does not mean I lack heart or merit. You see what you want, Marshall. The things you blind yourself to will surface. I hope it doesn't kill you in the end."

He turned, not giving Marshall a backwards glance, and spurred his horse down the road.

Marshall felt as if something new and fragile within him was breaking. The thing was—he'd been unaware until that moment that there was anything to break.

13

THE KHAZIRAKS

OBERION

THE PAIR OF THEM HAD MADE IT TO ADAVALE A BELL BEFORE MIDNIGHT. Oberion was inwardly agitated by the delay and doing his best to let it go. He couldn't hear the things Vaylin could last night and wasn't sure if she was having a laugh at him or being serious. She meant well and was doing what she thought was best, said the logical part of his brain. Her fear about these cracks or ruptures or whatever they were made him think that, for one impossible moment, the same thing was happening in the Wind District. He had thought all along that the disturbance in Mingalla was a mistake made by the shaman and nothing more.

What if he had been wrong…

The idea was unsettling.

It made him view this situation with a completely different perspective and regret his harsh behavior toward her. What would he have done if an entire village died without knowing the cause? What if it had happened when he first became an Elite?

He'd be here, doing exactly what Vaylin was.

The Mingalla stone was his biggest concern, and that was where he chose to focus. Whether the stone was the cause of or result of this crack, it was a dangerous magickal object that should be handled as little as possible until they knew more. Vaylin being the harbinger of such a power caused him unease. Someone like Aldwin, who was far older and more experienced with magick, would be a more suitable guardian of the stone. He'd tried to say as much to Hearthfire after Vaylin left his office that night, but the gatekeeper wouldn't hear a word against her.

Aldwin's words repeated in his mind. "You must trust her instinct. The stone came to her for a reason. Protect her, and you protect Panthea."

He gave up on sleep around dawn and went down to the yards to find the stable master. The Stronghold of Khazirak was three to five days from Adavale, depending on the weather, and he might as well get their new mounts for the trek ahead. Horses would be no good in the mountains compared to the climbing goats they would be taking instead.

The stable master was a sturdy old woman with weather beaten skin and thick, black-and-silver hair woven into a braid across her shoulder. Her name was Lena, and she barely reached his midriff. Her manner was nothing but confidence, and her commanding presence filled the stables, easily bending the animals to her will. He had known her for years and happily followed the little woman through the stables, which were impeccably clean. The animals were well groomed and all had a healthy glow about them. Lena cherished her animals, which was why he always chose her to trade with when near the mountains.

They reached the pen, and she opened the latch for him to see the climbing goats inside. He couldn't help but smile. These creatures were twice the size of their horses, with elegant horns curving off the sides of their head. Their fur was thick, excellent for cold weather, and varying shades of black, brown, white, and stone gray. They were perfectly camouflaged and had the uncanny ability to find sure footing on the icy rock paths that would cripple most horses. Despite their sure-footedness, once in a while they would randomly faint, dropping like a stone and causing mini earth shakes with their solid bulk.

"Which will you take?" Lena asked.

Some of them grazed, and others inexplicitly skipped and fainted with booms that shook the enclosure. He laughed as he watched them play.

There was a magnificent snow white one with muscles like corded iron. There was another that had beautiful, chestnut hues and horns a shade of ivory. That one was fainting the most and mainly responsible for the noise and shuddering coming from the pen.

"These two." He pointed at the ones he wanted.

"You have quite the eye, my guardian. Some of the finest beasts I've ever trained. The chestnut is named Loki and the white is Zama."

Oberion gave a warm smile. "You'll take care of those horses for us until we come back?"

"Of course! Of course! When are you thinking that will be, hmm?"

"We are not sure yet. I will send you a message when we arrive at Khazirak and let you know what our plans are."

"And what, pray tell, are you and the lady of the realm up to?" she asked innocently enough, but Oberion wasn't fooled. She knew as much gossip as the local bartender and always wanted the inside scoop.

He respected this woman and didn't want to offend her by rebuking her inquiries, but what he and Vaylin were doing was best left secret. "Some dwarven diplomacy. Nothing you need to worry yourself over."

"Very well, my Guardian. I shall prepare the goats for your journey and meet you in the stable yard," Lena answered with a bow of her head. She smiled warmly and her weather-beaten skin crinkled at the corners of eyes and mouth.

"Thank you, Stable Master." Oberion also bowed his head then walked out of the stables to find Vaylin looking around the yard.

"You're up early. Where are our horses?" she asked through a giant yawn. Her brown hair was braided on each side of her head, and those green eyes shone in the rising sun. Instead of her typical leather and tight clothing, this morning she wore long pants with knee-high leather boots and a white fur coat, her Eucalypta staff strapped across her back. She looked every bit an Elite Guardian, and Oberion was pleased to see her up early even though they'd gone to bed late.

"I've traded them to Lena for two of her climbing goats. They will be far safer for us to take into the mountains and much sturdier for the tougher terrain," he said.

"Two—what?" she repeated.

He was about to explain when Lena came trotting out of the stable behind him, leading two enormous goats. Vaylin stared at the animals, face a mask of shock and bewilderment.

The goats stood proudly next to Lena. The chestnut-colored one glanced at Vaylin and promptly fell over—shaking the whole yard and causing the horses to whinny nervously. Vaylin jumped back in fright at the force of the fall, and Oberion chuckled. Part of him did want to surprise her just to see how she'd react. Not many people got the chance to ride on these magnificent goats, and he thought she might like it, since those of Elder blood shared a unique connection to animals.

Lena laughed heartily, pet the beast lovingly on its side, cooing something in a different language. The goat replied in a chorus of neighing and wiggling on the ground, covering itself with dirt and bits of hay.

"You can't be serious right now," Vaylin said, aghast. "That thing could fall over at any moment and squish us underneath it."

"My goats would do no such thing," Lena said fiercely. "They are the best trained goats in the north. Ask anyone in Adavale or beyond. I guarantee you will safely reach your destination with one of my creatures."

Vaylin turned to Oberion, disbelief in her eyes. "Aren't we supposed to be communicating about these sorts of decisions?"

He didn't want to argue in front of Lena, who was listening intently. He gently ushered Vaylin to the side. "It slipped my mind until this morning. I knew we would need them once we got here and wanted to secure them for us before the day got busy. The goats are harmless, I promise."

She looked like she was trying hard not to smile as the second goat fainted to the ground with earth-shaking force. The pair of goats both squirmed happily in the dirt, and Lena laughed while scratching their bellies.

"They are rather cute," she whispered, turning away and failing to hide her amusement. He grinned at her smile.

"Just—tell me next time. I don't like being left in the dark. I feel like a gapping idiot."

Oberion was stunned. She had never called him out so openly before, and he sheepishly ran a hand through his hair, something he hadn't done in a long time. He dropped his hand quickly. "Starting now, I promise to be more informative. You can ask me whatever you want for the rest of our journey," he offered.

"Thank you." Shifting her posture, she turned back toward Lena with a smile and asked with genuine interest about the goats, the image of politeness.

Lena looked between Oberion and Vaylin, going along with everything and answering Vaylin's questions with a level of detail only a proud mother would know. Oberion stood back, mulling over Vaylin's words about trust and honesty.

A half hour later, the pair were on the enormous climbing goats heading westward into the mountains. Oberion rode the gleaming white goat and was pleased with her strength and stability. She was a magnificent beast and kept pace with ease up the slopes.

Vaylin looked uneasy on Loki, and Oberion could tell she was doing her best not to show it. He was good at picking up on people's little tells, and the more time they spent together, the easier it was to read her. Like how she bit her lip when she was feeling nervous or toyed with her hair when thinking deeply. Right now, she was focusing on her new mount with a little furrow between her brows.

The town of Adavale was far behind them and looked magickal from their vantage point on the cliffside. The hills were covered in emerald green grass, and sheep dotted the mountainsides like bunches of white clouds. Mist hung low in the air, and waterfalls ran off the cliffsides, feeding a teal blue glacier lake. The buildings were different shades of wood with trim like lace decorating windows and doors. Everything was painted with bright, vivid colors, adding a vibrant life to the town.

"It's a shame we didn't get to spend more time there," Vaylin said.

"We are coming back after we visit the dwarves. Maybe we could spend an extra day there to make up for it," he offered.

"Really?" She narrowed her eyes suspiciously but he could sense her hopefulness at his suggestion.

"Weren't you the one proclaiming the need for more communication?"

"I—yes," she said. "But the mission."

"Well, if we make good time in Khazirak, I don't see why we can't stay one day longer in a town we will have to pass through again to get home." He smiled at her, and she blushed, looking away from him.

As the days passed with no evidence of more ruptures or signs of distress in the countryside, Oberion felt more and more confident about this visit. The tension between him and Vaylin eased with each passing day, which would help once in the stronghold. Vaylin periodically stopped to observe the flora and fauna. She collected dropped feathers, leaves from bushes, samples of bark, and clumps of flowers, storing them in various bottles from her pack. Much to his surprise, she was able to better identify the local plant life than he was.

"Do you know how hard it is to come by these fresh in the market?" She picked a white mushroom poking up from rotting logs.

"If we keep stopping like this, we won't reach the stronghold until winter." He didn't spend nearly as much time in the wild as she did and preferred studying philosophy, logic, sacred geometry, and complex mathematics.

"I only have a few of these ingredients back at Panthea." She waggled the little bottle of mushrooms in front of her. Raising to her feet, she summoned a stone staircase to lift her back to the saddle before sinking it into the ground.

He watched their surroundings and tried to gauge how far they were from entering dwarven territory. "We're near the border of the dwarves. Half a day's ride and we will cross over into their lands."

Vaylin's mood shifted, and she fidgeted nervously on her seat. "All right." She attempted firmness while her cheeks paled and the freckles across her nose stood out. "I'm ready."

He could tell she was lying by the way she bit her lower lip.

"Are you nervous to meet them? I promise they are very hospitable and will welcome you into their mountain, even though you are of elven descent. You are an Elite Guardian of Panthea. They will honor that above the rest."

"That's reassuring but not my main concern," she said evasively.

She was working up to something, and he wanted to know what. "Then why so much hesitation? We need to get this cleared up before we enter the stronghold. Dwarves won't trust you if they think you're hostile or hiding something. They can tell if someone is being distrustful."

Vaylin bit her lip again, green eyes burning as she glared at him. "If you must know, I— I hate being underground," she admitted in a quick breath.

Oberion was dumbstruck by her words.

"Don't make fun of me, okay?" she said, clearly sensitive.

"How can you be afraid of being underground?" The notion was ridiculous. "Anyone with control over the terra element has nothing to fear, and you are an Elite Guardian. You can magick your way out of almost any situation. What's there to be afraid of?"

"I know that. It was the thing that pushed me to master the element in the first place. I'm fine with tight rooms or spaces, but there is something about being underground specifically that feels wrong. It's like I'm going to suffocate if I can't see the skies. My magick feels weaker too, and it becomes hard to summon. I don't know if it is an Elder thing or what, I just don't like it. Now, can we drop it, please?" Her cheeks had a light pink blush, and she avoided eye contact.

"You could have mentioned this sooner," he said in a kinder tone. "I had no idea this was even a thing. You won't go fainting while in the stronghold? I can't have my partner doing that on me."

His attempt at lightheartedness was met with cold resolve. "I'll manage."

He opened his mouth to reply and shut it. Never would he have guessed that a factor between elves and dwarves might be tied to a magickal one regarding weakness and strength of each race. Or that Vaylin, of all people, would have a sensitivity being underground. How long did she have to be underground for it to sap her magick? How long did it take to return? Would she be all right throughout their meetings? He wanted to ask her these questions but stopped himself. What kind of example was he setting if she would rather hide things like this from him than tell the truth?

Trust her.

"I'll make sure the dwarves don't hassle you too much. If you need to leave the stronghold, you can spend time with the goats. They keep most of the livestock in the fields outside of the stronghold. You could see the skies and feel fresh air whenever you want. The dwarves would never know. They have a special weakness for goats, and if they see you caring for these two giant loaves, they won't question what you're doing. It might even make them respect you more for caring about the animals the way you do," he tried to comfort her and felt like it was working.

Vaylin grinned weakly. "And here I thought I'd be trapped underground the entire time, doomed to certain misery."

"Elves can be so dramatic," he mocked, and her laugh was the sound of song birds and wind chimes.

The iron gray peaks and crevasses of the Khazirak Mountains plunged in either direction along the horizon. Evergreens grew from rocky soil, and bunches of grass sprouted in clumps of ochre, olive, and wintergreen. The land here thrummed with a raw and undisturbed power—wilderness unfolding around them.

The gravel path melded from neat stone to a road of paved bricks, not a broken corner or pothole in sight. The bricks were laid cleverly so the lines of the adjoining stone formed decorative square patterns that wove together perfectly. Endlessly. It was nicer than the sidewalks of Panthea Central.

Impressive. He appreciated the amount of time and craftsmanship it took to create such a feat. It added to the grandeur of the approaching mountain hall and was one of his favorite parts about this trip.

Vaylin looked around suspiciously, ears twitching at something he couldn't hear.

"Are you okay?" he asked.

"I dunno."

The goats were acting nervous as well, and he wondered if she could control them.

"We are crossing into the lands of the dwarves soon. They rule everything beyond that pillared arch in the distance. I doubt we will encounter any danger. The dwarves protect their boarders ruthlessly," Oberion said confidently.

"Right," she grunted. Her knuckles were white on the reins, and she kept an observant eye on the foliage around them.

They approached the stone pillars, reaching high above their enormous mounts. It formed a square archway and was carved from a single piece of rock. Veins of dark blue marble flecked with gold spread over solid black stone like nerve endings, glimmering darkly in the sunlight. It was polished stone and showed no signs of weathering. A rectangular mantel sat on top of both pillars, and runes were inscribed on it.

"What does it say?" Vaylin ran her fingers along the stone column as they rode by.

Oberion started, "It reads:

In the deepest, darkest reach
Born a race from earthen womb
With flame in heart and forges aglow
These lands are protected
By those below.
With hammer and axe,
No enemy shall pass
Into these mountain halls.

"I looked up the translation in Panthea's library after my first visit here," he said.

She peered at the marks. "This looks like it was built yesterday."

A slight shake of her head told him something wasn't right. It sent the hairs on his arms rising, and he could hear a slight popping noise. A subtle gesture from her hand told him to keep talking.

"Err—" he scrambled, resisting the urge to look around him. "Dwarven magick never tarnishes or shows the true age of an object.

It's like elven magick in that way." *What a stupid factoid.* It was the first thing that came to mind.

It worked.

Vaylin jumped onto the saddle of her goat and whipped her staff upward. The piles of snowdrift around the pillars rose skyward and transformed from powder to liquid as she pummeled a spot directly above them on the mantelpiece. Oberion covered himself and the goats with a blast of air and tried to see what Vaylin was attacking.

Before he could get a good look, Zama the goat let out a terrified neigh and fainted.

He pulled his foot from the stirrup, vaulted off the beast, and barely avoided being pinned to the ground.

Miraculously, Vaylin and her chestnut were still standing, fighting a patch on the pillars that was flaking off.

There was no way one human had the ability to corrode anything crafted from the dwarves. He froze some snow into an ice disk and glided toward Vaylin. The creature pinned against the pillar was flailing under her onslaught.

Icy water pierced eight tentacled arms lined with thousands of suckers, each one opening and closing like flower petals with tiny black beaks in their center. The tentacle was long enough to wrap itself around the column edges, holding fast against Vaylin's attack. The body of the creature itself was amorphous, shrinking and expanding, flashing colors, and changing textures to match leaves, twigs, clouds, water, pebbles, and pine needles.

Was this the thing that attacked the doe? How did it get into the mountains?

"What the hell is this, Oberion?" She withheld delivering a killing move without his direction.

"I have no idea," he yelled back. This was *his* district, and he wasn't sure what to think.

The creature looked like a octopus but was somehow surviving outside of the water. If it had been following them, it must have had some sentience or motivation to pursue them.

"Do we try to capture it?" She maintained a circular flow of snow, liquid, and ice to keep the creature contained.

He thought of the bottles she kept in her leather belt pouch. "Do you have any potions that cause paralysis?"

"I can try. A dose of water hemlock extract should work."

The pocket on her belt flipped open of its own accord, and a stream of muddy brown liquid mixed itself into the icy onslaught. It was about to reach the creature when the horizontal pupils of the tentacled thing widened, and several somethings whistled past Oberion's ear.

Four throwing axes embedded themselves in the black marble with a loud zing, as a substance blacker than the marble itself oozed from the decapitated limbs. A hideous wail came from the underside of the beast, and Vaylin wavered at the sound, her magick losing shape as she tried to see where the axes came from.

Four writhing tenacles fell to the ground with soft thumps as a pair of dwarves ran toward them, huffing and puffing like rhinos.

"Move out of the way," shouted a stout dwarf with bright blue hair, armor glinting in brightness of the snow and sun. He was closely followed by his yellow-haired companion who had hatchets in both hands.

"No, wait!" Oberion yelled.

It was no use. The two dwarves threw their weapons without hesitation, each one finding their marks.

Vaylin stopped her attack and moved away, watching the scene from astride her goat.

The agonized wail of the creature slowly diminished as dwarven hatchets and axes hacked it to pieces. It slid down the column with a lifeless flop and landed faceup, its curved beak clicking weakly as it bled out.

14

PUZZLE PIECES

ALDWIN

Two weeks after Vaylin and Oberion left for the Khazirak Stronghold, Aldwin sat at his office desk, poring over the pages Abraxas had given to him. As they agreed, Abraxas was now staying at Panthea in a lower apartment of the gatekeeper's tower. Aldwin chose this location particularly so he could be closer to his brother and keep an eye on him. Rowland Blackwell was thoroughly upset that Abraxas would be staying for the foreseeable future. The captain had insisted he be tailed while here, and Aldwin agreed, with the promise that whoever did it would remain hidden. It gave him some reassurance they would at least have eyes on Abraxas while Aldwin studied the mysterious document.

The pages themselves were grayish, and Aldwin wasn't sure what type of material it was. It had the dryness of parchment, the thickness of vellum, and left an oily residue on his fingers after handling it too long. Most paper was made from trees or plants, causing him to question the origins of this stuff. The ink itself was deep black with no evidence of fading or other damage. It made Aldwin think it was written recently, not twenty years ago.

It was a curious document, an amalgamation of symbols, numbers, and mechanical blueprints of different parts and pieces. There was something familiar about the script, and many of the mechanical draw-ings reminded Aldwin of the inventions Mundas had made them create. It was close to thirty pages long, and he had no clue where to start. Abraxas had given him the key to break the code, but Aldwin wasn't sure if he could trust it.

How had his brother even come up with a key to translate these pages?

Aldwin decided to use the key while creating his own and go from there. He had to make sure the key to the translation was accurate. It would be exactly like Maximus Mundas to hide something in plain sight, and Aldwin wasn't sure if Abraxas would recognize it if he did.

How had Abraxas even triggered those ripples, and were they acti-vated recently? Was it perhaps a time pocket spelled toward him or his blood?

Our blood.

He had heard some masters in the Psychic Union could create such things, usually to hide magickal objects away. It was immensely diffi-cult, and he had no memory of their father ever performing such magick. He was a historian born and raised in Panthea City, not a master psychic from the union. If that was the case, then it had to be Mundas sending these messages or someone who knew Abraxas, which was unlikely.

Abraxas's notes frequently expounded upon an object referred to as Ebony. The illustration detailing Ebony looked like an energy field with lines and circles radiating from a center point. Some of the circles looped back into the center, while others formed lines in random direc-tions and went off the page. It reminded Aldwin of partially formed spider webs and the orbital paths of planets.

The more he looked at it, the more incomplete the drawing seemed. Like a layer of something was missing.

A knock on his office door interrupted his thoughts.

"Come in." He dropped the notes he was examining.

The door swung open and in walked Neko Raneem, the Elite Guardian of the Terra Nation.

Aldwin smiled and shuffled his notes together. "How are you today, Neko?"

"Could be better." Neko was a robust Black man with the muscular bulk of a bull. A large, copper ring pierced his septum, and his brown eyes were kind, albeit weary.

"Does it have something to do with these ruptures?" Aldwin had sent messages over the CCs to the remaining Elite Guardians about the cracks Vaylin had warned of.

"I don't think so." Neko took the cushioned chair next to the desk. "I've been receiving reports from around the Terra Nation about a recent uptick in animal activity. Some beasts migrate with the seasons, like the Alizarik Bison or grassland gazelles. Others move throughout the lands at their own pace. I have reports claiming herds of elephants as far north as the Sound Federation's borders. Meanwhile, farmers are in uproar over flocks of vampiric bats. They've been sucking livestock dry across the countryside."

"Vampiric bats?" Aldwin repeated. "Don't those bats stay local to the forests they inhabit?"

"Yes. Not only that, I've had two reports in the last week saying werewolves are roaming the red sands. Werewolves, Aldwin. Can you believe it? I don't know what else to think. I've seen the pictures though, and I can't deny the injuries are nearly identical." Neko looked revolted.

"It's not out of the realm of possibility to have isolated contagion somewhere. Even so, there is little I can do otherwise. The Assemblage of Werewolves are granted certain areas of protection. So long as they reside within those limits, they are free to hunt at will. Have any humans been attacked?"

"Thankfully no. But if the werewolves think they can leave their regions to hunt in mine, they won't know what hit them when I reach them."

"Werewolves are forbidden to prey upon humans and other intellectual races without serious consequences. We could perhaps hold the assemblage accountable for an unprovoked attack on an innocent. Seeing that all the victims are animals, however, we cannot do anything more without further evidence."

"Something must be done though." Neko's eyes were hard and unfocused as he clasped his hands in front of him, elbows on his knees.

"What about the wanderer? Has anyone seen him around lately? Maybe he'd be able to stop this or have more information about what could be causing the animals unrest. I'd like to consult with him before making any decisions."

"He has been in the Southern Kingdom of the Elves. Due to a recent injury, he had to prolong his return to Panthea. I believe he will be making his way back here with due haste once he is fully healed."

"It's about time. What's the point of having a wanderer if he's never here when you need him?"

"Then you are perhaps lucky that he will be traveling through the Terra Nation to reach your embassy. He might discover something on his way to you that would be to your benefit. Much has transpired since we've last seen him, and it would be prudent to alert your citizens to keep their eyes and ears open for potential danger. If you are still concerned for the safety of your people, we can provide you with extra paladins as you see fit."

"Thank you, Gatekeeper. More paladins along the road would put me and others at ease. I still worry about those in the country that we can't reach. The Terra Nation is too vast to patrol and protect everyone thoroughly," Neko said heavily.

"The wanderer's job is to travel Chrysanthos to find and neutralize danger. You may be in luck when he returns. He does serve Panthea and all the countries in Chrysanthos, including your own."

"Point taken." Neko leaned back in his chair. "But he doesn't even know about these ruptures or whatever Vaylin and Oberion are dealing with. He's been out of CC range for weeks. You have to admit he should've checked back into Panthea last month."

Aldwin sighed greatly and rubbed his eyes, stopping quickly when he realized the residue from the gray pages was still on his hands. "Alas, I have to agree with you there. I allow him a certain amount of leniency that, in the current moment, is not wise. Trust me when I say that I will have words with him when he is back and re-affirm my expectations with him."

Neko nodded in approval and suddenly grabbed his forehead, wincing in pain.

"What's wrong?" Aldwin was halfway out of his chair to help when Neko waved him down.

"It's...nothing," Neko grunted. "Just a headache. I haven't been able to shake it lately. It twinges something terrible."

Concern filled Aldwin, and he was about to suggest a visit to the MediCenter when another knock came at the door. "Just a moment."

"Don't worry about me." Neko stood and shook his head. "This thing will go away soon enough. I swear allergies can be worse than any physical wound."

"If you're sure. When you see Marshall, send word to me immediately. And go easy on him."

"I will. Thank you again for your aid, Gatekeeper." Neko grimaced, palm on his temple as he stood and left the office.

15

FIRST IMPRESSIONS

VAYLIN

"THIS WASN'T HOW I WAS EXPECTING OUR ARRIVAL TO GO," VAYLIN muttered.

The creature they had killed—an octaped, as Oberion referred to it—was tied in a burlap sack onto a pole carried between the dwarves. Black blood that reeked of tar and decay stained the bottom and dripped like breadcrumbs as they went, staining the immaculate stone path to the stronghold.

"Me either," Oberion answered. "The octaped may or may not be related to these black ruptures. If an unknown entity is roaming the lands, it won't bode well with the khan, and he will be more willing to act with us.

"That thing sounded like the rupture in Mingalla. I'm sure it's related to those cracks somehow."

"If so, what on earth is it doing all the way out here? The dwarves would know if a crack was nearby. We would have heard about it."

"We've been on the road for two weeks and have no idea what's happening. I think the octaped was following us."

"Yes, I was wondering that too."

"Back in the forest, it didn't make sense that the deer was just left there. Most animals eat or hide their prey. I couldn't sense any life force near us but knew something was there. This creature has some sort of cloaking power, making it completely invisible to eye and ear, even my own. I think this octaped is smart and was trying to lure us into a trap."

"And how did you know it was there in the first place?"

"When we were talking, I could hear the suctions along the stone. It had a certain resonance I could trace. I didn't want the thing thinking we were onto it so I waited and guessed," she said with a little smile of satisfaction.

"That was one hell of a guess," Oberion said. "Why attack now though? What's different that would make it go for a direct attack?"

"I think it's this stone," Vaylin whispered, glancing at her pocket. "It was coming for me, not you."

"Oi, you two!" the yellow-haired dwarf shouted.

Vaylin jumped and looked down to see the two dwarves watching them intently.

"Save your jabbering for the khan. We're nearly there."

The dwarf eyed her suspiciously. She wasn't concerned about it. Not when she had bigger issues on her mind. If the octaped was hunting the stone, she was endangering Oberion and all the dwarves in the stronghold.

The creatures do not stop. They must not get the stone.

Could other creatures sense it? Would more come after her until they finally got what they wanted? The memory of the exsanguinated bodies in Mingalla rose in her mind. There had to be more of these creatures, and they must have been coming from these cracks.

They turned a corner on the cliffside, and Vaylin gasped as she beheld the dwarven Stronghold of Khazirak. It looked as if a giant had scooped the valley out of a mountaintop. Built from the cliffside was an ornate entrance way with two robust towers on either side of a gaping entrance into the mountain. Atop the entire thing, a grandiose stone carving of an angry dwarven warrior head had been carved from the mountain itself, its mouth open in a silent war cry as it overlooked the valley. Her gaze wandered up the massive guard towers, to the colossal stone sculpture of a dwarf's head, intimidating all who approached. She felt small in comparison. Maybe that was why dwarves-built things so large.

"By the gods," she whispered. If the sheer size of the entranceway was indicative of the insides, she was in for an architectural wonder, the likes of which she had never seen before.

The fields in front of the entrance were equal parts farmland and guarded fortress. From their vantage point, she spotted small dots moving around the grounds, going in and out of the entrance into the darkness beyond.

She gulped as her mouth suddenly went dry.

Thank the skies for Oberion's suggestion about the goats. It wasn't just kind; it was a lifeline he gave her. One she was desperate to cling onto throughout the duration of this visit.

As they neared the entrance, two sentinels on either side halted their progress. Almost all of the dwarves were dressed in heavy chain-mail and thick plate armor. The sentinels wore half helms with a piece of metal protecting the nose and square shields strapped to their backs. One sentinel carried a battle axe, while the other held a war hammer the size of Vaylin's goat's head.

They dismounted their goats and approached with Digli and Rigli, the two dwarves that had taken down the octaped.

"Greetings, my fellow dwarves. I am Oberion Watson, Elite Guardian of the Wind District. This is Vaylin Carina, Elite Guardian of the Aqua Realm. We are here to meet with your khan and clan leaders regarding an issue of utmost importance." Oberion somehow managed to be graceful and authoritative as he bowed to the guards, Vaylin mimicking his example.

She couldn't mess this up. There was too much on the line for her, and Oberion could tell Aldwin anything about this trip. Vaylin was determined to succeed.

The dwarf looked at his companion with the battle axe and nodded somberly. Indicating the burlap sack, the sentinel with the hammer asked, "What do you got there?"

"Not sure," answered Digli, the blue-haired dwarf. "The border alarm went off, and by the time we got there, these two were already fightin' it. Came to aid and finished off the beastie."

"All right," the other sentinel said. "Let them through. I can't stand the stink of it. Leave your things and your...goat beasts. They will be cared for."

Rigli followed as Digli lead the way, and the guardians followed suit.

The air felt like a vacuum, pulling her into the darkness and freezing her solid. There was a loud bang from behind her, and she jumped what felt like a foot into the air.

Everyone turned. Her chestnut goat had fainted in the middle of the road, rolling around joyously as many dwarves came out to pet its big belly. The beast deserved it after the fright it had with the octaped.

"There's a way to make an entrance." She feebly tried to laugh at Loki, the mischievous and attention-seeking goat.

Their group entered the mountain, and after crossing the threshold, it felt like a lead blanket was draped over her magick. She swallowed, hard. Bracing herself for the trek downwards.

Before them descended a grand staircase made of polished gray stone. Digli and Rigli were halfway down before the guardians reached the bottom step. How did they move so fast? The ceiling was impossibly high, and their escort reached the bottom quickly and disappeared. Droplets of black blood still fell from the sack.

Oberion let her lead the way, and she wasn't sure it was to prevent her from turning around or if he was trying to support her through this. His mood had changed considerably since nearing the Khazirak Stronghold, and the comradery that was easy with other Elite members had finally started to form between her and Oberion.

They crested the last steps, and Vaylin's mouth dropped open again. If she was surprised by the paved road and sweeping fields before the stronghold, it was nothing compared to the main hall.

It was a cavernous space, the ceiling so tall she couldn't see where it ended. Hundreds of columns spread throughout the hall, connected by archways that crisscrossed the space and illuminated by glowing quartz crystals at the base of each pillar. Despite being underground, there was a slight air current here, and it smelled clean and warm. The never-ending chorus of hammers, squelching metal, and pickaxes on rock were the music of the hallowed hall. Her gaze traveled up the blue marbled veins of the walls. It took little imagination to see the lifeblood of the mountain pulsing through those lines.

It reminded her of the Mingalla stone. That made her hopeful.

Oberion prodded her gently in the back. "If you don't shut your mouth, you're going to swallow a moth. I'd hate for that to be the first impression you give our hosts."

She laughed. The suffocating claustrophobia released its tight grip by a fraction. "I think the octaped and goat ruined that for me already. I thought it would feel cramped and dark in here." She shook her head in astonishment as they followed their hosts, turning in a slow circle to take it all in. "This...this feels like a canopy of stone trees."

"People never quite realize how much space there can be underground. The thousand years of digging helps."

Digli turned around and called out. "Keep up please."

They picked up their pace a little. For someone two feet shorter than her, this dwarf was making it his mission to power walk the whole way to his khan. She couldn't blame him. Other dwarves moved in all direction as they went about their business, carrying sacks or pushing wheelbarrows of ore, coal, chunks of metal, and rough hued stone. The dwarves on average stood around four feet tall and all wore a similar combination of outfits of chainmail, leather, bits of armor, heavy boots, and different bits of brightly colored clothes and hats that distinguished them from one another.

And the hair. Vaylin had never seen people with so much hair on their heads and faces. Some of them had bushy nests of hair atop their heads. Others had perfectly trimmed mustaches that ranged in all manner of sizes and shapes. Some had dyed their hair to match the colors of their clothes. She snickered to herself as a dwarf passed by with an electric goatee, crooning to a fire salamander held in their arms.

Vaylin thought she even saw a few female dwarves. They were dressed similarly to the male dwarves, but gods save her, they had facial hair too. Not as prolific as the men but enough she had to choke back her surprise when a female passed by with a thinly trimmed mustache and unibrow long enough to be pulled into the braided strands on their head.

The dwarves stared as they passed, ignoring her elf ears for the much more interesting and reeking sack between Digli and Rigli.

"I didn't realize dwarves are so...colorful?" she whispered to Oberion, trying hard to maintain her composure and not giggle or stare too much.

"If you are surprised by this, it's nothing compared to the khan. He has a thing for purple," he said conspiratorially.

She smiled at the thought. "Who would have thought."

"Never presume to know a dwarf. They are as different as any human can be." He looked at her from the corner of his eye. "You all right?"

"Not bad." It was hard enough to admit her weakness, and she didn't want to voice it now.

He seemed to read her expression carefully and dropped it. Instead, he leaned in close. "I'll handle most of the introductions with the khan, if that's all right. I'll let you explain what happened in Mingalla and the octaped. They will want to hear it from you, not me. I will have your back if you need it in there."

"You promise?" There was a lot on the line here, and she wanted to trust him.

"Of course. The khan can be a little extravagant at times and reminds me of Fabien. I swear, he is quite sane and easy enough to deal with."

"What do you mean, 'quite sane'?"

"I think the fumes from the forges gets to the dwarves' heads a bit. Makes them a little insane—or brilliant. I haven't decided which yet," joked Oberion.

At least she thought he was joking.

Before she could respond, the two dwarves halted and looked back at them.

"We are here," they said in unison.

The stone doors in front of them were banded together with black iron and anchored into the wall ahead. Square designs and repeating geometric shapes decorated the framework, and an enormous iron knocker fashioned into a hammer hung in the middle of the door.

There was a crown etched onto the hammer. This had to be the khan's residence.

Digli knocked three times. The door opened of its own accord, and the two dwarves stepped into the room. Oberion gave her a quick smile and gestured forward. She strode past him, shoulders back and head high with as much poise as she could muster.

A long, stone table in the middle of the space rose solidly from the ground. It was currently filled with a host of dwarves as they sat, eating, drinking, and talking. Fires burned in grated hearths along the walls, filling the room with pleasant heat. A stone throne was fashioned on a raised platform against the one wall. It was relatively plain compared to the dwarf sitting on it.

His hair was vivid purple, and he was adorned in silver metal from crown to boot. Each finger was covered in sparkling rings, and his armor shone like liquid mercury.

Vaylin and Oberion made their way toward the khan, who watched them as they approached. The volume in the room dropped, and many watched covertly from behind their tankards of ale or mead.

"What do we have here?" asked the khan.

"Greetings, Khan Kharak Druzy. It is good to be in your mountain hall once more, and it warms my heart to see you alive and well. The forges are burning brightly, the ale is flowing, and the food smells delicious," Oberion announced to scattered grunts of approval.

Sweat prickled at Vaylin's forehead. Oberion was usually quiet, never drawing attention to himself, and composed to the point of indifference. Now he spoke in a way that reminded her of Marshall's jovial tone and acted like everyone was his best friend.

"It is a pleasure to see you in our halls again, Oberion Watson. Who is your friend?" the khan said in a deep and gravelly voice. "It seems you bring grim tidings with you."

"May I introduce to you my esteemed companion and fellow Elite member, Vaylin Carina of the Aqua Realm." Oberion stepped to the side and let Vaylin step forward.

She bowed at the introduction. "I am humbled to be here and to receive such a fine welcome."

"I haven't seen an elf in my halls for over three centuries," Khan

Druzy responded. He squinted at her before sniffing greatly. "Or should I say, part Elder? You aren't full blood, are you, girl?"

Vaylin didn't appreciate the manner in which he addressed her. "Begging your pardon, Khan, but I am no girl."

The khan kept his stony expression, and Oberion's eyes implored her.

Right. Diplomacy. "Your speculation about my heritage is correct. My mother was human, and my father was an elf, likely from the Northern Citadel, though I am not certain."

The khan's gaze flicked between hers and Oberion's. "I like her," he said. "It must be a matter of great importance to warrant both of you coming here."

"They were attacked on the border," Rigli said, yellow hair coming out of its braid.

Khan Druzy snorted in disgust. "By what? Rockhounds? Trolls? We've killed more than enough goblins lately that it will be a while before we see their likes again."

"It was not one of your common enemies, Khan," Oberion said calmly.

"It was a bleeding cephalopod. Out of the water and in our mountains." Digli dropped the sack and untied it.

The stench had all the dwarves gagging and retreating from the table. Many of them shouted angrily, shocked by the mysterious creature.

The khan showed no reaction besides a lip curling in disgust at the octaped.

Oberion motioned to Vaylin to take the floor.

She spoke clearly. "We have come here regarding a matter of great distress to all of Chrysanthos." She glanced at Oberion, who nodded encouragingly. "We seek aid in our time of need and have come to ask for help."

Khan Kharak Druzy ran a hand through his purple beard, assessing the woman in front of him. "Let us speak in private. I'd not have rumors spreading through these halls like poisonous gas. Dorian, Gizmo, and Oaken, come with us. Digli, Rigli, burn this creature and make sure every fowl bit of it is cleaned from this hall."

He stood and went to a side door, waving at them to follow. Three dwarves from various spots at the table got up and made their way toward the end of the room. Oberion glanced at Vaylin, who kept her face a mask of calm as they followed. Her head ached slightly, and her magick squirmed under the weight of the rock above.

"This is a good start." Oberion ushered her along.

"We shouldn't let them burn the octaped. We should study it."

"Don't." He took her arm to stop her from saying anything. "What the khan says is law. Contradicting him will only irritate him and make asking for his aid more difficult."

"It's such a waste," she said regretfully.

Digli and Rigli were surrounded by a cluster of dwarves, all determined to make assessments and help dispose of the creature.

"I know."

There was disappointment in his eyes, and she was strangely comforted that he agreed with her. She didn't want to kill that creature in the first place. If the dwarves hadn't interfered, what would they have learned from it?

PERSUASION

VAYLIN

A SOLID STONE WALL AT THE END OF THE DINING HALL WAS ENGRAVED with dwarven glyphs and knotwork designs of squares that twisted around the edges. In the center was a depression the size of a hand. The khan placed his adorned appendage in the space, and the wall shuddered to life.

Glyphs filled with purple light, and the wall slowly sank into the floor.

The chambers were nothing short of lavish. Stone shelves were built into and out of the walls, holding an assortment of books, gemstones, odd gadgets with exposed gears, weapons, and pieces of armor. Sofas and chairs scattered around the room looked comfortable, despite being a little worn. Side tables carried beer, liquor, more food, and a variety of smoking pipes. Several hexagonal chandeliers hung from iron hooks and chains in the ceiling, casting a warm glow around them.

The three dwarves and the khan helped themselves to tankards of ale.

Vaylin stood there awkwardly. Mounted on the wall directly across from her was the grotesque face of a howling giant. The thing was hideous, with short, bristly hair and wrinkled, gray skin. Its head had been chopped clean off, long-dried blood browned with age lining the neck. She avoided the giant's murderous face and looked for Oberion.

He had wandered across the room to examine an enormous tapestry.

It took up the entire wall and was a perfect rendering of the underground layout of the Khazirak Stronghold. Vaylin was entranced by the many levels, halls, and passageways the dwarves had carved deep into the mountain. It was amazingly complex and reminded her of the inside of an ant hill.

"I see you have an eye for fine things," the khan remarked. At his full height, he barely reached her shoulders. She couldn't deny the solid strength that emanated from him. "Every year, I have one of my engineers come in and add the new passageways to that map. Are you impressed by the giant head?"

"It's...very ferocious," she said.

"My great-great grandfather Zür killed the beast himself. It was a massive giant, nearly twenty feet tall and more vicious than a hoard of goblins in a blood rage. It terrorized the dwarves trying to settle here, eating them by the dozen after smashing them to death. Grandfather Zür went off by himself, ready to spill our mortal enemies' blood and stop the murder of our kin."

"I can see he was quite successful," she said earnestly. Was Khan Kharak telling her this to frighten her? Or to impress her with their bravery?

"Indeed, he was. He fought for three days and three nights. On the fourth day, he swung his mighty battle axe into the neck of our foe and toppled the giant once and for all. He and my clan have ruled under these mountains for fifteen hundred years since. There is no grander stronghold in Chrysanthos than our own."

"Truly impressive. This is my first time in a dwarven stronghold. I am honored that this is the one I am so privileged to see."

The khan beamed at her, his chest swelling with pride. "Come, I doubt you have made such a hasty journey here to listen to the glory of our forefathers. Let's hear what you and Oberion have to say." He rummaged for a smoking pipe in the folds of his clothes and packed it with a fragrant, green leaf. He waved vaguely toward the goods as he continued his ministrations. "Help yourself to any refreshment."

"Thank you." Vaylin glanced at the food but felt no real hunger.

Oberion walked over and offered her a glass of red wine, having poured one for himself. "If the khan offers you refreshment from his table, he means no ill will. Guests are protected by the law of hospitality in dwarf culture and by taking refreshment, you agree to it."

She took the wine with a nod of thanks and sat with him on a couch opposite Khan Kharak. Once the khan was satisfied with his pipe, he lit it with a snap of his fingers, inhaling a deep drag and exhaling gray smoke into perfect rings.

"Mmm." He smacked his lips approvingly. "The Terra Nation still produces the finest herbs in all of Chrysanthos." He pulled once more on his pipe before speaking. "Let me introduce my dwarven chieftains."

Gizmo Forgeworm of the Firekeeper Clan wore goggles on top of his head, flaming red hair teased out in all directions beneath them. Soot was smeared across the broad expanse of his forehead, and although he had bushy eyebrows, parts of them looked as if they had been recently singed off. The second dwarf, Rathir Stoneborn of the Icebane Clan, had hair of the purest white. It shone moon bright, and his waist-length beard was silky smooth. The third dwarf, Oaken Tourmaline of the Whiteoaks, had coarse, black hair pulled into a thick braid down the center of his skull, and his eyes shone dark green under hooded lids. They all wore an assortment of gleaming leather and armor that covered their chests, arms, and legs. It was finely made. The metalwork expertly crafted and inlayed with copper, brass, and silver shone against the dark steel of the plate.

"They have lived in the Khazirak Mountains for many generations." Khan Kharak finished.

"It is an honor to meet you all," Vaylin said.

"As it is mine, fair lady," Rathir, the silver-haired dwarf, answered. Oaken slightly inclined his head, and Gizmo, remained silent. He reminded Vaylin of an owl, with those round eyes.

"Don't mind Gizmo," the khan said. "He's the most brilliant engineer we've ever seen, but he can be a little…odd sometimes. Isn't that right, Gizmo?"

"Khan, I was simply puzzling over the strangeness of our new guest." He pulled his goggles down to stare at Vaylin, making his eyes appear buggy. "Ah, now I see it."

"See what?" Oberion asked.

The dwarf was distracted completely by this, and glee filled his face as he focused on Oberion, like this was the first time he'd seen the man all evening. "If it isn't my most favorite tinkerer and fellow mad man! What will we be experimenting with this time, Oberion? Flaming weapons, catapults, or harnessing energy into portable devices?"

Now the burnt eyebrows made sense.

"I've told you a dozen times—it's Fabien Prince's work, not mine. I am merely the messenger." Oberion grinned like a fiend. "But perhaps this will keep you entertained."

Oberion pulled a tightly rolled scroll from inside his pocket. Gizmo's face lit up, and he squealed. The scroll had the orange wax seal of flame of the Igni Territory on it.

"I knew you'd have something for me," Gizmo said. "You know where my forge is and are always welcome to visit me at any hour and—"

"To business," the khan interjected, returning his focus back to Vaylin. "Now tell me, dear lady, what business it is that Panthea wants with the dwarves."

Vaylin reached into the leather satchel on her belt and pulled out the Mingalla stone. It shone, white aura pulsing and red stones twinkling across the pale pink surface. Immediately, the dwarves all straightened and looked eager at the treasure she presented. The khan's eyes grew wide as he took the stone from her proffered hand. Gizmo pulled his goggles on again and stared inquisitively at the stone.

She spoke for nearly a half hour about the Mingalla village, the crack, and the stone she used to seal the rupture. "What we need your help with is identifying this stone. We have no idea what it is or where it came from."

Vaylin held her breath as she watched the dwarves and their reaction.

"How peculiar," the Khan mused. He took a long drag from his pipe.

"The stone is alien," Oaken said. "How does she come by such a thing? In a fey inhabited forest, no less?"

"Alien?" Oberion repeated.

"It is no ordinary stone," Oaken said.

"Yes, we have ascertained that already," Oberion said. "Please, explain more."

"I think," Rathir said with a glance at Oaken, "what Oaken means is that not all stones found on this earth are created here. Things fall to us from space, whilst others were embedded into the foundation of our world during its creation. This stone has clearly not originated in Chrysanthos." He had a scholarly air about him. "In the creation legends of dwarves, many believed that when this world was formed, it pulled in various elements from the sky and space to form our world. This is how we have metals like mithril and gold, for they are a metal beyond anything this little earth could create. Some stones in Chrysanthos are not stones at all but glass formed from meteors. I suspect this stone is of similar origins."

"Do you know what this is called?" Vaylin asked.

"Alas, I do not," Rathir answered regrettably.

Her heart sank. Mining for more was off the table then. Half-formed ideas about arming paladins with this crystal fell away to nothing. If this were a stone from space, who could they ask about it, and how would they ever find more? Would Madame Zahira of the Psychic Union be willing to help them?

"What is more concerning to me is the nature of this blackness," Khan Kharak said quietly. "The dwarves are all too aware of the dark places in the world and the horrors that reside there. Those who have dug have not always returned, swallowed by shadows and nightmares born in the chasms of the deep."

A chill went up Vaylin's spine, and she imagined colossal fiery demons. "The Mingalla tribe aren't miners or cave dwellers. They are foragers and isolated from the modern world."

"Forest dwellers, eh?" Oaken said. "Perhaps the fey Folk have something to do with it. It would be just like them to create a pointless and dangerous object to drive humans mad."

"The fey have nothing to do with this," Vaylin said firmly. "They told me of a shadow in their forest that they were not able to kill. They have a duty, a stewardship to the forest, as you do with these mountains. I think the shadows they were tracking were released from the crack in Mingalla." Her pronouncement raised eyebrows from the dwarves and Oberion. A thrill went through her stomach at the impressed look he gave her.

"If what you say is to be believed, then the dwarves are at highest risk. Our homes are underground," Khan Kharak said. "Many of us do not venture to the surface for years at a time. Creatures of darkness have always been our enemy, and few surface dwellers understand this or care."

"We care," she said. "That is why we are here asking for help and offering our own."

"You only want help with the stone, girl, and then you'll forget about us," Oaken accused.

"That is uncalled for," Oberion cut in. "Panthea Central wants to aid the dwarves, and nothing about our past dealings would indicate otherwise. Vaylin Carina is here on behalf of her country and its people. Surely you can sympathize and understand what she is going through. An entire tribe was wiped off the map because of it. We do not want to see *anyone* suffer that fate again." His voice commanded respect.

Oaken's face was furious as the khan raised a hand to silence him.

"Nevertheless, you have come here in a time need, asking for our help, and now we must consider the risk this puts us in." The khan's voice was as unyielding as metal.

"Panthea offers the Khazirak Stronghold allyship and protection for your knowledge on this subject," Vaylin said. "We also have a powerful stone that has proven effective in combating the effects of the ruptures. Should the same fate as the Mingalla people fall upon you, we would use it to help your stronghold."

"What if we visit Skyminer?" Gizmo dreamily tilted his head sideways as he examined the crystal.

"Skyminer is a myth," Rathir said. "No one has seen hide nor hair of the collector in over a century."

"Who is Skyminer?" Oberion asked.

"He doesn't exist," Oaken said stubbornly.

"Oh, yes he does." Gizmo's eyes were still magnified with the goggles on. "*I* have met him."

Oaken snorted so loudly Vaylin was surprised nothing flew from his face.

"How come you have not mentioned this until now?" Khan Kharak reprimanded.

"No one has ever asked me," Gizmo said like it was the most obvious thing in the world.

"Great mountains above, Gizmo. Are you kidding me?" the khan demanded. "You mean to tell me you know where one of the most notorious dwarves of our history is and you never once found it relevant to say anything?" He slammed his fist onto the arm of his chair.

"I'm saying something now, aren't I?" Gizmo said. "He wasn't that special. A little touched in the head if you ask me."

Vaylin tried hard not to laugh at the disbelief on Khan Kharak's face and Gizmo's innocence, who looked like a demented owl. *Really, they might all be touched in the head.*

"Who is Skyminer?" Oberion urged. The air around him stirred, and the dwarves all looked at him in alarm. His wind magick felt like a balm to her aching head, and her magick lifted at the touch of it.

She only had to hold on until this meeting was over. Then she could sneak outside and lay with the chestnut for a while.

"Skyminer is one of the oldest dwarves to have ever lived in these mountains." Rathir's eyes flashed like chips of ice. "His collection of crystals is so vast, so precious, that many tried to steal it for their own. He grew paranoid and moved it deeper within the mountains to keep it safe from prying eyes and greedy hands. No one has seen him since. It is rumored that he has one of every crystal to have ever been found in Chrysanthos."

"It's true. I have seen it for myself," Gizmo proclaimed.

"What!" all three dwarves said in unison.

A laugh finally escaped Vaylin at their indignation.

"Gizmo Forgeworm, not only have you met the infamous Skyminer but you've laid eyes on his *hoard*?" The khan's eyes narrowed as purple eyebrows contracted.

"It was beautiful." Gizmo seemed completely unperturbed by the khan's annoyance.

"And when exactly did you see Skyminer and his collection?" Disbelief was etched across Oaken's face, and he sat with his arms crossed tightly. "Have you imagined all of this, or have the fumes from your forge rotted your brain?"

"Hmm...two years ago," Gizmo answered.

"Two years!" the khan exclaimed.

Oaken grumbled something in dwarfish under his breath, and the khan nodded his agreement. Rathir looked like he wasn't sure what to believe.

"I was wandering the Chazakül Mountains for a place to test one of my inventions when I stumbled across the most peculiar set of stairs. None but a dwarf would have recognized them, for they were well hidden. Even then, I wasn't sure they were real. I took a chance and decided to follow them. Wouldn't you know it, they led me straight to Skyminer's Keep. The poor fellow didn't trust me at first, but he could see I was in a right state and needed a hand."

"Just like that, you found the most mysterious and well-hidden dwarf of our time," the khan said in disbelief. "I have heard you say some outlandish things in my time, Gizmo, but this tops them all."

"You do listen to me then." Gizmo happily missed the insult of the khan's words.

Vaylin seized the chance to speak up before the dwarves could start arguing again. "Did you see anything like this stone there? Did Skyminer have another?"

She held her breath in anticipation. Two stones would be better than one.

Gizmo turned to her, eyes wide. "I do not remember. Skyminer has many rooms in his hole and many treasures hidden throughout. Only he knows his collection."

"We need to get to Skyminer. He's our best chance at finding out the truth of this stone." She turned toward Oberion, excitement ebbing away from her. How long would it take to get to Skyminer? How would they even find him?

"That is, if he is willing to help at all." Oberion rubbed his hand across his jaw, thinking hard.

"Can you take us? How long will it be to get there?" Vaylin asked Gizmo.

"About nine rotations of the sun if we can take the Lumbrinica Tunnel," he answered.

"Nine turns?" she repeated numbly.

The weight of the mountain pressing on her was unbearable. She couldn't breathe and needed to leave. Just before she stood, Oberion placed a hand on her leg to keep her steady. It didn't matter if he saw her fear right now.

"Excuse me," interrupted Khan Kharak in frustrated tones, "do you plan on taking one of my chieftains and running off into the horizon without asking my permission first?"

Vaylin jumped, completely forgetting that she was in front of the khan and it was his decision if Gizmo was to help them.

"No, of course not, Khan Kharak," Oberion said quickly. "Time is not on our side, and Vaylin only asks out of care for her people. Considering how adamant you are about the safety of the Khazirak Stronghold, I'm sure you can understand her urgency, and Panthea's, to deal with this problem swiftly."

Oaken snorted again. "If you let Gizmo lead you into the mountains, you are both fools and will be lost within a day."

"Enough, Oaken." The khan had a shrewd look in his eyes. "Well played, Oberion. I grant you permission to take one of my chieftains as a guide into the Chazakül Mountains to find Skyminer's Keep. You learn about this Mingalla stone and share your intel with me. Should any misfortune come to Khazirak Stronghold while you are gone, we expect help from Panthea without question. Is that understood?"

"Absolutely," the guardians said at the same time. They looked at each other in surprise.

The khan nodded in approval of their synchronicity and immediacy to agree. Dwarves hated lengthy discussions and got bored arguing the nuance of things—best to be firm and decisive.

"I have one condition," the khan said. "I want Rathir and Oaken to accompany you on this journey."

FOLLOWING LIGHTNING

MARSHALL

MARSHALL WAS STUNNED BY AVON'S SUDDEN DEPARTURE AND AT A LOSS for what to do next. He never actually considered that the elf would leave him, despite wanting that from the beginning. Now that he was absent, it felt as though something was missing. For all of Avon's posturing about following him and feeling a pull between them, how could he have left so easily?

This whole situation was silly and exactly why he felt stupid for letting himself get attached to Avon. The lingering disappointment and hurt an unexpected twist. One that he hadn't known or felt in a long time.

Perhaps Avon was trying to prove his point by leaving, and this whole thing was an act to see how Marshall would respond. Either way, he had little patience with drama of any sorts. He spurred his horse on, expecting Avon to come into view at any moment if he stayed on the road and kept up his pace.

But the longer he rode, the more it dawned on him that, if Avon didn't want to be found, he probably wasn't going to be. Avon talked openly about his skills in stealth and was riding one of the best horses from the Southern Kingdom. He was a natural with horses, and Marshall doubted he would catch up even if he tried.

It did nothing to increase his morale.

Mile after mile went by. Marshall started to feel disquieted after the third day without any sight of the elf and wondered if he had booked it all the way to the Terra Embassy. It was a ten-day journey across the desert at top speed. Unless Avon swapped his mount for a fresh one, he would need to stop to give the horse a rest.

Frustrated beyond measure, Marshall pulled on the reins of his horse and dismounted. He needed to collect himself and walked beside the horse for a time to give the beast a break.

No matter what happened, Avon would be going to the Terra Embassy and most likely reach it first. Whatever was between them, Avon was obligated by the southern king to deliver his message to Panthea. Which left Marshall with two options: head to the Terra Embassy with due haste to arrive before Avon or continue as he was and show up whenever he damn well pleased. If he arrived after Avon, so be it. Avon would recount the tale to the gatekeeper without him, and Marshall could confirm details once he got there. Aldwin would not approve of Marshall's lack of courtesy. He was already facing some type of reprimand for his lengthy time away from Panthea.

He groaned aloud and led his horse off the road to a low over-hanging of rock. There was a stream nearby, and Marshall summoned water in a glittering ribbon for the horse to drink while he set up camp for the night. He felt no hurry anymore.

In fact, he was positively dreading going back and considered staying out here for another few weeks just to avoid the drama. He didn't want to face Avon, not after their argument or whatever that was. He sat against a boulder and wondered why he was feeling so bitter and resentful.

I'm the mirror you don't want to face.

Marshall didn't think there was anything wrong with his behavior. He kept to himself most of this journey. What was wrong with that? And he had loads of friends all over Chrysanthos. Granted, he only bothered to visit or get in touch when he was in the area. He never had time to write letters to people during his work for Panthea and his CC only worked within the embassies or Panthea Central itself.

There was a dull ache in his chest, like he'd been hollowed out. He tried to find the familiar comfort of being alone again, but something was off. Everything he did felt foreign and wrong.

He thought about their conversation about eclipses and planets and wondered if he was feeling this way because of their influences. He watched the skies and could see the moon and sun drawing close to one another. True, the moon effected the tide. One could argue that it had power over their world that way, which made more sense.

Avon's ideas were impossible, improbable really.

For some reason that thrilled him. It was a freedom in his normal construct of reality, and the corner of his mouth twitched into a smile.

Was this what the elves were taught growing up? He didn't know much about the elven educational system and made a note to ask Avon about his upbringing.

He quickly stopped himself. Avon was nowhere to be seen and probably wouldn't want to share with him after this anyway. It was foolish to think that, after one fight, they would never be able to speak to each other again. Friendship meant dealing with the bad shit as much as the good. Avon should know that.

Marshall lay there as twilight crept across the skies, thinking about Avon and unable to find a comfortable position.

The eclipse wasn't due to happen until tomorrow around sunset. He had never seen an eclipse in person before. It required precise timing and location, depending on which hemisphere one was in. He was excited to see it, and the desert seemed like the perfect place to witness such an event. There was no noise or light pollution from the cities out here. The night sky was a blanket of darkness above him. His had the most surreal feeling as he realized gravity was the only thing keeping him, and everything else, here on earth. It was easy to forget that invisible force.

He thought absently about what to do and decided that he needed to find Avon before reaching the Terra Embassy. How difficult could it be? He knew this land well enough and was confident that he could reach the elf. Marshall dozed off with that comforting thought.

When he woke the next morning, he set off across the horizon with high hopes.

By midday, his midnight hopes were deflating. He had spent hours looking across canyons, trying to decipher tracks in the heat waves coming from the sun and off the ground. Besides a few trade caravans passing him in the opposite direction, none of which had seen an elf when he asked, he came up with nothing.

There was no sign of the elf, and Marshall was in a foul mood because of it.

How could he have let this happened? He wanted to send Avon a message but had no bird with him, only the pen and paper. What good was writing a letter with no way of delivering it? Maybe there was another way to send some sort of signal.

Marshall had an idea.

Scrambling to his feet, he went over to his horse and rummaged in his bags. After a moment, he withdrew a coil of string, a few jars of powder, and a tube-shaped metal rod in his arms. He knew that stop in the Igni Territory for these powders would be worth it. Arranging the materials before him, he sat and thought—what signal would Avon recognize that no one else would? His first thought was of the crest for the Southern Kingdom, but it didn't seem good enough.

Then it came to him. He poured different powders and stones into the tube, whispering a spell that the shopkeeper taught him while he worked. A pinch of this, a dash of that, and soon it was ready.

The sun was getting low in the sky by the time he finished.

He had gathered up his belongings started down the road again. Sitting astride his horse, he aimed his signal toward the sky and held his breath. He summoned a ball of fire to his fingertips with a snap. It burned bright yellow before catching the wick on fire, and sparks blossomed from his hand as he directed his signal toward the skies. It fizzled in his hand and shot out of the tube with a muffled thump then soared into the air like a firework.

When it reached its zenith in the sky it burst into a black, swooping shape.

Terrible in its familiarity, the chiro formed above him, darker than the orange-and-indigo sky.

He urged his horse down the road, and the signal followed him like a kite, looking for all the world like a real threat as it appeared to pursue him along the path. Within twenty minutes, hooves approached, and he turned to see Avon galloping over the ridge beside him, eyes blazing with fury and swords drawn in each hand.

Marshall grinned and, with a snap of his fingers, extinguished the shadow above him in a puff of smoke. He knew he would come. No one else would have recognized the chiro and come running. Only Avon.

"You," Avon growled.

"Listen to me…" Marshall called.

"Why should I waste my time and energy on someone so ignorant as yourself?" Avon was clearly offended. Which was exactly why he had chosen the chiro. "Using the chiro to summon me like that, the audacity."

"I'm sorry. I knew you would come if you saw it. I've been trying to find you for days and didn't know what else to do," Marshall pleaded.

"Why is that?"

"I'm just— I don't want to be alone. I'm sorry for how I acted. I'm not used to taking criticism, all right?" Marshall explained. "I was angry and defensive, and I didn't mean to act that way. It's…hard for me to trust."

"That doesn't give you the right to take your discomfort and insecurities out on me," Avon said swiftly.

"You are right. I shouldn't have." Marshall didn't want to fight Avon, only make amends.

"What changed your mind?" Avon asked cautiously. He sheathed his weapons and looked fractionally less menacing.

"I don't know. Being alone didn't feel the same anymore," Marshall admitted. "I'm used to having people to care about when I'm with them. Otherwise, I have no one. It never really bothered me until I was sitting there alone the other night and wanting to talk to you."

Avon continued to give him that penetrating look, like staring down a bird of prey.

Marshall continued, "I didn't want you walking into Panthea without me. The gatekeeper would not be impressed with me, and I want to prove that you can rely on me, especially after that life debt I owe you." It felt awkward saying it, but it was the right thing to do.

Avon looked smug as he sat on his high horse. Literally.

Marshall had said what he needed to, and the next move was Avon's.

After waiting for what felt like forever, Avon cleared his throat. "We should find somewhere to camp for the night."

"So...I take that as a yes, then?" Marshall said hesitantly.

Avon's eyes danced. "Yes. Know that I will not tolerate being treated as anything less than your equal during our time together. You respect me, and I respect you. I think that can be mutually agreed upon for both of our best interest."

"Of course." Marshall was relieved that his scheme had worked and Avon was once more beside him.

They hurried off the road and up the cliffside to a wide cave to set up camp. It would be the perfect location to witness the eclipse, which Marshall was grateful to view with Avon. There was thunder in the distance, and the sun and moon were nearly overlapping. There was something volatile and strange about this approaching storm, albeit more ominous with the eclipse starting soon.

Intense energy in the air tingled along Marshall's nerves. Was this what Avon was describing to him about the power of such events?

"There's nothing like a desert storm," Marshall said.

"This is the power of the eclipse you are feeling, not the storm," Avon replied.

"Is it, now?"

The red glow of the sun highlighted the low-hanging clouds, making them shine burnished gold. Around the two celestial orbs, the sky was turning black as they began to cross in front of each other.

Marshall and Avon sat there, watching the slow progression of the eclipse.

It started as a sickle shape before morphing into a burning ring of fire with an empty black hole at its center. The skies along the eastern horizon flashed with lightning.

"This is incredible," Marshall whispered.

"Do you believe me now when I say there is power in such things?" Avon asked smugly.

"Yes." Marshall trailed off as the eclipse filled his vision, making him woozy. The longer he stared, the more he felt like he was out of his body.

"Careful now," Avon warned. "It can be dangerous to stare too long without practice. You might start seeing visions."

Marshall tore his eyes away to look at Avon, who smiled at Marshall's obvious captivation.

Marshall blinked a few times, the image of the eclipse blurring his sight. It was over quickly, and he felt a loss when the sun descended over the edge of the world, leaving the inky dark in its wake.

They sat in silence for a long time after night fell. The storm in the east was louder now, lightning striking frequently to the ground.

Strange, it kept hitting near the same spot.

"Does that seem normal to you?" Marshall pointed toward the spot the lightning kept striking.

"I'm not sure. It is natural in some environments to have lightning storms."

"Yes, but always hitting one spot like that? Something must be attracting it. I've seen at least five bolts hit there."

"Do you want to investigate?"

"It is my duty as wanderer to do so," Marshall said with an official tone. He stood up and collected his battle axe and a few hatchets to hang on his belt. Avon gathered his swords, and together they went into the night.

They followed the arcs of lightning along a dried riverbed. The air was thick and alive with electrical current. A boom from the heavens ricocheted the earth, and lightning barreled into a hollowed canyon nearby.

Marshall and Avon crouched as they approached the ledge.

Below stood a hooded figure, directing the lightning at a small, silver ball.

QUANDARIES & QUESTIONS

ALDWIN

ALDWIN AND CAPTAIN BLACKWELL WERE WALKING AROUND THE PANTHEA Academy training grounds, a mix of elemental obstacle courses and sparring rings mostly used for higher level students who were about to graduate. Nearly every race of Chrysanthos was born with some type of magick and were welcome to join the academy and choose any element to study. Most studied at least two elements or trained in the basic four. Only those who had higher aspirations went on to study the more complicated magicks of sound, psychic, and storm—the combination of elements to create something new.

They both walked with their hand behind there back and spoke in hushed voices.

"He seems to be spending the majority of his time in the libraries," Captain Blackwell said. "Abraxas spent the first few days in the library at Panthea Central, but lately he has been spending his time split between the Terra Embassy and Aqua Embassy collections. I don't know what he's looking for. None of the books he's going through have an obvious connection to these pages."

"What sort of books is he reading?" Aldwin asked.

At Aldwin's request, Captain Blackwell had ordered a few paladins to watch Abraxas and remain hidden while doing so. Aldwin felt bad having someone tailing his brother without him knowing, but he wasn't going to give Abraxas free rein at Panthea. If he was being honest with himself, he wanted Abraxas gone and to burn these pages. He hadn't finished translating the pages but successfully created his own key of the notes. Most of what Abraxas had done lined up with his own conclusions. He'd started calling these pages the "Mundas Grimoire" and was left with riddles after spending hours decoding the nonsense.

"Things like *Fantastical Faerie Tales and Folklore* and *The Mythos of Mermaids*," Captain Blackwell said. "Then he pulls down half a dozen map scrolls of Chrysanthos and a copy of the *Universal Language of Mathematics*. Then more books about Panthea's history and the first Elite Guardians who created portals. He has star charts everywhere and books about different planets littered all over his space. There is a room in the east wing of the library that he has taken over."

"I'll have to go there myself and see what he's up to."

"If you don't mind me asking, sir, what are the two of you up to?" It was his duty as much as Aldwin's to keep Panthea safe. The man was twice as thick as Aldwin, who was more on the leaner side, and carried himself with regal countenance.

Aldwin squared his shoulders and spoke honestly. "He has come to me with information about our adopted father and asked for my help with something he suspects to be his. It's a sort of grimoire."

He explained the book in detail and Mundas's obsession with portal magick.

"Things that appear out of nowhere usually bear no good will to the user," the captain said. "By the sounds of this character, Mundas, it very well could be his work that your brother discovered. Mundas would make sure it survived even if he didn't."

"I agree with you. As of now, this grimoire is in my possession, but trust Abraxas to have his own copy. I have yet to ascertain the danger in any of it and am still trying to understand its meaning."

"I'm telling you, this is a bunch a nonsense, and you need to stop entertaining your brother. It can't lead to anything good for us, or Panthea."

"How often is he in the libraries of the Terra Nation and Aqua Realm?" It puzzled him as to why Abraxas was visiting those two libraries specifically. From all the indications of the grimoire, there was an object that needed to be found to complete the final equation. Was it in one of these countries?

"Mostly in the Terra Nation, sir. I've had many complaints about it from Neko Raneem. He has seen Abraxas about the Terra Embassy and doesn't like that he's been going through old records. Neko specifically said he wants him removed or permanently restricted from coming there. The man seems on edge of late, to be honest."

"We all are on edge lately. Something is happening in the world, and we don't know what it is yet. Neko has written to me this very morning about Abraxas, which is why I am seeking your counsel. I have half a mind to burn this grimoire and ask Abraxas to leave Panthea. I cannot get rid of this feeling that something is wrong. It is my duty as gatekeeper to learn about these things and ascertain their meaning. I know I'm missing something here."

"Sir, if you want my counsel, here it is: Remove him from Panthea immediately and destroy the grimoire. No one would oppose your decision, and we'd all be better for it," Captain Blackwell reasoned. "You could put this matter to peace without causing anyone harm."

"I fear it will damage my relationship with Abraxas beyond repair," Aldwin said woefully.

The captain's face relaxed slightly. He clearly understood the position Aldwin was facing and what it would mean for his reputation as gatekeeper if his brother was caught in something illicit. He'd be jeopardizing his position, and much worse, if he allowed this to continue. What would Abraxas say and do if Aldwin chose Panthea over him—again?

"It's never easy when it comes to family," the captain said. "You've done the best you can with Abraxas, as far as I can tell. He's damn lucky to have a brother like you, and if he had any decency, he wouldn't disrespect you and compromise your position here."

Aldwin's chest clenched. He didn't know if their relationship could withstand a blow like this one. The captain was right; if his brother had any true love for him, he would understand the folly of this ordeal and see its better left alone. If Aldwin had said no in the beginning, he wouldn't be in this mess now.

Except he couldn't help his own curiosity over this grimoire and its implications. If he knew Abraxas, there was something more happening, and whatever he wanted from Aldwin, he couldn't ask for it outright.

"You're right. I'll discuss this with him tomorrow and ask him to leave Panthea." Aldwin squared his shoulders. He wanted to believe that Abraxas would take the news well but knew he wouldn't. "We've survived worse. Perhaps this won't be so bad."

"If you don't mind me asking, sir, why did you even agree to such a thing in the first place? It would have been more prudent to settle the matter then, rather than give it hope and set roots."

"Our adopted father died when I was ten. Brax was six, and he idolized the man. He was desperate for any father figure, even an abusive one," Aldwin said. The captain sucked in a short breath, and Aldwin grimaced. "I thought this would help give him closure to work through this and show him I still care after all these long years apart. I just can't get rid of this feeling that he's up to something, and I wanted the chance to watch him. I need more time to understand this grimoire."

"Your heart is in the right place, Al. But as gatekeeper, you cannot tolerate this. Out of respect for you, I will not apprehend him. I'll give you three days to find something more. He's gone on sunrise of the fourth day." He clearly wanted to resolve this situation and was being fair with Aldwin.

"I will handle it," promised Aldwin.

Later that evening, Aldwin went to investigate the east wing of the library and find Abraxas. The last paladin report said he'd be in there. A paladin might have overlooked a clue or something if it didn't appear to be dangerous or harmful outright. The snooping didn't make Aldwin feel better, but what choice did he have? All hard things were worth doing, and there would be no easy out for him on this one.

The library at Panthea Central was filled with floor-to-ceiling windows on the east and west sides of the building. The glass looked like the surface of water, allowing some visibility to the outside world while blurred enough to have privacy. Wooden buttresses rose from marble floors to the cathedral ceiling and led to the upper levels of the library, where desks and comfortable lounge chairs were scattered about. The lower levels of the library had an assortment of classrooms, historic records, and little nooks of privacy hidden away from the main aisles. The library exuded a calm that only a place of great learning could, and it was easy to get lost through the endless shelves and thousands of book spines.

Aldwin was at the tiny classroom Captain Blackwell had described to him and looked through the window. No one was in there. This was an excellent opportunity to go through Abraxas's notes himself.

He checked the hall to see if his brother was coming. He searched through the scattered notes and drawings around the room, all while keeping an eye on the door. Aldwin found a copy of the grimoire sitting nearby and reached for it. He was right about Abraxas making duplicates then.

Flipping through the pages, Aldwin noticed the content was consistent to his own pages, only this version was written on parchment instead of that gray, hide-like vellum. He flipped to the page that had the drawing of Ebony, the same image he had been staring at for hours.

There was no handwriting in the margins or any marks on the page. Other notes lying around had Abraxas's scrawl along the sides or sentences underlined. It didn't even look like he'd touched this page. Considering this was what he wanted help with, Aldwin assumed he would see more evidence of further research.

He tossed the copy aside and kept searching.

Nothing he found made sense. The subject matters of the books varied from modern history to magick theory to geographical schematics of Panthea. Here and there, a book about aboriginal cultures and other creation tales stood out. It almost felt as though Abraxas was studying for a test or something. It was absurd.

Frustrated, he left things the way he'd found them and headed out of the tiny room. Maybe Abraxas was in the apartment and he could catch a private word with him.

Aldwin turned down a corridor to see his brother barreling toward him.

His normally sleek hair flew in all directions, and realizing it was Aldwin who stood there, he skidded to a stop, and tried to look casual as he approached. He had sweat around the temples and a faint flush in his cheeks.

"Where are you going? What's wrong?" Aldwin immediately summoned magick into his hands and fingertips.

"There is nothing wrong," Abraxas said quickly, chest heaving. "I'm on my way out—in a hurry, as you can see—and I forgot something in there."

Aldwin stared at him incredulously and lowered his arms. Was there a clue in there this whole time and he'd missed it? "What the hell is so urgent that you're flying through here like a tornado?"

"I'm already running late and need to go." Abraxas tried to side-step Aldwin.

Aldwin slammed his foot down to block him, melting the stone he stood on and twisted it up his ankle.

Abraxas swayed and whirled his arms to find balance. "What the hell—" Abraxas groaned. "Is this necessary?"

"I'm not letting you go until you tell me what's going on." Aldwin could always follow him into the room and demand to see what he was taking.

Abraxas balled his hands into fists, trying to gain some composure as he stood there with his foot awkwardly stuck in the ground. "I am on my way to the city. I—I have a date and left a book in there that I promised to bring them. We're meeting at the Tipsy Portal."

The Tipsy Portal was one of the oldest bars in Panthea and everyone's favorite place to eat, drink, and relax.

Aldwin laughed at him. "You can't seriously think that I'm going to buy that, are you?"

"It is really that impossible to believe someone would be interested in me?" Abraxas feigned great injury. It wasn't enough bravado to cover up his annoyance.

"Not impossible, just highly unlikely," Aldwin stated. "Aren't we supposed to be focusing on this grimoire?"

"I can do both. Now, can I go? I'm already running late, and this isn't helping."

Aldwin wanted to believe him. There was a note of urgency in Abraxas's voice that Aldwin only heard when he was trying to get away with something or get something he wanted very badly. He could still read all of Abraxas like a book, even after all these years. Maybe there was someone who genuinely liked his brother. Who was he to interfere?

"Fine." Aldwin twisted his foot in a half circle and released his hold on Abraxas. He gestured for his brother to go back into the classroom and watched him carefully as he picked up the book on aboriginal cultures in the Terra Nation, flashed it impatiently in front of Aldwin, and hurried out of the room again.

Aldwin's feeling of unease increased as he watched his brother go.

"We need to talk," Aldwin said before Abraxas got too far away.

"Now?"

"Tomorrow." Aldwin knew when it was the right time to push, and now wasn't it. He wouldn't get anywhere with Abraxas with how distracted he was.

"Okay. Send a message with details, and I'll be there."

"Good luck on your date," Aldwin called. "What's her name?"

"Who said it was a her?" Abraxas asked evasively.

Aldwin grinned unexpectedly, wondering if it was actually possible that his brother had a romantic interest in somebody.

UNEXPECTED COMPANIONS

VAYLIN

THREE DAYS LATER, VAYLIN AND OBERION WALKED DOWN THE TUNNEL entrance together. The quickest way to get to the Chazakül Mountain Range, which stretched up the middle of Chrysanthos, was through the Lumbrinica Tunnel at the base of the Khazirak Stronghold. Khan Kharak explained that the tunnel was built by one of his ancestors as an escape route in case their home was ever compromised by dragons or hordes of goblins.

Vaylin was having a hard time controlling her anxiety. Her lips were raw and close to bleeding from biting them so often. Oberion had found her in the goat pens after the meeting with the khan and sat with her for hours, discussing everything. It was a bit dingy, but they had privacy and Vaylin felt like she could breathe again away from the oppressive mountain.

"What's it like? Is your magick okay? You looked like you were about to lose it in there for a moment." Oberion's awareness of his surroundings, and her, was precise enough to know when her mood shifted. His hand on her knee had been the only thing keeping her from running from the room and making a break for the exit.

"It feels like a fire that has no air. It can flicker at first, but after a while, it gets smaller and smaller until not even an ember remains," she said dolefully. Being underground took more energy than she was expecting. Sitting out here was rejuvenating, but how on earth was she going to make it nine days?

"I know we're going to be underground longer than you were expecting, but this is the fastest way there," Oberion said. "No matter what happens, we will get out of here. I promise."

She only nodded, eyes focused on the path before them. It was nice that he was trying to make her feel better. He handled most of the delegations with the khan so she wouldn't have to—and she was grateful.

Ahead, Rathir, Oaken, and Gizmo stood in the entranceway of the tunnel, laden with bags and various weapons and armor. Among them stood the khan, flanked by Digli and Rigli and a strange female dwarf beside Rathir.

"Rathir's wife, Mavil of the Blue Ridge Clan," Oberion whispered conspiratorially.

"So?" Vaylin asked, not understanding his tone. "What's the big deal?"

"Most dwarves are polygamists. The fact that Rathir is committed to Mavil is most unusual."

"What about Oaken and Gizmo?"

Oberion raised his eyebrows in contemplation. "I don't know anything about Oaken. As for Gizmo, I'm sure he considers his forge the only lover he wants or needs in his life."

Vaylin nodded and felt sad as she thought of the jungles and how much she missed being there instead of in this dark hole. Oberion placed a reassuring hand on her shoulder. The comfort of his touch eased the grip of her anxiety; it was easier to put one foot in front of the other with a comrade at her side.

"We will be out of here soon," he promised. "Time feels different down here. Faster than you realize without being able to watch the skies. The dwarves can be quite fun to travel with."

He smiled at her, and she attempted one of her own. It became a rictus, and she quickly stopped.

"If you say so." She broke away from his touch.

She had a lurking feeling that being the only female on this journey was going to be interesting—good thing her cycle passed before they reached Khazirak. She was also thankful Oberion was being kind to her and had proved that they could work together to some extent. It made the whole journey feel easier, even though her magick was being suppressed with each passing minute.

They approached the small group of dwarves, and the khan turned to them.

"You took your time," grumbled Oaken. "Can we go yet?"

"Nearly." Gizmo was going through his pack and talking to himself as he sorted through a manner of different metal gadgets and parcels. "Yes, magnetized compass, air breather, troll gobbler..."

"What in the world is troll gobbler?" Oaken asked.

"It's a marvelous little invention of mine that can cross any terrain, including water. It makes noise and heads in whatever direction you want, causing a lovely distraction. It has a heat sensor too, so if any threat manages to get close enough, it blows up." Gizmo placed the troll gobblers in his pack with the gentleness of handling a newborn.

Vaylin made a mental note to walk as far away as possible from Gizmo during this trip in case one of those things went off.

"That's something," Oberion said sarcastically. "Any other potentially dangerous items in there we should be aware of? We wouldn't want to blow up the whole mountain by accident."

"I won't blow up the mountain," Gizmo said, eyes ablaze with an inner fire. "These are all my latest creations. They have been thoroughly tested and are ready to go. We won't be in any danger during this trip from me, I promise."

In an exaggerated flourish, he pulled out two items with a long, steel barrel extending from a handle.

"What are those?" Suspicion crossed Oberion features.

"I call them Fire and Fury—my special guns." Gizmo kissed the barrel of each one. "They shoot bullets, bombs, sprout flames, and cause all sorts of destruction."

He laughed wildly and grinned like a fiend. Vaylin's eyes widened in shock.

"You're one mad dwarf." The khan looked at the guns. "These are ingenious. When did you make them?"

"The plans are in my workshop if you want to peek. I think you'll find them highly interesting and entertaining." Gizmo looked positively mad as he exulted in his own creations. He latched Fire and Fury to the holsters on his belt and closed up his pack.

"You weren't wrong about this being interesting," Vaylin said in an undertone to Oberion. "Fifty gold marks he blows us all up."

"Deal," Oberion said.

She smiled for real this time.

"If you're done showing off your guns, can we please go?" Oaken pressed. "We are wasting time here."

"Yes, yes. It is time to be going," Rathir said briskly. He turned to Mavil and spoke soft words of dwarfish.

Before Vaylin knew what was happening, Rathir wrapped his arms around Mavil's waist, lifted her up, buried his face into the impressive swell of his wife's breasts, and blew hard. She gave a squeal of laughter and, once her own feet were on the ground, returned the gesture to Rathir, who chuckled modestly.

Vaylin choked on her laughter and hid her face behind her hands. Oberion had forgotten to mention this custom.

"Oh, will you two get a room." Oaken crossed his arms in frustration. "You've had all last three turns to say your farewells."

"You're just jealous that you have no one blowing you," Rathir replied coolly, eyes never leaving his wife's face as he gently pecked each cheek. Their facial hairs mingled, and the intimacy they shared touched Vaylin. While here these last few days, she had not seen dwarves being overly affectionate, as far as she could tell, and it was nice knowing they were capable of such tenderness.

Oaken tightened his pack straps. "Then I'm leaving. See you when your done being lovesick."

He turned to the khan and crossed his arms before him and bowed shortly.

The khan inclined his head in return and waved farewell to him with a bejeweled hand. "Be well, Oaken. Try to enjoy yourself for once."

Oaken gave Rathir and Gizmo a disgruntled look before walking down the tunnel alone. His figure slowly disappeared into the darkness.

Oberion stepped forward and extended an arm to the khan. "As always, it has been a pleasure being in your hall. Thank you for your help and hospitality. If you learn anything new, please send word to the gatekeeper at Panthea. He will help you however he can."

"It will be done." The khan made an X shape with his arms, fists bumping against his own shoulders in farewell.

Oberion copied the gesture before the khan turned to Vaylin.

"It was an honor to meet you, Lady Vaylin Carina, Elite Guardian of the Aqua Realm. Our mountain is your mountain, should you ever need safe refuge," he said graciously.

"Thank you, Khan Kharak Druzy. Your hospitality has been most appreciated. I shall go forth after this day and speak nothing but praises of your magnificent home." She copied Oberion's gesture, bowing low to the khan.

"Take care of those dwarves. They are special to me, the best chieftains I have ever had." The khan's eyes shone with admiration.

"I will do my best."

"A word, Oberion, before you leave," the khan said casually.

Vaylin looked questioningly at Oberion.

"Go on. I'll catch up with you," he said.

Without another word, she turned down the tunnel to follow Oaken. All she had to do was take this journey one step at a time, and she would make it through. Before long, Oaken was next to her, who nodded once in acknowledgement, and they continued on in silence.

2 0

THE LOW ROAD

OBERION

OBERION STOOD THERE, MIND NUMB, AS HE STARED INTO THE KHAN'S black eyes, trying to register what he was hearing. Gavin and Rathir watching covertly from the sides.

"All I'm saying, lad, is that you need to watch yourself around anyone with Elder blood. They are a tricksy folk, and they never tell you the full truth, which is as good as lying to your face." Khan Kharak clearly thought he was doing Oberion a favor by warning him about Vaylin.

"You got it all wrong. She is an Elite Guardian of Panthea and one of the highest-ranking women in the capital. She has taken oaths of fidelity to Panthea and has proven her loyalty to the council and the country. What were these last few days to you? A show for her benefit, all while harboring antiquated and, frankly, idiotic notions about each other's race?" Oberion's magick shuddered to get out as his emotions rose.

"You shouldn't be shocked by it," the khan said. "There are years of dispute between the dwarves and elves that cannot be forgotten."

"Why not? It seems to me like you're limiting yourself and your people by holding onto these old judgements. What was the point of even entertaining us these last few days if this is truly how you feel?" The khan's words were opposite of Aldwin's. *Trust her.*

The khan waved his hand dismissively. "You humans always have such strange rules that make everything unnecessarily complicated. Those of Elder blood never change. The dwarves know this and time will prove me right, you'll see. I pray that it doesn't cost you in the end, my friend."

He was turning away from Oberion, finished with the conversation in typical dwarfish manner—stubborn and straight to the point. Oberion wasn't done however.

"This is about basic respect and decency that need to be honored and upheld, especially by the khan," Oberion said fiercely. "If you do not trust Vaylin, then you do not trust me or Panthea by extension. Is that the sort of khan you are?"

The khan stopped mid-step and looked over his shoulder. "Heed my warning or not, boy."

Oberion held his stare for a long moment, neither of them willing to speak.

Khan Kharak broke away first and left without another word. Oberion fumed for a few minutes, considering his subtle threat to the khan and glaring at Gavin and Rathir as they stood there dumbfounded. They said nothing and he knew they would not bring this up again. Turning, he propelled himself forward with a gust of air and rushed after Vaylin into the darkness.

The cold chill of the earth was nothing compared to what was in his heart. The khan, who Oberion had no previous issue with, had shown a side of himself that Oberion didn't know existed until this moment. He hated how prejudices caused pain.

Do not trust those with Elder blood. Hadn't Oberion himself been distrustful of Vaylin at first?

Trust her, said the voice of Aldwin.

When Oberion had trusted her at the dwarven border, she had

saved them both. He hadn't seen and had barely heard the octaped that day. He would have ended up like the doe if he hadn't given Vaylin a chance and trusted her.

There was no light in the tunnel. Ahead, he could make out Vaylin by the flame in her hands and Oaken beside her. Maybe using her magick underground would help her stay connected to it. He'd tried not to show too much concern over her magick faltering in case it increased her unease. It must be agonizing and she had trusted him enough to say something in the first place. That was something. The least he could do now was expedite their journey through this tunnel by whatever means.

Oberion jogged at a casual pace to catch up. She spread her flame wide at his approach, filling the air with tiny lights like fireflies. Oaken grunted at the impending company and increased his own pace, leaving Oberion alone with Vaylin.

His cheeks were flushed from running as he drew besides her.

"Good thing you left. I was this close to punching the khan." He held up his fingers a hair's length apart. He told her about the khan's warning, and she looked amused and not at all surprised.

"Did he accuse me of stealing something precious or enslaving one of his dwarves?" she asked sarcastically.

"Not exactly," admitted Oberion.

"I thought he was treating me too kindly."

"It was better that you left. The khan has some old prejudices that hinder his judgement. I reminded him of that fault."

Vaylin opened her mouth to speak and shut it again. Was he sensing guilt in her expression?

Her flames trailed after them and he hesitated before reaching out to touch her shoulder, sending a breeze of cool air and reassurance across her back. The effect was immediate as her muscles relaxed instantly.

"Thank you for standing up for me. It means more than you know." The darkness covered most of her blushing.

"The khan is wrong. Despite our differences, I would never allow any man, or dwarf, to treat someone I know that way. I know I haven't been the easiest to deal with, but we are right and we are on the same side."

"I'm sorry if my presence jeopardizes your relations with the dwarves."

He waved her comment away. "Better me than you. They are a hardy folk who won't take offense over such things. The khan won't do anything to upset Panthea or the Elite Guard anyway and I reminded the khan of that. He's too scared that Panthea might not help him, especially after seeing the octaped."

"I'll take your word on it."

They grinned at each other, and this time, he held her gaze, those deep evergreen eyes near black in the tunnel. His pulse raced and for once he was happy they were on this mission together. Did Aldwin suspected this from the beginning which is why he made him come here with her in the first place? He marveled at the woman before him.

He had never experienced a dwindling or repression of his own magick like she was now. Her willingness to go through all of this to help Panthea and the Aqua Realm was commendable.

The voice in his head ticked back and forth like a metronome.

Trust her. Don't trust her.

He had always relied on logical thinking and her actions had proven honorable and true. It was the stone and this whole situation that had him on edge. Not Vaylin. She just happened to be tied into this whole damn thing. Hadn't she warned him about the dwarven prejudices? He thought his presence would've been enough to vouch for her honor and it wasn't. He had been wrong.

Without thinking, he reached forward and touched her cheek. It was warm under his touch, like a fire living under her skin. It sent sparks of energy through his fingertips and into his chest as traced the slightest line across her cheek bone.

"Oberion," she said quietly as his hand fell away and she stepped back the flames around them dimmed, casting them into flickering light.

What was he doing?

"I—"

A pointed cough came from behind them.

Oberion whirled to see Gizmo and Rathir standing there. Rathir glanced between Oberion and Vaylin, while Gizmo tinkered with a metal contraption in his hand, not paying attention.

The moment between him and Vaylin broke.

It took all of his self-control to keep the anger at what the khan had said off his face as he took in the two dwarves.

"Isn't this cozy?" Smugness crept across Rathir's face, despite the tense mood.

Gizmo looked up, and his eyes fell on the fire Vaylin was conjuring.

"How long have you been there?" growled Oberion.

"Not long," Rathir said innocently. "You were blocking the way, see, and we didn't want to be rude and interrupt anything."

"Do you want a worm jar?" Gizmo interjected, completely oblivious to what they walked in on and distracted by the flame in Vaylin's hand. "I have a few in my bag, and they are infinitely more convenient than wasting your energy keeping that thing going."

"Err—a worm jar?" Vaylin was clearly taken aback by the sudden change of topic and was trying to keep her composure. She kept glancing back at Oberion.

"Yes. A worm jar." Gizmo reached around and pulled something from a side pocket in his pack. It was a glass jar filled with wriggling worms that glowed soft blue. "Use these, and your eyes will adjust better to the darkness. You're technically blinding yourself by keeping those flames alight right now, and it's making it harder for the rest of us to see too. It's really quite rude, actually." He held out the jar. "Take it," Gizmo persisted.

Vaylin looked nonplused and took the jar, extinguishing the last of her embers. Oberion blinked spots from his vision as everything except the worm jar went pitch black.

"See? Better already. All you have to do is feed them one rock a day. I won't have any of them dying on me, you understand. I've been raising them since they were precious little eggies, got it?"

"Okay, one rock a day, got it," she said.

Gizmo gave her a final warning look before focusing on the metal object in his hand and trotting onwards. The three of them stood awkwardly, illuminated by the blue light of the worm jar.

"We mustn't fall to far behind Oaken." Rathir patted his silver beard. He passed by Oberion, who was watching him suspiciously.

Unspoken words and feelings crossed between them, questions that neither had the answer to. He wondered for the first time if he had to be weary of the dwarves and if they would report any hint of trouble from Vaylin back to the khan.

Vaylin looked between him and Rathir. Without saying more, she began walking, the blue jar illuminating her way. It struck him then how annoying it was going to be traveling with these dwarves.

VAYLIN

Vaylin could feel the weight of the world above her, a daunting mass of rock and rubble excavated by these dwarves and somehow still intact. The terrain under the world was full of odd echoes. They passed underground lakes surrounded by stalactites and stalagmites, the water flat and clear enough to reflect the cavernous ceiling above in a perfect image. Pale salamanders and see-through fish swam like ghosts beneath the surface, the steady drip of water feeding hidden pools.

Unlike her magick. That felt like a dying bird inside her chest, and she wondered idly if it would vanish entirely if she was down here too long. But that was her fear speaking. She had to believe that, once she was out of here, she'd be back to her normal self. Her normal magick.

Days had passed since they'd entered the tunnel and Oberion had touched her. It felt like an eternity ago. With Oaken, Gizmo, and Rathir, the guardians had barely had any alone time, which was a good thing. Gizmo spent hours talking to her about his ideas, inventions, and many, many failures, ruining all her plans to keep as far away from the dwarf as possible. She had listened and laughed at his stories, most of which involved him blowing something up. That was why he insisted on having a shaved head—fire safety and prevention first. It was easier for her to listen to him than worrying endlessly about her magick and trying to dissect whatever had happened between her and Oberion the other day.

Gizmo had fashioned Vaylin and himself helmets made of leather and metal with a long, arching piece of metal that ended in a small hook to hang the worm jar from. It reminded her of a fishing pole. He had offered to make some for the others, who had all refused, saying two lights were plenty to see by. Vaylin accepted the helmet in good humor, committed to distracting herself with these odd inventions. What did it matter if she looked silly? These dwarves were half sane anyway and it helped keep her mind off her magick.

She caught Oberion looking at her and stuck out her tongue in response. Joy radiated in her at his attention and he smirked at the ridiculous thing.

"Wanna try it soon?" Vaylin nudged Oberion in the arm.

"I like watching you wear it. I don't think it would be very amusing on me."

"Nonsense. I would find it *very* amusing."

What on earth was happening between them?

She shouldn't be touching Oberion in these little gestures or thinking about him as much as she had been. Was it because he was the only human with her or that he had defended her to the khan? They were here on a mission, one that was paramount to the safety of Panthea and all of Chrysanthos. For the first time, she felt like she could genuinely trust him. Which was good to feel from one's fellow Elite.

That didn't stop her from absentmindedly running her fingers along her cheek, recalling the fire at Oberion's touch.

Rathir watched them constantly. He was subtle about it. Times when she laughed with Oberion or talked to him more than the others, the dwarf would always catch her eye before looking away pointedly. She felt no threat from him, only mild annoyance that he was so interested in their relationship, which was strictly professional.

There was too much on the line. She could be ousted from the Elite, and she wasn't ready for her time at Panthea to end. It had barely started. A few more days and she'd be free of this tunnel and the close proximity to Oberion and the dwarves. Her magick would be back and she would feel like herself again.

The incline of the tunnel rose and fell as they crossed perilous stone walkways spanning fishers in the earth that plunged vertically.

Vaylin made the mistake of looking into the depths too long, and vertigo took hold.

The yawning void on either side of the bridge was eerily similar to the darkness she felt in Mingalla. The longer she peered into the space, the more it felt like it was calling to her, pulling her down. Nudging a loose rock over the edge, she listened for an answering click of stone on stone. She watched the descent of the little rock until it disappeared, nerves tingling as she waited.

There was nothing. Nothing but empty space.

The darkness stirred, snaking tendrils of denser black creeping upward. It was coming for her, gaining speed as it ascended.

Her eyes had to be playing tricks on her. It couldn't be real.

A sharp pain wrapped around her midriff and yanked her away from the ledge.

"What do you think you are doing?" It was Oaken, and he looked livid.

"I-I wasn't going to lose my balance." Her voice shook slightly as she righted herself, heart pounding in her ears.

"Be mindful of your footing. Only a fool would willingly throw stones into the darkness," he said.

"I didn't throw anything." She kept one eye on the sides of the bridge in case there was something in the darkness. The octaped tentacles flashed in her mind, little suckered beaks imbedded in her skin.

"Yer big feet knocked a stone off the ledge. I heard it with my own ears. You might as well have dropped a boulder down there and announced our arrival to all the creatures of the underworld."

"It was an accident. It won't happen again, I swear it," she said earnestly.

Oaken glared at her. Of all the dwarves, he was the least talkative, content to take the lead for miles at a time and avoid the others. Vaylin often wondered if he could listen to the earth around them in the same way she did with nature.

Rathir stepped between them and rested a hand on his shoulder. "Oaken, calm down. Our ancestors wouldn't have built an escape route over any dangerous nests or beasts."

"It's been thousands of years since our ancestors took a chisel to these walls. Anything could have made homes in here unbeknownst to us," Oaken said doubtfully. "Only a few know these passages existence, meaning we've had no reports about anything that may be going on down here. Unless Gizmo has anything useful to share about his last trip through here."

All heads turned to Gizmo, who said in a singsong tone, "A lone dwarf who makes no noise meets no trouble."

Oaken rolled his eyes and pulled an axe from his belt, raising it defensively.

"We should be on our way." Rathir stepped between Oaken and Gizmo. "The more distance we can create from this spot, the safer we will be. The exit must be getting close now."

Rathir was the ice of the dwarves, where Gizmo was fire and Oaken, rock. Rathir tempered their behaviors and always kept them levelheaded.

Vaylin understood why someone like that would be valuable to any court and the purple pig-headed khan.

Still, Oaken breathed through his nose like an angry bull. He ignored her entirely and crossed the rest of the bridge. He pulled a second axe from his belt and glanced suspiciously over the sides, quickening his pace over the gaping maw of the chasm.

Vaylin was annoyed he'd grabbed her but grudgingly thankful he had. She only knocked a stone over the ledge to hear when it hit the bottom.

The impulse of her curiosity suddenly felt like an idiot's blunder. What if that movement had landed them in a dangerous situation? Or awoken a monster? Her magick was weakened, and she wasn't sure how well she could fight without it. Help was so far away that it would be too late for them.

Oberion made his way next to her and tilted his head, silently asking, *Are you okay?*

She nodded imperceptibly and turned back to the bridge, praying the exit was as close as Rathir said it was.

THE CONJURER EXPOSED

MARSHALL

THE LONE FIGURE STOOD IN THE BOTTOM OF THE CANYON, CLOAK billowing in the wind. During those brief lightning strikes, all Marshall could see of the figure's face was a white mask with black holes near the eye sockets. It walked in circles around a circular object on the ground.

Lines and alchemical symbols drawn in the sand radiated from the object. Every few moments, the figure raised their hands and channeled another bolt of lightning into the object. The spell work in the sand burned red hot then faded to black.

As they watched, the silver ball grew bigger, opening with every hit of lightning.

The figure spoke in a tongue Marshall couldn't decipher. The language was archaic and sonorous. The enchantment grew, conducting and conjuring far too much energy here for his comfort. He had a foreboding feeling—whatever was in that silver ball needed to remain there. Every instinct in his body told him this was a dark and forbidden magick, something never taught at Panthea. It was exactly the sort of thing the wanderer was supposed to investigate and stop. He couldn't let the figure finish casting the spell.

Marshall looked at Avon, who mouthed the words, *Attack?*

They had come to the same conclusion.

Marshall nodded and drew a diagram in the sand with his finger to silently explain the attack plan. They would converge on the figure at the same time from opposite directions.

Avon nodded, and they looked at each other for a moment.

Marshall wasn't sure what he was feeling. He wanted Avon's help with this but didn't want anything bad to happen to the elf. If something went wrong, Marshall's first priority had to be Panthea. He had to stop this enchantment and get the object away from the conjurer. If Avon helped him achieve this, all the better.

Taking a deep breath, Marshall grasped Avon's forearm firmly, the gesture they had used at their wrestling match. Avon exerted equal pressure on his own arm before moving into position.

The sand was warm under Marshall's hands as he crouched and crawled away from Avon. He squinted against the dust and blinding flashes of light, the sand whipping in all directions by the potent magickal storm being conquered. Was this conjurer harnessing the energy of the eclipse to do this? The clouds were roiling masses of apocalyptic yellow and black, churning with ribbons of dark blues and purples. It was like watching colored smoke mixing and the figure below was the one stirring it. No normal person would be able to do this.

Marshall was in position as he rose quietly to the ledge and pulled two hatchets from his belt. The space was too cramped for his two-handed axe, which was strapped across his back. Across the clearing, he could see a shadow moving—Avon was directly across from him. Marshall looked to the skies, waiting for the next lightning strike to make a move. His nerves fluttered, grateful that Avon was here and praying that they'd make it out of here.

When the figure raised its arms to channel another strike into the object, Marshall launched himself down, wrapping himself and Avon in a cushion of air magick as they landed in the canyon. Both men ran toward the conjurer in perfect synchronization.

The figure twisted at their movements and roared to the night.

Not knowing which one to attack first, the figure made a sweeping motion with their arms and directed the streak of lightning toward

Avon. It missed him by inches, and the deflected bolt hit the ridge, shattering rocks and sparks onto some of the dry grasses.

An ember of fire jumped to life, smoldering and filling the air with whisps of smoke.

Avon used his momentum to roll toward the figure, circling around and engaging the figure into combat with his twin swords. They blocked Avon's blows with shields of red and purple psychic magick, retreating slightly with every flurry of blows Avon landed.

Marshall skidded onto the ground near the sphere and knelt over it. His eyes darted from the geometric lines of the spells in the sand to the glowing etchings on the metal to the object itself hovering several inches off the ground. He sheathed his hatchet on his belt and raised hands to either side of the metal object.

It was a ball of concentric rings and half shells, each spinning freely on its own axis. In the center of the space was a sphere of solid metal, roughly the size of an egg.

Was there something inside that?

He opened his hands wider to feel more of the energy and wondered how to remove this object without hurting himself.

Marshall blasted backward by an invisible force of magick. He was so absorbed that he didn't see the attack coming. He fell several yards away from the sphere, all the air knocked from his lungs.

Through a haze of dust and smoke, another bolt of lightning came hurtling from the sky.

He rolled sideways to avoid being hit. Where the lightning struck, the sand transformed into glass shrapnel. Marshall curled into a ball to avoid the worst of it, and slices of pain exploded across his back.

He gritted his teeth. He couldn't stop. If he stopped, he was dead.

Crouching to his feet, Marshall felt bits of glass slicing his skin further. He steadied himself as he assessed the fight.

Avon was engaged with the conjurer and unleashed fiery blows from his swords at an impossible speed, effectively distracting the figure and giving Marshall time. He had to hurry.

Running back toward the sphere, he pushed the pain of his back away and crouched over it. He didn't have much time to puzzle out the spell or develop a counter enchantment. He pummeled the ground, sending shudders of earth magick through the sand to try to erase the marks.

They flashed yellow when his magick connected with it but didn't fade.

The masked figure's attention whipped toward Marshall with every hit of his magick that connected to the spell. They sensed his intention to disrupt the enchantment and hissed angrily.

To Avon's credit, he did a fantastic job at keeping the conjurer distracted while Marshall worked on the sphere. He couldn't undo the spell work around the object and wondered if he could physically pull it out of the enchantment and force it shut.

Brute force, it would be, then.

The sphere hummed and buzzed audibly over the sounds of fighting as he inched closer. Spreading his feet shoulder width apart, Marshall pulled every ounce of earth energy into his legs, torso, and arms, grounding himself in the core of his strength.

Holding both hands out and taking a deep breath, he pressed toward the metal.

An electric current pulsed against his palms. It felt like a thousand bee stings, the electricity in his veins, as he focused and directed the current through his body and out his feet, channeling it into the ground and disbursing the magick safely out of his body. Closer and closer he got to the sphere. The pain seared up his forearms.

His hands touched the warm metal of the object, and he gasped as a surge of electricity rushed through his body. The sphere trembled, and the metal pieces whirled beneath his fingers, closing itself neatly. It took all his concentration to direct the diminishing current of electricity away from his heart, through his limbs, and into the earth. Sweat poured from him, and his blood boiled, burning him from within as he pulled the sphere away from the center of the spell.

It was working.

The metal cooled rapidly, and the intensity of the pain lessened as the spell broke down. The markings in the sand faded, and the winds subsided. His muscles cramped with the effort as he pulled inch by inch.

Finally the tether snapped.

Marshall fell backwards, panting and smelling of burnt hair. The sphere was in his hands. The reverberation of electricity spasmed through him and granted little control over his muscles.

A scream of frustration came from the masked figure, and with a bang, Avon flew backward, hitting the canyon wall with a crunch. He fell to the ground and didn't move.

The figure turned on Marshall, who was shocked and horrified to see Avon fall.

Marshall needed to move.

He tried to pull a hatchet from his belt, but his hand spasmed and he couldn't grab the handle. He tucked the sphere closer to his body. There was no way this thing was taking it back from him.

"You!" The masked figure advanced on him. "Do you have *any* idea at what you've just done?"

Purple lightning danced around their fingertips, and Marshall could tell by the way their magick writhed that they were extremely powerful—and pissed off. The flames around them smoldered from the sparse grasses, filling the space with smoke and making it difficult to see and breathe.

Marshall's eyes burned, and he kept retreating, hoping to press against the canyon wall.

"Let me guess, I ruined some grand scheme of yours?" He tried to buy some time for his limbs to cooperate. At least he didn't fry his vocal cords to a crisp.

The figure let out a sound of amusement. "Give me my sphere, and I will end your life quickly. Refuse, and we will see just how much lightning your body can handle."

The purple lightning grew along their hands and arms, alighting the blank white mask under the hood. He was going to have to fight them if he wanted to find Avon and get out of here. It always came down to more fighting.

Marshall stared coldly at the figure, forcing his legs to obey him and rising to his feet. He growled a single word. "No."

It didn't matter that he could barely move. There was no way he would relinquish this sphere.

"I'm going to enjoy ripping that sphere from your corpse."

"Like hell you will," Marshall shouted.

He had no idea where the walls of the canyon were. They had to be close behind him and if they were he might be able to magick himself out of the canyon.

The figure spoke in that archaic language and moved their fingers and hands in the air in front of him, drawing shapes that floated ominously toward Marshall. The purple lightning wicked off his fingers and amassed into a network of electricity in front of him. Cursing, Marshall backed up in the direction he thought the canyon wall was, never taking eyes off the conjurer.

The hooded figure jerked violently forward, a black, tar-like substance gushing from their empty eye sockets and over their mask. The spell work in the air dissipated, and Marshall froze, not believing what he was seeing.

Two silver points stuck out of the center of the conjurer's chest.

Avon yanked his swords free and kicked the figure to the ground in one fluid motion.

Elven knight indeed. And dammit, he was being rescued again.

Avon stood victoriously over the fallen conjurer, covered with red dust and a splatter of black gore. A gash on the side of his head was leaking blood. He toed the robes open, and gray dust fell from them, along with a broken, white mask.

"You're okay!" Marshall couldn't see anything past the smoke and was surprised at Avon standing there and the amount of relief he felt at seeing the elf.

"Of course I'm okay. It takes more than that to best me." Avon spat on the crumpled black robes. "The body disappeared, and the only dark magick I know that does this is the creation of a golem, a puppet of sorts that can be controlled remotely. We need to get out of here. The danger has not passed, and whoever is controlling this thing could be close by."

"We did it," Marshall said blearily. He couldn't think straight. Every muscle in his body ached, and his mind felt jumbled. Being electrocuted wasn't helping his thought process, and his vision was going in and out of focus.

"Yes, we did. You make a fine distraction. That's twice now I've been able to save us with you acing like bait." Avon grinned.

Marshall was too exhausted to respond.

The solid weight of the sphere pressed on him, and he couldn't help but feel repulsed by the thing, whatever it was.

"Here, take this." He held out the sphere. He felt as though he was going to pass out and trusted Avon to keep it safe.

Marshall faced the wall, placing a hand against the rocks. He would use the last bit of his energy to get them out of here. He slid clumsily into a pose and stomped his foot, twisting his heel as the ground beneath their feet cracked and lifted them away from the pit. Dirt streamed off the sides of their platform, and he flung his arms upward, propelling them up the canyon through waves of heat, smoke, and ash.

They reached the top, and Marshall toppled over, falling to his knees, coughing and retching. Black spots floated in his vision, and he felt as though he could lay here forever.

"We need to go," Avon insisted.

Marshall was trying to hurry, but passing thousands of volts of electricity through his body had taken its toll. He only needed a moment to rest, and then he'd be able to walk back to camp.

Avon held out his hand for Marshall to take.

He hesitated, seeing six hands instead of one. He looked at Avon closely, vision going in and out of focus. Another tally for Avon for saving his life.

Marshall was really doing a terrible job staying out of life-threatening trouble lately.

22

THE HIGH ROAD

VAYLIN

THEY HAD BEEN UNDERGROUND FOR NEARLY TEN DAYS, ACCORDING TO Oberion, when they finally reached the end of the tunnel. Vaylin felt drained beyond measure but could sense a lifting of the weight above her as they climbed upwards. The winding passage opened to an antechamber where the exit had been sealed. Rathir lifted the lid off a stone chest set in the corner and removed a square disk that must have been a key. He slipped it into a hidden slot near the door, and suddenly, they were all blinking back daylight.

Vaylin's eyes watered as the pain of her magick returning flared in her veins. It was a fire bursting to life and made her feel utterly alive for the first time in days. Her limbs tingled, and her heart soared with joy. She felt powerful, more powerful than when she first entered the Khazirak Stronghold and she couldn't stop herself from beaming happily.

The fresh air washed over her, and she automatically oriented herself to face east. She imagined she could see the green tops of the Aqua Realm jungles far, far away. All of this was for the land and the people she protected.

"I didn't realize how good it would feel to finally be out of there again," she mused to Oberion.

She couldn't help herself and spun in circles under the sunlight, spreading her arms wide and letting the breeze caress her skin.

Oberion smiled. It seemed being outside was as much a balm to his soul as it was for hers. Together, they quietly took in the sounds and sights of the mountains around them. They were high enough up that the air was thin and white clouds rolled around the peaks beneath them.

"The Storm Peaks of Titan," Oberion said in a wondering voice. "It's one of the highest elevation points in all of Chrysanthos. I've always wanted to come here."

"All we have to do is traverse the wild mountain side for an ancient dwarf that only Gizmo knows the location of. Should be great." She gave a sarcastic thumbs up.

Each moment with her magick was a gift as it swirled around inside her, wanting to be used. She was giddy. It didn't matter that these mountains were steeper, the weather more erratic, than the Khaziraks. She had her magick back, and nothing they were about to face would be as bad as being underground.

"I swear if Gizmo gives me one more invention, I'm going to start breaking them on purpose," she whispered.

Oberion grinned. "It wouldn't do you any good. He'd just fix it. I like the glow worm helmet the best. Shame you won't need it anymore. It was very stylish."

Vaylin smacked his arm lightly and grinned at the joke, knowing all too well that Gizmo would and could fix anything. "In his defense, it was very convenient for me to not hold the jar the entire time."

"Maybe you'll have to break it out at night again. For old time's sake."

"I've managed to keep the worms alive, haven't I? I should name them if I'm going to keep them." The feel of sunlight on her skin was divine, and she relished being free of the Lumbrinica Tunnel. Peering around Oberion, she called out to the dwarves, "Which direction are we heading, Gizmo?"

The dwarf rummaged through his pack, as always, and pulled out a few pairs of black glasses and passed them to Rathir and Oaken, who took them hesitantly.

"Sunglasses," Gizmo said in a matter-of-fact way. "Don't be thick. We've all just spent ten turns in near total darkness, and we'll have a harder time adjusting to the light than the humans."

After traveling with them, she had learned that a dwarf's sight in the dark was just as good as, if not better, than a fey. Like most earth-dwelling creatures, their eyes were more accustomed to long periods of darkness and were sensitive to sunlight. Gizmo walked over to the guardians and offered them each a pair. Oberion raised his eyebrows at Vaylin, and she could almost hear his words in her head. *Are you going to break these?*

She put them on, and her vision became a shade darker. She was surprised by the ease she felt in the protection they offered.

"I think I'll keep these," she said in an undertone to Oberion. Clearing her throat, she asked Gizmo again, "So, which way are we heading?"

The Storm Peaks of Titan were in the middle of the Chazakül Mountain Range and as remote at the polar ice caps. From where they stood at the tunnel exit, three winding paths led in different directions.

"We take the middle one south." Gizmo pulled his goggles over his eyes and rolled a side dial on them that dimmed the lenses to a cool black. Sighing in appreciation, he withdrew a detailed map of the Chazakül Mountains and a strange-looking metal box. It had a screen similar to her CC and a few dials along the bottom. "I've been trying to retrace my steps from my last visit up here, and I think I got it."

"It's about time you did something useful," Oaken grumbled.

"I create useful things all the time," Gizmo protested. "Maybe if you bothered to listen to me once in a while, you would know this."

"I've listened to you for days now, and I haven't heard anything interesting."

Gizmo rolled his eyes. "If I'm so useless, you can give me back those sunglasses."

He held out his hand expectantly. Oaken crossed his arms, not saying anything.

"I thought so." Gizmo retracted his hand and turned back to his map. "Anyway, from the tunnel, I went south undisturbed for days. On the third day, it started to storm, and upon looking for shelter, I stumbled across these trolls. There were two of them, both ten feet tall and cleverer than they should have been. It was dark and rainy, which made it easier for me to stay hidden. You know how they can be, sniffing me out all over the mountainside. They knew I was close and kept up their pursuit."

"It's too bad you didn't have something useful in your pack to help you," Oaken said bitterly.

"For your information, I did," Gizmo said.

"The troll gobblers," Vaylin exclaimed, suddenly understanding. She was continuously impressed by his inventions and understanding of mechanics, navigation, and engineering, despite all his oddities.

"Indeed, my fair lady." Gizmo gestured dramatically to the metal box in his hands and pulled a small cog from his pocket, pushing it into a hollowed space on the back of the box.

It shifted, and metal scraped on metal as little bug shaped robots emerged from the box. They had six spindly legs, a flexible metal body, and propeller on top that folded open and closed like wings.

"It was an all-terrain, programmable, walking bomb." Gizmo's face relaxed in a deep sigh of admiration.

"Why not axe the trolls and be done with it?" Oaken said.

"I came to these mountains to test my invention. Not swing a blade."

"How do you coordinate the bomb?" Oberion asked.

"You set a marker of your choice, and it charts a course from there," Gizmo said. Vaylin had never heard of anything else that could do what Gizmo's troll gobblers did.

Rathir asked, "After you launched your device, how do you know it worked?"

"Well, I knew where I had sent it and wanted to follow its progress. I found a nice peak to watch. Didn't have to wait long either. I could feel the explosion from my lookout." His eyes glinted with fervor as only he recalled the memory. "It was glorious."

"You spent all this time planning a distraction for you to get away to then stay and watch?" Rathir asked incredulously.

Oaken snorted and turned his back on the group.

"Yes," Gizmo said. "I found Skyminer's Keep soon after I examined the damage. The noise gave him a fright, I can tell you. He knew something was happening up here."

"You're the craziest dwarf I've ever known, Gizmo Forgeworm." Rathir shook his head in astonishment. "But I suppose there is no sane way to greatness. Without risk, what is there to gain?"

Gizmo grinned appreciatively.

"So, you generally went south after that? Once we pass the explosion mark, what should we be looking for?" Oberion asked.

Gizmo thought for a moment, placing an oily hand on his chin. "Now that you mention it, I remember thinking there was a funny rock formation that looked like an eagle."

Vaylin turned to Oberion, a smile blazing across her face as she took his hands. "This means we nearly have a direct route south of Skyminer's Keep to Panthea when this is all finished."

Everything felt like it was falling into place now that she had escaped the tunnel.

"Come on then. Let's move," Oaken said. "These mountains are treacherous. Storms of hail and freezing rain can come up quickly, and we don't want to get caught in one."

After two days of trekking south through the mountain, Vaylin almost wished she were back underground, where there was no wind or rain. Almost. The winds at the high altitude were frigid, and the ground was made of shale. It was slippery and would shift under foot so often that she was constantly summoning earth magick to keep her upright and steady. Clouds blew around them, and moisture clung to their clothes, dampening them and freezing her to the bone. Often, the skies were gray, and rain fell on distant peaks.

"Why would the dwarves make an escape route into such a formidable place?" she asked Rathir through chattering teeth.

He considered her question. "I imagine it was to be as far away as possible from any threat that attacked Khazirak. If this came out within the Krakhammer Mountain Range north of Khazirak, most creatures, like a dragon or giant, would be able to sniff us out again. No threat could follow us here. Dwarves could seal themselves off at the entrances or exits with keys like the one I used. They'd be able to keep this spot as a base until they found another home."

She nodded. "I guess most dwarves wouldn't want to be out in the open when they were most vulnerable."

"Precisely," he said. "It is rather difficult to find solid mountains to dwell beneath. If there was a chance of going back to Khazirak to liberate it after an attack, you can imagine why this would also be an advantageous spot to protect and potentially infiltrate from."

Vaylin nodded again and was quiet. She looked to the skies. A dense, gray mass was forming above them. Tumbling rocks could be heard falling down the side of the mountain. The winds picked up strength.

Rathir cast a wary eye toward the tumultuous skies. His sleek, silver beard shone in muted light. He called toward Gizmo, who was at the head of the line. "Should we head for shelter before this gets worse?"

Gizmo shook his head. "This might pass in an hour or so. We're only a few miles away from the detonation spot. Skyminer's Keep isn't far from that."

"Conditions could potentially worsen and slow us down. I don't want to be caught in the open with rain, hail and rock falling around us," Oaken shouted.

Vaylin agreed. A charge in the air promised a storm was brewing.

"We can't stand here much longer to debate this. This next ridge looks narrow, and we'd need to get through it quickly if we want to find a decent shelter," Rathir said.

The skies grew darker. They were wasting precious time arguing and needed to go.

"Let's put it to a vote," Oberion offered. Vaylin shot him a look, but he didn't meet her gaze. "All in favor of continuing to Skyminer's Keep." Gizmo and Oaken raised their hands, and to Vaylin's horror, so did Oberion.

"Are you mad? We're going to get blown off the mountain before we can reach Skyminer," she said, furious.

His eyes were sympathetic, but a steely hardness told her his mind was made up.

"You and I can keep the majority of rain and wind away from us. I know it will be exhausting, but there's no point risking more time poking around caves and possibly disturbing whatever may live there. We know there's absolute safety with the Skyminer and it gets us one step closer to knowing more about that stone. Why not make the run for it?" His eyes serious reflected the grays of the storm. It had a startling effect.

"We can't fight Mother Nature forever," she said begrudgingly.

"It'll be enough," Oberion promised, wavy brown hair whipping about in the winds. "You and I can do this."

She believed him, even though her gut was warning her. Together, the group set off at a brisk pace into the gathering storm, the guardians bending the elements for their protection as they went.

OBERION

Vaylin disagreed with the decision, and part of Oberion couldn't blame her. The clouds had turned into a churning, roiling mass above them as the world turned darker. The dark of night tinged with an eerie yellow-grey of catastrophic storms. There would be no hiding from this without proper shelter. Color was leeched from everything as they rushed onwards. Droplets of rain peppered them as they jogged, occasionally slipping on the shale and water. Vaylin held a protective shield above them to keep the majority of the rain off. But it couldn't prevent the mountainside itself from getting wet, and rivulets of water snaked down from the peaks above them, making the path nearly impossible to walk.

"I told you this was a bad idea," Vaylin yelled over the deep rumble of thunder. It boomed and echoed between the steep passes.

"Keep going!"

Oberion had never felt the power of sound so acutely. Doubt filled his mind.

No, he wouldn't regret this decision if they could make it to Skyminer's Keep. It would be worth it. They had to persevere a little longer. The storm cast dancing light and shadows on the cliffs, and it felt like they were being watched by a sinister giant. The hairs on his arms rose.

"How much further?" he asked Gizmo, who was ahead of them by a few paces. They still hadn't come to the demarcation line of the dwarf's exploding device.

"Not far now. If my calculations are correct, the detonation spot should be twenty-five meters that way, around the cliffside." He pointed toward the path ahead, which curved around the mountain in a long arch, blocking their view beyond.

A bang of thunder roared through the skies, and Oberion's eardrums rang with the force of it. The rain came down hard now, and the pressure in the air spiked his anxiety. "*If* they are correct? Gizmo, you better pray they are, or else I'm throwing you off this mountain myself!"

They plunged on, safe in their bubble of magick, knowing that with each step they were getting closer to shelter. It took all Oberion's concentration to keep the outside wind from brushing them off the path, and he was sure Vaylin must be struggling too.

When they finally turned the corner, Oberion gaped at the massive crater in front of him.

In the center of it ran a deep, black crack.

23

RUPTURES

VAYLIN

VAYLIN'S HEART STOPPED.

"No!" She let out a strangled cry as she gripping the cliffside for support. She was too late. Again.

Here was another one of those void-sucking cracks, which meant they must be spreading through Chrysanthos. The black fissure stretching across the crater was just like the one in the Mingalla, only drastically bigger. Rocks disintegrated inward as the crack spread infinitesimally onward. Its energy was boundless, alive, and free, not held into place by any human. Vaylin was overwhelmed by it. On the other side of the crater, a path continued south down the mountain.

"Holy gods." Oberion's eyes went wide. Although he'd taken the situation with the octaped seriously, he clearly didn't grasp the gravity of the magick they were dealing with until now.

The three dwarves stood there with equal horror on their faces. The power of the rupture was otherworldly and pulled on the mind and body in an invasive way. It was hungry.

Her hip blazed with warmth, and the belt pocket that held the stone shone from within. It felt like a talisman, begging to be used against this fowl darkness. She resisted, remembering the attack in the shaman's place.

"Did you cause this?" Oaken rounded on Gizmo, eyes wide under his goggles, as he stared into the crater.

It was clear by Gizmo's face he thought he'd caused it too. "I-I couldn't have. The bombs wouldn't do this much damage."

Oaken was having none of it. He grabbed Gizmo by the throat and slammed him against the cliff wall. "I am going to smash in that boulder brain of yours!"

Oaken scowled at Gizmo, eyes like green fire, and punched him square in the nose. Blood burst from Gizmo's nostrils, and he squealed in pain. Oberion grabbed Oaken's arm before he could deliver another swing, and Oaken nearly threw him off. Distracted with the dwarves, Oberion dropped his protective magick, and the air hit them like shards of ice.

Vaylin redoubled her effort to keep the group shielded against the relentless storm and the limitless nature magick that fueled it.

"It wasn't him," she shouted over the storm. "Do you hear me, Oaken? It wasn't Gizmo! This is the darkness I saw in Mingalla. You have to stop!" Her words felt like whisps against the screaming storm.

Oberion and Rathir struggled with Oaken, who was working himself into a towering rage. She knew the dwarf had a temper but to get this worked up? The sight of that crack would make anyone in their right mind terrified. They needed to leave and put as much distance as possible between them and this crater.

Rathir reached around Oberion and grabbed Oaken's arm.

The raging dwarf instantly relaxed as vivid blue ice spread from Rathir's fingers and around Oaken's wrist. His angry green eyes softened as they clouded with white frost, and his limbs stiffened.

This was going from worse to terrible.

"Stop! What are you doing to him?" Vaylin said.

"It's not harmful," Rathir explained. "I am calming the fire in his blood."

"You've had the ability to keep him calm this whole time?" she asked.

"I only use it when the forge within it gets too hot. Why do you think the khan keeps me on his council?" Rathir replied coolly.

Vaylin couldn't even respond to that. Her only thought was to get them out of here.

"Oaken, we need to move." Oberion held the dwarf's arms, even though the fight had gone from him. "No dwarf could have done this. We need to get to safety."

"The dwarves have awoken the unholy darkness before. They all died." Oaken's voice was peculiar, filled with sorrow and loss as he spoke. Tears welled in his eyes.

Vaylin wondered what he had seen in his lifetime beneath the earth and the consequences of digging too deep. A question for another time if she dared to ask, after they were out of here.

"Now is not the time for grief. Now is the time to live," Rathir said.

Oaken blinked slowly, and Rathir released his arm. Oaken took a shuddering breath as the ice vanished from his sleeve and frost cleared from his eyes. He shook his head doggedly.

"I hate it when you do that." Oaken rubbed his wrist and grimaced.

"I hate seeing your anger," Rathir said ruefully then turned to Vaylin, face serious. "Is there any way around this thing, or do we turn around?"

"We can't leave here knowing this exists and do nothing about it. There might be a way through." She wanted them all safe and the vague idea forming in her mind was a mad one.

"How?" Oberion replied. When she met his stare, his eyes grew wide as he realized what she was implying. "No," he said hoarsely, "You can't. There must be another way. It's too dangerous to attempt."

"What other choice do we have? I have to try. If it goes right, then we can solve two problems with one."

"No, I won't allow it." His usually flowing cloak was drenched and his hair looked black plastered against his wet skin.

"You can't stop me from doing this. It must be me. I can't sit back and let this happen. We need answers. We need to cross here." She refused to break eye contact with Oberion.

The lines of his face were harsh as he dipped his head. "This is a terrible idea," he conceded. "I'd hate to tell Aldwin about this if you die."

"Then don't let me die."

Lifting her chin, she walked in front of the group and touched the stone in her pocket. A pulse of power went up her arm, and she was acutely aware of its unique composure and the difference in its magick from her own. After the tunnel and torturous days of feeling faint from her own suppressed magick, it felt like she had developed an extra sensitivity to all magick and its defining source.

The stone from Mingalla was warm and welcoming, unlike any crystal she had ever worked with. Taking deep breaths to steady her racing heart she reached for her Eucalypta staff and removed her beloved opal from the end of it.

She could do this.

She *had* to do this.

For Panthea and the Aqua Realm. And for those lost souls in the Mingalla nuca she couldn't save. She would not be afraid.

Without further thought, she pulled the shining stone from her pocket and placed it into the end of her staff, unleashing a radiating blast of power that snapped through the world.

OBERION

Her conviction was his undoing. Her strength propelled him to act, to meet this situation with no less bravery than what the woman in front of him had chosen. What she was about to do. Nothing could have prepared him for the sight of that darkness when they had turned the corner. And nothing he had ever experienced could have prepared him for the sight of her standing in front of them, a lone figure against the gaping black hole of the void beyond.

It all felt wrong.

She shouldn't be doing this alone. Yet he had no weapon against this foe.

Fear, sharp and real, rose unbidden in him as Vaylin led the way with her staff out, the Mingalla stone nestled in one end. The black pit was moving, directing its attention toward her. Toward the stone. She was the only thing standing in its way.

"Go!" She thudded her staff on the ground, and a staircase of stones erupted around the edges of the crater, creating a pathway up and around the void.

"Come with us." Oberion grabbed her hand before she could run.

The storm continued to ravage the mountain peaks like a wrathful god. She was his partner in all this and he had to protect her.

"Get everyone safely across, and I'll meet you there. I promise," she said.

It was a lie, and he knew it. He couldn't let her be the distraction. It wasn't fair. It wasn't right. He was about to say something when a keening emanated from the void, and he grabbed his ears reflexively. Snaking tendrils slithered up the crater walls toward them.

"Go!" she yelled.

Then Vaylin was out of his grip and running. She leapt into the air with the grace of a dancer, landing on disks of solid ice underfoot that floated her through space, away from the group.

The tendrils swayed and turned to follow her. Or the stone.

Damn it. He could only help by getting everyone across this crater and out the other side. The sooner he managed it, the sooner Vaylin could join them and leave.

Oberion concentrated on his footing as he shepherded the dwarves up the staircase. They were a quarter of the way around the crater when a lightning bolt descended from a purple sky and hit the cliff above them. Rocks blew apart at the collision, and debris barreled toward them. Without hesitating, Oberion slammed both fists into the cliffside and pushed out a section of wall above them to form a protective roof. Boulders the size of elephants smashed into it and rolled into the crater, hitting the black crack without a single sound. The rocks imploded, fragments disintegrating to sand and sand into dust within seconds upon touching the void. How was that possible?

Shouting drew him back. Gizmo lost balance and slid toward the rupture.

Oberion moved out of instinct again, forming a ledge of stone in Gizmo's path. The dwarf hit the surface, smacking his head against the stone with an audible thump. He landed on his back, and a trickle of blood fell from his head toward void. Oberion pulled the stone ledge bearing the little dwarf upward as the blood from Gizmo's head touched the void.

The black mass shuddered, tendrils coalescing in its center as new tendrils went directly for Gizmo.

"Everyone move, now!" Vaylin made her way toward them.

She hadn't attacked the void like Oberion thought she would. Instead, she moved evasively, defensively. He suddenly remembered back in Aldwin's office she had said none of their elemental magick could touch the black stuff, meaning he couldn't attack the thing directly. They could only run.

The tendril of black was almost upon Gizmo when Oberion summoned the platform toward himself, the dwarf on top of it.

At the same moment, Vaylin swung her staff at the tendrils and bellowed into the night.

A dazzling beam of white light shot from the end, lighting the entire canyon. When it touched the darkness, it shattered the black mass into a hundred ribbons of smoke, rainbow sparks flying in all directions and muffling the mind-numbing keening. The tendrils withdrew into the mass, and she landed gracefully on an outcrop of stone high above them, like a protective angel. *A Guardian angel.*

Rain poured from the skies and dripped off Vaylin's features, those evergreen eyes he had come to know intimately filled with golden light not their own. Silver threads of power swirled and blended down her staff and into her arm.

She looked like a goddess of war and water, of stars and moonlight. She was transformed. Terrifying and beautiful in a haunting, forbidden way.

"Get them out of here!" It was and wasn't her voice, a layer of indefinable power beneath her words, brooking no argument.

There was no choice but to listen and obey.

A voice in his head shrieked to get away, and adrenaline coursed through him. Where was this power coming from?

Rathir and Oaken lifted Gizmo between them. He looked a mess with a broken nose and gash across his forehead. He swayed as they righted him, and Oberion ushered them along.

"Once you all are safely across, I'll double back to help her."

Oberion had to believe she could handle herself a little longer. He didn't want to think of the alternative.

"We can help." Gizmo made to turn around and almost fell back into the crater.

"Oh no you don't." Oaken grabbed the other dwarf and hooked an arm around his stomach as they hobbled along.

"Your elements and brute strength won't work here," Oberion said. "We are helping her by getting you lot out of here. She won't stop until we're across so get moving."

The dwarves listened and ran. Through the veil of rain, Oberion saw the path that led southwards and away from this accursed crater. *We are almost there. Just a few more steps.*

They were off the staircase and running down the path. Oberion skidded to a stop and looked back, watching Vaylin and waiting for a chance to help.

To his stunned disbelief, she was blasting hit after hit of that white light from the staff toward the black crack, which was shrinking. The darkness seemed agitated, causing pointed ripples on the surface as she attacked. There was a flash of lightning.

A tendril timed its attack with the lightning, shooting directly at Vaylin like an arrow of pure darkness.

"No!" Oberion ran toward her. Time slowed, and he couldn't move fast enough. His limbs were impossibly weighed down, and it felt as though he were running through water.

The blot of blackness connected with Vaylin's chest.

The silver light that had wrapped itself around Vaylin quivered, and the world froze around him. The darkness couldn't penetrate her silver web of power, although it was trying. Black and silver tendrils merged, and Vaylin was in the heart of it. A rushing noise filled the space, but for once, it wasn't coming from the crack in the earth.

It was coming from Vaylin.

She was hovering midair and encased in an orb of white-and-gold light, a thread of darkness woven into the mass. The stone from Mingalla shone like a star at its center. Oberion watched, mystified, as she pointed the end of staff at the center of the darkness below.

Flames burst from her staff and doused the blackness in a burning, golden light.

The canyon walls flared as if it were broad daylight, and Oberion covered his eyes from the brilliance of her attack. A keening came from the crack fading, and Oberion's eyes watered at the sound. The intensity of the fire grew.

Vaylin's eyes were no longer her own. A whiteness covered the familiar green irises, and her brown hair flowed around her, pulled from its braid. The flames turned from gold to red then pink, before finally blazing to a blinding white. It encompassed the void entirely, weaving and stitching what looked like iridescent spiderwebs from the edges and creating a seal over the entire rupture.

The darkness shrank, and his knees wanted to buckle in the relief he felt.

The white light of Vaylin's eyes spread across her forehead, down her cheeks and neck. Light under skin that seemed to pulse into her, along with that thread of blackness.

Oberion didn't know what was happening. He took two steps toward her, arm outstretched to help, when the white light faltered and fell away from her and the darkness pulsed into her. She convulsed, dropping from midair and letting go of the staff.

"Vaylin!" He reached for her and the staff with all his remaining magick, demanding the air bring her toward him. He caught the staff in one hand and, a second later, grabbed Vaylin, laying her gently on the ground.

She looked weaker up close, like the husk of a starving person. There was a black stain under her skin, and her eyes rolled back as she stopped moving.

MIDNIGHT ILLUMINATIONS
AVON

IT TOOK A WHILE FOR THEM TO REACH THEIR CAMPSITE. AVON WAS FEELING the aches and pains of the fight, and lugging two hundred fifty pounds of dead weight across a desert wasn't helping. Part of his elven battle training was learning how to heal during a fight. He concentrated, and his wounds knitted themselves closed. One of the first lessons taught by the Sun Warrior was: to be a great warrior, one must know how to heal the hurt they have caused. Balance must be found in all things.

Everything at the camp was how they'd left it. The horses were happy at their return and seemed otherwise unfazed by the storm. Avon grinned with pride at them; it took much to scare the horses from the Southern Kingdom. Marshall was mumbling to himself as Avon propped him against the side of the cave and pulled out their sleeping mats and healing supplies from his pack. It was too risky to light a fire and might give away their position if the golem master was lurking about.

He faced Marshall, ready to assess the extent of his injuries. Marshall was half conscious, and it did nothing to ease Avon's frustration over him. This man, Baxter Marshall, had idiotically risked his life to stop that enchantment with his own two hands. He could have died, letting that much voltage pass through him, and somehow didn't. It validated some suspicion Avon had about Marshall's inner strength and his "throwaway" attitude about life.

Elven kind were nothing short of diligent when it came to preserving their lives and communities, especially since they could live thousands of years if they didn't sustain a life-threatening injury. Human lifespan was a blip compared to their own. Perhaps that made the opposite true about Marshall, that his extraordinary strength and willingness to go through so much danger was precisely because he was human and had little time to waste being cautious.

Avon pondered the man before him.

He was beautiful for a human, burly and bearlike with the perfect amount of hair covering his body. It was mostly black and, in the right light, had a shining red-auburn hue. The hair on his arms was burnt from the electricity, and the skin of his arms and hands were dry, red, and shining with burns. Avon had been with more males than females over this past century and seldom attracted to humans the way he was toward Marshall. Was this something more than the gentle guidance of the Sun Warrior?

The elven race didn't often mate with humans, due to the shorter life spans. It wasn't impossible, of course, and the elves of the south were generally more open to that type of bonding than their northern brethren.

Still, romance was not what he was here for.

"Marshall, can you hear me?" he said in a clear voice.

Marshall looked up blearily and had a hard time focusing on Avon.

"Hey youuu," he slurred. "High five back there." He raised his hand briefly and, without waiting for Avon to return the gesture, dropped it limply back to his side.

"All right," Avon said slowly. He lifted Marshall's eyelid and snapped his fingers. A beam of sunlight appeared.

Marshall's pupils contracted when the light hit them, and he flinched backwards. "Hey—don't do that."

"Contrary to the evidence before me, you don't seem to have any serious brain damage. I'm going to move you to your sleeping mat so I can heal your injuries. I think all that voltage seared a majority of your nerves endings. I'm shocked you didn't blow your own heart out."

"I'll show you heart." Marshall pulled at his shirt collar, delirious. It didn't do much to show off his physique and only caused him to fall sideways.

"Whoa there." Avon righted him again and had a hard time not laughing. A small part of him was thoroughly enjoying seeing the man without his usual stern defenses.

After a moment, Avon found himself admiring Marshall's body as he sat there before his senses clicked back into place. He shook his head to clear his mind. It was exactly that effect that caused him to lose the wrestling match that night. No matter what he was feeling toward Marshall, he wouldn't do anything sexual to him while he was in this state. It was highly unethical, and he would rather have Marshall conscious, present, and active if something intimate were to ever transpire between them.

"Come on," the elf said. "If we're trying to leave in the morning, you need all the rest you can get. I have a tonic that you can take before going to sleep that will help."

"Whatever you say, pointy ears." Marshall lifted both arms above his head like a child waiting to be picked up. Avon gripped his broad chest and lifted him toward the mat.

Great Warrior above, this man was massive.

He laid Marshall down and propped his head on a bundle of clothing as a makeshift pillow. A stain of red on Avon's hand caught his attention, and he lifted Marshall's undershirt to see a scattering of cuts and scrapes across his back. They were perfectly sliced open, filled with dirt, sand, and glass pieces.

Avon let out a long breath. That would require cleaning before his magick could heal the flesh completely.

He pulled Marshall's filthy and torn shirt off. His eyes lingered on that broad chest, down his abs, and along the waistline, where he noticed a tattoo peaking above Marshall's trousers. It intrigued him and looked like two snake heads rearing up on either side of his hips. The lower half of the tattoo was covered, and Avon couldn't help his curiosity as he tugged the waistband down slightly for a better look. The bodies of two entwining snakes continued south along his pelvic bones and presumably wound around his....

Avon let go of the pants and sat back on his heels, his heart racing and a stirring in his groin.

"That's a unique tattoo," he remarked under his breath.

"Got it as a teenager."

"That's a...pretty ambitious design." The pointed tips of his ears heated.

"It goes all the way down and around."

Avon's jaw dropped, and he quickly shut it again, suddenly very hot despite no fire in the cave. His heart rate increased at the thought of exploring the details of that tattoo personally, and he had to take several deep breaths to calm down. He had to remind himself that this was not part of his mission. This was a medical situation, and he would not be distracted.

Some part of Marshall was emotionally struggling and suffering. Avon could sense the pain of it and saw its manifestation during their brief time traveling together. He could only heal the physical body. Marshall would have to figure out the rest. There was a particular power that it took for a person to heal spiritually. It always had to come from within and of one's own will. Avon passionately believed that anyone, no matter how victimized, could always heal themselves. No one was every truly trapped in the pain of old wounds.

Lucky for him, Marshall didn't seem to notice Avon's discomfort. Pushing the erotic thoughts from his head, he rolled Marshall onto his stomach as gently as he could.

The process of pulling the glass out took a while. There was a pile of bloody glass next to him by the time he cleaned the wounds on Marshall's back completely. His healing magick was careful, knitting the wounds shut and leaving no mark behind. Healing was an artform and required him to sense the workings of the body using his hands and inner eye. Avon was good at it, and his suspicions about the electrical damage were correct. Most of Marshall's nerves had suffered some degree of high voltage during that fight.

Astonishingly, the nerve endings had started to grow back of their own accord.

Avon was amazed by the rapid biological response to the damage. Most humans wouldn't show that type of response unless they had crossbreed with another magickal species of Chrysanthos blood or had some type of medical care immediately after the injury. Even then, nothing could explain the nerve growth taking place. It made Avon's life easier as he worked from head to toe, silently repairing the last of the burns and nerve endings.

Marshall fell asleep at some point, and after hours of healing, Avon finally finished. He felt tired but nothing more. Stretching, he left Marshall where he slept and went to check the perimeter of their campsite. There were no tracks or indication of anything wandering near them in the long hours Avon healed Marshall.

He returned and brought fresh water and some dried mango slices. He gently patted his companion on the shoulder. "Marshall, if you can hear me, I need you to wake up now."

Marshall cracked an eyelid open and groaned. "I feel like shit." He rubbed a hand over his forehead. "What happened?"

"You electrocuted yourself. What do you think happened?"

Marshall responded with another groan.

"You passed out once we were out of the canyon, and I brought you to the campsite. Have some water. You must be parched."

Marshall propped himself on one elbow and reached for the canteen Avon passed to him. He gulped it down eagerly. A trickle of water fell down Marshall's chin and neck, a glittering rivulet going down, down, down.

Avon coughed. "Easy there. You don't want to make yourself sick."

Marshall, who was panting slightly, gave back the canteen and sat up straighter. The color had returned to his golden-brown skin, and he sat with his eyes closed. "I don't remember anything after we left that pit."

"I got you along and healed your injuries. Your back was pretty bad, but I got all the glass out and it healed fine. Your nerves took the biggest hit. You're an incredible healer, did you know? I did what I could for the nerves, but your body was already taking care of it. I have an elven tonic you can take if you want, though you might not need it at this rate."

Marshall nodded vaguely while Avon spoke, seemingly uninterested in what he was saying but gasped suddenly.

Avon whirled behind him, thinking something was entering the cave, which was absurd since he would have heard anything approaching them a long ways off. "What in blazes was that for?"

"Where is the sphere?" Marshall touched his shirtless body and trouser pockets, panicked to find them empty. His hands flew over the blankets and mats while he searched for the mysterious object.

"Calm down and be quiet. I have it right here." Avon pulled open the straps of his bag nearby to show the metal ball inside.

Marshall sagged in relief and laid back against the wall. He looked pale, and Avon had no doubt he wasn't feeling good.

"You need to take it easy," Avon said tentatively.

"I'll be fine. This isn't the worst I've ever been," Marshall said, the lack of self-love evident. Even though he was good at hiding it, Avon saw right through him. "My gut says there's something terrible inside that thing."

"What do you mean?" Avon had been so absorbed in healing Marshall that he hadn't given the sphere a second thought until now. Once he focused on it, he sensed the wrongness of the object.

"When we were down there, the sphere was partially opened. It has some sort of inner compartment. I think something is hidden in there and that was what the golem wanted. That's what that person was after."

Avon eyed his bag suspiciously. "There is a peculiar energy coming from it. What do you think might be inside?"

"No clue. Something dark if it required that amount of natural magick to power the enchantment. They could have been using the eclipse's energy too."

"Although possible, I don't think it's likely. Not many people can channel cosmic power like that. The eclipse are powerful, but not recommended for spell work. The chaos energy is too unpredictable." Avon grinned then despite the morbid topic. He was slightly stunned that Marshall would connect the two. "What I said *did* make an impression on you, then."

"Maybe." Marshall avoided Avon's eyes, which made him grin even further. "Maybe being electrocuted fried my brain enough that I don't know what to think anymore. You were the one who said cata-clysmic energy."

"It is never a bad thing to question the world around you. Inquisi-tiveness is as vital as imagination. Both are conduits to vast amounts of knowledge."

"Yeah, yeah. Save it for when I'm better." Marshall laid back on his mat and looked drained. "What were you saying about a drink for me?"

"It's a healing tonic, not alcohol." Avon pulled a bottle from his pack. It was filled with pale blue water with swirling, shimmering gold dust inside.

"What is it? It looks like a faerie drug."

"It is an elixir my people made with the waters from our sacred pools and a few other rare and magickly potent ingredients," Avon said with pride. "It is a must-have for any journey away from the kingdom."

"And what exactly does it do?"

"It will rejuvenate your mind, speed up your body's natural healing processes, and temporarily increase your magick flow. In short, a healing potion. Many of the elven warriors will take it before battle to improve their fighting. We call it Telrithian."

"Never even heard of the stuff."

"It is an integral part of elven culture used in sacred rituals and causes altered and euphoric states. If you don't want it I won't waste it on you." Avon tucked the bottle back into his bag, slow and deliberate.

Marshall seemed more interested and sat up straighter, trying to show some respect. "No—come on now. I want to try it, all right?"

Avon grinned wickedly. Why not have some fun with him, after all? "It can be intense for humans. Too much of a good thing, you know. It can overwhelm the senses, make you feel connected to the things around you, or knock you out cold."

"Oh?" Marshall raised an eyebrow. "Are you sure this is a healing tonic, then? Not some sorta love potion?"

Avon grew hot and protested, "Don't be ridiculous. You can't craft love. Everyone knows that. Besides, even if you could, I would never use a love potion on someone. I'd want the real thing. No magick can ever fake that."

Marshalls eyebrows rose even higher.

"You should drink some *Telrithian* yourself."

The idea hadn't occurred to Avon. He wanted to ration as much of the elixir as he could while he was away from the Southern Kingdom.

"Come on. I don't want to drink alone, and if it's good for you, then why not? You've had one hell of a night too."

"I— Well, all right."

Marshall grinned at him. "That's the spirit. Nobody likes drinking alone."

"You're not alone," Avon said bluntly.

Marshall opened his mouth to reply then stopped at the look Avon was giving him.

Avon looked away and pulled two small cups from his bag, pouring them each a measure of the shimmering blue liquid. It twinkled like sunlight and had the dry, rocky aroma of his kingdom when he opened the bottle. A little bit of home.

He passed a cup to Marshall, who reached forward for it eagerly. Their fingertips brushed ever so slightly against each other, tingling with electricity. Maybe some voltage had remained in Marshall's system and Avon got a dose of it at their touch.

Avon raised his glass. "To our health."

"To not being alone." Marshall stared intently at Avon, who felt like butterflies were in his stomach.

There was that current running through him again, like gravity pulling him closer into Marshall's orbit. "To not being alone."

They clinked their glasses together and drank.

25

THE TERRA EMBASSY

AVON

MUCH TO AVON'S DEEP AMUSEMENT, MARSHALL FELL ASLEEP INSTANTLY after he drank the elixir the previous night, as most humans did. He had held out longer than most yet Telrithian was not a typical spirit. Marshall had slept the whole night with a big, dreamy smile on his face, and Avon chuckled at the sight of it. He was completely rejuvenated himself, having no trouble falling into a deep meditative state, as elves did not sleep like humans. The sun crested over the horizon, and Avon was checking the perimeter when Marshall finally woke.

"Feeling better?" Avon said smugly. He was tending the horses for the day of riding ahead.

Marshall stretched and moved his newly healed body. "Better? Is that a joke? I feel better than I did when I left the Temple of Sakhet."

"Well, it's against their code to give Telrithian to mortals. It's sacred elven magick."

"Is it? Should I consider myself lucky you gave me some?"

"I'd say so. I doubt any other elf would have given you some. I'm a bit of a rebel when it comes to breaking those sorts of traditional rules. Probably why the elders don't want younger elves like me on the councils. We challenge the old ways of thinking too much, wanting to adapt to this modern world and have the elves take greater part in shaping it. There are more of us then the older gens. We should have more say."

Marshall raised his eyebrows. "A rebel knight, then?"

Avon scowled. What did he know about the challenges of society when he chose a life of wandering about the country side? "I believe in change and being the example. That is why I am here and not sitting in a river villa, remote and protected, while the world moves forward around me and my kingdom." He breathed sharply through his nose and turned away. *This man does not care about your burdens. Do not waste your energy.*

Marshall approached him, face full of concern and conflict. "I cannot get involved in your politics." Avon's gut wrenched, and Marshall kept speaking. "For what it's worth, I think you're right and justified in your beliefs."

Marshall's broad and freshly healed hand was inches from his own. Avon grasped it firmly.

"Thank you for your words and kindness." Avon looked into Marshall's dark brown eyes, spots of gold reflecting on his skin from where the sunlight shone off his own dermal piercings. He liked the effect it had on Marshall, who smiled and tightened his grip on Avon's fingers.

They left the sands of the red desert behind for a rocky path that leveled into sprawling fields. Light green and yellow grasses swayed lazily under the beaming sun, long stalks whispering against one another and indistinguishable from the buzzing of insects. As they traveled west, towering mushroom-shaped trees appeared in the distance. Although tiny on the horizon, these beauties towered over two hundred feet. The stalks had thick, white bark that curled up off the towering stem in places. Avon had to crane his neck to see up the underside of the massive trees. Smaller mushroom caps peppered the stems up to the behemoth cap on top, which was brick red on the outside with an underbelly full of ochre colored gills, waving like velvet curtains. Occasionally, a trickle of what looked like pollen would fall from the gills to be carried away on the winds like yellow dust.

"The Red Giant Pass," Avon said in wonderment. "These are

magnificent. I hoped our route would take us through here. I wasn't sure how many of these giants were left after the Colonizer's Revolt." They had cut and harvested these mushrooms to boost their magick and create an army to try to overthrow the Terra Nation. Legend said the spirits of the mushrooms were vengeful and poisoned the Colonizers, ruining their plans in the end.

"They got what they deserved," agreed Marshall. "There are shamans and aboriginal tribes that live here and protect the Red Giants. The Terra Nation considers the tribes people and the mushrooms a national treasure. Anyone caught destroying these groves is at the mercy of the shamans. Terra Nation gives them full jurisdiction over these lands."

"Will they bother us?" Avon eyed the stems of the mushrooms and pondered the rumors of the extreme psychedelic powers in these plants.

"No, they have their own magick that alerts them to dangerous presences. We're traveling through and mean no harm or ill intent to our surroundings. They will let us pass unhampered."

He was right too. Avon didn't see anyone along the Giant's Pass, though he could feel hidden eyes follow their progress. They rode in silence for a while, passing through bars of shadow cast by the long mushroom stalks.

"Have you ever been to Panthea before?" Marshall asked.

"I have not, surprisingly. The first one hundred years of my life have been spent in the Southern Kingdom, training with the legion and completing my studies. We are free to go to Panthea, of course, but many elves prefer the education they receive from our Wisdom Holders and are discouraged from leaving the island of the Southern Kingdom altogether. They understand and keep all of our oldest traditions, passing them onto the younger generation of elves."

"I think you will like it there."

"Will you be my personal guide?" Avon teased.

Marshall reddened slightly. "I er—it would be quite rude of me to not give you a tour of the grounds. You are a diplomat and an honored guest at Panthea after all."

Avon cocked his head sideways. "Honored guest, am I? My how your opinion of myself has evolved."

"Strictly speaking, it's what I've been telling myself as a coping method for your presence."

"I appreciate the title. It makes the whole thing sound more official." Avon held his head a bit higher and squared his shoulders, making himself look more regal. Marshall snickered, and Avon relaxed his posture again, laughing along.

"Speaking of official, there is some…business I want to discuss with you before we arrive." Marshall's tone became serious. "I will have to meet with the Council of Panthea after our arrival. It is all the Elite members, the gatekeeper, and the captain of the paladins. You will be expected to give testimony about everything from the chiro to the sphere."

"Of course," Avon said. "I expected nothing less and look forward to meeting your fellows on the council."

"That being said, I think it would be best to discuss these events privately with the gatekeeper before we have the council meeting. It will take some time to assemble all the Elites, and I've been thinking about this golem and sphere all day. Whoever is controlling it must be powerful. What if they are within Panthea or somehow spying on us? We need to make sure this sphere doesn't fall into the wrong hands."

"You suspect someone in Panthea could be associated with the sphere?" It went against the very image of the Elite Guardians and ideals of the capital. Yet, humans were notoriously fickle and selfish. It wouldn't surprise Avon if someone in a powerful position there would use their influence to increase personal glory and status. That was the nature of power after all.

"I can't honestly say. Everyone's a suspect until proven innocent. The golem, or whatever that thing was, got a good look at both of our faces. They might have recognized me and know I would come back to Panthea with the sphere. There is a good chance someone in the Terra Nation could be doing this. Lots of powerful politicians and elementors come though the embassies, and they have the advantage of watching and waiting for us while we have no clue who they even are."

Avon nodded in agreement. "There were no signs of a disturbance around our camp in the morning. I scouted the surrounding areas before you woke and saw nothing out of the ordinary."

"All I'm saying is we need to tread carefully, and the only person we can trust with the knowledge of the sphere is the gatekeeper."

"I understand. We bring many dangers in our tidings to Panthea. It must be handled with care and caution." Avon wasn't going to do anything to jeopardize this or hurt Marshall in the process. Not when so many of his own future plans were tied into this whole thing.

"Good."

A stream slowly descending along the roadway with them created a calming sound, and the temperature grew hot next to the bleached canyons around them. The walls reached high above their heads and created a naturally hollowed cathedral of sunlight. Everything around them was cast in shades of orange, brown, and gold that shone through the coral-like branches of the canyon ceiling. Water and wind had carved a path through the cliffside over eons, creating organic twisting bends and turns.

It was quiet down here in a simple and meditative way, peaceful, and Avon connected to the space around him. His own Elder magick always had a better sense of rocks, earth, and fire than wet and woody forests of the north.

"We are approaching the outer gate," Marshall whispered.

A thrill of anticipation coursed through Avon as they rounded the corner and found an enormous slab of dead-end wall. His excitement deflated as he stared at the solid mass in front of them. Ten paladin guards stood there, looking like ants compared to the expanse of stone behind them. They wore hooded white robes lined with red trim and orange embroidery. Each of them carried a long spear and shield, standing shoulder to shoulder and barring the way.

"I'll do the talking," Marshall muttered as they approached the paladins.

Avon nodded. He wasn't sure how many elves the paladins were used to seeing and hoped they wouldn't cause him too much trouble. There was an old tension between the Southern Kingdom and the

Terra Nation that caused many prejudices between the two races to this day.

"Hello, and welcome to the Terra Embassy of Panthea. Please provide your identification and state your purpose," the guard said politely and held out an armored hand expectantly, waiting for their documentation.

"I'm Baxter Marshall, the Wanderer of Chrysanthos, and this is Avon Nehym, representative of the elves from the Southern Kingdom," Marshall said with an extraordinary amount of charm Avon had never heard him use before. In his palms, he flashed a burnished piece of metal to the guards, who immediately recognized it and bowed.

"The Wander and an elf," the paladin mused and stared at Avon's pointed ears. "We were not expecting you to have company."

"Neither was I," Marshall said with a wink. "Now, unless you have more questions for us, we are rather late and must be on our way."

"No, sir. There isn't anything else." The man bowed. "Aldwin Hearthfire has given us orders to alert Panthea Central as soon as you pass into the embassy. We will send him a message of your arrival."

"You needn't bother." Marshall pulled out a clear square of quartz wrapped in metal that Avon had not seen until now. "I can alert him myself."

"As you wish, sir." The paladin bowed again. He turned on his heel, white-and-red robes swishing as he gestured to the other paladins on guard.

They split into two groups and performed the same sequence of body movements, grounding their energy and opening the gate. Their hands balled into fists as they crouched, leaned sideways, and held their fists inches away from the cliffside. There was rumbling, and a gap opened from floor to cavernous ceiling. It grew wider and wider, forming a space big enough they could pass comfortably through to the other side.

Marshall spurred his horse forward and Avon followed.

Avon leaned close to Marshall and whispered, "What was that metal thing you showed the guards?"

"Oh this?" Marshall pulled out the square of quartz. "This is my Comm Crystal. It allows us to send messages within the embassies and

Panthea Central. Damn useful too. I know Fabien Prince is working on getting these things into all the major cities."

"Not that, although it's fascinating and I want to know more. The other thing."

"It's the insignia of the wanderer. The paladins recognize it and know who it belongs to. Perk of the job, I suppose."

"Can I see it?"

"That would completely violate the secrecy of my position," Marshall said in mock afront. "But I think I can make an exception for you." He opened his hand for Avon to see. It was a copper pendant with a triangle on it, except each point of the triangle was folded over and on top of itself, making an infinite loop.

"How unique," Avon remarked.

"A Penrose Tribar, symbol of the wanderer. It's an optical illusion in physical form."

"An apt sign for your position," Avon said with amusement.

The gate shut behind them with a dull thud that made the ground shudder. Ahead was a meandering azure river along the base of a hill. Trees with dark green leaves and clusters of small, red berries lined the dirt pathway toward the main complex. Multiple bridges crossed the river and connected to several paved roads carved from the hillside. Each one led toward an elaborate gate set into the terracotta walls that surrounded the embassy. Squat towers and flag posts were decorated with the red-and-black banners of the Terra Nation and the sigil of the cracked rock printed on it. The wooden lattice gates were open, and groups of academy students were in the midst of terra lessons around the grounds. Instructors shouted commands at their students, who were moving boulders at targets or running obstacle courses. There was a lightness here and comradery that made Avon smile.

"It's expanded over time. The original temple is in the center of the complex, with the portal entrance to Panthea Central inside. There are resident halls, lecture halls and amphitheaters, a modest sized library, and other park and recreational areas. All six embassies have unique and different features about them that cater to the magickal arts taught there."

Avon raised his eyebrows. "Impressive."

"It is impressive, isn't it?"

They passed through the gates and several groups of students who watched as they entered. Avon knew instantly why Marshall had asked for discretion upon arrival. People covertly stared at them over books or around shoulders. Even a few teachers paused their instruction to watch their progress.

They dismounted their horses, and Marshall started to walk away.

"Are we leaving our horses here?" asked Avon.

"Yes. We won't need them anymore. Most horses don't like using the portals and get very skittish around them."

"These are the finest horses in the Southern Kingdom. They would follow us anywhere without issue." It was a foreign idea to leave the horses here. What if they would need them? He would be thousands of meters away at Panthea Central.

"I promise you, they will be fine. We can return here whenever we want in an instant. If you're truly feeling uncomfortable in a day or two, we can try to bring them along to ease your worry."

Perhaps he needed to trust Marshall on this. "All right. I get your point. We can try it for now, but I don't like it."

He walked away from the stables, resigned. People stared shamelessly as they passed through the embassy. Avon ignored it entirely. Marshall was right, and anyone could be watching. He would show no weakness for a potential enemy to exploit.

Avon stepped closer to Marshall. He kept his face a mask of calm and moved his lips as little as possible as he whispered, "Are they always like this when you come back?"

"No." Marshall chuckled. "Most don't even know who I am. They are probably more curious about you. Not many elves around these parts."

"How can no one here know who you are?" Avon said in disbelief.

"That's not what I mean. They know of the wanderer but not who the wanderer is. Most of my business is with people and places *outside* of Panthea. I spend little time here otherwise. The wanderer is incognito and gathers intelligence for the capital. I'm not meant to teach classes or boast about perfecting arcane magickal arts. That's for the Elite Guard to do, not me."

Before Avon could say more, his ears twitched at someone approaching them from behind. Marshall's face changed from happy to stern amusement.

"Look at what we have here?" The voice dripped with contempt.

Avon turned to see a man like a bull assessing him curtly and staring daggers at Marshall. His robes were solid black and lined with bright red bands around the hems.

"Do you realize how long it's been since anyone has seen you? Nearly two months, Marshall. It's unacceptable. Do you have any idea what we've been dealing with here without you? Aldwin has been covering for you, but the rest of us won't tolerate such a lack of communication."

Avon instantly disliked this man and was almost saying a prayer to the Sun Warrior for an opportunity to fight him.

"Hello, Neko Raneem. It's nice to see you again too." Marshall completely disregarded Neko's admonitions.

The man, Neko, was positively fuming and appeared on the verge of charging Marshall down. His nostrils flared irritably as his hands curled into fists. The muscular bulk of Neko was sufficient enough to rival Marshall's own.

"This isn't a joke, Marshall." Neko rubbed a palm against his temple. Sweat beaded from his forehead.

"I didn't think it was," Marshall said easily. "My orders are to report to the gatekeeper. If you have an issue with that, then take it up with him. Until then, you're being rather rude to me and our guest. This is his first visit to Panthea, and I'd hate for him to get the wrong impression of you."

"Guest? Since when do *you* invite guests to Panthea?"

"Just because I haven't in the past doesn't mean I'm not capable of it now. I think you'll find its well within my authority as wanderer to do so."

"Your authority? I'd believe your authority when you've earned it. You can't just come and go as you please."

"Actually, I can," Marshall said. "It's literally in my job description."

Neko looked irate and instead turned to glare at Avon, who

smirked and straightened his spine to its full extent, giving Neko a piercing look of his own. They were almost the same height, except Avon was fractionally taller.

"Who are you?" Neko snapped.

Avon was reluctant to answer before deciding he would not sink to this level of rudeness and spoke clearly. "Avon Nehym, Warrior and Knight of the Southern Kingdom of Elves."

"Welcome to Panthea, Avon." Neko spread his arms in mock gesture. "Might I suggest not getting wrapped up in whatever affairs Baxter Marshall has landed himself in now. You'll find he only cares about himself."

"It's exactly because of those affairs that *my king* has ordered me here."

Neko seemed to register Avon's meaning and didn't deign to respond or apologize for his unpleasantness. Avon felt a strong urge to throttle him.

"We can have a nice long chat at a council meeting," Marshall said. "I'll send you a message with the time and date. I need to check with Hearthfire first, so if you wouldn't mind, get out of our way."

Neko crossed his arms.

"You have no idea what type of serious matters *we've* been dealing with." He spoke in a softer voice, and it was clear Neko was preoccupied with something.

The tension between the three of them was high.

"Something has been happening at Panthea too?" Marshall quieted his voice and gave Avon a significant look. "Is anyone hurt?"

"No one within the capital," Neko said.

"What do you mean?"

"I suppose you will find out when we have that council meeting." Neko was clearly enjoying holding this information over Marshall, and it did nothing to improve Avon's impression of this man. "I'll see you then."

Without another word, Neko walked away.

"He's a pleasant one," Avon said sarcastically when he was out of earshot. "Should I expect welcomes like that from everyone here?"

"No, he is unjustly taking his frustrations out on me and you. Don't judge him too harshly. Usually he isn't this hostile. Something bad must be happening if we're seeing this side of him. He didn't become known as the Iron Bull for nothing." Marshall stared after Neko, concern on his face. It took a certain strength of character to show concern for someone even when they were being a complete jerk. It made him appreciate Marshall even more.

26

THE GATEKEEPER

MARSHALL

AVON WALKED BEHIND MARSHALL EVER SO SLIGHTLY, OBSERVING EVERY inch of the Terra Embassy as they passed through varying courtyards toward the portal. Here and there, a paladin stood guard, white robes standing out against the red stone. The portal archway was at the center of the embassy, and the courtyard was decorated with beds of desert blooming flowers, cacti, and gnarled trees. Boulders were artfully placed around the square, surrounded by meditative sand gardens. Several students traced a mandala design into the sands.

There stood the Terra portal. It was an archway of great height made from smooth, tan stone. Ornamental filigree was carved along the arch, and crystals were inlayed into the stone like a stained-glass mosaic. Garnets of deep red, orange, and pink were scattered amongst smoky quartz, clear quartz, hematite, and onyx, all pulsing with power. In the space of the archway glittered a pale gold veil, eternally undulating and swaying. As they approached, a few apprentices stepped through the arch and disappeared to Panthea Central.

"This is incredible." Avon's jaw was slightly open in disbelief, and his usually sharp eyes had gone round and glassy.

"It's really something special," Marshall agreed. "Can you believe some people are frightened of them? They have been stable for over a thousand years."

"What does it feel like to pass through?"

"Why don't you find out?" Marshall gestured toward the portal. "I swear, it doesn't hurt *that* much."

Avon gave him a reproachful glance, clearly not amused with his little joke but also not taking him seriously.

Marshall had gone through the portals often enough that he didn't register the feeling anymore. "You will be fine, I promise."

Avon walked up to the edge of the golden veil that separated them from Panthea Central. He raised his fingertips and let them hover inches above the veil, closing his eyes and sensing the energy. Taking a deep breath, he stepped through, and a ripple emanated from where he vanished.

Marshall waited a few seconds, oddly enjoying the feeling of leading Avon here and sharing this experience with the elf. He focused on the sensations he felt when he stepped through the portal this time. It was a forward-rushing momentum and slight compression around his whole body. Colors swirled around him, and in a blink, he had gone from the Terra Nation to Panthea Central in the middle of the continent.

The compression released its hold, and he saw the familiar portal Nexus of Panthea Central. Five other archways shone and twinkled around them on a circular platform, each with banners of different colors.

Avon stood in the middle of the room, directly under the pointed glass dome as he turned around in amazement. The sight was enchanting and made him pause midstride to watch. Was it the way the afternoon sun hit the glass at this particular angle so patches of color danced across Avon's skin? Or was it the impressive silhouette of the warrior elf that made Marshall feel like he was glimpsing something from a myth?

Someone bumped into Marshall from behind, and he stumbled forward. It was a student whose face was buried in a book, returning from a day of lessons.

"Sorry," Marshall muttered, stepping out of the way and hurrying over to Avon.

"This is marvelous." Avon's eyes gleefully flickering between Marshall and the portals.

"Yes, they are, and er— won't go anywhere. The gatekeeper told us to come to his office straight away." Marshall had his CC out and showed Avon the message.

"I should get one of those while I'm here. And you can teach me about it."

"Sure thing. Right after we deliver our report." He placed a hand on Avon's shoulder and steered them away from the portals.

They knocked on Aldwin's office door fifteen minutes later.

There was a gentle, "Come in," and they entered.

The office was a beautiful room with panorama windows that overlooked the capital grounds. A stone engraving of the Panthea crest was carved on the wall behind Aldwin. It was two triangles overlaying to form a six-pointed star, encompassed by a hexagon with a smaller hexagon in the center of the star. Below the carving of the crest was an inscription of the Panthea words:

As Above, So Below. Balance in Magick, For Source to Flow.

The desk was littered with parchment, ink wells, pens, and gray pages of a book filled with complex diagrams of shapes and numbers. They looked vaguely familiar to Marshall, but he couldn't place it.

"Ah, Baxter Marshall. Good to see my wanderer again. It's only been two full moon cycles and eighteen turns of the sun." Aldwin walked around his desk and greeted Marshall with a firm handshake and pat on the back. "I see you have a guest with you. Who do I have the honor of meeting today?"

"This is Avon Nehym of the Southern Kingdom of Elves. We met recently while I was in the kingdom, and he has traveled here with me as a diplomatic liaison for his court," Marshall said in a stately manner.

"It is an honor to be here, Gatekeeper." Avon bowed low. "Panthea is beautiful in its antiquity, and the portals are the glowing gem at the center of it all."

"The pleasure is all mine." Aldwin also bowed low. "I am glad you are here and hope you feel welcomed in our city and on these grounds."

"Yes, all have been hospitable except for that man, Neko. He accosted us on our arrival, which I found to be most discourteous. If one of my own had treated a guest that way in our kingdom, they would have been severely punished," Avon said somberly.

Aldwin's purple eyes looked confused, and he raised a questioning eyebrow at Marshall. "What is he talking about?"

"Neko decided to take it upon himself to reprimand me for my lateness upon our arrival," Marshall said.

Aldwin glowered at him. "What was said?"

"I told Neko to mind his own business. And that if he had an issue with my responsibilities to take it up with you."

Aldwin pinched the bridge of his nose and sighed deeply. When he took his hand away, he looked exhausted and turned back to Avon. "May I offer you my humblest apologies for his behavior. The man has been under a lot of stress and has not been acting like himself recently. There are issues—attacks really—arising in the south that have been troublesome for him. I will speak with him regarding this incident and beg your forgiveness until then."

"That is appreciated, Gatekeeper." Avon brought his hands together in thanks and bowed slightly. "As for your wanderer, he has shown me the treatment I expect from those who belong to the esteemed establishment of Panthea."

"Tell me how you met and all that has transpired. The message I received from your king was both troubling and illuminating." Aldwin gestured at the chairs before them. "Tea or some other refreshment? I have some brandy here if you'd like something a bit stronger."

"Tea," Avon said at the same time Marshall said, "Brandy."

Marshall raised an eyebrow at the elf and scoffed, settling into his chair and groaning as he stretched. He couldn't feel any spasms of electricity in his muscles, but the memory of it was still fresh. Avon really was an incredible healer. More efficient, too, than all those nurses at the temple.

"I can do the measure." Aldwin supplied Marshall with a brandy in a round glass goblet and waved a hand to clear his desk and make room for a teapot and three cups. With a pointed glance between Marshall and the teacup, he said, "In case you change your mind."

"You know me better than that," Marshall said. "Just put the bottle on the table and we'll go from there, eh?"

"If you insist," Aldwin conceded. "Now, do tell me what you've been up to these last few months. Much has happened at Panthea recently. I would prefer to hear your tale before I tell you mine."

Marshall took a small sip of the brandy and let it slide over his tongue. It was a fine vintage with subtle notes of rich oak and smooth caramel. He swallowed a mouthful of the amber liquid and smacked his lips appreciatively. "You got fine taste, Aldwin. I can't deny you that."

He told his story haltingly, starting with his time in the Southern Kingdom, the chiro attack, and how he had been taken to the healing Temple of Sakhet afterwards. Marshall took off his boot to show him the puckered, black scars around his foot and ankle.

"Positively gruesome." Aldwin tapped a metal piece behind his ear to release a monocle and examined the wounds.

Marshall involuntarily flinched when Aldwin's fingers got close to touching it.

"You've gotten yourself into sticky situations, but I'd say this one takes the cake. I've never seen an injury like this before. You're lucky to be alive," Aldwin said.

Marshall felt a pang of guilt at the tone in Aldwin's voice.

"The letter I received from King Darius explained this to me already. Yet, seeing it is a rather different matter altogether."

"The healers at the temple weren't sure what attacked Marshall at first," Avon said. "We have several chronicles of beastiaries from around Chrysanthos, and one of them described creatures from an underworld known as Nimrothag. I have brought several books from the Library of Xanthus for you that explain this world that sits below this one and its creatures in further detail."

A strange expression crossed Aldwin's face that made Marshall uneasy.

Marshall had heard that word tossed around in the Temple of Sakhet but was too weak and befuddled then to comprehend its meaning. Aldwin's eyes went round in astonishment, and Marshall glanced between him and Avon.

"Are you certain this place is real?" Aldwin asked. Marshall had never seen this awed disturbance from the gatekeeper.

"I'm not surprised that you doubt what I am saying. Knowledge of Nimrothag has long passed from human memory, but I assure you it is real. The elves remember. Our records are extensive, and we have never forgotten the threat of that evil place. It is why the Southern Kingdom keeps a standing army to this day, though many humans misunderstand it's true purpose and fear us."

Aldwin's eyes flicked toward the paperwork he had removed from his desk.

"It is a true realm of darkness, opposite to Chrysanthos," Avon said into the silence. "Eons ago, the door between our world and Nimrothag was opened. Our ancestors, elves and humans, had established relations with Nim, and for a while there was harmony. Alas, the nature of that realm is of darkness and corruption. It wasn't long until fighting broke out, and we waged a war with them and had to seal ourselves off from that world. As you can imagine, they didn't want to be closed off and fought back. Many were lost. We aided Panthea in the battle and were able to conquer our enemy, thus entering an age of peace."

Aldwin stood up abruptly and walked to the window of his office, clenching and unclenching his fists.

"Are you okay, Aldwin?" Marshall asked.

"Did you find any evidence of nature decaying or magickal ruptures in the landscape on your way to the embassy?" Aldwin looked panicked.

Marshall dug his pinky into his ear, unsure if he heard Aldwin correctly. "Say what now?"

"There was an incident in the Aqua Realm involving Vaylin. An energetic rupture occurred that destroyed an entire area of the Numinbah forest. Trees and plants atrophied to the point of dust. The wildlife and the people were gone. An entire nuca was lost. It was no ordinary scene of magick, as you can imagine."

"Neko mentioned something bad was happening. Is this what he meant?" Marshall asked.

Aldwin turned toward them and paced his office. "Neko has been dealing with various attacks on livestock throughout the Terra Nation. He thinks it has to do with the werewolf assembly, but it doesn't fit. After seeing your injury, I'm inclined to think that these...chiros are responsible for the damage." He rummaged through a desk drawer and dropped some photos between them. "As you can see, the attacks aren't pretty. I can understand how one would assume werewolves without the knowledge of chiros."

"Burning hells." Marshall poured another healthy measure of brandy into his empty glass as he thumbed through the gruesome attacks. There was no mistaking it—those bite marks matched the one on his foot.

"Perhaps these ruptures are somehow allowing the chiro to access Panthea. Seems to be a one-way trip though," Aldwin said.

"How did Vaylin escape the rupture?" Marshall liked the newest Elite Guardian and wanted to see her succeed. Vaylin's energy matched his own wildness, and they had formed an instant kinship. Much about Avon reminded him of Vaylin.

"As fate would have it, she found a powerful crystal in the nuca and used it to counteract the magick coming from the rupture. A rather lucky turn of events for us, if I may say so," Aldwin said.

"What type of stone?" Avon sat up straighter.

"We are not sure. She and Oberion have gone north to consult our dwarven brethren. They should be returning here soon, I hope," Aldwin said. "I know they reached the Khazirak Stronghold and haven't heard anything since."

"Bet she wasn't too pleased by that." Marshall turned to Avon and said in a stage whisper, "Vaylin and Oberion don't get along well."

"Whatever tension there is between the two has been set aside while we figure this out," Aldwin said to Marshall. "They are both members of the Elite Guard, and I expect them to act as such. This is no time for petty squabbles."

"So you think." Marshall took another sip of brandy.

"Enough." Aldwin dropped a fist onto the desk. "Vaylin understands the gravity of the situation far better than anyone else. Including you. She nearly died in the Numinbah forest. You would have known that if you had gotten here sooner or bothered to check in with us."

Marshall's stomach twisted uncomfortably at that. "I nearly died myself, you know."

"Yes but she at least bothered to tell me where she was going and with whom and when she would be returning. If something had gone wrong, we knew exactly where to find her, unlike you," Aldwin reprimanded.

Marshall put his hands up in a gesture of surrender. "You're right. I'm sorry for being a colossal idiot, and it won't happen again. You have my word as wanderer."

Aldwin and Avon both snorted in unison, and Marshall would have found their distain amusing if he wasn't the one being yelled at.

"I'm not completely useless. We didn't come across any ruptures but we found something else." From within his satchel Marshall pulled the sphere out and placed it on the desk.

If Aldwin looked shocked at the mention of Nimrothag, it was nothing compared to the look on his face when he saw the sphere. If Marshall hadn't known better, he would have said it was equal parts recognition and terror. Aldwin dropped his teacup, which broke and spilled pale green liquid across the desk.

"Geez, Al," Marshall said. "What's gotten into you?"

"Where did you get that?" Aldwin didn't even bother clearing the tea away as it stained several sheets of notes, bits of porcelain scattered between the pages.

Aldwin listened intently as Marshall spoke about the conjurer, the golem, and the fight for the sphere. The gatekeeper tapped his monocle back into place and gingerly picked up the sphere to examine it. It was unusual to see Aldwin unnerved. It made goose pimples rise on Marshall's skin and confirmed his feeling that this sphere was wrong. It didn't belong here, and they were right to trust Aldwin with it.

"What do you know about this thing?" Marshall gestured to the sphere with his glass and took another sip. "When we found it, it was opened to reveal some sort of inner chamber."

"The glyphs along the edges fade and change constantly," Avon said. "It matches the spell work that was drawn on the ground that night."

"It is an amalgamation of an invented script and several archaic languages," Aldwin said softly. The glowing red font shifted and undulated beneath his fingers.

"Can you read it?" Marshall asked disbelievingly.

Aldwin looked up and gave no indication of what he was thinking. It made Marshall uncomfortable.

"Perhaps. All locks can be broken, one only needs the right key." Aldwin turned the sphere over and over in his hands, observing every inch of it. It was a solid mass of silver, precisely formed so no grooves or rings were apparent on the surface.

"Will you call us when you are close to opening it? There's something dangerous inside. That's what the conjurer wanted. The sphere is its protection," Marshall said.

"I can see that." Aldwin offered no more information, frustrating Marshall. Something was wrong, and Aldwin wasn't saying more. There seemed to be a tipping of the balance in their world, and no one knew why this stuff was happening.

Cataclysmic energy, whispered Avon's words in his head.

"What does this mean for us? For Panthea?" Marshall asked.

"I don't know." Aldwin placed the sphere on the desk and tapped his monocle again. It flashed and folded neatly behind his ear.

"Clearly something is wrong," Marshall said frankly. "What could be causing these ruptures or the chiro to come into our world?"

"I cannot say for certain," Aldwin said. "I am monitoring the situation closely and will stop anyone I suspect to be involved with this. No ruptures have appeared elsewhere in Chrysanthos to the best of my knowledge. Leave me a map detailing your travel route through the Terra Nation. I will inform Neko of these chiros and have him send me the locations of where these attacks have been occurring; there may be a pattern we're not seeing. Skies above, I hope Vaylin and Oberion return soon with the information we need."

"If I may, Gatekeeper," Avon said, "I need to inform my king of all information we divulge here, for the safety of our kingdom and our people."

"I want complete transparency between us. This is a threat to everyone in Chrysanthos, and we must all work together to end it. The world will be looking to us for answers, and Panthea will have them."

Marshall drained the last of the brandy from his glass. The warmth of the draught coursed through him, burning away the fear at the edges of his mind and heart. Aldwin had reassured him, but the man was hiding something. That didn't sit well with Marshall.

CRYSTALLINE HEALING

OBERION

OBERION'S EARS RANG.

No, he couldn't let this happen. Vaylin was unconscious, cold to the touch, and gaunt. Her lips were blue, and there were dark circles under her eyes. The rain continued to fall, and he didn't care. The voices around him sounded fuzzy.

There was one thought in his mind, the silent prayer of her name.

Vaylin. Vaylin. Vaylin.

He fumbled for a pulse, knowing an agonizing moment of dread as he felt nothing under his shaking fingers. Pressing. Hoping to feel life in her veins.

"Please," he whispered. "Stay with me."

A flutter. A beat.

A stuttering pulse so weak it barely registered through his numb fingers.

Oberion relaxed minutely and brushed wet hair from her face. He focused on what little energy he had left to summon heat to his hands and placed one on the side of her neck, trying to warm her blood. It was a feeble attempt that did nothing to change her deathly appearance.

He felt helpless.

The stone from Mingalla glowed faintly beside him, and the power and energy of the stone called to him. Without thinking, he wrenched the stone from the end of the staff, and it flashed, burning his palm briefly as he held it to Vaylin's chest, covering it with his own shaking hand and focused on healing her.

Heal her. Save her.

He felt it then, tugging at his magick and in his heart.

The stone beneath his fingers grew hot, and a sudden chill spread through him. It wasn't his magick. He sensed the stone's power like a northern wind through his veins and clenched Vaylin closer to him, focusing only on healing her. On bringing her back. Light shone beneath his palm, and silver-white threads spread from the stone into his arm and over Vaylin's chest. The threads brought them closer, pulling him toward her body. His senses seared in a flash of pain, and he couldn't let go of the stone or Vaylin if he'd tried. The stone was binding them together.

Please, this has to work. He couldn't think of the alternative—it was too terrible, too real in this second to comprehend her death.

"Oberion, we need to move," Rathir said. "We aren't safe here."

Oberion heard the words and couldn't react. A wave of power rolled through him again, and he gasped at its enormity, the demand in it. He was paralyzed, and the pain his only anchor to Vaylin, to the world around him. Somehow, the stone was using his magick, guiding it to do what he was asking.

Vaylin's eyes suddenly flew open.

They were evergreen once more, and she gasped for air, coughing and retching.

The painful tugging vanished, and he loosened his grip, fingers stiff as he rolled sideways, the stone still on Vaylin's chest. Her chest moved up and down, and Oberion let out a strangled cry of relief.

She was back.

She was going to be okay.

He looked toward Oaken, one arm around Gizmo who was bleeding steadily, and then over to Rathir, whose eyes shone with concern. Oberion dropped his gaze back to Vaylin. She was unconscious again but clearly breathing. The stone actively pulsed, alternating between bright white and deep red.

His own vision blurred as he looked back at the crater.

The crack that had nearly spanned the entire crater was sealed. It looked like an ugly, glistening scar on the rock, but it was sealed. No void. No disintegrating rocks. He stared. Vaylin had managed to seal the rupture.

At what cost? He looked at Vaylin's unconscious form.

"We need to get to Skyminer's Keep," Rathir shouted.

The path beyond led south. An effigy of a stone eagle rose on a crooked rock formation, beaconing them to safer passage. That was enough for Oberion to get up and moving. He pocketed the stone, strapped the staff to his back, and scooped Vaylin up. They took off down the path without a second glance backward.

Oberion had no idea where Skyminer's Keep was. He had one eye constantly on Vaylin, the other haphazardly on his footing. Her eyes shifted under closed lids. The rain was falling, and exhaustion was finally taking its toll on him.

The dwarves had stopped several paces back, and it took him a moment to realize that he had walked beyond them. All three were examining the ledge of a rock wall. It looked like every other ledge Oberion had seen in these damn mountains. But this must be the spot if it had caught the dwarves attention so completely.

"How do we get down?" Oberion panted. The ledge looked like it dropped at least forty feet before hitting solid ground.

"Like this." Gizmo weaved slightly as he stepped out of reach and dropped his foot into open air.

Oberion shouted a warning.

Gizmo's foot fell on solid stone instead. It was a narrow step and camouflaged perfectly against the wall, making it nearly invisible. Gizmo kept walking down, one hand resting along the cliffside for balance. The other dwarves followed suit, and Oberion continued behind them. His arms were numb with Vaylin's weight, and he didn't dare shift his grip for fear of dropping her.

Oberion had counted over fifty steps before he lost track. They were far enough down the stairs that the rains and winds of the storm couldn't reach them anymore. It was dark and marginally warmer from the lack of atmospheric assault. If Oberion had any energy left, he would have conjured a warm breeze to dry their clothes. Gizmo pulled a glowing blue worm jar from his bag and placed it on his head harness. The stupid contraption was ridiculous, but Oberion smiled at recalling Vaylin wearing it a few days ago.

The stairs bottomed out into a flat, dry landing, and Oberion's legs shook as he knelt to place Vaylin on the floor.

"How is she?" Gizmo had a swatch of cloth pressed against his head, stained with blood. Of the dwarves, he had grown most attached to Vaylin.

"Her breathing is steady, and she seems stable." Oberion hesitated. "But I can't be sure."

"Gizmo," Oaken said, "how much further do we—"

His words were cut off by an unfamiliar voice.

"Hello, strangers," it said squeakily.

All four of them turned to the speaker. Just outside their sphere of blue light was a shadowed figure. It was small. Smaller than the dwarves by at least a foot, maybe two. Had they come to the right place?

"Skyminer!" Gizmo shouted jovially. Everyone jumped as he whirled toward the small figure, blue light illuminating his features and making him look positively terrifying.

Oberion took in the patched and frayed clothes and dirty skin of the smallest dwarf he had ever seen. Skyminer had a gray beard and tangles of hair that stuck out at odd angles under a dirt-stained, cone-shaped hat. The dwarf had a hooked nose and seemed very timid to be around so many of them at once.

"Yes, yes. I knew you'd be back here someday." Skyminer twisted his hands together nervously and took little steps toward the group. His black eyes jumped between each dwarf to Oberion then down to Vaylin. "Great prisms. Whatever happened to her?"

Faster than Oberion expected, the tiny dwarf took steps toward Vaylin. Oberion placed himself in front of her, blocking Skyminer's way. He towered over the small dwarf, who trembled slightly but held his ground.

"I cannot help her if you do not let me see her." He stamped his foot on the ground.

He gave Skyminer an appraising look and stepped aside. Oberion was no great healer, and he had only gotten her breathing again by using the stone. Foreboding crept up his spine. The stone, using it to save Vaylin—it had to cost him something.

The small dwarf sat by her side, lifting an eyelid and touching pressure points on her body.

"She needs healing," Skyminer said, voice quiet. His eyes kept flicking to Oberion's pocket, the one that held the stone from Mingalla. Oberion surreptitiously covered the spot with his hand.

"What's wrong with her?" Oberion pressed. He wanted answers, needed to know she was going to wake up and everything would be fine again.

He needed her to come back. It was his fault if she didn't.

"Her physical body is fine, but her magickal one has been drained, near to the point of collapse. She needs immediate energetic healing, or she could lose her magick permanently," Skyminer said.

Oberion couldn't let that happen. Not after she had braved the Lumbrinica Tunnel and they were this close to finding some answers. "Magick regenerates naturally. How could she be in danger of losing it?"

"Because it was no ordinary draining of magick. It was ripped from her by something else. Something powerful. If you want to ensure she lives *with her magick* beyond this night, you will stop arguing with me, pick her up, and get into my home. We have very little time," Skyminer demanded.

Oberion pushed all his doubts away and, without questioning further, scooped her up again and followed the little dwarf over the threshold.

He barely noticed the exquisite details of Skyminer's home as they rushed down the hallway. Skyminer was surprisingly fast and nimble. He led them into a back room that was part laboratory, part apothecary. Tables were filled with dried herbs, glass jars, tubes, Bunsen burners, scales, magnifying lenses, and crystals. Hundreds of crystals lined the walls in jars and bowls on countless shelves. Each one was neatly labeled with the type and origin of the stones.

Oberion didn't spare them more than a glance as he placed Vaylin on a stone worktable in the center of the room. The table stood two feet tall and had sacred geometric markings carved onto its surface. Ones Oberion had recognized. Seven circles spanned from one end of the table to the other, each painted with a different color of the rainbow and filled with ornate mandala patterns. Skyminer adjusted Vaylin's arms and legs so they aligned with the designs on the table. Oaken, Gizmo, and Rathir filled the space behind him and watched the little dwarf work his magick.

Skyminer trotted to a side cupboard and pulled it open to reveal a meticulous arrangement of stunning crystal specimens. Oberion was no stranger to gemstones and minerals, having used them throughout his magickal training, but these stones were beyond anything he had seen in Panthea. They shone with the light of stars, and the vibrations from them could be felt from across the room.

The Mingalla stone pulsed with power in Oberion's pocket. He had the strangest thought then that the stone was somehow conscious. His suspicion was immediately confirmed when Skyminer snapped his attention to Oberion and eyed him up and down. However, the little dwarf said nothing and placed more stones in strategic points around and on Vaylin. He arranged stones into swirls and patterns, quickly encompassing her entire body with gemstones. She looked like a corpse laid out on a funeral altar, and Oberion was nearly sick at the morbid thought.

Skyminer set a large smoky quartz point by her feet, clear quartz points in each hand, and an amethyst cluster near the crown of her head. Then with immense care, he picked up a white, pyramid-shaped stone and placed it on her forehead, directly above her third eye. When he let it go, the effect was immediate. Glowing golden lines radiated across her skin, connecting to the other stones placed on her body and around the table. The light spread and arched over her, cocooning her in a web of delicate light.

"Give me that stone in your pocket," Skyminer said sharply to Oberion.

He was taken aback by the severity in Skyminer's voice and recoiled. How could he know about the stone?

"I don't know what you're talking about." Oberion was hesitant to reveal the stone and wasn't sure if he trusted Skyminer yet.

"Don't be stupid." Skyminer held out his hand expectantly. "I know what it is that you carry, and it's the last thing we need to reconnect her magick. I need it unless you want her to lose her magick forever."

At the urgency in Skyminer's voice, Oberion pulled the stone from his pocket and passed it to the dwarf, whose eyes went round as saucepans when he beheld the stone. Skyminer walked back toward Vaylin's unconscious form and pointed the stone like a brandished sword at Vaylin.

Oberion shouted at him to stop, but the dwarves around him grasped his arms, effectively pinning him.

A loud, humming vibration echoed around the room, and Oberion watched, transfixed, as Vaylin's body relaxed and fleshed itself out again. Muscles reformed in her limbs, and the hollowed, gaunt look of her face faded. Relief swept through Oberion, and his knees went weak beneath him. The dwarves released him, and he stayed on his knees watching.

Watching.

Waiting.

He needed to make sure she was going to be okay. Light circulated around her for a long while until it dimmed and dispersed like mist into the air.

Skyminer approached her and removed the stones and crystals one by one. They weren't glowing with the same brilliance anymore. They were duller, some of them stained with black streaks as Skyminer placed them in a dish of salt. It reminded Oberion of that sentient darkness from the void.

Skyminer turned and offered Oberion the Mingalla stone when he was finished. Oberion expected it to look like the others, faded and with black streaks. The stone was in perfect condition, unaffected by whatever spell Skyminer had performed using it.

"She will live and keep her magick," Skyminer said kindly.

"Thank you," Oberion said.

The little dwarf bowed low, his hooked nose almost touching the ground. "It appears that there is quite a tale to tell here." Skyminer looked around at the assembled dwarves and the bloody and disheveled state of them. "Once you've had some rest."

"That would be an understatement," Oberion said wearily.

28

SKYMINER'S KEEP

VAYLIN

VAYLIN FELL THROUGH DARKNESS AND SHADOW.

The void stretched around her. How did she get here? There had been rocks. Rain. A black arrow then—nothing. When opening her mouth to scream, she had no air. No voice. Only strained muscles and silence. She was trapped.

Panic flared.

She had to get out. To get back to...where exactly?

Vaylin wasn't sure.

The emptiness pressed on her. Suffocating. Pinpricks of pain spread over her entire body, the darkness worming its way into her. Savoring her.

Taking from her.

Small bites at first. Then more.

The darkness wanted more from her. It ripped in through every pore of her body. She tried to hold on to herself. Tried to keep the pieces of herself together. Her thoughts were smoke, forming in her mind to be blown away. Unable to remember. Unable to focus.

The darkness surrounded her. She was drowning and there was nothing.

Vaylin, a voice echoed. Familiar.

There was endless space. Spreading and consuming.

Vaylin.

Everything was pain as she twisted, peering through the blackness for something. Anything to hold on to.

Vaylin, come back.

There was a light in the distance. A single star in the sea of darkness.

That voice. She knew that voice. She clung to it like a lifeline, reaching for it with every shred of will she possessed.

The light shone brighter and brighter, filling her vision with shapes and colors.

She was so close, needing to breathe and to find her way out. The light touched her like the finger of Oneness and forced her upward.

Bursting forth from subconscious waters, Vaylin gasped and saw Oberion's face for the briefest moment. Then she crashed back into her body. Her bones rattled with the force of it, and nerves flared white hot before burning cold. Everything hurt, and she shook violently. It took a tremendous effort to open her eyes, and when she did, blue-gray skies with clouds floated in front of her. Or was this a window into another world? It was a pretty world. So much nicer than that crushing darkness.

Moving her hand, she reached for the clouds, wanting to touch them when through the mist he appeared. Vaylin's fingertips brushed the side of Oberion's cheek before the tides of unconsciousness swept her back into the abyss.

OBERION

Oberion knew it had worked when she looked at him. Present behind those evergreen eyes, if only for a moment. All thanks to Skyminer and the stone he contemplated in his hands, glowing faintly in the dim light of the room.

His apprehension toward the stone grew stronger. It felt like they were using magick far more powerful than any of them truly knew. Yes, it had saved Vaylin, but just because they were the Elite of Panthea didn't make them impervious to danger. She had almost lost her magick. What if the same happened to him? It was jarring to see the change her body went through in the last few hours. From withered to full, she was completely rejuvenated.

These were powers best left alone.

When she'd touched his cheek, Oberion had wanted to cry aloud, overwhelmed with gratitude at her survival. He pressed his lips tight, not wanting to unravel at her touch. Something about it caused him immense longing. He tried to rid the thoughts and feelings from his mind. He was confused, exhausted, and needed to sleep. He was simply happy she wasn't dead and they'd saved her magick; that was all.

A brown curl had fallen across her forehead, and he reached forward, brushing it back. His fingers moved lightly as he traced her jawline with his thumb, like he had in the tunnel. The insane urge to run his hand through her hair coursed through him.

Would her hair feel like woven strands of water? Would she wake and see him touching her and be upset with him? What was he thinking? What was he doing?

He shouldn't be touching her at all. He withdrew quickly.

"You are both connected," a voice said behind him. Oberion did not turn to see Skyminer as the little dwarf continued. "She will make her recovery, though there might be some lingering damage to work through."

"What type of damage?" Oberion didn't mean to sound accusing. He was drained and hollow by this night or nights. There were no windows in Skyminer's Keep, and he couldn't tell what time it was.

"Her body was in this world, but her spirit was not." He paused. "My stones were able to follow the lines of her energy and reconnect them. It was only possible because of Dyadralite, the stone you gave me, for that is its true name. I know of the darkness in our world and what you are facing. It has clearly touched this woman, and now it has touched you too. Powerful forces of nature are at work. You and Vaylin are in the middle of it, bound together by magick and friendship. I think you are aware of this and are scared. Rightfully so, I might add. The stones are deadly when used apart, let alone whole. Once touched by them, one cannot simply walk away from it."

Oberion swallowed hard. The world was spinning. He put his head in his hands, trying for stillness and clarity to sort out everything Skyminer was saying. Some type of bonding? What was this darkness? How did it come into being? And these stones. Dyadralite? The impossible crystal that now resided in his pocket stirred at his very attention, a foreign magick pressing against his own. He turned toward the dwarf, who stared at him, head cocked to the side curiously.

"Dyadralite, you say?" Oberion said.

"Yes. Dyadralite. It is a glorious stone, making it all the more terrifying."

Despite his exhaustion, Oberion sat up straighter and peered intently at the dwarf. His body protested at the movement, his sluggish mind trying to start up again. Answers to his questions at last. "You know what this is, then?"

"Yes, I do."

It was worth it. Everything they had risked and done to get here was worth it with that simple statement.

"Let me take you to your room. The road has been long and unkind to you," Skyminer said. "We will speak more in depth after everyone has had time to heal and settle."

The idea sounded wonderful, and Oberion turned to face Vaylin one last time, that lock of hair still tucked behind her ear. It struck him then how beautiful she truly was. Her delicately pointed ears and freckles across her nose and cheeks. She was the fire that burned in the sun, the galloping of horses across open fields. The energy of the jungles clung to her, and the wildness of it made him yearn for her. He saw, for the briefest moment, himself running through the forests with her beside him.

Oberion was in a dead sleep when Skyminer came in and poked him hard on the forehead to wake him up. He wasn't sure how long he had been sleeping. It must have been a while, judging by his tousled hair and the gunk crusting his eyes. The tacky feel of his tongue made his dehydration unbearable, and he gulped down the water at the side of his bed. A cluster of pointed amethyst sat on the table, light from beneath by a yellow glow.

He realized Skyminer was standing next to the bed and jumped. "Bleeding hells, I didn't see you there."

"Vaylin is conscious if you would like to see her," Skyminer squeaked.

"Really? How long have I been asleep?" He stumbled to his feet and threw on some clean clothes.

"Nearly a full turn, sir."

"Please, call me Oberion." He ran his fingers through his hair and dashed from the room to check on Vaylin.

When he got there, she was disoriented and upset by the turn of events. She put a hand on her head and winced as she sat up. "What-what happened?"

"Easy there." Oberion placed a hand on her shoulder to steady her. "You've been out of it for a while now."

She looked drained, wincing as she pressed shaking hands against her sternum and left ribs. Lifting her shirt away, she peered down at herself.

He pointedly turned his head. "Anything?"

Vaylin didn't answer right away. "It feels like I got hit with a cannon ball," she said grimly. "I can't see any markings or blackness. That's good, right?"

"You kind of were, in a sense." He didn't want to overload her with the details of what had happened, but he had to ask. "Your magick, can you feel it? Can you summon it?"

Vaylin looked even more confused, brows furrowed as she withdrew into her pillows. "What's gotten into you?"

"Show me."

Perplexed, she turned to her water glass and waved her fingers through the air. A thin stream spiraled upward and then splashed back into the cup.

Relief swept through Oberion. Skyminer had done it. He had saved her magick.

"Is everything okay?" she said. "Are *you* okay?"

No.

"Yes," Oberion said bleakly. He didn't want to meet her gaze, not sure what he was feeling or what exactly to say. The last thing he wanted to do was burden her with all his troubles. "Skyminer said that you were cut off from your magick. That it was being ripped from your soul. I think he was right too. You looked different, changed somehow, after the darkness hit you. It was all I could do to keep you alive."

"Changed how?" She examined her body. "I'm still me."

"You are now." It wasn't her fault. They'd had little choice in the mountain pass, but why did he let her take on the darkness by herself? He should have tried harder to work out the best strategy and then attacked. "Skyminer called the Mingalla stone 'Dyadralite' and apparently knows what it is."

Vaylin looked flustered. "Then what are we waiting for. Let's go."

She moved quickly before grabbing her side dramatically. Concern rushed through Oberion, and he moved to help her.

"Stop. I can do this." She moved gingerly at first then more steady movements as she found her balance. "I'll be fine."

He wanted to believe her.

You cannot trust those with Elder blood.

The khan's words rose unbidden in him, and he ignored them. Vaylin was his comrade, his fellow Elite. She had sealed that rupture and nearly killed herself to do so. He trusted that she would give anything to the Aqua Realm, even using Dyadralite and overextending herself. His concern for her wellbeing came from that and nothing more.

Now, he felt like liar.

29

BANISHMENT

ALDWIN

ALDWIN WAS DONE WAITING FOR ABRAXAS. THE THREE DAYS HAD PASSED since he'd intercepted Abraxas running through Panthea Library, and he hadn't seen hide nor hair of his brother. Aldwin was angry with their circumstances, and none of the paladins or the captain had any useful information. He had only wanted to improve their relationship by helping his brother, and now, there were such strange things happening. Aldwin wasn't sure if it was coincidence that Abraxas appeared at Panthea now, of all times. Vaylin had acquired the Mingalla stone. Then Abraxas *found* this grimoire. Marshall was attacked by a chiro from Nimrothag and then showed up with Avon and a silver sphere, the exact same one he remembered from his childhood—if he wasn't mistaken.

It had been that fateful night, when Mundas finally got his portal working, that Aldwin had first laid eyes on it. The power source for Mundas's portal. Aldwin had assumed it had gotten sucked into the collapsing portal after Mundas left.

It was a dreadful shock when Marshall deposited that object on his desk, even more so realizing that Maximus Mundas must still be alive. Not to mention Nimrothag being a real place, an underworld no less.

Who else would be controlling an object from Nim, if not Mundas?

This also meant that Mundas was after Abraxas or they were working together and conspiring against Aldwin and, subsequently, Panthea.

"Brax, are you in here?" Aldwin called through the closed door of the apartment, pounding on the doorframe. He was on the first floor of the gatekeeper's tower, where Abraxas was staying while working on these pages. "This is a serious matter. I need to talk to you."

The door remained closed. No shuffling of feet or movement of any kind.

Aldwin jiggled the handle to no avail. Sighing, he pulled the master key of Panthea out from under his robes and fit it into the lock. He was trying to give his brother a chance to be civil, but he was done waiting. He walked purposefully into the room, expecting to see a sleeping figure on the couch or in the bedroom.

No one was here.

There were some clothes in the bedroom. Otherwise, the place was empty and lacked signs of life. No dishes, bits of trash, or rumpled blankets of recently vacated cushions. The place was bare. Books were scattered on the apartment surfaces, and he picked a title up at random, *Aboriginal Tribes of the Aqua Realm*. It unnerved him to see this. Did Abraxas know about the ruptures in Mingalla? Was he aware of what happened to Vaylin and investigating the matter himself? Aldwin was sure that the Mingalla stone was still a secret. Maybe Abraxas was after something at Panthea too. Could that be it?

Neko had intersected Abraxas on several occasions and was increasingly frustrated by his presence. He made it a point to say something to Aldwin every time he was at Panthea Central. Was Abraxas the cause of these chiro attacks? If so, how was it even possible? There was no way he would have the means to create a rupture, could he?

Aldwin examined the room for any indication of where his brother was or what he was up to. It was a longshot coming in here. Abraxas would be too clever to leave anything incriminating behind. He should have never let him leave the other day. His gut told him something was wrong, and he ignored it. He'd just let him go.

What a fool you are.

Damn Abraxas for making him do this. He didn't want to be the detective or the authority. He only wanted to have a normal relationship with his brother, not this perverse game of cat and mouse.

Aldwin recognized a stack of notes on the desk in the corner as Abraxas's copy of the grimoire translations. He flipped to the last page again, curious to see if Abraxas had made any notes on the Ebony diagram yet. Last time Aldwin had checked, the page was completely blank. This time, however, the page had a set of coordinates printed at the bottom in neat script. He could tell by the numbers it was in the southern hemisphere, likely in the Terra Nation. He examined the image, gazing at the concentric circles that surrounded the dodecahedron shape in the middle of the page, intersected with lines into the nucleus at the center.

Something clicked into place.

This was a drawing of the sphere. The silver sphere from his childhood. The one Marshall had brought to Panthea. It had taken seeing the forgotten thing again to trigger his mind. There was something about the sphere, or in the sphere Abraxas was after, and Aldwin had beat him to it.

His hand shook as he folded the page and slid it into his pocket, rubbing a hand over his jaw. Abraxas already believed Mundas alive and must have been close to accomplishing his quest to bring him back. Had he left that night to go to these coordinates and find the sphere, given to him by Mundas? Aldwin was certain that, if he confirmed with Marshall the rough location where the fight with the conjurer took place, the two would line up perfectly. Mundas obviously wanted Abraxas to use whatever was in the sphere, and Abraxas would do whatever Mundas wanted, especially if it meant returning him to Chrysanthos and proving Abraxas right—and Aldwin wrong.

How could he stop this? How could he save his brother?

If Abraxas wanted to be saved at all.

If Aldwin kept the sphere a secret and acted like nothing had happened, Abraxas would never know otherwise. His three days were up though, and Captain Blackwell wouldn't give him more time. The only way he could protect Abraxas and stop all of Mundas's plans was by banishing his brother from Panthea. If he stayed, it might be furthering an agenda for Mundas that Aldwin was still unaware of.

The sphere was the priority, and he needed to protect it. He left quickly for his office and tried to think of better hiding places for this wretched thing.

Twenty minutes later, Aldwin was panting and sweating as his office door unlocked under his touch. All was still and seemed to be exactly how he had left it. He rushed to the engraving of the Panthea crest behind the desk and placed his hand on the smaller hexagon in the middle of the crest.

A portion of the wall slid down to reveal several hidden shelves of rare objects, strange inventions, and books too precious to be kept in the library. These were ancient relics used by previous gatekeepers who had given their collections to Panthea after their deaths. A metal cabinet was set into the wall, doors locked and held shut by an enchanted iron padlock. Pulling the master key of Panthea from around his neck, Aldwin opened the cabinet doors and sighed in relief.

There it sat. A perfectly smooth ball of silver on the center shelf with those shifting red symbols across its surface. The thing felt wrong and brought back fearful memoires. Avon had mentioned Nimrothag in their last conversation.

It was a real place the elves knew about.

According to the elf's books, it was all that Avon said it was, a realm of darkness and terror. If Mundas knew that, then why would he insist on going there? What was in Nimrothag that was worth leaving Chrysanthos for?

Aldwin removed the sphere, his notes, and the copy of the original grimoire, setting them on his desk. He shut the cabinet doors and pressed a button to conceal the secret compartment again. He opened the grimoire to the mysterious diagram of Ebony and placed the sphere next to it. The image wasn't identical to the sphere, but several of the symbols across the sphere's surface matched the ones inked onto the gray pages. He held the silver ball and turned it over in his hands, trying to puzzle out a coded sequence to open it.

Banging at the door made his heart jump into his throat, and he dropped the sphere in panic. It rolled off his desk and landed on the ground with a metal clink.

"Aldwin, are you in here?" It was Captain Blackwell, and he sounded livid.

"Yes, just a minute." Aldwin hastily covered his notes and bent over to retrieve the sphere from the ground.

It wasn't there.

He searched the ground frantically for it, not seeing it anywhere.

His office door crashed open. Straightening quickly, he cast covert looks between the floor and the captain, trying to see where the sphere was. A glimmer of silver caught Aldwin's eye. It had rolled out of reach against one of his many bookshelves that lined the walls, visible to anyone who looked down and to the right. Thankfully, it was far enough away to be inconspicuous.

Captain Blackwell dragged Abraxas over the threshold by the collar. The former looked outraged, while the latter looked dreadful. Abraxas had two spectacular black eyes, and his nose was blotchy and swollen. His normally sleek hair was disheveled, and he seemed exhausted and coated in dust as he wrenched himself free from the captain's grip.

"What did you do to him?" Aldwin said, aghast at the captain.

"This wasn't me, although I wish I knew who did do it so I could thank them," Captain Blackwell said. "I found him entering the grounds thirty minutes ago and apprehended him immediately for you."

"What has happened? Who did this to you?" Aldwin demanded from his brother.

Abraxas grinned and stepped out of the captain's reach, staring at Aldwin. "Got into a bit of a fight, didn't go s'well for me, as you can see," he slurred his words a bit and shrugged. Was he unhinged or concussed? Possibly drunk?

"Who did this?" Aldwin stood up and edged his way around the desk, covertly putting himself between the men and the sphere to his right.

"Some blokes in the city. That date I went on...didn't go great. Turns out her boyfriend didn't approve of me taking his lady out for drinks."

"You got into a fight at the Tipsy Portal?"

"No, the barmaids kicked us out so we brawled in the alleyway. I would have had him too, if his friends didn't jump me. Outnumbered by cowards, I say. Cowards!"

Aldwin stared at Abraxas. Was he acting like this because he had lost the sphere and needed to cover it up?

"What lies," Captain Blackwell spat. "With all due respect, Gatekeeper, if Abraxas was hurt and in the city, we would have found him. You've been missing for three days, lad. We saw you enter the Tipsy Portal that night, but you never came out. Where did you go?"

"Having me followed, brother? Here I thought we were working on our trust issues," Abraxas said.

Aldwin's heart raced. The moment was now. He would have to do this now.

"I— It was a precaution on behalf of Panthea," Aldwin said. "I had no other choice, and as gatekeeper, it was my duty to make sure that all who dwell here remain safe."

"Including me? Or from me?" Abraxas's normally purple eyes looked black with the bruising around his sockets. It was like seeing a shadow of Mundas wearing Abraxas's features.

Aldwin repressed a shiver. His imagination was playing tricks on him. "This isn't a game. I didn't know what we were dealing with when you first came here asking for my help. This grimoire explains about dangerous magickal objects and portal theories that are outlawed. I had to take steps for others protection, as well as your own."

"Panthea is so lucky to have you guarding it," Abraxas simpered.

"How dare you speak to your own brother in that tone." Captain Blackwell seemed to swell with anger, like he was growing bigger with every passing minute.

"You don't know him like I do, Captain. Aldwin may seem to carry himself nobly, but deep down, he is a selfish bully who uses his power to control others." He gave Aldwin a look of hatred mixed with disgust. "He doesn't care about what anyone else thinks or wants. He will do whatever *he* wants so long as *he* gets his way. All under the guise of protection. I should know. That's how my older brother raised me."

"It sounds to me like he did what any decent older brother would do," the captain said.

"If he was a decent brother, he wouldn't lie to me and always put Panthea's needs before my own," Abraxas shot back.

"Panthea was our home. You forget that this was all we had when we had nothing. I kept us safe after Mundas left that night." Aldwin didn't want a fight to break out, especially with the sphere so close. His eyes flicked to it for a second.

He should have known better.

Ever observant, Abraxas followed his line of sight, and a sheen of recognition lit in his eyes as he beheld the sphere on the ground.

Several things happened then. Abraxas lunged for the object at the same time Captain Blackwell moved to grab him, like a lion lunging for escaping prey. Abraxas blasted a ball of fire toward the captain, who moved fast enough to deflect the attack with a whirlwind of air, charging forward to tackle.

It gave Aldwin the split-second advantage he needed to put up an impenetrable shield of sound and psychic force between the sphere and Abraxas. Abraxas slammed against it, and Aldwin dove, fingers closing around the metal ball, a feeling of repulsion climbing up his arm and throat at the touch.

The rage and pain was plain in his brother's face as the captain pinned him against Aldwin's protective force, squashing him between transparent barrier and body.

"I knew you'd betray me," Abraxas seethed. Spit flew from his mouth, and a cut on his temple bled into his eyes. "I knew you would turn on me, just like you did with Mundas. He told me all about what you did."

Fear prickled at the core of Aldwin's heart. "I have always done what I've had to. I've protected us. You know this."

"He was *my* father! And that never mattered to you."

"And we have known nothing except pain at his hands. He's using you, just like he did when we were children. He is using you, and you are letting him by going after this sphere. I have to stop you."

"He promised me a life that you could never understand. We're better off without you," Abraxas said.

Aldwin sucked in a breath, trembling with the effort to remain calm as this last cornerstone of his life deteriorated. Abraxas was the only person Aldwin considered family. The only person he truly had left.

"I have done everything for you," Aldwin whispered. "Always for you. For us. He would have killed us, Brax. He would have taken you and killed you if I didn't stop him."

His throat constricted, and he fought prickling in his eyes. He wasn't sure how to reach his brother anymore. He wasn't even sure if this person before him still was his brother. Shadows of Mundas kept flashing across his face. Was Mundas using some sort of magick to corrupt him? Was Aldwin already too late?

"I don't want anything from you ever again." Abraxas's His hollowed face looked aged, and he diminished slightly as the captain yanked him backward and away from Aldwin.

As the door shut behind them, Aldwin collapsed onto the floor and cried.

DYADRALITE

VAYLIN

THE DWARVES, OBERION, AND VAYLIN ALL SAT AROUND THE TABLE AND waited for Skyminer. The little dwarf cleared his throat and held a steaming mug of tea before him. On the table was an assortment of bread and fruit, a pot of honey, a wheel of cheese, and dried strips of lamb and goat jerky.

Vaylin found the tea immensely comforting and nibbled on some figs. The warmth of the liquid that seeped through the cup and into her fingers was deeply satisfying.

"Before I begin, place Dyadralite on the table. It is the centerpiece of our story and deserves to be seen," Skyminer said.

Oberion acquiesced, and Vaylin tried not to feel annoyed he had the Mingalla stone—no, Dyadralite. He had Dyadralite since she had fallen to the rupture. It shouldn't bother her, but it did. She shoved the feelings away. It was better that Oberion held on to the stone while she recovered her strength. This entire journey long and she had to fight death itself to keep her magick, something she wasn't expecting. The rupture had taken more from her than she first realized, and she never wanted to be in that suffocating darkness again.

She'd tested her magick more thoroughly in private and found everything in working order. Whatever Skyminer had done, she was indebted to him for saving her life and her magick. She shuddered at the thought of truly losing her magick. It felt like a core part of her. Who would she be without it? Certainly not an Elite Guardian.

Skyminer's crisp voice got her attention, and she looked up.

"The story of Dyadralite starts with Panthea," Skyminer said.

Vaylin was surprised by this. Oberion's face reflected the same reaction.

"Panthea, as you know, was founded by the Master Elementors, who we now call the First Guardians. Any magick wielder can call themselves an elementor, but these individuals were highly skilled in the magickal arts. They were searching for a place to build Panthea when they discovered Dyadralite deep in these very mountains. Taking it as a sign of fortune, they started construction on the very spot they found it. The First Guardians experimented with Dyadralite when they accidently created the first portal of Panthea. Instant travel between two locations. The Master Elementors were ecstatic with their discovery and continued to expand Panthea, creating five more portals to all the regions of Chrysanthos. You can imagine the lure that caused for any aspiring Elementor of the time. Everyone with magickal ability flocked there to watch, learn, build, and grow."

Skyminer paused, taking a sip from his mug.

"In the proceeding years of Panthea's conception, the First Guardians had created six portals, but there was also a seventh, secret portal that was made, and it led to the underworld known as Nimrothag, a place with similar but opposite magicks as Chrysanthos. A domain of shadow and illusion."

There was silence from everyone except Oberion, who looked agitated.

"Nowhere in our history does it say anything about a seventh portal being created," Oberion said. "There's no physical evidence of such a thing at Panthea. The six portals are aligned in a perfect hexagon. There was no room for a seventh. How can you claim this to be fact?"

Skyminer gave him a long, contemplative look. "Do not ask me why humans cover up their history. It makes everything so confusing. I imagine knowledge of this seventh portal was dangerous and the

Master Elementors did not expect blood to stain *their* grounds due to its construction. It was foolish, as all magick comes at a price. The Master Elementors were betrayed by the ones from Nimrothag, and thousands were killed before they could close the rift."

"How do you know this to be true?" Oberion asked. "The portals were connected to Panthea long before you were born. I've studied the origins of Panthea and have never read any evidence of your claims. Everything in the Zetzu Monastery confirms a six portal history."

"Because I can hear Dyadralite whispering to me," Skyminer softly answered, eyes round. "It has been telling me its story ever since you arrived."

"Impossible. Stones don't talk."

"Is it?" He quirked an eyebrow up. "What do you know of the gnomish people and our abilities? I knew it was in your pocket when you arrived because I could hear it buzzing, full of energy."

Oberion didn't say anything, and Skyminer sat straighter.

"You came here to ask for my help, remember? So you would do well to listen to me, or else face dire consequences."

"You're a gnome?" Gizmo ask. "Here I thought *time* had shrunk you. Now you go telling me you're gnomish? How could you keep such a thing from me?"

Skyminer was not amused. He crossed his arms and glared at Gizmo.

Oblivious, the dwarf continued ranting. "I thought gnomes kept to gardens. Where are all of your plants? Aren't gnomes supposed to have plants and green thumbs and grow things?"

"I have a garden, you idiot." Skyminer's face pinched slightly, and he squared his shoulders. "It's a crystal garden."

"Well then, let's see it. Take me there." Gizmo made to stand up.

But Oberion raised his hand to halt him. "We are not going anywhere until we finish discussing Dyadralite. Gizmo, save it for later, all right?" He gave a withering look before turning back to Skyminer. "So, are you claiming you can communicate with Dyadralite?"

"Yes," Skyminer said. "Of a sort."

"And it has been telling you about the history of Panthea?"

"Yes, parts of it, some of which I don't understand. I'm telling you what I've pieced together since I've tuned into its frequency."

Oberion raised his eyebrows. Vaylin couldn't tell if it was the gnome or his outlandish claims that caused Oberion's scrutiny. It was almost amusing.

"Only two realms, I believe. This one, where Chrysanthos is, and Nimrothag," Skyminer said. "I imagine if you searched deep enough within Panthea, you would find evidence of this for yourself."

"But this is impossible." Oberion shook his head.

"I am simply repeating what I am interpreting from Dyadralite." Skyminer's eyes flashed at Oberion like chips of onyx. "Do not blame me for the inadequacies of your history. I have no reason to lie to you about this, especially when Vaylin and you are connected to the stone."

Vaylin's heart skipped a beat. "What do you mean?"

All eyes flicked to her, and Oberion's face stiffened.

Skyminer leaned in. "You have the Incandesite stone, Vaylin. It was broken after Panthea sealed the seventh portal all those years ago, and it has been alone ever since, separated from its other half. This is the light half of Dyadralite, and it has found you. Marked you as one of its own."

"What do you mean *marked* me?" she asked through numb lips.

"Dyadralite is actually two stones. One represents the darkness of Nimrothag, while the other is the light of Chrysanthos. The stones are meant to be together. They feed from each other. They have been calling to each other over time and space, alone and desperate to be whole again. If they cannot, they will take the life force or magick of their bearer. If used unknowingly or for too long, the stone will kill the user, sucking them dry in the process, to fill the void left by their separation. It has marked you as a source of energy in place of Ebenosite, the dark half of Dyadralite."

TRUTHS AND WARNINGS

VAYLIN

T HE STONE V AYLIN THOUGHT WAS THEIR SALVATION WAS A LIE.

A false hope.

They were left with a tool they couldn't use. A blade with no handle. If she used Incandesite, she would risk her magick and her life. Anyone who attempted to use it would, unless they found Ebenosite, the mysterious other half of Incandesite. If they could find Ebenosite, they could unite Dyadralite and use it without consequence. If they had Ebenosite, no harm would come to them or Panthea. They only needed to find it before it was too late.

"Can Incandesite tell us Ebenosite's location?" she asked. If the stones were connected and Skyminer could communicate with the stone, then perhaps they could discover where the other one was.

"No," he said. "That is not how Incandesite communicates. It is not a demanding of questions and extracting of answers. It is a slow and steady process, a stream of shapes, consciousness, and emotion."

Vaylin tried hard not to let her frustration show. "All right then, how does its consciousness react if you focus on Ebenosite?"

Skyminer closed his eyes, and his ears twitched. "There is a sense of loss and longing. The connection to Ebenosite was cut off for many centuries. It can only call to it."

"Is it in Chrysanthos? Do you see a city, a specific location? Maybe a land marker?"

"No," Skyminer said with finality. "It only knows it is here, in this world and on this continent."

Disappointment crashed over Vaylin. "What good is talking to stones if you can't even get useful information from them?"

"Do you realize how valuable that information is? These stones are immensely powerful and have the ability to travel between worlds under the right circumstances. What you want to obtain is in Chrysanthos. Far easier to get to than Nimrothag, I dare say. There is no way to Nimrothag without Ebenosite, as that is the stone that can create portals to or within that place. Incandesite works the same way but only in Chrysanthos. Panthea connects all this together, and it is there I would begin your search for Ebenosite."

"Why Panthea?" Oberion asked.

"Ebenosite is drawn to Panthea as Incandesite is. It is a signature of their energy because the magick of Dyadralite was used to create the portals network at Panthea. Like calls to like. When lost, does one not try to return home? I would say the stone is already there or will find its way to Panthea in due course. Especially now that Incandesite and Ebenosite are both active in the world once more. They are calling to each other, and they will be brought back together."

Incandesite twinkled innocently on the table.

"If something that powerful was at Panthea, someone would have found it by now," Oberion said.

"Perhaps. Perhaps not." Skyminer shrugged. "Panthea is an ancient place surrounded by a sprawling city. I imagine there are many secrets hidden there that none but the cleverest amongst you can find."

"Is there danger in the act of uniting them?" Rathir had sat with his fingers clasped together this entire time, listening intently, and observing the conversation.

"Of course there is danger. These stones are capable of altering the fabric of reality," Skyminer said, clearly exasperated. "If you weren't scared of them, I'd question your sanity."

"But if the only way to seal these ruptures is to unite the stones," Vaylin said, "then we have no other choice."

"It would appear that way," Skyminer said. "However, Ebenosite and Incandesite are meant to be together. I would imagine they will not harm others in their reunion. I would exercise extreme caution if you reach that point, as bringing together such forces is likely to create an energetic reaction of some sort."

"Great, we're damned if we do and damned if we don't." Vaylin buried her face in her hands.

Oberion cast her a concerned glance. "What is the likelihood that uniting the stones could create another rupture in our world?"

Vaylin flinched at the stark coldness in his tone. He was always first to reach to the worst possible outcome of any situation.

Skyminer pondered for a moment. "I cannot determine the extent of its reaction. I would caution not to unite them on Panthea grounds. The portals are too powerfully magickal, having been born from Dyadralite. It would be best not to tamper with the magick. However, away from the Vale of Panthea, I think uniting them would be advantageous for whoever manages it. The stone has a sense of allegiance to those who have aided it. The one who unites them controls the power."

"Not all is lost then," Oberion said without any real hope in his voice.

Vaylin had more questions than answers after speaking with Skyminer. Where was Ebenosite? What would happen if she tried to use Incandesite again? Would it immediately take her life force, or would it be a slow drain? Was it worth trying and testing the limits?

She took refuge in Skyminer's crystal garden on the eve of their departure. The gnome had shown them after Gizmo begged him for a peek. It was a beautiful, intricate, and delicate space filled with globes of natural gas that cast a shifting, sparkling light across the stones. Crystalline wonders popped up from the earth like glistening, geometric flora. Clusters of amethyst grew over walls like purple crust, and rainbow-filled quartz points erupted from the ground, standing several feet tall. Bunches of citrine, garnet, aquamarine, and peridot sparkled in nooks and crannies set into the walls. Each crystal emanated a different vibration of magick, and Vaylin focused on their familiar energies.

It was strange to think these stones gave their magick freely, while Incandesite had a cost. It went against everything she knew about working with stones.

There was a scuff on the stone, and Vaylin turned to see Skyminer in the doorway.

"May I join you?" he asked.

"This is your house."

"Be that as it may, it is still important to ask if one wants company or not."

She nodded, and he sat on the ground beside her.

"Your garden is magickal," she said after a moment of peaceful quiet.

Skyminer looked around appreciatively. "It is, isn't it? I've spent years caring for and cultivating these crystals. They are my life's work."

"Do you hear all stones or only a few?" His gift with the crystals was fascinating. She wondered if she could hear the stones if she focused.

"All of them. Some are louder than others, just like people. They keep me company and share their gifts with me. I talk back and share my own stories. Crystals have long memories and a penchant for tales. It makes the stones happy to hear their owners stories and improves compatibility with the user."

"What do you mean?"

"Well, crystals spend most of their time underground being pushed and squeezed by natural elements. Only if there is a natural displacement or we interact with them do they see sunlight and are given the chance to be used, which is what they are meant for. They enjoy hearing the stories of their users. It gives them purpose and helps them know us. By forming any bond with any stone, you enter into a symbiotic relationship with it. You call on it when you need aid, and the more it knows about you, the better it blends with your magick."

Vaylin thought about that for a moment. "It's like my opal. I've used it since I was eighteen, and I swear it has gotten stronger over time. Do you think all stones want that?"

"In some fashion, yes. Meditate with it and see what comes to you. They are a part of our world and serve their own purposes, like everything else. I believe the things put on this earth are meant to be used. For better or worse. Where would our magick or medicine be without their influence? What type of technology would we have if crystals weren't used in them? They are crucial to our wellbeing and livelihood in all ways."

"There would be no Panthea if it weren't for Dyadralite."

"That's not entirely true. There might still be a Panthea but not how it is imagined now."

"For a little gnome holed up in the far reaches of the continent, you're pretty cool."

Skyminer chuckled. "What a lovely compliment, dear. Thank you for that one."

"Thank you for healing an elf." Vaylin paused, not sure how to voice what was troubling her. "Last night, you said that Incandesite had marked me. I was wondering, what exactly does that mean and can it be removed?"

He pondered. "I don't know. When you arrived here, I could see tangled states of your magick and the stones. It shows us how deadly Incandesite can be when we let its power merge with our own. What surprised me most was your ability to come back from such an attack. You have a strong will and a strong companion. I think you are uniquely capable of withstanding Incandesite with Oberion by your side. I also think you would have been lost to us without him."

"What does Oberion have to do with this?" She had known he'd carried her here and refused to leave her side. The idea of him caring about her to that extent was strangely comforting, and she wished she'd been conscious to see it for herself.

"You two are close, are you not?"

Vaylin was caught off guard by his question and fidgeted slightly. Yes, they'd known each other for a few years, but it was a professional relationship filled with animosity and bitterness. "Not until recently have we been...cordial."

"But you are close? Why else would he sacrifice himself for you?" Skyminer pressed.

"Sacrificed himself? What are you talking about?"

"Oberion was what kept you tethered to your life that night. He used his own magick in conjunction with Incandesite to bring you back and give you more time. I used my power to return your magick. Together, we saved you and your magick."

"How is that possible?"

"Incandesite is no ordinary stone. Its powers are vast and incalculable. He took it from you after you fell. He tried to reach you while you were unconscious, out of love and concern. If I'm not mistaken, he connected you both through Incandesite, creating an anchor for you through himself."

"Does he know what he's done?" Vaylin asked.

"I think he suspects it. I have not told him what I'm telling you. Not yet, at least, but I will. He deserves to know the truth."

"Then why are you telling me at all?"

"Because you are clearly marked by Incandesite. Your life is intertwined with the fate of Dyadralite, whether you like it or not. Others will be drawn to you and its power. Oberion is the first. If you manage to see it be reunited with Ebenosite, then you could be the one most suited, most capable, of wielding its power. Which means it is your responsibility to watch over and care for the lives of those closest to you. They will not understand Dyadralite's influence, seeing only you and your magick. Some will remain allies, while others become enemies, depending on how the stone sways them. It amplifies one's natural abilities and tendencies, for better or worse. Like calls to like, remember."

"Are you trying to warn me about my friends? They would never do something like that to me." She was insulted by the very thought, the accusation stinging.

"I am trying to make you aware of the possibility. For your safety, as well as others," he said tenderly. "Make no mistake, Vaylin— Dyadralite serves itself. It will answer to whoever has it for its own purposes. You are the vehicle it wants to use. Should you lose control of the stone and someone else acquire it, Dyadralite will do their bidding, not yours. If you are not careful, you will be left in a withered and drained state, pining over the lost stone."

She thought of Sloane and Henrietta Scyth, the Elite Guardian of the Sound Federation, the two women she trusted most at Panthea. Would they become enthralled to her? Was Vaylin already enthralled to the stone? And what about Oberion? He was caught up in all of this too. Was he being influenced by the stone? He knew the truth of Dyadralite. Would he advocate to destroy it, protect it, or take it for himself? How could she trust him or anyone now? She hated thinking this way about her friends, and the pressure of the situation bore down on her, heavy and relentless.

It felt like she was back in that oppressive darkness.

"It's too much," she said weakly. "I wanted to be a guardian, but no one has ever dealt with anything like this before. Now, it all comes down to me."

She was ashamed to admit it, but it was the truth. This responsibility scared her, and for the first time since being on this journey, it felt like she was in over her head. She had stubbornly held on to the belief that she could figure this all out with time. Yet everything was crumbling around her.

"Those who don't seek power and have it thrust upon them are often best suited for it. You have a strong and gentle heart, Vaylin. You are beyond capable of doing anything you want. Do not fear. Do not despair. If it's any consolation, you were the one who found Incandesite, the stone of goodness and light. It takes an incredible individual to find such a thing. You have survived, twice now, in the face of darkness. Take solace in knowing that you were meant to find Dyadralite and use its power to help those around you."

"If I use it, it will kill me. You said it yourself last night."

Skyminer shifted in his seat. "If you find Ebenosite, you might be safe. I cannot say for certain, but with Oberion by your side, it could be enough to keep you anchored in your body and magick while using Incandesite, should you need to. I still caution against it unless absolutely necessary, but if anyone could navigate the power of the stones, it is you two."

Skyminer stood up and stretched his skinny little arms, making his way toward a watering can along the side wall. He picked it up and poured water over a small cluster of quartz growing from the ground. It grew a few inches as she watched. There was something so nurturing and tender in the way he cared for the stones that eased the weight of her burden.

Maybe, just maybe, she could do this.

The next day dawned with everyone packed and ready to go. Vaylin was still uncertain about what to do regarding Incandesite and Dyadralite, but she would figure it out.

One step at a time.

She, Oberion, and the dwarves were leaving for their return journeys home. The dwarves would take the same route back to Khazirak Stronghold, and the guardians would continue south along the Windora River at the bottom of the peaks into the northern rim of Panthea.

Vaylin surprised herself by finding she was sad to leave the dwarves. Their banter and odd behaviors were a nice diversion while underground.

Butterflies flapped in her stomach at the thought of traveling alone with Oberion. They were different now than when they first set out on this journey. They had resolved whatever ill feelings they'd had toward each other, and now Incandesite had forged some sort of bond between them.

Sooner or later, they would have to learn what that meant.

The group stood outside Skyminer's Keep in front of the long staircase that led back to the cliffside path. The sky was blindingly blue as she looked up. She'd had her fill of underground adventures and was ready to be on the open road. Vaylin would stay above ground for the next few years at the very least if she could manage it.

"Thank you again for your healing and hospitality." Oberion bowed deeply toward Skyminer. "We owe you our lives."

"It was nothing, nothing at all." The gnome tittered. "You will return, won't you?"

"We will do our best." Vaylin bowed slightly and gifted him a few of her healing tonics and foraged ingredients, thanking him for everything.

"I'll be back soon, Skyminer," Gizmo piped up. "I want to see how your crystal garden is fairing. I'm starting one in my own home. You'll have to come to Khazirak to see it and give me tips."

"I doubt it will be as magnificent as my own. Perhaps in time it will be worth my effort to visit. Until then, your enthusiasm over the prospect is most exhilarating," Skyminer said.

"I think the dwarves would be fascinated if you paid us a visit," Rathir said. "The khan would be most eager to start a line of communication with you."

"We shall see. Big journeys are ever so daunting. Who would water my crystals for me while I'm away?" Skyminer asked earnestly.

Vaylin chuckled, and he turned to her again.

"Take care of yourself, and Incandesite," he said.

"I will." She gave him her warmest, most sincere smile and hugged him. Turning, she looked toward the dwarves before her. Rathir had stepped forward and crossed his arms across his chest. She gratefully repeated the gesture.

"You saved us from that void," he said. "We will carry tales of your valor back to the khan and the stronghold. Panthea has our allegiance, as do you Vaylin Carina of the Aqua Realm."

"It was a pleasure getting to know you," Vaylin said. "Panthea's aid is yours, should the time arise." She repeated the crossed arm gesture to Oaken, who bowed and did the same for her. Finally, she stood before Gizmo, kneeling down so she was on eye level with him. "Can I keep the glow worms? I've grown rather attached to them."

His features lit up with a smile, and from the corner of her eye, she could see Oaken grin and roll his eyes.

"Of course, you can. They are yours to keep, my fair lady," Gizmo said. "I also made these for you." He pulled from his pocket two long, silver chains with an empty cage-like setting dangling from the end.

"What is it?" Vaylin studied it curiously.

"It's a necklace to keep Incandesite in and another for when you find Ebenosite. If I may." He held his hand expectantly to Oberion, who was still carrying Incandesite since she had fallen.

Oberion glanced between Vaylin, Gizmo, and then Skyminer. He pulled Incandesite from his pocket and handed it to Gizmo.

A few seconds of twisting and turning, and Incandesite was set effortlessly into its metal cage.

"There you go." Gizmo handed it back to Oberion, who looked at the necklace and then looked at Vaylin. Her stomach swooped at his attention.

"I believe this is for you, not me." Oberion held the necklace forward, and Incandesite sparkled under twisting bands of spun silver.

"Are you sure?" she asked.

"Yes." He winked at Skyminer, who beamed encouragingly. Vaylin wondered briefly what the little gnome had said to Oberion while they were here.

If she accepted this, she was accepting all the risk and responsibility that would follow.

She could do this.

She would do this.

Vaylin looked directly at Oberion, brimming with certainty. She smiled wide and accepted Incandesite.

"May I?" he asked, voice a low purr that sent thrills of excitement through her.

She turned and pulled her hair off the back of her neck. His fingers traced her collarbone slightly as he draped the necklace over her. It was lighter than she expected, unlike the heat coursing through her at Oberion's touch.

32

SECRET KEEPING

VAYLIN

They traveled along the Windora River for over a week, and the white rapids gurgled southward toward the Vale of Panthea. They were a day away from Panthea now, and Vaylin had thought about little besides Dyadralite, Oberion, and their newly forged bond since leaving Skyminer's Keep.

"What are we going to tell everyone once we're back?" she asked.

"To be honest, I'm not sure," Oberion said. "I've been thinking about it constantly, and I don't have any good answers. We are dealing with a dangerous magickal object, and I fear the more people who know about it, the more potential for harm there is. We need time, if possible, to fact check any of this. Skyminer said a lot of outlandish things, and I, for one, would like to know how much of it we can believe."

"He could hear Incandesite though. It's not like he made it up."

"And you believe him?"

"He had no reason to lie to us. And that would be a pretty big tale to lie about."

"Fine, if everything he said about Panthea and Dyadralite is true, that still leaves us with a dark object we need to lay hands on before someone else does."

"If all the guardians are searching for Ebenosite, we might stand a good chance of finding it and keeping everyone safe," Vaylin offered halfheartedly.

"I think we have long since bypassed safety." He ran his fingers through his wavy dark brown hair, something he usually did when he was puzzling over a problem. "Aldwin would have told the other guardians to search their regions for those ruptures. They know about Mingalla and the stone and that we're involved in it. Dyadralite is the only thing we know of that is capable of sealing ruptures permanently. We *must* find Ebenosite then figure out where to unite Dyadralite and under what conditions, assuming we all don't blow up in the process."

Vaylin grimaced. Hearing what they had to do out loud made the insurmountable tasks before them feel like a precarious pile of blocks teetering on collapse. "Ebenosite is the stone of darkness. If we make it our mission to find it, I think we need to be cautious of whoever finds it. It will influence its user. If it took a good heart to find Incandesite, what kind of person would it take to find Ebenosite?"

"Does it feel like Incandesite is influencing you?"

"No," she said automatically. "Skyminer said something to me about being the type of person to attract this stone. Like calls to like, so that means Ebenosite will call on the darker parts of whoever finds it, won't it?"

"Fair point." Oberion nudged her elbow. "That's quite the compliment to you then, isn't it?"

"I suppose." She grinned sheepishly. She had always felt like a good person, but seeing Oberion impressed by Skyminer's remark elated her. "Back to the situation at hand, we can't leave the ruptures to fester if there are more out there."

"I know we can't," Oberion said, frustrated. "From what we can tell, the rupture in the Storm Peaks is sealed. We don't know what the repercussions of energy like this can be. What if the longer they are active, the more deadly they become? We'd have to conduct sweeps of the entire continent. The organization for such a task is nearly impossible."

"Incandesite worked well enough in the mountains."

"And it nearly killed you. I don't consider that working."

"Technically, it was the darkness that attacked me, not Incandesite."

"Incandesite was tearing your magick from you to fight that darkness. That's not even the point either. Your life, our lives, can't be the asking price every time we come up against one of these things. We can't even use the one thing we have to our advantage."

Vaylin felt the sincerity of his words but didn't want to hear the defeated tone there. She gave him a challenging, defiant look.

"I choose what to do with my life, and I chose this." She gestured at the stone hanging around her neck, and he scowled darkly. "That's what you've been saying to me this entire time, right? This is a guardian's responsibility. I cannot go back, nor do I want to. I'm willing to risk my life to stop these things, Oberion. You need to understand that. Skyminer told me that if anyone could use Incandesite or Dyadralite safely, it would be me. Well, us, actually."

Vaylin kept her mask of cool disposition while her heartbeat ticked up a notch. Now was as good a time as any to talk to Oberion about this. She could sense his moods without speaking and read his body language effortlessly. There was an unspoken and caring connection between them. When one of them stumbled, the other was there with a proffered hand. She felt safe with him, despite the precarious situation they were in. He had helped her throughout this entire journey, and she would not be here without him.

When she wasn't obsessing over Dyadralite, she was thinking about Oberion and their bond—the way he moved, how he observed his surroundings, the care he took when performing any task. Once or twice, she had found herself thinking about the feeling of his arms around her. Then the absurdity of these fantasies would sink in, and she'd force them from her mind. She wondered if it was her own emotions making her feel this or if it was Incandesite's steady influence. The stone had marked her and bound them together. Was this a by-product of that?

After a moment, he spoke in a calm voice. "Us?"

"Yes, us. You and me."

"What else did he say?"

She wasn't sure how she wanted to answer. How much did Oberion know or suspect of this growing connection between them?

Did she want to bring attention to it and potentially alter their relationship irrevocably? Skyminer had specifically told her the bond he had created to keep her alive. Surely that meant something. Something worth exploring, even if Incandesite was a factor.

"He told me that on the night we arrived, you had taken Incandesite and somehow used it to heal me and connect us. That's why I didn't die or lose my magick. I'm not sure if you used the power of Incandesite consciously or unconsciously, but Skyminer thinks we are bound by the stone. He seems to think there is less risk for us to use it, or at least, we would be able to slow its effects without Ebenosite."

"Did he, now?" Oberion said darkly.

"Oberion, I think he is right. It was your voice I heard when I was stuck in empty darkness. It felt like my body was being pulled apart, the pain was excruciating, and I was drowning. Then, I heard your voice echoing across the space, and a ribbon of light emerged. The light was so bright, and when I touched it, I came back to my body." Vaylin cast a sideways glance at him.

His face was inscrutable. Her heart sank at the expression, and she felt like an idiot for saying something. He was probably appalled at the idea of being connected to her. It didn't make their situation at Panthea any easier.

"Skyminer told me everything about the connection when we first arrived," Oberion said softly. "I wasn't sure what he meant by it or what I had done exactly. I was trying to heal you, that's all. You were dying in my arms, and I didn't think about it. I just acted. I had no idea this would be the result. I was waiting for you to bring it up until you were ready."

"I'm glad you did. Do you regret it?"

He sighed deeply, and she held her breath, needing to know his answer.

"No. I would never let anything hurt you or anyone I cared about, if it was within my power to keep them safe." Oberion stopped walking to look at her, eyes like blue sapphires against the bright sky. "If this connection, this bond, is real, then what does this mean for us? For the Elite? I did what any Elite in my position would do, and I don't regret it. I don't want to leave Panthea or forfeit my place in the Wind

District because of it. I assume the same is true for you with the Aqua Realm."

"Oberion, I have the same concerns. I am willing to find out what this bond means for us and to take a chance on it. Through all of this, we have proven we are stronger together. I wouldn't be here if it weren't for you, and I owe you my life."

"If it weren't for me, we wouldn't be bound together. I made that choice for you out of desperation. It wasn't right for me to do that. Now, we are both at risk because of it."

"I'd rather be at risk then dead. You couldn't have known this would be the consequence when you made the decision."

"I knew something would be the asking price. You never asked to be bound to me, and we are in this situation through my ignorance. We have no idea how to use Incandesite, and now, no matter what, we have to see this to the end." He ran a hand through his hair. He looked sad and it confused Vaylin.

"Do not think for one second that *I* regret this. I would have done the same thing for you if it meant keeping you alive. Even knowing the consequences of Incandesite I would have chosen to save you."

Awkward silence hung between them, like they were in uncharted territory and had somehow gotten here together.

"So, you're not upset with me?" he asked tentatively.

"No. Why would you think that that?"

"Because this compromises our future."

"Our futures were compromised the moment we became Elite Guardians. Whatever challenges come our way, I'd rather have you by my side than not."

Oberion smiled, and his hair was slightly windblown, stray strands of silver catching in the light. Her heart beat strong in her ears.

"Together, then," he said earnestly.

They grinned at each other, and he opened his arms for a hug.

Vaylin stepped close to him and felt inexplicable comfort as she wrapped her arms around him. She thought she was floating as she breathed in his scent of cold northern winds and petrichor.

"Perhaps I got lucky when I bound myself to you then," Oberion said.

Her grin widened and she felt Incandesite beneath her shirt, warm and nestled between her breasts, a comforting weight on her chest. A lightness spread through her, and her cheeks got hot. Oberion grinned back, and it thrilled her to see him smiling like that at her. How had there even been so much animosity between them?

"What were you saying about exploring this bond?" His hands had slid down her sides, and his thumb curved along her hip bone.

"Err—" she started. Why was it so difficult to think straight? "Not exactly. I only meant that if we are both acknowledging the bond then we should figure out what that means for our own sake."

"Mmm." Oberion turned away from her and stared into the distance. "At least we know one thing."

"What's that?"

"This is going to land us in a bigger mess of trouble."

OBERION

Oberion was grateful Vaylin had brought up the subject of the bond. Whatever this meant going forward, they were on the same page and could talk about it. Her suggestion to explore the bond made him excited and slightly reluctant. An overwhelming instinct made him want to always be near her, and he wasn't sure if it was him or Incandesite.

He couldn't get what Vaylin had said about "like calling to like" out of his mind. If they made it their mission to find Ebenosite, weren't they condemning one of their own to fall victim to its dark power? If one among them could be corrupted by Ebenosite, then weren't they at the same risk with Incandesite? He had a hard time thinking how a stone of light could be less dangerous to them, but perhaps that was the point. It almost didn't seem dangerous, which was why he didn't trust it.

Vaylin was marked by the stone, and he had bound himself to her, marking himself by extension. Had Incandesite somehow manipulated him that night so it had two souls to use, not one? The idea was unpleasant. It also suggested that Vaylin was subject to being influenced by it, despite her frequent rebukes on the topic. If he hadn't always known Vaylin to be headstrong, he might believe it was the stone, not her. Perhaps it was that trait in her that made her capable of withstanding Incandesite. He resigned to keep a close eye on her until they knew the full ramifications of the bonding.

He would keep them both safe if it was the last thing he did.

33

CONVERGENCE

ALDWIN

THESE NEXT FEW DAYS AFTER APPREHENDING ABRAXAS WENT BY IN A HAZE. Aldwin was drained.

"How is he?" he asked. Not only was his brother occupying a holding cell at Panthea, but Vaylin and Oberion had finally returned from their trip north and had called for a council meeting. They had been gone for a moon cycle, and after a late night meeting with them, Aldwin had a hard time getting out of bed that morning.

Fall was in full swing at Panthea, and the trees around campus were burnished gold, brick red, and burnt orange. Aldwin didn't enjoy any of it as he and Captain Blackwell made their way to the council chamber.

"He made a break for it when we first brought him down there. I hate to say it, but we lost track of him for a moment before apprehending him. He's not saying anything or eating anything we give him." The captain held his hands behind his back as they walked. "I have two guards posted on watch as we speak. They rotate every three hours so each one is fresh and ready to act, should the need arise."

"I doubt it will. I'm the one he has a problem with."

"I know he is your brother, but this is best right now. Something dangerous is happening, and he is directly involved in it. Keeping him away from the sphere is our top priority. I understand why you tried to help him. I really do. Thing is, sometimes it doesn't matter how much you help someone, if they can't help themselves first. You can give and give, and it will never be enough. That's when you need to realize it and set boundaries. For your own good, as well as the other person."

"Setting boundaries doesn't resolve any of our issues." Aldwin barely registered the vibrant foliage as they walked through breeze-ways and down long corridors. Everything with Abraxas had gone to shit, and he could see no way of fixing it without compromising his integrity or Panthea, which he refused to do. "I suppose he was right about me always choosing Panthea over family."

"Your choices gave you both life and time to have these arguments and hardships. Be grateful for them. And I, for one, am damn grateful you are choosing Panthea, and so are the people within it. Abraxas will come around if he knows what's good for him." The captain's salt-and-pepper hair was combed off his broad forehead, giving him a resemblance to an old, proud lion.

"What if he doesn't and I have lost the only person I've ever cared about my entire life?"

"You can't lose what is meant to be yours. I'd say, since he's your younger brother, it's likely your influence will wear off on him and he'll come to his senses. Eventually."

"That's what worries me. If he takes too long, I fear his path will lead to death and destruction. If I know the risk beforehand and cannot stop him, then I have failed him."

The pair turned the corner. The ornate metal doors of the council chamber were propped open at the end of the hallway, and people already moved around inside.

The captain placed a hand gently on Aldwin's shoulder. His hazel eyes studied the gatekeeper. "Do not despair over what has not yet come to pass."

He is a good man. The corner of his mouth twitched upwards into a half smile. "I am grateful to have such a wise and caring friend around me in this time. Thank you for all you have done and the discretion you have taken while handling my brother. This is a complicated situation, and you have performed admirably."

Captain Blackwell beamed as the pair of them walked into the chamber.

OBERION

The lure of Vaylin was like a magnet, and Oberion had gotten no sleep last night because of it. He kept finding himself thinking about what she was doing and wanting to be next to her.

When he did manage to fall asleep, he dreamed he was wandering the jungles and trying to follow her through the trees, Incandesite a glowing light upon her breast and wings like a fey on her back that shone metallic purple and turquoise. He couldn't catch her. He ran, trying to get close enough to touch, and when he finally did, she shuddered horribly, black power oozing from his fingertips as her golden skin turned to stone. He watched, terrified, as she struggled to fly, limbs weighing her down until she was naught but a statue on the jungle floor.

He'd woken violently and fell out of bed, dry heaving onto the floor.

What in the burning hells was wrong with him? His eyes streamed as he clenched his fingers. His mind went to Incandesite and the bond. Their friendship. The brief and intimate moments they had shared. He wondered for the hundredth time how her lips would feel on his if he would be so bold.

Stop it, you're driving yourself mad. This wasn't the time or place to think like that.

The relief after seeing her in the dining hall at breakfast was palpable. If he wasn't mistaken, she had beelined right for him, that magnetic pull that had been tight and strained all night finally loosening with her next to him. After a near silent breakfast, Vaylin and Oberion were waiting for everyone to arrive at the council chambers, standing on opposite sides of the room, awkwardly catching each other's eye and looking away hurriedly.

Steps approached, and in walked one man and one elf. By the looks of it, the elf was from the Southern Kingdom, with his dark complexion, dermal piercings, pointed ears. It wasn't unusual for elves to be at

Panthea, but in their current predicament with the ruptures, the presence of an official representative seemed ominous.

"Well met, friend," said Oberion as he approached Marshall and shook his hand. "It's been an age since we've seen you. I hope you are well."

"As well as ever. I figured it was time to get back. Seems like you lot are all in a bit of trouble, eh?" Marshall replied.

"You could say that. We thought you were in a similar situation with your prolonged absence."

The elf snickered, and Marshall narrowed his eyes playfully. Oberion must be tired if he was seeing Marshall flirting with this elf.

"Nothing that couldn't be managed. I'd like to introduce you to Avon Nehym of the Southern Kingdom," Marshall said grandly.

"It is a pleasure to meet you." Oberion bowed.

"The pleasure is mine," Avon said, voice deep and soothing.

"Well, well, well. Back so soon, Marshall?" Vaylin had walked over from the windows, and Marshall smiled broadly, wrapping his enormous bear arms around her in greeting and lifted her off her feet. Vaylin giggled, and Marshall laughed as they fell into easy conversation.

This irked Oberion more than he cared to admit. Turning away, he saw the same distaste on Avon's face.

"Have you...er—known Marshall long?" Oberion asked, trying to distract himself from the animated chatter behind him. He should have realized Vaylin had her own relationships with the others here and didn't usually spend all her time with Oberion. It was nothing to be jealous about.

"Not very," the elf replied in clipped tones. "He was in the Southern Kingdom recently, and we met under...unique circumstances. Hence, my presence here. There are issues facing our kingdom that are also plaguing your own, I believe."

"I see. You aren't the only ones who have some news to share then."

Avon nodded as another man walked into the chambers, his exuberance and flaming orange-yellow hair causing all to turn in his direction. A look of disapproval crossed Vaylin's face, but it didn't bother the man as he waved.

"Hello, darlings! This is going to be a juicy meeting. I can feel it in the air."

Fabien Prince removed his electric blue sunglasses with an elegant flick of the wrist and pocketed them. Looking around the room expectantly, he spotted Oberion and made his way over.

Oberion hugged his best friend while avoiding being skewered on his flaming orange mohawk. He didn't know how or when he was going to explain to Fabien what happened while he was gone. His CC had half a dozen unread messages from Fabien on it when he'd turned it on last night, hoping for a distraction. But this sort of thing wasn't something you explained in a message.

"Glad to see you back in one piece," Fabien said into his ear. "Little Aqua Miss didn't cause you too much trouble, I hope?"

"Don't call her that," Oberion murmured.

Fabien raised a manicured eyebrow at Oberion's hushed tone.

"Something did happen then?" Fabien said. "I knew it would. You've always had a thing with her and just couldn't admit it. That's why you never liked her. You'll have to tell me everything once this meeting is done."

"Will you shut up? The only thing that happened was both of us nearly being killed." Fabien waved his hand. "You clearly made it back in one piece. It couldn't have been that bad since you both seem to be intact and…am I sensing some type of connection between the two of you? Your energy is completely different than when you left."

"Fabien, this is Avon Nehym." Oberion pointedly ignored the probing questions and gestured toward Avon for a distraction. Fabien was too sharp for his own good and as clever as a fox. Oberion had completely neglected to think that others would sense a change in his energy. Perhaps only Fabien could since he knew Oberion better than the rest.

"Pleasure." Fabien bowed his head and nearly hit Oberion in the face with the tips of his waxed orange hair.

Avon looked slightly offended and impressed by Fabien. "By the Sun Warrior, man, you look like a flaming rooster."

"I say, that is the politest way I've ever been called a cock," Fabien replied.

Oberion's jaw dropped.

Avon burst out laughing. "You are a funny one, aren't you? I like you."

"If you think I'm funny now, wait till you see me after hours. We'll have to take you to the Tipsy Portal for drink while you're here. It's the best place to experience the unique diversity of Panthea."

The trio all chatted as Neko Raneem and Madam Zahira from the Psychic Union walked in. Her white-gray dreadlocks were twisted into an elegant beehive on her head, and butterfly wings pressed in glass hung from her ears. She looked ethereal, with crystals dangling in her hair and bands of sliver wrapped around her arms and wrists. Waving graciously at everyone, her lilac robes floated in her wake like clouds as she quietly took a seat at the round table with perfect posture.

Neko cast a weary look in the direction of Oberion, Avon, and Fabien, a pained expression on his face as he pulled out a chair and sat down, jaw locked. Avon stiffened, and his smile was rather fixed as he watched Neko, who rubbed the heel of his hand across his forehead like he had a bad headache.

"You two have met?" Oberion hadn't had the chance to speak to any other Elite members since arriving back at Panthea last night.

"Very astute of you." Avon nodded in appreciation. "Yes, we have met already, but it wasn't a pleasant interaction."

Oberion's gut lurched in apprehension. "Really? What happened, if you don't mind me asking?"

Avon relayed the story to Oberion, who at the end of it was inwardly shocked at Neko's reaction to their arrival. Why would Neko be unhappy to Marshall and Avon?

Before he could say as much, in walked Captain Blackwell and Aldwin Hearthfire.

VAYLIN

Vaylin knew immediately that something was wrong with Aldwin when she saw him and heard Oberion's intake of breath over her shoulder. He looked wan and depressed, with dark circles under his pale purple eyes. His normally close-shaven hair was shaggy, and the lines around his eyes and forehead were deeper. What had happened in the last month to cause such a drastic change?

She couldn't pinpoint the cause but his energy was different and the stone around her neck warmed against her skin. Captain Blackwell shared the same concerned and tense energy but hid his emotions better.

Was Incandesite giving her the ability to sense these things?

The captain took the chair to the right of Aldwin and sat down. The low murmur of voices in the room quieted as everyone sat themselves.

"Welcome, all, and thank you for coming today," Aldwin said.

Vaylin sat with Oberion on one side and Fabien Prince on the other, uncomfortable with Fabien's proximity. He kept glancing between her and Oberion and made knowing glances at her covertly. She ignored him and that stupid hair. There were bigger issues than Fabien's prying, and she needed to focus on those.

Aldwin, addressed the room. "As you know, we are here today to discuss recent events regarding the energetic ruptures and other disturbances in Chrysanthos."

"Will Henrietta be joining us?" Madam Zahira asked in a soft voice.

"I don't believe she will make it," Aldwin answered. "She is dealing with some troublesome sylphs at the moment in the Sound Federation."

Neko blinked a few times at the mention of Henrietta's name before crossing his arms and looking out the windows, eyes distant. Henrietta had told Vaylin that the two of them had a long and complicated relationship. Vaylin interpreted the look in her friend's eyes when she said it to mean some sort of romance.

"The air spirits should know better than to trifle with her," Madam Zahira said. "What is the issue disturbing them?"

"That remains to be seen. Many magickal creatures are on edge as of late, and it is indicative of the changing times," Aldwin said.

"It certainly seems to be the case," Neko said. "The migratory animals of the Terra Nation have all altered their traditional routes this summer. Something has been terrorizing the countryside and killing herds of livestock and other animals."

"You bring up a fair point, one that we will get back to in due course," Aldwin said. "First, we need to hear from Vaylin and Oberion, whose mission in the north, I believe, ties into what is happening in the Terra Nation. As you all know, they have been gathering information about a stone Vaylin found during the investigation of a magickal anomaly in the Mingalla nuca. If you may."

He gestured to her and took a seat.

Vaylin's mouth went dry, and her hand trembled slightly as she stood up, unclipped her necklace, and placed it on the table so all could see the stone for themselves.

There was a collective, audible gasp as everyone beheld it.

For nearly twenty minutes, she talked in complete silence as everyone absorbed her tale. She told them the truth about everything that had happened. Everything except the bond between her and Oberion. The idea of Dyadralite caused a split reaction from the group. Some looked disturbed, while others were excited at having an answer to the problem.

"What good is a weapon if we can't use it?" Marshall asked, frustrated.

"We can," Vaylin corrected patiently. "Only...we need to find its other half to use it safely. Then we aren't without risking our lives or our magick to do so."

"This stone is not safe to use, whole or not," Madam Zahira argued. "My dear, it nearly killed you. Should that not be enough for us to pause and question the nature of using such an object?"

In the corner of her eye, Oberion nodded.

"Madame," Vaylin said with forced politeness, "I understand the risks involved with using the stone, but I'm not going to stand by and risk more innocent lives if I have the ability to stop a threat."

"You miss my meaning," Madame Zahira said. "It is not for any of us to use. What makes you so special? This crystal, Dyadralite, was hidden and separated for a reason. We should not meddle in these affairs further without more knowledge, or we endanger ourselves and Panthea with our foolishness."

"I agree with you, Madame Zahira," Oberion said.

Vaylin hid the scandalized feeling surging through her. He was mistrustful of the stone and had cautioned her about it many times. It still annoyed her.

"I have witnessed its power of Incandesite for myself," he continued, "and I think we underestimate the gravity of the situation we are in. Skyminer warned that Dyadralite could split the fabric between our realms and that Ebenosite is currently somewhere in Chrysanthos. If anyone but ourselves were to find it... What if someone tears the veil between worlds? What else has the capabilities to create these ruptures? I saw the power of Incandesite in the Storm Peaks, and although it seems impossible, no other solution explains it."

"What evidence is there of that?" Neko asked.

"The first rupture that came to our attention also had Incandesite there. I don't think it was a coincidence," Oberion said.

"There haven't *been* any other ruptures except the ones you've encountered," Neko answered.

Vaylin was confused as she looked to Aldwin for confirmation.

"He's right," Aldwin said. "The only strange thing we have to report are these creatures of Nimrothag infiltrating the southern continents, primarily the Terra Nation. We cannot pinpoint their location of origin, but they have left a violent and bloody trail of destruction behind them."

"It's true." Marshall shifted back in his chair as he undid his shoe and lifted a bare foot atop the table so all could see.

Avon covered his face with his hand, exasperated by Marshall's crassness.

"Gross, Marshall." Vaylin covered her mouth as he wiggled hairy toes midair. It wasn't the most eloquent posture, but it had a visible effect on the room at large. A ring of black puncture marks encircled his foot and heel, standing out against his tanned skin like a dark halo.

"By the skies," Oberion muttered. "You were attacked by one?"

"Yup, never seen the like of it before," Marshall said. "The thing would have gotten me too if it weren't for Avon. That's how the southern elves come to be involved in all this."

"Ahh," Neko said.

Heads turned when Avon cleared his throat. "They are vile and foul creatures of darkness, from a land called Nimrothag. Their appearance to the elves suggests a deterioration in the barriers between our world and theirs. We think the beasts are coming through weak points. We don't know where these points are or how to sense them. After hearing Vaylin's story, I have drawn two conclusions. The first, Incandesite has the capability to open and seal these ruptures. The second is these stones are either acting of their own accord, or there is someone or something eroding the barriers between our worlds."

Fabien whistled under his breath, and Oberion rubbed his hand over his mouth.

Avon broke the silence. "In our lore, the Star of Creation was used to seal off the barriers and protect this world from the corruption of Nim."

"The Star of Creation." Oberion glanced at Vaylin with a meaningful expression. "Rathir told us that Dyadralite is not from Chrysanthos. He talked about stones coming here from space. This fits with what Skyminer said about Panthea having conflict in its early days, if it all turns out to be accurate."

"If that is true, then the Star of Creation and Dyadralite, are one and the same." Vaylin turned to Avon. "In the elven tales, what happened to the star after it was used? Who took it? Where did it end up?"

"It is said to have returned to the natural world when it dissolved to seal the doors between worlds," Avon answered.

Vaylin deflated slightly. "What does that mean?"

"I have always interpreted it to mean a return to spirit or to the natural state of magick, which is non-being," the elf said.

Vaylin gaped at him. Ebenosite had to be in Chrysanthos, not 'non-being.' Skyminer said it was here.

"If this stone is the only thing that can find or patch these weak points, what do we do in the meantime? Let the south bleed while we search the entire continent for an ancient lost crystal? If these chiros continue to infiltrate my lands, how do we stop them from attacking my people? If we need to find Ebenosite to have the slightest chance of stopping it, I'm in," Neko said.

"King Darius would lend troops and horses to patrol the southern lands as a mark of good faith in aiding one another in our quest to rid these creatures from our world," Avon offered.

Neko looked sourly at him. "Invite a whole elven army to take up residence in my lands? I don't think so. The people would revolt."

"If all this is occurring in the south, then perhaps there is a connection there that we aren't seeing," Captain Blackwell said. "It would be best to ally with others who are affected by the same issue in the same lands. Now is a time to forget our differences in the face of our enemy. We work together, and that's final."

"Ebenosite." Aldwin stood suddenly.

Everyone stirred as they watched him.

"Holy gods," he muttered. "The sphere!"

"What sphere?" Vaylin, Oberion, and Fabien all asked at the same time.

"Marshall and Avon apprehended a golem while they traveled to the Terra Embassy. It was trying to get into this sphere, but they stopped it. This sphere is covered with a language that none of us could recognize. I just realized it's the language of Nim. It matches the scripts in the books Avon lent Panthea. What if the sphere was sent into this world though the ruptures?"

Vaylin gasped. "What if the appearance of Incandesite triggered the appearance of Ebenosite? Something must have triggered them to start reacting to one another. Skyminer said that both stones would try to find each other after being separated."

"That doesn't explain the sphere itself," Marshall said. "If the stones had vanished into 'non-being,' then it wouldn't have developed a metal shell. Something wanted us to find it."

"It's a possibility," Vaylin agreed. "Where is the sphere now?"

"It's here. At Panthea," Aldwin said.

34

TRICKS & THIEVERY

ALDWIN

ALDWIN SLUMPED BACK INTO HIS CHAIR AT THE GRAVITY OF THEIR discovery. Maximus Mundas had found Ebenosite.

He'd been a historian at Panthea in his youth, and if he'd found information about Dyadralite and learned how powerful that stone was, he would have made it his mission to discover it. Aldwin was sure of it. Once Mundas had found the stone, he'd created the sphere to make it compatible for his portal. That was why he was able to make the connection to Nim in the first place.

Mundas had found Ebenosite.

His memory was in overdrive as the night of Mundas's leaving overrode his senses.

"If you ever want to see your brother again, you are going to come with us without a fight." Mundas sneered, holding a paralyzed Abraxas in his arms. *He had a knife pressed against the boy's throat, the blade covered with a pale yellow poison. "If you decide to stay here, I'd run away fast unless you want to be sucked into the collapsing vacuum of my portal and end up in Nim with us — that is, if you survive the transference."*

Aldwin came back to himself and to the meeting.

Oberion was speaking. "If we truly have Ebenosite at Panthea, we need to keep the two halves of the stone separated until we can find a safe location to try to unite them. Skyminer warned us not to unite them in the vale."

"If the stone is trapped in a sphere, we have to figure out how to open the damn thing first to use it," Marshall said. "That thing was charged with more electricity than I would've thought possible that night, and that stupid ball still wasn't opened all the way."

"Incandesite can probably break the sphere," Vaylin said.

The suggestion silenced the room.

"No. It's too risky." Oberion looked angry and, if Aldwin wasn't mistaken, protective of Vaylin.

Seeing this gave Aldwin some comfort, knowing that they had worked through their differences at last.

"The interaction alone is unpredictable," Oberion said.

"These stones want to be united, right?" Vaylin said. "They have the capability to open rifts between worlds. I don't think some metal and an enchantment will be much trouble for Incandesite."

"There will be an energetic exchange of unknown strength," Oberion said. "You can't ignore that and simply hope for the best."

"Hope is the only thing we have right now. Skyminer said the stones would aid those who aided them. I don't think it would hurt us." Vaylin's cheeks were flushed, and her green eyes flashed in defiance. "Someone has to do it, and I already have Incandesite. It should be me."

They were carrying on without realizing everyone in the room was watching them go back and forth.

"Even if we unite the stones and can counteract the deterioration of the veil," Oberion said, "we still don't know how or why this is occurring. Something wants you to use the stones. What if there's something else happening that we're not seeing? This could merely be a side effect of a much bigger problem."

"What are you suggesting?" Fabien asked.

Oberion turned to him. "If this is a natural occurrence, then why now? We know the stones were separated ages ago. It must have been for a good reason. If someone wants Dyadralite, the evidence of which is obvious, it would be pretty convenient to have someone else take the risk of uniting them and do all the dirty work without realizing it."

"We are in the season of eclipses at the moment," Avon said.

Madam Zahira closed her eyes and nodded in understanding.

Avon continued. "Perhaps this is related to some cosmic interaction."

"Eclipses are not uncommon. They happen every year," Oberion said. "By that logic, we'd constantly be plagued by ruptures, and this is the first time any of us have dealt with something like this. Someone is pulling the strings and using us like puppets."

Aldwin sat up in his chair. "Captain, send a message to the holding cell immediately."

They shared a significant look, and Captain Blackwell spun a ball of light into existence on his fingertips and flicked it from his hand. It passed through the stone wall in a whisp of light. This was the secret method of communication between the paladins. They used a special type of spirit magick to stay connected to one another, like an invisible spider web across the entire continent.

"What is going on? Who is in the holding cell?" Fabien glanced between the two men.

The captain looked at Aldwin beseechingly. Aldwin didn't want to admit the truth about his brother to the council, but there was no other choice. "My younger brother, Abraxas Mundas, came to Panthea after Vaylin and Oberion left. He wanted help decoding a grimoire he believed to be our father's. He came to me asking for help with these notes, hoping for closure. I agreed and discovered information about the sphere and the presence of someone, or something, manipulating my brother. We apprehended Abraxas three days ago when he tried to take the sphere from me with force."

"You knew he was up to this and you let him into Panthea?" Neko said. "He has been lurking about the Terra Embassy for weeks now, and I haven't done anything about it because you vouched for him."

"The paladin guard has been tailing him since he arrived at Panthea," Aldwin said. "I did not fully trust my brother and was only trying to help him. It turned out to be an error of judgement on my end with some unexpected windfalls."

"So he is the one causing all of this? My people have to pay the price for his unrequited grief?" Neko stood up, chair toppling backwards and nostrils flaring as he stared at Aldwin. He looked like an enraged bull, black flickering in his eyes, covering the whites for the briefest moment.

Aldwin blinked, not sure if he had seen what he thought he saw. "Neko, please sit down."

"Burning hells I will." Neko kicked his chair out of the way and made for the door.

Captain Blackwell moved quicker than Aldwin and blocked the exit. All around the room, everyone rose from their chairs in anticipation, not sure what to do.

"Calm down, man. We are on the same side and mean you no harm," the captain said.

"If you don't let me pass, we are going to have far worse issues than my anger to deal with," Neko growled.

"Let him go, Captain," Aldwin said. "It's not worth fighting over."

The captain never took his eyes from Neko as he stepped to the side. Neko bristled as he left, flexing his shoulders and hand pressed to his head as he walked away.

The silence in the room was different now, tinged with potent, anticipatory energy.

"This is awkward," Fabien said in an undertone that carried throughout the room. "Shall we call for a recess?"

"I think so." Foreboding crept up Aldwin's spine.

VAYLIN

Marshall and Avon went with Aldwin to check on the sphere, and Vaylin couldn't stand sitting between a scowling Oberion and curious Fabien. She left the chambers and went down a few side hallways for some peace, the bright foliage a blur in her peripheral vision as she turned corners. She was frustrated and angry that Oberion, of all people, was advocating for caution and restraint with Incandesite. Wasn't he on her side with this?

The solution to their problems was right there and she wanted to run toward it with all her might. Why didn't he see it?

A vision of her holding Dyadralite was vivid in her mind's eye, shortly followed by the moment she fell in that crater. The shame of the memory crashed around her, reminding her of her mortality.

Was Oberion right to caution her?

The thought tore at her that he might be right about this.

Rustling clothes from behind made her turn to see Oberion approaching. Sunlight streamed through the windows, and highlighted the navy blue trim of his dark gray robes. They fit him handsomely and were far more impressive than his rustic travel wear.

Her heart beat a little faster when he stopped next to her and she could smell the wind and rain that clung to him.

"Oh, it's you." She brushed out her cream-colored tunic reflexively.

"Hello," he said cautiously. "Before you say anything, let me explain myself."

"You've already done that," she said.

He took her gently by the arm anyway and led her down another hallway further removed from the council chambers. They stopped in a small nook, and his wind-and-rain scent filled her senses. She'd hardly slept last night, thoughts of him making her toss and turn uncomfortably.

"I want to unite Dyadralite," he said. "I agree it's the only way to solve this problem. I only urge us to be careful. Our lives are at greater risk than the others, and you know that. We are energetically bonded to the stone, and there is no way of knowing what will happen to *us* once the stones are joined. We need to find a safe space away from Panthea to do this. That story about the golem reminds me of the octaped attack. I think it was following us, trying to get the stone. It knew somehow it wouldn't be able to once we crossed into the stronghold so it made its move before we entered."

"The message I got from Mingalla said the creatures were after it," Vaylin said.

"Exactly. What if they are being controlled like the golem? It would be a clever way to act without being seen."

"The time to act is now," she replied earnestly. "I swear, Oberion, I don't think the stones will harm us. If Aldwin is right about what is in that sphere, we have both halves of the stones right here. We must do this before something happens."

"But you can't *know* that." He reached for her hands and held them tightly, pulling them toward his chest. She didn't fight it. "I watched you nearly die the last time you used Incandesite. You can't ask me to go through that again. Not with both of our lives on the line."

She heard the plea in his voice and wanted to soothe his worry. "Oberion, the stones have been at Panthea for a day. If something was going to happen, it would've. They want to find each other."

"Do you hear yourself? You're talking like these stones have minds and wills of their own. This is what Skyminer warned us about. These stones aren't long-lost lovers that will be nice to us for bringing them back together. They are powerful and dimension altering. What if we get sucked into Nimrothag and are stuck there? Then what do we do?"

"I don't know. Skyminer said these stones want to be united. That, to me, is a type of sentience, and it will recognize our will to help."

He looked at her with that familiar shadow of skepticism. "They are dangerous objects that can manipulate the very fabric of our worlds. Do not forget that."

"Listen, I know how to listen when my gut is telling me something. My gut is telling me we can do this and we will not be harmed. You have to trust me on this."

"What if this is Incandesite manipulating you?" he asked in a low voice.

The question caused Vaylin to pause and consider its implications. Her first reaction was to instantly deny, but she probed her own conscience. Was this really what *she* wanted? Oberion was trying to keep her grounded. Keep her alive.

They stared at each other for a long moment, hands still wrapped around one another. The hallway was so quiet that she heard the wind outside rustling leaves on the branches. His touch was soothing, and she wondered, felt, a longing deep in her soul. An old ache wanting to be satisfied.

"I trust you." She peered into those blue-gray eyes.

"I trust you," he said gently. "You have both of our lives in your hands, and I do not underestimate that. I only urge you to remember and think before you act."

He spoke with such tenderness that she wondered how she could be so blind as to forget that detail. She was only thinking of herself. Stupidly and selfishly about herself. It was one thing to know and accept her own fate. Quite another to be responsible for Oberion's life. Her heart ached at the thought of hurting him by being reckless, and she shifted closer to him.

"I will do everything in my power to keep you safe," she whispered. "You were the one who saved me from the darkness."

Oberion's eyes blazed with emotion. He raised his hand to touch her cheek, and it warmed under his touch. A wave of dizziness rushed through her, and the heat of Incandesite poured between them. Moving as if on gliders, she tilted her head up, close enough she could see his every blemish, every hairline wrinkle, and every fleck of silver in his dark brown hair. His eyes fell to her lips, and the energy between them thrummed, Incandesite heavy around her neck, as they came together like magnets.

Their lips met, and she was transported.

Colors rushed behind closed eyelids, and her body vibrated with an overwhelming surge of emotion and feeling. She thought her heart might burst from the sensation of it. If it were possible to fall into somebody, she did so in that moment. All the unspoken tension of the last few weeks left them, fueled by Incandesite, and released the pent-up energy.

She could feel the bond between them, like a golden thread of light that anchored them together at the core of their magick. It grew thicker and brighter the longer they kissed, lips glued together as they held onto each other.

Slow clapping registered in her mind.

She was lost in Oberion, in his kiss, and pulled herself back, disoriented. They were no longer alone. The light of Incandesite faded between them as Fabien Prince stood there, looking as smug as a cat who finally caught the mouse.

PART II

THE BEST LAID PLANS

VAYLIN

THE GOLDEN MOMENT OF OBERION'S FIRST KISS BROKE AROUND HER. AFTER weeks of thinking about it and resisting, they had finally come to this point. Why couldn't Fabien have left them alone? Why did he have to come nosing after them?

"For the record, I did warn Oberion this was a possibility before he left and that he had my full support." Fabien's purple eyes glittered mischievously as he glanced between them. "No need to look so terri- fied, Vaylin. Believe it or not I'm on your side. I have no wish to tell anyone about this or the bond."

"Really?" Her mind was still reeling as it tried to catch up.

She and Oberion had kissed. Fabien had witnessed it and knew about the bonding from Incandesite. Great.

"I'm wounded. Have I not always shown you courtesy?" Fabien touched his heart. "I could tell the moment I saw Oberion something was up between you two. What else could it be? I don't want to see something bad happen to him, and that extends to you as well, beyond being my fellow guardian."

"It's not what you think it is," Oberion said.

Fabien rolled his eyes and scoffed. "I know exactly what this is."

"No, you don't." Oberion launched into an explanation about using

Incandesite to heal Vaylin and how he accidently bonded them. "We aren't entirely sure the details about this bond, except that both of our magicks are tied to this stone. Vaylin and I shouldn't get anywhere near that sphere or Ebenosite until we are off Panthea grounds. I think it will be safe to try once we're away from here. Until then, I don't want to take any chances."

Fabien nodded and tapped his jaw with a perfectly shaped fingertip. Vaylin's own nails were uneven and slightly stained from years of working with alchemy ingredients. Fabien dressed and groomed himself better than most women, including herself. Many people of the Igni Territory put a lot of time and money into their appearance. Beauty was an important part of their culture.

"I have no problem with the two of you doing this," Fabien insisted. "As I've told you before, I think that rule is archaic and should be absolved. Panthea needs to keep up with the times. The borders haven't changed in over six hundred years. We should be able to change them for the betterment of modern people."

"That's a very admirable sentiment," Oberion agreed. "Perhaps we can fit this into our agenda after we solve the problem with Dyadralite and ruptures destroying the fabric of our very world?"

Fabien chuckled and clapped him on the shoulder. "You know me. I have many pokers in the fire."

Vaylin bit her lip in uncertainty. Was she ready to do something like that? And what about her and Oberion? Was anything between them natural or being influenced? What if intimacy and proximity strengthened the bond to Incandesite? Would it merge their energies into something stronger? Something more? Did she want that? She remembered back to the Lumbrinica Tunnel and how she had felt before their bond was forged. There was a part of her, even then, that wanted more from Oberion.

The thought was a spark of hope.

"Fine," she answered. "I know you wouldn't do anything to hurt Oberion, and I trust that you will keep this a secret until we are ready to act. Until that point, I'm not going to take my eyes off you."

"Oh, please don't," Fabien said. "I love knowing someone is

watching me. I'll make sure to give you a show." He winked, and a traitorous part of her wanted to grin.

"How this man is your best mate, I will never know," she said to Oberion, who ran a hand through his hair sheepishly.

"It doesn't hurt that he's dead clever when he isn't using his skills to sneak around on his friends or woo romantic interests." Oberion's expression clearly meant he was supposed to be exempt from Fabien's little games.

"You can't blame me for this," Fabien said. "I knew something was up, and it would have taken you ages to admit the truth about this. I'll let it pass this time since you just returned to Panthea but no more secrets. This will have to come out soon if we attempt to join the stones and you two are magickally bound to it. That's no laughing matter."

A commotion came from the council chambers, and all three of them turned in unison.

"Something has happened." There was shouting, and Vaylin moved instinctively, magick on high alert.

"Where is Hearthfire?" Captain Blackwell demanded, forehead peppered with beads of sweat.

"He's checking on the sphere." Madam Zahira rose in her seat. "We aren't sure where exactly, but the hour of our adjournment is almost up. He should be returning here shortly."

Captain Blackwell let out a groan of frustration.

"What has happened?" Oberion asked.

Before the captain could answer, Marshall, Avon, and Aldwin rounded the corner. All the men wore similar expressions to Captain Blackwell's.

"There you are! We have a problem," the captain started.

"So do we," Marshall said. "The sphere is gone."

"And I'm guessing Abraxas isn't in the jail cell anymore," Aldwin prompted.

"Yes. I have no idea how either. The guards I posted outside his room and hallway reported no disturbances. I told them to open the cell, and the only thing different in there was a pile of dust in the corner. Can you believe it? What kind of magick leaves a mark like that?" the captain said.

Vaylin and Oberion stared at one another. Fear and panic bubbled in her chest. If the sphere was gone, so were their chances of uniting Dyadralite. They had no more time.

"We must act quickly," the captain said. "Where would Abraxas go once he had the sphere? Aldwin, is there anything in that grimoire that would give us a hint?"

Aldwin's face paled. "I found this in his quarters the other day."

From his pocket, he pulled out the crumbled diagram of the Ebony drawing.

Vaylin saw the coordinates on the bottom of the page and knew it was somewhere in the southern part of the continent.

"I thought it was the coordinates of where the sphere was supposed to arrive, but maybe it's more. Whatever Abraxas is planning, it can't be anything good." No sooner had Aldwin stopped speaking than a faint rumbling like distant thunder emanated across Panthea. It sounded like it was coming from underground and was followed by a booming clap of lightning. Panicked yells rose from within the grounds.

Vaylin looked anxiously at Oberion as the room erupted in chaos. Everyone left at top speed for the portal courtyard, which was the center of the disturbance. Vaylin's imagination raced as she imagined what Abraxas would do with the sphere. She'd had no idea that Aldwin even had a brother.

If Ebenosite called to the darkness within him and Abraxas had the stone, he was the most dangerous person in all of Chrysanthos. And she shouldn't be anywhere near him with Incandesite.

She trailed Aldwin, Avon, the captain, and Marshall as they turned into the nexus.

The courtyard housing the portals was a mob of terrified students, teachers, and politicians moving in all directions and covered with a thin layer of red dust. Vaylin grabbed Oberion's hand in the chaos, and he gripped her fingers tightly. In all the confusion, no one noticed. She didn't want to be separated from him.

Marshall grabbed someone passing them at random. Thick arms covered with hair tangled in the robes of the whimpering politician. "What is going on?"

The man shook from head to foot. "It-it was Neko. He's lost his mind, demanded that everyone leave the embassy. Some tried to calm him down, and a fight broke out. He went berserk and attacked. It all happened so fast. It was all I could do to get myself out of there."

Marshall looked disgusted and pushed the man away from him.

Aldwin's face was set as he turned toward the crowd.

"Silence!" he bellowed across the nexus, amplified by sound magick.

Everyone in the vicinity stilled and turned in his direction. Vaylin felt like she was standing in a spotlight as hundreds of eyes fell upon them, the Elite Guardians and their gatekeeper. Her fingers dropped away from Oberion's.

"Anyone who is injured, partner up with someone who isn't and go to the MediCenter. Those of you who aren't, we need everyone to vacate the area. Go to the city or one of the resident halls and wait there until further notice. If anyone has information for the Elite, come forward now. We must remain calm and stay safe," the gatekeeper commanded to quell the anxious crowd.

"Do you think what happened in the council has made Neko act this way?" Vaylin asked Oberion.

"I'm not sure," he said. "Neko is one of the most down-to-earth guys I know. This isn't his character. It doesn't make sense for him to act this way. I know the pressure of the ruptures is wearing on everyone's nerves, but to do this? It's wrong."

"The man hasn't been the same since we came back." Marshall had been listening to their discussion.

The crowd had thinned enough that the guardians were able to make their way closer to the portals. A ring of paladins covered in red dust formed a protective ring around the Terra portal.

"Gatekeeper," they addressed Aldwin as he drew near.

One paladin said, "We tried to stop Neko, but couldn't. He was too strong."

"What did he do?" Aldwin asked.

"He ordered everyone in the embassy to leave, saying there was some sort of emergency and that we'd be safer at Panthea. A few of us tried to stay and help, but he wouldn't let us. He has some sort of sphere, sir, and he forced us out of the embassy with it. Never felt the likes of that sort of magick before. It was unholy."

Vaylin's stomach dropped. Neko had the sphere, not Abraxas. How did that happen?

"We need to go there at once." Marshall stepped forward, about to pass under the Terra arch, when a sizzling noise began and he was flung backwards into the air, landing fifteen feet away. Vaylin and Avon rushed over to him as he groaned and coughed.

"Neko has done something to the portal," Oberion said. "They used Ebenosite to do it."

Captain Blackwell pressed, "Are all the portals compromised or only the Terra one?"

"There's only one way to find out." Fabien turned toward the Igni portal and stepped through. He disappeared and returned seconds later.

"That was perhaps the stupidest way to test a theory," Oberion said.

"I thought I'd be right." Fabien casually straightened his jacket. "And I was."

"Here's what we're going to do," Aldwin said in a loud, clear voice. He seemed detached to the situation as he gave orders. "We need to get to the Terra Embassy as soon as possible. If the other portals are working, we can take a zip train from the Igni Territory into the Terra Nation. It shouldn't take us more than a few hours. Hopefully, we can reason with Neko and try to come to some sort of compromise."

"I'll come with you," Marshall said.

"As will I," Avon said. "There are some kindnesses I need to return to Neko."

"No one will be attacking him unjustly." Aldwin's pale purple eyes flashed dangerously. "We only use force if it is absolutely necessary and only to subdue him. We do not move to kill. He is still an Elite Guardian and will be treated as such, understood?"

Everyone nodded.

"Captain, stay here and organize the paladins," commanded Aldwin. "I want eyes and ears on all of the portals at both ends in case something happens. Get in contact with the paladins at the Terra

Embassy and tell them we are on our way. No one is to engage further with Neko until we arrive."

"Yes, sir." Captain Blackwell bowed and left for the paladin barracks, sending balls of light in various directions as he summoned the paladins to him.

Vaylin watched, fascinated by these little comets of communication.

"Right. As for the rest of you"—Aldwin turned to Vaylin, Oberion, Fabien, and Madam Zahira—"I think we need to take caution and halt all travel through the portals. Even if nothing is wrong with them, we need to make sure none of our people use them if something goes astray. Send messages to your regions and bar anyone from using the portals until further notice. We will arrive at the Terra Embassy before sundown. Make sure you are here to monitor the archways and keep others out of harm's way by then. I'll be in touch via the CCs."

"Understood," Vaylin said, echoed by the other guardians.

BELLY OF THE BEAST

MARSHALL

MARSHALL AND AVON MET ALDWIN IN FRONT OF THE IGNI PORTAL AFTER retrieving their weapons and gear. He had no idea what they were about to face, but he wasn't going to go in there unarmed. Avon seemed to be thinking along the same lines, as he was now dressed in his Sun Warrior uniform, the same one he had worn when he first visited Marshall in the Healing Temple of Sakhet. It was slightly distracting, the way his uniform accentuated the smooth lines of Avon's body and certain parts of his nether region. A curious feeling struck Marshall then, one that he hadn't felt in a very long time—if ever.

Was he feeling—attracted—to Avon? The idea sent a thrill of excitement through him.

"You're staring," Avon said without looking at him.

"How can you even tell if you're not looking at me?"

"Elven sense."

"Yeah, what else does that elven sense tell you?" Was he actually flirting?

Avon grinned, the golden disks along his eyebrows flashing. "Much more than what is appropriate to discuss with the Gatekeeper of Panthea coming our way."

"He—what?" Marshall coughed.

Sure enough, Aldwin Hearthfire walked briskly across the courtyard toward them. He bore no weapons, only a bag strapped to his waist.

"Are we ready then?" Aldwin said as he got within earshot.

None of the other Elite members were there to see them off. All were alerting their own embassies. They stepped through the Igni portal, and the familiar compressing sensation enveloped Marshall.

The Igni Embassy was the most modern of all the embassies connected to Panthea and was located on the outskirts of Kia Ora, the coastal capital city of the Igni Territory. Everything here had a yellow tint, and scents of the ocean permeated the city. The buildings of Kia Ora were made of shining metal plates and glass that reached impossible heights, connected by an intricate system of electric rails and powered carts. The ore and natural gas deposits in the Igni Territory were inexhaustible and used it to their full advantage. The wealth and technology developed in Kia Ora was changing Chrysanthos in a way never seen before, especially under Fabien's guidance.

Out the windows of the zip train, the skyscrapers of Kia Ora shrank to golden needles as they headed southward. Palm trees and vivid green grass grew near the coastline, but inland was a dry and barren plateau of white sand and rock, stretching for miles until reaching formidable mountain ranges formed by long-dead volcanoes and tectonic activity.

There was a noticeable change when they passed over the border into the Terra Nation. The dark brown and black of the Igni Mountains were slowly replaced by a gradient of familiar red hues and grasslands that expanded in all directions. A herd of Alizarik Bison had red fur that blended perfectly into the backdrop of red rock with horns curling upwards off their blocky heads. Something about the bison reminded Marshall of Neko, and he felt a pang of unease.

"You know how unlikely it is that Neko was actually the one who stole that sphere, right?" Marshall asked Aldwin, who sat a few seats away, poring over the grimoire as if it still held some secret he was missing.

"I know," Aldwin said. "Which is why we are going there to talk or apprehend Neko, not beat him unconscious or murder him."

Aldwin flashed a look at Avon, who was unfazed by the remark.

"What if he fights us?" Marshall asked. "No offense, but I'm not just going to put my hands back and let him get his punches in."

"I'm not asking you to." Aldwin sighed heavily. "I'm not fool enough to think fighting won't break out, but we will control ourselves. You are both highly skilled fighters. This is a task that will require the finesse and restraint I know you both have."

"If what you told us about your brother is true, then maybe he's done something to Neko and will be there hiding. This could all be one big trap," Marshall persisted. "If it comes down to it, will you be able to act without bias toward your brother?"

Aldwin snapped the book shut, glaring at Marshall, who didn't flinch. He had to push the gatekeeper to know where his heart was, that he could handle this situation. If Abraxas was truly behind this, Aldwin faced some increasingly difficult decisions in the very near future. Marshall wasn't planning on dying anytime soon.

"Do not think for one minute I'm letting Abraxas off the hook for this because he's my brother. I have warned him time and again to stop this folly, and he's refused to listen to me. What other choice do I have besides letting him face the consequences of his action? Just because I have to be the one to determine his punishment doesn't mean I'll waver." Aldwin's normally kind expression was gone, and his pale purple eyes were tinged red, as if he hadn't slept in days.

"All right, all right. All I know is shit will hit the fan as soon as we arrive and we need to be prepared for anything. Your brother is somehow involved in this. If one of us has to apprehend him, just remember it's nothing personal," Marshall said.

"I am aware of the possibility and do not need a reminder." Aldwin coldly opened the grimoire again.

Despite the gatekeeper's reassurance, Marshall didn't believe him.

ALDWIN

A thin stream of smoke was rising into the sky above the Terra Embassy. Scattered groups outside the perimeter walls talked in hushed tones. Aldwin, Avon, and Marshall dismounted their borrowed horses near a group of paladins, who recognized Aldwin and all burst into various explanations of what had happened.

"Calm down." Aldwin raised placating hands. "You"—he pointed at a dark-skinned paladin woman nearest him—"take a breath and tell us everything that happened."

The woman spoke in a tremulous voice. "Neko told everyone we had twenty minutes to leave the embassy before he destroyed the portal. Several politicians and teachers tried to speak with him, to no avail. He overpowered them all and forced them through the archway. Most people left after that. Those who tried to remain behind were attacked by Neko or forced over the walls. I think most of us got out, but I'm not sure if anyone is still in there."

"Where did you leave the embassy from?" Aldwin asked.

"The south gate. I managed to get out right before he blocked the gate. I don't know how you're going to sneak past Neko. He can see through the earth and knows if we get close to the entrances. He's already forced us back three times."

"It's a good thing that I have a plan and will need your help," Aldwin said.

Marshall and Aldwin sneaked along the walls of the Terra Embassy while the group of paladins split off and made for each of the four gates. The sun was setting, and shadows crept across the landscape.

Aldwin tried to remain calm, but his heart was a nervous drum beat. This was all his fault, and now people were hurt, possibly dead, because he'd allowed Abraxas into Panthea.

You couldn't have known Abraxas would do such a thing.

Didn't he though? Part of him wanted to believe his brother wouldn't be capable of such treachery, but the other part knew how impressionable Abraxas was and how, once he was onto something, it was impossible to deter him. It would be far too easy for him to be manipulated by someone or something. Particularly an estranged father figure.

"I still think we should have knocked. Clearly someone is home." Marshall was not happy at Avon's willingness to sneak through the drainage pipes of the Terra Embassy while they and the paladins caused a distraction at the gates to keep Neko occupied and give Avon time to sneak in.

"Avon insists this is what he was trained to do. We would only slow him down if we attempted to go with him, and we need every advantage we can get right now." Aldwin sighed. He and Marshall waited near the southern gate. The distraction taking place around the embassy was causing a racket.

"The elves won't be too thrilled if one of their own was killed here on our behalf."

"Shh," Aldwin hissed. "I hear something."

There was a slithering noise as a length of rope fell from the parapet above.

Avon was there and tying the end off as he waved at them. Aldwin went first, quickly followed by Marshall. Once Aldwin was steady, he peered through a gap in the walls toward the portal gate.

Something was happening down there. Glinting metal surrounded the archway.

"Any trouble underground?" Marshall asked Avon. Sewage grime stained the bottom of the elf's robes, but he paid no attention to it.

"None," Avon answered. "It seems Neko is too focused on our distraction and the archway, blind to all else that moves around him."

"We need to get closer," Aldwin whispered.

Moving quickly and silently, they disappeared down a staircase and made their way through the vacated embassy. It was astonishing the transformation that had taken place here in a few short hours. The paving stones along the ground were cracked and covered with debris and rubble. Several buildings were partly destroyed, and fires burned inside some.

Aldwin stepped carefully through the mess, trying to not disturb anything as they flitted between shadows. A faint buzzing rose as they neared the inner courtyard. Aldwin's hands shook with nerves as he remembered everything Vaylin had told them about the ruptures, running the facts through his mind and trying to formulate a plan. They approached the entrance to the portal courtyard, pressing themselves into the wall and peering around the corner.

It was as if he had stepped back in time.

Where there had once been an elegantly carved stone archway now stood a replica of the archway Mundas had created, only this time it was so much worse.

Blasphemous dark metal formed a cage around the ancient stone pillars, ugly and brutish, covered with spiky symbols etched into the metal and burning red like a forge. Wires ran in thick ropes off the sides and into several control boxes covered with an array of buttons next to the portal. At the zenith of the archway was a silver-white sphere, gleaming like the eye of a monster, its dark power pouring into the archway in pulsing waves. The golden veil beneath was stretched tight and fading in brilliance with each passing second

"What has he done?" Aldwin said in a tremulous voice. *What have I done?*

Leaning back into the wall, he took several breaths, forcing himself to calm down.

"No matter what happens, we have to get the sphere from the portal," he said to Marshall and Avon. "Do whatever it takes to remove it. I don't care which one of us does it, as long as—"

"Welcome, brother," said a showman's voice from the inner courtyard. "I was beginning to think you were going to miss the show."

A chill of horror and disbelief went down Aldwin's spine at hearing Abraxas address them. Aldwin had suspected this, and the overwhelming truth of the moment did nothing to soften the blow.

Marshall and Avon both drew their weapons.

"Do not kill," Aldwin reminded softly. "We bring them back alive if it can be managed."

"Magnificent, isn't it?" Abraxas had a dagger hanging from his fingertips, one edge shining with a red enchantment scrolled across it. "Why don't you come out so we can have a proper little chat?"

Aldwin dug his fingernails into his sweaty palms and feigned confidence he did not feel as he stepped around the corner and saw

Abraxas standing near the control boxes. Marshall and Avon flanked him instantly, assessing the ruined courtyard and trying to find Neko, who was nowhere to be seen. Aldwin only had eyes for Abraxas as he walked closer to the archway. His brother's hair was slicked off his head, and he wore a black robe over traveling clothes.

"See, isn't that better?" Abraxas asked in mock courtesy.

Aldwin wasn't going to play these games with him. If he wasn't mistaken, time was running out before Ebenosite corrupted this portal. He didn't want anything or anyone coming through that thing if it went online. "You need to stop this, Abraxas. It's not too late to shut this down."

Abraxas grinned like a wolf. "Oh, but it is too late, Al. All I must do is flip a switch here, and the entire portal will be hijacked by my device and open a gateway to Nimrothag. The life I was always promised is just a moment away. Guess who will be waiting on the other side for me?"

Aldwin said nothing. A quiet rage built as his brother taunted him.

"You realize that Maximus Mundas has been alive all these long years, right? He's been helping me this whole time, guiding me through the grimoire and giving me the sphere. What interesting things he had to say about you. Would you like to hear a few?" Abraxas ran a finger over the edge of the dagger.

"We don't have time for this. Let's go, Avon!" Marshall shouted, surprising Aldwin.

Aldwin couldn't do anything as the two men stepped from either side of him and charged the archway.

"I don't think so." Abraxas cast purple lightning from his fingertips, and the two of them split in different directions, gaining ground toward the archway as they went.

Aldwin registered a tremor in the earth. Neko was nearby. He exploded from the ground like a sand kraken right under Avon, who was lifted ten feet off the ground as rock and dirt propelled him upward.

Twisting gracefully through the air, Avon used the momentum of Neko's attack to jump from various rocks and land in a crouch on the low courtyard wall. Avon rose like a warrior, beams of orange sunlight highlighting his silhouette from behind. Neko, whose eyes were completely obscured by black, stared at Marshall, who froze mid-step.

"What have you done to him?" Aldwin demanded.

"Nothing drastic," Abraxas said. "A little help from Ebenosite was all it took."

"Illegal portals, kidnapping, and violating the law of free will—do you really expect to get out of this? I can't protect you from this," Aldwin said.

Abraxas chuckled. "Don't worry, Al. I don't intend on being here much longer, nor do I want your protection."

"You're not going anywhere if I have something to do about it."

"Like you did when we were kids?" Abraxas laughed coldly. "Maximus Mundas told me an awful lot of things about the night he *died*. It seems to me you played a far greater role in it than you ever let on."

"Whatever he said is a lie." Aldwin's pulse raced. "That's all he ever does, and he puts us against each other. Can't you see it?"

"I think you're the one who has been lying, Al," Abraxas said. "He told me he was successful that night. That he used Ebenosite to create a portal to Nim and we were all supposed to go there as a family. You didn't like that, did you? So, you caused the portal to malfunction and take him away, while we stayed in Chrysanthos."

Aldwin's ears rang. "Mundas poisoned you that night. That's why you have a scar on your neck and can't remember anything. He used you to threaten me, tried to manipulate me into going to Nimrothag by taking you with him. He doesn't truly care about either of us. It's always about him and what we give him."

Abraxas scoffed. "Mundas would never hurt me. I'm the son he always wanted. He taught me everything about portal energy and the mysteries of Dyadralite. Oh, yes, brother, I know about Dyadralite. It was only a matter of time until the stones returned to Panthea, the origin of their greatest magick, and I would be there waiting when they did."

"You knew," Aldwin said in disbelief.

"Of course I knew. Mundas is far more forthcoming with me than you have ever been. He told me Incandesite had arisen in the Aqua Realm. I was on my way there and missed that girl, Vaylin, by only a few days. Mundas had to send me Ebenosite if this plan were to ever work. Ebenosite can only create portals to Nim, as you know. Mundas was trapped there unless he found Incandesite or someone from Chrysanthos found it and helped him. He told me I'd have to be careful using Ebenosite, as it drains the magick of the user. I've become rather skilled at puppeteering this year, if I say so myself." Abraxas gave a rictus grin.

"You were the one controlling the conjurer that night." Marshall said. Avon, perched, waiting on the low wall.

"That's right. It's also how I managed to escape from that cell in Panthea and take Neko's mind hostage so he could steal the sphere without anyone noticing," Abraxas said.

Marshall ran toward Abraxas, who looked unconcerned as he snapped his fingers. Neko, like a puppet on strings, rushed to intersect Marshall, who lifted his axe defensively and blocked the blow. Avon leapt from the wall and onto various obstacles to join Marshall as the three of them began fighting outright.

"Stop this at once!" Aldwin shouted. His anger could no longer be contained, and thin streams of fire shot from his closed fists like daggers.

"No." His brother's glare was cold. "You should have let us go that night. Dad and I would have been happier in Nim without you."

The shadow of Mundas crossed his features and Aldwin couldn't stand the resemblance he saw there. In a flash, Abraxas sliced the dagger across his palm and squeezed his hand. Aldwin's gut clench as Abraxas grabbed a handle on the control panel and lifted it into position.

The golden veil beneath the arch shuddered, and its color leeched out into a dark gray.

37

INTO THE INFERNO

VAYLIN

VAYLIN TRAVELED TO THE AQUA REALM AND INFORMED SLOANE AND THE others about what was happening with the Terra portal and Neko. Sloane flat out told Vaylin there was no way Neko would be this volatile and reckless and that something else must be going on. Vaylin agreed with her and they discussed Ebenosite while she strapped on leather armor and hid several poisoned blades on her person. Vaylin wasn't sure what was about to happen, but she felt better armed than not. Her Eucalypta staff was strapped across her back with her trusted opal at the end once more.

"Sloane, I need you and a group of paladins to guard the Aqua portal here," Vaylin said as they approached the blue-glowing archway.

"I should come with you," Sloane said.

"The other guardians will be at the nexus with me. I need someone I can trust protecting the Aqua Realm while I'm gone. You're the only person who can."

"Be careful. There have been too many close calls with this stone, and my gut tells me something is wrong. Promise me you won't do anything stupid?" Sloane's black hair cut across her face, making her look fiercer than Vaylin remembered.

"I promise I'll come back in one piece."

Sloane gave her an appraising look. "You shouldn't lie to me, you know?"

Vaylin clenched her jaw tightly. "I'm not lying to you. I will come back. I have many reasons to survive this night. Keep the Aqua Realm safe. I'm counting on you!"

Without another word, she turned and walked through the portal.

She was the first Elite back and sat on the steps of the circular platform, absentmindedly watching the paladins block people from entering the nexus. Her eyes flicked to the Terra portal every other heartbeat. It seemed normal, a thin glimmering sheet of gold like all the rest. But something about it was strained, as if it were being pulled tight. Her feeling of foreboding increased.

Neko had no idea about the sphere or Dyadralite until they discussed it *today*. How could he have taken it? There was hardly any time for him to do it after leaving the council meeting.

She was toying with the edges of her leathers, lost in thought about Neko, when she felt a slight shudder in the air and turned to see Oberion walking out of the Wind District portal. Her breath caught. He wore the traditional fighting robes of the Northern elementors, a flowing and functional garment that amplified the user's ability to move quickly and direct air current effortlessly. It was pale green and lined with yellow, and across his back was a glider, commonly given to those who studied air magick. When he got nearer, the faintest aroma of wind and rain caressed her, and she relaxed slightly, the weight around her neck feeling a little lighter with him next to her. A pulse of Incandesite echoed against her own, and warmth emanated from the stone.

Stop it. It wasn't going to influence her. She wouldn't allow it.

"You look ready," she said.

"As ready as I'll ever be." He leaned against a stone column and joined her vigil as the sun descended in the west. "Are you okay?"

Vaylin laughed and stood up, brushing nonexistent dirt from her pants. "I honestly can't tell anymore. One moment I'm good, and next thing I know, the world is flipped upside down. It's all I can do to adapt and keep moving forward."

"True. I don't think any Elite Guardian over the last two hundred years has had to deal with anything this complicated."

"Yay us," Vaylin said in mock celebratory tones. "I still can't believe Neko is involved in all this."

"I know. I have a hard time believing he was so upset at the council meeting that he would do something as radical as separate the Terra Nation from Panthea. Breaking a thousand-year-old portal is no laughing matter."

"I came to the same conclusion. Hopefully the others will be able to stop him without too much trouble. They are there now. Marshall sent out a message a half hour ago." Her voice trailed off as she turned southward.

"Listen, I need to tell you something." Oberion brushed his fingers against hers as he stepped closer.

The impulse to reach out was automatic, and she forced herself to resist. The other Elite members were due here any moment, and a group of paladins surrounded the nexus. She had to control herself. Her stomach swooped apprehensively as she waited for him to continue.

"First, when they return with Ebenosite, I don't think you should be in Panthea Central. You need to remain in the Aqua Realm until we find a safe location to unite Dyadralite. I'd tell you to leave it protected somewhere, but seeing as how the sphere got stolen, it is something that needs to be personally guarded."

Vaylin wanted to argue but held her tongue. She needed to listen to him, not talk over him.

"The second thing I want to say is that no matter what happens, from this point forward, I do not want you using Incandesite under any circumstances. This bond is dangerous, and we don't know what it can do to us. No matter what happens, we need our magick and Incandesite can cripple us by stealing it forcefully. Promise me you'll resist. Promise me you won't use it." His blue-gray eyes were beseeching as he grasped her hand, fingers tangling together.

Why is everyone asking me for promises? Didn't they understand Vaylin had to solve this? It was her responsibility and she wasn't promising something she wasn't sure she could keep.

"Oberion, I can't—" she tried to say.

"No. This is not up for debate. You need to make me this promise. Now."

"What if I can help?" she asked. "It worked in the Storm Peaks. Why not here?"

Oberion sighed and looked to the heavens. "It is not helpful for anyone if you and I end up dead. If something serious happens to Neko and we meet an unfortunate end, Panthea will have lost three guardians in one night. Let that sink in, Vaylin. It would take years to recover, and with Dyadralite in the picture, Panthea can't afford that right now. The whole continent will be clamoring for explanations."

Her mouth went dry, and she felt trapped by his words.

His promise.

"Oberion, when we first started on this journey with Dyadralite, you told me that this is what it means to be an Elite Guardian. It isn't about the magickal prowess or titles but the strength and willingness to make sacrifices for the greater good of Chrysanthos. For my people. When we took our oaths to be guardians, it was our life that we pledged."

"I know what our oath says. But this is different."

"It isn't," Vaylin said firmly.

Oberion didn't respond.

"Our lives have always been the asking price to be a guardian. Yes, we are bonded with Incandesite. But if we weren't, this is still a life-threatening situation. If we die here tonight, we will have done what every generation of guardians did before us."

Oberion gave her a contemplative look before chuckling softly. "Here I was, thinking I was the wise one."

She smiled faintly. "I learned a few things from you during all this."

"I'm glad you've learned some humility too," he joked, but something like pride and admiration lingered on his features.

Vaylin scoffed and tried to pull her hands away. His fingers tightened on her wrist. She was about to protest when he wrapped his arms around her. The weight of him was awkward at first. Then the smell of rain and damp earth filled her senses, and she relaxed, feeling transported to a forest she had never known but longed to explore as she settled into his embrace.

She felt compelled to hold him tighter, but was it her feelings suggesting it—or Incandesite? It was hard to tell anymore, and the memory of their recent kiss made her ache for more, clouding her judgement.

Oberion straightened his arms suddenly, holding her a few feet away from him. Color tinged his cheeks, and they were both breathing heavier than warranted for a hug.

A dizzying rush of emotions assailed Vaylin—first lust, then rejection, and then confusion and anger. The heat from his body was gone, and she was cold without it, craving its return. She wanted to hold him, to pull him closer so they could never be parted.

"We need to be careful," he said faintly, pressing a hand to his head.

"Why?" Her voice was low and sultry. Her gaze followed his hand as he adjusted his nether regions and felt her own ache between her legs.

"Because I might not be able to stop myself from taking you north and having my way with you." The baritone of his voice resonated down their bond and straight into her heart, thrilling her at the notion.

Her knees went weak, and she had half a mind to say fuck it and get away from here before this glorious feeling vanished.

"You know, if I keep finding you two like this, you'll be hard put to keep this a secret for very long." Fabien wore his familiar electric blue sunglasses and a sleek, black leather jacket with sharp shoulders and pronounced collar lined with orange. His flaming orange mohawk was tinged with red on the ends.

"You always were one for dramatic entrances," Oberion said. "I see you've dressed for the occasion too."

"My timing is perfect." Fabien dusted off his shoulders and adjusted the sleeve of his jacket. "If this is going to be a fight, I might as well look good doing it."

Vaylin rolled her eyes. If she was feeling generous, Fabien did look rather remarkable. It was a wonder he'd ended up a guardian instead of a model.

"Any news yet?" Fabien removed his sunglasses. He had coal smudged around his purple eyes.

"None besides this first message from Marshall," Oberion replied.

"Great, well before this starts, I have gifts for you." Fabien reached into a pocket and pulled out three golden wrist bands. "I have one for Madame Z when she gets here too. They are defense bands. It's the latest breakthrough from my company."

"Is it pertinent to give us IgniTech watches right now?" Vaylin asked sarcastically.

"Although telling time is one of its many features, there's much more to them than that," Fabien said. "They are highly intuitive magick boosters that can aid the user during battle. It will also sense danger around you and automatically shield you if you are compromised."

"How do we use them?" Oberion clipped his onto his wrist.

Vaylin looked at hers suspiciously before doing the same.

"Imagine it's like a crystal where all you have to do is channel magick and intent through it. It naturally synchronizes with your magick and will respond only to you once it's imprinted." Fabien was adorning himself with little metal contraptions, placing one band on each wrist and the heels of his boots. He pulled a strange pair of black gloves from his pocket and put those on too. They were form fitting, with the fingertips removed. The wrist band clicked and whirled, extending strange metal appendages like an exoskeleton of a hand, following the lines where actual bones were. The appendages magnetized to the glove and clinked as he flexed his fingers. Fabien turned expectantly to the other two. "Just a few other prototypes from Igni-Tech that need testing."

Oberion gaped at him. "Do you think now's the best time to test this?"

"Of course. What better time to test something than when one is in imminent danger?"

"You're unbelievable," Oberion said. "I hope for your sake they don't malfunction."

"I would never be *that* reckless. These have already seen a few rounds of external testing." Fabien calibrated his gloves, which sparked yellow and twitched as he dialed the tiny nobs at the base of his wrist.

"Why don't we get any gloves or extra components?" Vaylin asked.

"The bands I gave you have already been proven safe. The upgrades *I'm* testing are still in the experimental stages of development," Fabien said. "The one great cost of any inventor is that you are always test subject number one."

Vaylin snorted and crossed her arms as Madame Zahira came through the Psychic Union portal to join them at last.

"What are these?" she asked as she approached. She wore white robes, and her dreadlocks were tied up with a length of deep purple silk.

"Fabien's latest experiment," Oberion answered.

"Ingenious." She clasped the golden band around her own wrist. "You've enchanted the metal with psychic abilities to complement the users magick. Nicely done."

"You flatter me." Fabien fanned himself. "If you're impressed now, Madame Z, wait until I have time to explore the alterations I received from the dwarves. Your little friend Gizmo sent me some very curious schematics." His excitement was evident as he winked at Oberion. "I haven't had time to implement them yet."

"So, that was what I delivered to Gizmo?" Oberion appraised his wrist band with new interest. "I'd be careful if I were you. Gizmo has a knack for blowing things up."

"It's one of the many things I have in common with that brilliant little dwarf," Fabien said.

Vaylin smiled at that and clipped her own wrist band on, turning at the sounds of people coming toward them. It was Captain Blackwell with a troop of paladins standing in rank behind him. The sun hovered above the mountains that surrounded the Vale of Panthea and cast a burning red hue over them all.

"Good, I'm glad to see you're all here. I have news from the paladins in the south," the captain said mechanically. "Hearthfire, Avon, and Marshall all reached the Terra Embassy without issue. They came up with a plan to gain entry to the embassy, and according to the paladins, it was successful. We haven't heard anything since, but the paladins have the Terra Embassy surrounded and will let us know if anything develops."

The tiniest shift of vibration caused everyone in the vicinity to freeze.

Incandesite twitched toward the shimmering golden veil of the Terra portal. Vaylin froze.

The veil of the Terra portal stilled, no longer eternally swaying with the currents of time. It rippled violently, as if hurricane gales tore through it. An enormous force of suction pulled on everyone in the vicinity, growing louder until the pressure finally released.

A loud crack sounded through the air, and the Terra portal blinked out of existence.

38

UNRAVELING

MARSHALL

THE CLANG OF ROCK ON METAL RATTLED THROUGH THE COURTYARD. THE decorative sand pits blew apart, and boulders and bricks crumbled into the ornamental plants and foliage.

Marshall panted heavily as he fended off blows from Neko, whose empty, black eyes were haunting, a constant reminder to act defensively, not offensively. It wasn't an easy task. Neko was equal to his own strength, and having the power of Ebenosite behind his magick made him ruthless enough that even Avon was sweating, something Marshall had never seen. Every time Marshall formed any type of terra magick, Neko would sense it and overwhelm the magick with his own sheer force. Marshall focused on his speed instead, delivering swift strikes of fire in a flurry of jabs and quick movements.

The vibration around them changed when Abraxas turned on the metal archway, and it increased Marshall's panic. The energy grated on his nerves, and the shock of the familiar golden veil turning a murky gray made him numb all over.

His lapse in attention cost him when Neko threw a volley of earthen disks in his direction. Marshall dodged most of them. The ones he didn't left stinging gashes across his calf and left shoulder. He was lucky his bones didn't shatter from the impact.

Neko stumbled, and Avon rushed forward. He hit Neko's legs with the flat part of his sword, which was sharp enough to leave parallel slits on the exposed skin. Neko fell to his knees, roaring in pain.

Avon circled, ready to make another swipe when Neko reached out, glaring at the elf, and squeezed his hand midair. Avon jolted to a stop as his foot and ankle sank in quicksand.

Neko laughed and made toward Avon, but Marshall cut him off, driving the heel of his axe into the back of Neko's skull. He staggered, grabbing his head with both hands before falling unconscious onto the ground.

Marshall ran over to Avon and undid the terra magick to free his foot.

"Can you stand?" he asked.

"I think so. It is only stuck, not broken." Avon grimaced as he put weight on his leg.

In the distance, the brothers fought, bursts of yellow and purple light flashing between them. Abraxas delivered a hit that almost had Aldwin toppling backwards into the archway.

The gatekeeper caught himself at the last second.

Why was Aldwin so close to the portal?

"We need to get that sphere." Marshall panted. "I'll guard Neko and provide backup. Give me the rope to bind his hands." Avon tossed him the rope, and Marshall started knotting Neko's wrists and ankles together. "This won't do any good once he's conscious. He can burn the ropes away, but hopefully it will give us some time if he wakes up."

"It is elven rope," Avon said. "It cannot be severed by blade or magick."

"Good to know," Marshall said.

Avon's jaw tightened. "How do you suppose we get the sphere? That thing is thrumming with the power of Ebenosite. We won't simply be able to take it. It might drain our magick if we try."

"Maybe we can shut it down another way." Marshall wildly looked toward the control boxes. They were right next to the battling brothers, impossible to get to without entering the fray. "Abraxas must have thrown one of those switches. How hard could it be to figure out which one?"

"We need to lure them away from the portal to try. I can help Aldwin while you figure out the controls."

"Let's go for it." Marshall grasped Avon's forearm near the elbow like they had the night of the wrestling match.

Without warning, the elf tugged him forward, and their lips met for the briefest moment. Fireworks exploded through Marshall, and he was overcome with emotion at the sensation of Avon on his lips. The kiss was light and quick, full of intention and promise.

They pulled away from another.

Marshall's head swam worse than when the chiro had bitten him. "Wh-what was that for?"

"For luck. And something worth fighting for."

"Right." He couldn't process everything he was feeling and thinking in that moment. The horror of the portal, the hope of more time with Avon.

The earth shuddered beneath them, and Aldwin yelled as a bolt of purple lightning hit him in the shoulder. He fell backward, illuminated by purple light as the portal shimmered like a pool of liquid silver.

Everything about it was wrong. Somehow the damned thing was connected to Nimrothag.

They were too late.

Aldwin barely stirred, and Abraxas looked triumphant as he stepped closer.

"Come on!" Marshall and Avon ran toward Abraxas and Aldwin.

Aldwin looked defeated, tears streaking dirty cheeks as he pleaded with his brother. It hurt Marshall to see the gatekeeper begging for his brother to stop.

"I'd say try not to kill him, but I'm having a hard time finding reasons not to," Marshall said to Avon.

"Don't worry. I'll take care of him." Avon spun his twin swords in both hands and looked like a deadly praying mantis with the head of a hawk.

Marshall really wanted to help Avon pummel Abraxas but forced himself to stay off to the side as he got closer to the control boxes. Avon went for a direct attack and caught Abraxas off guard. He knocked him away from the gatekeeper and the portal, fire dancing along the edges of his swords. Abraxas had an ugly look on his face as he shot purple lightning at Avon.

Marshall approached the control boxes and stared at the variety of buttons before him. Some were blinking, while others read different numbers or dials. There was a quartz screen in the middle of one control box, and on it were the words: portal engaged.

"Obviously," he grumbled. He was hesitant to push any buttons in case something adverse happened instead. He carefully tried a few out. Nothing significant occurred so he took a step back to observe the entire thing. Some panels had many small buttons clustered together in neat rows, while others had larger ones spread apart. Several large ones were the same size, and a few looked as though they had potential.

His gaze fell on a rounded handle with rust flaking off the metal. He reached forward and grabbed it. An electric shock surged through him as his hand clamped down on the handle. It was worse than the night they found the sphere.

He flew backwards from the control boxes, landing hard on his back and smoking slightly. Why did this always happen to him? Dust filled his eyes and lungs as his muscles convulsed. He dug his fingers into the ground, channeling his magick as he focused on dispelling the electricity from every strand of his muscle.

Marshall rolled over. Abraxas and Avon were still fighting. Aldwin was rousing from the ground, painstakingly slow, half his robes covered in sticky red as he forced himself up with one arm. Marshall wasn't sure what to do.

Then a cry from Avon caught his attention as Abraxas gained momentum in the fight.

Each strike of lightning that hit Avon's blades traveled up them and into his arms. His blows got weaker and sloppier with every parry and swing.

Marshall launched himself forward. His body responded instinctively, but it was no use. He was never going to get there in time. Abraxas landed two more strikes, closing the distance between in a few steps, and on the third lightning strike, plunged a dagger into the elf's ribs.

Avon's eyes widened, and a sickening intake of breath wrenched from him.

A trickle of blood touched the corner of Avon's lips.

The lips that were so recently on his own. This couldn't be happening. Avon couldn't die.

Abraxas withdrew the blade violently from Avon's gut and turned in time to see Marshall hurtle toward him. Abraxas raised his hands in defense, and a smoke screen plumed into existence around him.

Marshall couldn't see anything and blindly kept his course. Within moments, he hit something solid and tackled it to the ground. The dagger skittered away, and the figure beneath him writhed angrily.

He punched every inch of Abraxas that he could. Abraxas felt like a rag doll beneath him as he swung.

Again.

And again.

Marshall couldn't stop himself. He didn't want to. Years of rage and pain burned in him.

Abraxas had caused all this suffering, had killed the one person who had bothered to get close to Marshall after years of isolation. If Avon was dead, diplomacy be damned.

A hand grabbed his arm and twisted. He fought back until he realized it was Aldwin trying to stop him.

"What are you doing?" Marshall growled, blood and pulp dripping from his knuckles.

"Stop, Marshall. Stop!" Aldwin was pale, and the flesh of his shoulder was blackened and burnt, bits of fabric melted into his skin.

"Why?" Marshall demanded furiously. "He deserves this!"

"He's my brother," Aldwin said desperately.

Marshall fell back, all the fight vanishing from him at the words and the expression in Aldwin's face. The smoke dissipated, and he had no space for Aldwin's dilemma as he half ran, half crawled toward Avon.

Avon lay on the ground, hands pressed to his lower ribs where bright red blood leaked from the wound.

"Avon! Tell me how to help you," Marshall yelled.

"I hear you." Avon groaned and curled inwards, covering his injured side. "Pointy ears, remember?"

"Then tell me what to do." Marshall ripped off his shirt and pressed it to Avon's side.

Avon didn't respond.

Marshall cursed, frantic to help his dying friend. "Come on. Don't you dare stop breathing on me. We're not done yet."

Avon's eyes were half closed, and his breath came in labored gasps.

Frustrated, Marshall searched the elf's pockets. It had to be on him somewhere. There was no way Avon would come here without it. Marshall's shaking fingers touched a smooth glass and pulled out the vial of Telrithian. Relief washed over him as he cradled Avon to him, one arm pressing against the elf's side.

He held the bottle and ripped the cork out with his teeth. He tipped the entire bottle into Avon's open mouth and held him steady as the liquid went down his throat.

Marshall waited with bated breath.

This had to work. It healed his own injuries seamlessly, and it would do the same for Avon. He refused to believe this was an ending. They needed more time.

He needed more time with Avon.

It had been too long since he'd felt like this, and he didn't want to let it go. The elf had awoken something inside him that now screamed to be heard. To be seen. To be felt.

Not yet.

Avon's eyelids fluttered like the wings of a butterfly freed from its chrysalis, and for the first time in over twenty years, Marshall cried in earnest.

ALDWIN

His shoulder throbbed, needles of pain splintering through him. It was nothing compared to the pain gripping his heart, ripping it to shreds while he sat there, unable to do anything about it.

Abraxas truly hated him this much.

Did he somehow deserve this for trying to protect his little brother?

Aldwin knelt beside the beaten figure of his brother, face a bloody and bruised mess. Grief and exhaustion weighed on him as he took it in, thinking about all that had been lost today.

How could they ever come back from this? Abraxas would face capital punishment when they returned, and if Aldwin was still gate-keeper by the end of this, he would be the one to make the final verdict. It was what was expected of him as gatekeeper. That made him every bit the traitor Abraxas claimed him to be.

It didn't matter anymore. Abraxas was here, and whatever Mundas was planning with him wouldn't come to pass. Aldwin had prevented him from going through the portal, and the only thing left to do was shut it down.

The travesty of the portal thrummed, still activated.

With great effort, Aldwin forced himself up.

Pain lanced through his shoulder and down his spine as he steadied himself. Colors and light swirled in his vision, making him dizzy. He took one step toward the portal then another.

He froze. There was already a figure before it, and for one-heart stopping moment, Aldwin thought he saw Maximus Mundas standing there, the vision of his nightmares come to life.

"My, my, brother. You really know how to take a hit, don't you?" said a familiar, sly voice. Abraxas. He was a dark silhouette lined with silver before the archway, a bulbus shape of a rucksack on his back.

Aldwin blinked.

It was Abraxas. But how?

His mind felt slow, trying to keep up with what he was seeing. He looked stupidly between the Abraxas standing near the portal and the Abraxas lying on the ground.

The body on the ground deflated, turning to dust before Aldwin's eyes.

Another golem.

THE BREAKING OF PANTHEA

VAYLIN

THE GOLDEN PORTAL HAD TURNED GRAY.

The paladins erupted into confusion, and Captain Blackwell yelled instructions over the chorus of voices. The guardians looked anxiously at each other. Cold dread crept in as the reality of the situation settled around them.

Neko had done something to the portal using Ebenosite.

There was nothing they could do, no message heading their way with reassurances and tales of success. There was no gatekeeper to give direction, and one of their own had cleaved a strike at the heart of Panthea.

They were on their own.

It was up to them to protect Panthea. She'd had a feeling it would come to this and thought about the stone around her neck.

She never had made that promise to Oberion. Would he hate her if she chose to use the stone to fix this?

Not yet. Not now.

A constant vibration started underground.

"Do you think a rupture will form here?" Vaylin forced herself to be calm and quelled the panic in her chest. "If one does, the devastation and loss would be unfathomable with the portal network."

"I don't think that is what's happening." Oberion gestured at the other portals.

Another rumble came from the earth, stronger this time, and the multicolored panes of glass shook in their frames, clinking faintly like breaking icicles. Dust fell like snowflakes from the ceiling, and Vaylin's mind raced. Was all of Panthea feeling this right now, or just them in the nexus? The Terra portal had a misty sheen under the archway, a gray phantom veil.

"Oberion," she said nervously, "what do we do?"

"I don't know," he answered, muscles tight in his jaw.

"We fight, obviously." Fabien flicked both hands, and the whirl of gears buzzed over the commotion.

"We don't even know what we're dealing with," Oberion said. "Our first response shouldn't be attacking what we don't understand."

"This isn't a diplomacy," Fabien said. "Neko took a sphere that contains a stone full of dark energy and can connect to a realm of demons. Clearly, this issue has moved from 'proceed with caution' to full blown danger. If this thing connects to Nimrothag, who knows what will come through."

Oberion let out a sound of frustration.

Captain Blackwell joined their circle. "Do we have any idea what's going on here?"

"Fabien is right. It's connecting to Nimrothag," Vaylin said through numb lips.

"What?" Captain Blackwell said.

Everyone turned to her, and she knew she was right. "That's what Neko has done. Maybe he tried to sever the Terra portal connection to Panthea and accidently created a portal to Nimrothag. What else would explain this?"

"That can't be," Oberion said.

"I think she is right," Madame Zahira said. "The energy coming off that portal is vastly different than the others."

"But-but..." Oberion seemed to struggle with the gravity of the quickly changing situation. "What if this is showing us the Terra Embassy? There are only three of them down there, with a handful of paladins, dealing with something that has clearly gone wrong. I don't care how talented any of them are. They can still be killed."

His eyes flashed like chips of ice. Vaylin stood her ground and squared her shoulders. The portal behind them changed with each passing moment.

"I want to help too, Oberion. But does that look like our world? Does it feel like our world?" she urged. He had to know, had to sense the wrongness of whatever was forming in there. "Everything beyond that arch feels off. A world full of monsters and demons are on the other side of that veil, intent on killing us. The chiro, the octaped. We need to stay here and stop those foul creatures from entering our world. It'll be a massacre if we're overrun."

"If we're about to prepare for an invasion, the paladins will not back down," Captain Blackwell said proudly. "Our ancient order has protected Panthea from the beginning, and we are honored to defend her."

"Good," Vaylin said, addressing him. "Have them form a perimeter around the dais and courtyard. Call any able-bodied paladin to us. The guardians will remain on the platform and be the first line of defense. If anything slips past us, it's up to you lot to take care of them, got it?"

"Yes, ma'am." Captain Blackwell shouted commands at the waiting paladins, and they moved into position, balls of light flying into the night as spears and shields encircled the platform for the impending fight.

"Right." She turned to the other guardians. They all looked at her, astonishment and impressed approval across their features. She stood a bit taller, was proud she could elicit such a reaction.

Oberion beamed at her. "If demons cross into this world, we need to stop them from escaping through the portals. If these things figure out they can travel through them and into Chrysanthos, the damage to the embassies could be irrevocable. We have paladins standing guard at the other end, but I'd rather not give these demons the chance to get that far."

Their panic subsided as they formed a plan. Oberion and Fabien worked out a quick strategy for them, their minds calculating all possible outcomes of this scenario. Seeing this made Vaylin finally understand what made them such good friends.

A shuddering, roaring cry came from the archway.

It was molten silver, and although they couldn't see into Nimrothag, the dead chill of the place raised goosebumps on Vaylin's arms.

"We should form up," Fabien said. "We each guard the portal leading to our region. If any of us move out of position, the rest will cover you." Vaylin had never seen him looking this severe as he triple-checked his gadgets. "If we can't kill the beasts, toss them to the paladins. Their numbers should be enough to take care of what we can't."

They all nodded in agreement and moved into position.

Madame Zahira cracked her neck and shoulders, shifting her feet to shoulder length apart, and raised both arms above her head, bringing her hands together in prayer. She stood there, eyes closed and as still as a statue. Whisps of purple-white light coalesced around her, like butterflies landing on her skin. This was highly advanced psychic magick, drawing and transforming raw ether into a cocoon of magick. It was hypnotizing to watch and deadly to behold. One touch of those psychic tendrils would be enough to cut a body in half or block access to one's magick.

A crescendo of sound and force erupted from the archway. Vaylin ducked and covered her eyes as several panes of glass fell from the ceiling. They exploded like bombs, releasing glass shrapnel on impact. When it stopped, she looked up again, and bits of glass fell from her like droplets of water.

The air around them was sucked toward the dark portal, and Vaylin had the strangest sensation that Nimrothag was breathing in Panthea's scent, tasting the promise of their world. It sent shivers up her spine.

The sudden change of atmosphere was unnerving.

Vaylin caught Oberion's eye. He responded with a weak smile, lips pressed together tightly. This was the last moment of peace they were going to share together before all hell broke loose. She had to focus on the fight—she would never survive this if she were distracted.

"Steady," Oberion said in a commanding voice.

Vaylin unstrapped her staff and crouched into a fighting stance.

"We are the guardians. We are the shield that protects Panthea, the sword that meets every enemy, and we will not falter." Oberion's hands were at his sides with tendrils of air and ice dripping from his fingers, glider on his back.

Sniffing and scratching sounds grew louder, their magick a lure to these things.

The rank odor of the creatures hit Vaylin, and she gagged, eyes watering. They smelled like hot sewage water mixed with the pungent sweetness of rotten leaves. Long, black talons groped around the edge of the archway. The head and torso of an enormous monster materialized underneath.

It was grotesque. Humanoid in body and shape with huge, leathery wings that curled upwards from its back. The slits it had for nostrils flared as it sniffed loudly, ropes of saliva dripping from a mouth full of razor-sharp teeth. Matted, black hair covered its body.

It was a chiro.

The creature that Marshall had described was more terrifying than she'd imagined, and two more followed the first.

There was a blast of fire from Fabien, and the fighting began.

The chiros shot through the archway and made for Fabien. Madame Zahira covered his flank with a shield of psychic force. The beast howled, and in another heartbeat, a chiro leapt for Vaylin. She attacked with her staff, impaling the beast with an icicle as large as her body.

She lost track of time, moving impeccably as she directed waves of water from her staff, shooting spears of ice that expanded upon contact with the chiro to freeze off limbs and wings. The chiro Oberion was fighting got in her line of sight, and she threw several ice blades along the creature's spine. It screeched in misery as black blood gushed from its wounds.

Vaylin winced, grabbing her head as the sound made her eardrums ache and bones shudder. Oberion covered her lapse in fighting by sending pulses of magick from him, forcing the sound of the creature to dissipate quickly.

On they fought.

They ducked, whirled, and attacked as each successive foe came through the portal.

The chiros were only the first wave. Soon, other nightmarish things made their way into Panthea.

A swarm of mosquito-like insects ballooned out of the portal and aimed directly for the guardians. One landed on Vaylin, and pain pieced her thigh. It immediately started sucking blood, and she was instantly faint. She burned the bug to ash, but several more landed on her. Pricks of pain radiated down her back, arms, and legs. There were too many, and she couldn't concentrate on all of them as another wave of dizziness overcame her.

The metal band around her wrist whirled to life and unfolded around her arm like a bizarre gauntlet.

Vaylin blinked, and flames erupted from it, encasing her entirely and incinerating the bugs feeding on her. She looked across the body-strewn floor to see Fabien grin at her and tap on his own metal contraption as a similar cocoon of fire encased him. Oberion and Madame Zahira were both surrounded by shields of flame, the bands on their wrist flashing in the light as they battled.

The paladins were less lucky as the flying pests descended upon them instead. The paladins pointed their spears toward the heavens in a synchronized movement, and a solid mass of light bloomed over them like a web of starlight and vaporized the blood-sucking insects instantly.

"Vaylin, look out!" Oberion shouted.

A chiro barreled toward her, claws extended as it swiped furiously for her neck.

She dodged and rolled away clumsily, hitting a column of stone near the Sound Federation portal to her right, exposing the entrance to the Aqua Realm. She wheezed for air, all the breath knocked from her. The momentum of the beast was too much to stop itself, and it hurled into the portal, disappearing from sight into the Aqua Realm.

The action suspended as every eye watched the beast vanish.

"No!" she shouted.

Images of the creature feeding on Sloane or any of her other companions filled her mind. The chiros made weird clicking noises to each other, and Vaylin's own fear also showed in the faces of the other guardians.

Could the chiros sense freedom from this slaughter if they went through the portals?

The chiros redoubled their attack, focusing on maneuvering instead of bloodlust. It was all Vaylin could do to keep fighting and block the portals.

Madame Zahira bellowed as she ducked and twirled between creatures, disks of psychic energy encasing her hands as she severed limbs and amputated wings. Two chiros forced their way through the Psychic Union portal. Vaylin tried to yell a warning over the madness.

The flow of chiros slowed, but there were a dozen surrounding the guardians and more scattered amongst the paladins. The creatures that fell moved no more, but the ones fighting attempted to escape the onslaught. One broke free and flew into the indigo night. It was fifty feet in the air when it collided spectacularly with a giant flying lion. The griffin screeched its call to the night and, with a ferocious grip tore the chiro in half, spraying black blood like rain.

Henrietta Scyth, the last of the Elite Guardians from the Sound Federation was astride her caramel-colored mount named Tiny, a griffin with a fifteen-foot wingspan, flanked by Beast, her other griffin. Her long, red hair glowed in the light of Panthea as she raised a thin sword skyward, letting out a war cry that rang throughout the grounds. Her mounts echoed her, along with half of the paladins. Vaylin added her own war cry in answer, elated that she had come to protect the skies.

Her relief was short lived, as the howling of wolves approached the veil. More demons were making their way here. How long could they keep fighting? If Aldwin couldn't reverse this portal to Nimrothag, should she?

"Do you think we can shut the portal down?" Vaylin yelled to Oberion over the noise of fighting.

"We can't do anything without *both* stones!" he shouted back. "It's too risky."

Enormous shapes emerged from the archway. Coarse, wiry hair

covered these four-legged mongrels, whose long snouts sniffed in their direction. Their mouths were filled with teeth the size of her hand. The biggest one led the pack. Its angry, beady red eyes locked onto Oberion, who was directly in front of them. When they walked, embers of flame dropped from their paws.

Hell hounds.

The creatures reminded her vaguely of werewolves. Their intense, wild ferocity seemed to panic in the chiros, who tried to get away faster than ever, only to fall at the hands of the paladins or be torn apart by Henrietta and her griffins in the skies.

The five hounds advanced.

Fabien whirled a few dials on his mechanical gloves, held his hands before him, and little pistons emerged above his fingertips, a blueish gas leaking from them. He hurled a fireball from his hands, and the blue gas reacted violently with the flames, exploding into a blistering deluge of brimstone aimed directly at the hounds. The temperature of the air rose, and Vaylin had to retreat behind a stone column as the heat of the attack seared her whole body.

She lowered her arms to see the aftermath of the destruction.

The hell hounds shook their matted fur, bits of ember and flames rolling off them like morning dew. Fire could not quench other fire. They were impervious. Fabien looked terrified that his trick didn't work, and all five hell hounds bore down on him.

"Oberion, surround the guardians with air," Vaylin shouted.

In a sweeping gesture with her staff, Vaylin filled the space before with water, knocking two of the five wolves sideways. Steam rose from their skin, and they whimpered in pain as their flesh burned raw and fell from their bodies.

The remaining three turned to face her, ignoring Fabien and his fire.

She held her staff before her. She was not going to back down.

They howled in unison, and it was surely the cry of death coming for her. With another flourish of her staff, she produced a second wave of water, freezing blades of ice in the mixture and pummeling the beasts with it. The two flanking the leader fell back and tried to attack Fabien and Madame Zahira.

The leader kept coming for Vaylin. It stood nearly as tall as her on all fours, swiping and biting its way through the water by sheer force, trying to break through her barrage. The beast was gaining, and Vaylin stepped backward.

It was impossibly strong. She tried freezing the water surrounding its feet, but it broke free every time.

Oberion moved toward her with a rushing, billowing air tunnel, trying to lift the hell hound backward. It rose from the ground and crashed into the paladin ranks, who immediately stabbed the animal, spears encased in white light, as it fought to stand. Another remaining hell hound leapt for Oberion and tackled him to the ground. His green robes ripped and tangled with the limbs of the beast, and Vaylin couldn't attack for fear of hitting Oberion.

The flare of his wrist band went up, but the heat did nothing to deter the animal. Vaylin felt an echo of pain in her arm and chest as though fangs sank into them—it was Oberion's pain she was feeling.

"No!" Vaylin shouted, and the crystal she had been diligently resisting all night came to life with a sudden, blinding fury. The power of the stone coursed through her body, giving her strength and boosting her magick.

Oberion's pain was her pain as she glared at the beast on top of him, eyes white with power. The hell hound flew off Oberion, crashing into a stone pillar. The stone cracked, and chunks fell from the column.

But Vaylin didn't stop.

She couldn't stop.

An invisible force pressed the hound against the wall, refusing to lessen now that it had been released after all this time. The energy of Incandesite flowed through her, filling the wretched beast with the force of a comet, the true power of the stone.

The hell hound was no match and disintegrated into nothing.

The last hounds battled Fabien and Madame Zahira. Vaylin reached for the beasts and poured Incandesite's power into every aspect of the foul beings. Like its fellows, it evaporated from cosmic power.

An eerie calm settled over the platform, and nothing emerged from the silver portal.

Vaylin rushed to Oberion.

He was covered in blood. His one was arm badly bitten, flesh hanging in ribbons and bending in the wrong direction. A glint of white poked out from the severed flesh, and a tar-like substance edged his wounds.

Of all the terrible things she had seen tonight, this was the worse. Shadows surrounded her, and everything felt threatening. She knelt over Oberion, his brown hair plastered to his forehead with dirt and sweat, blood running from gashes across his chest and neck. He seemed to hover somewhere between consciousness and unconsciousness, barely able to move or speak. She called on Incandesite and demanded it to heal Oberion, just like he did to her all those weeks ago.

Sensing the bond that connected them, Vaylin strengthened it with her magick.

Black poison extracted from his wound as she wove together flesh and bone.

Fabien and Madame Zahira stood beside her, watching her work with the light of the stone.

"He needs to be moved," Vaylin said once she was finished. It was her voice—and not her voice.

Oberion had made her promise not to use Incandesite, and she broke that to save him.

It was worth it.

The world tilted dangerously around her, and she seized, nearly collapsing over Oberion as Incandesite flared brighter, heavy around her neck. It pulled her toward the silver portal.

Fabien grabbed her shoulders to keep her upright and withdrew his hand quickly, shaking his hand in pain. "We can get him out of here, but we won't get far with this portal opened."

They needed more time, and she could fix this. She could seal the portal like she had in the Storm Peaks. How bad could it be if she used Incandesite one more time?

She'd survived the darkness once before. She could do it again.

"Take Oberion and get him away from here," she said.

Fabien and Madame Zahira looked at her apprehensively.

Vaylin burned with the power of Incandesite. She had to do this. Every instinct in her body screamed at her not to, but she ignored it. The only thing that mattered was sealing the portal.

She turned and ran for the Terra portal, stepping out of Chrysanthos and into the dread world of Nimrothag.

40

THE BREAKING OF BROTHERS

ALDWIN

ABRAXAS CONJURED ANOTHER GOLEM IN THE SMOKE SCREEN.

Aldwin had been fooled once again.

Marshall looked up when Abraxas spoke. He laid Avon gently on the ground and stood up. The elf wasn't bleeding anymore, and Aldwin didn't know if Avon was alive or dead.

The wanderer seemed to swell in size and looked positively grizzly as he rose to his feet, towering like a bear ready to charge Abraxas.

"Not another step closer if you know what's good for you," Abraxas warned, pulling another dagger from his belt and pointing it their direction.

Marshall, breathed heavily as he glared at Abraxas.

"Once I step through this portal, the whole thing is rigged to collapse after me. The ensuing vacuum will bring Ebenosite to Nim for me and generate enough power to destroy this entire embassy, along with anyone in it," Abraxas said triumphantly.

The memory of escaping the barn played in Aldwin's mind. He would not let that happen here, not to Panthea.

Aldwin took a step forward, holding his arm to his side. "It is not too late to stop this, Brax. There is nothing to be gained by going to that realm. Mundas lied to us. It's a world of darkness and evil."

"You don't give orders to me anymore. I choose my own destiny, not you."

"I am not the one you should be fighting, Brax. Mundas is messing with your mind and forcing you to do this stuff. I have always been on your side. I'm your brother, and I have always loved you." Aldwin fought to keep his voice calm and steady. His patience was wearing thin, and he knew he had one chance to stop Abraxas.

He managed a few more steps toward the portal, hand raised in a surrendering gesture. The pain in his shoulder throbbed. He'd be close to useless in a fight.

"Shut up!" Abraxas shook his head and swayed slightly. Dirt smeared his hollow cheeks.

Aldwin saw a flash of the little brother he knew behind those cold, dark eyes.

"Mundas only wanted to give us what we didn't have, and you could never accept that, could you?"

"Brax, I wanted to believe Mundas when we were kids, truly. But he wasn't the man we thought he was. Parents are just people in the end. He abused us, and when I finally refused to do what he wanted anymore, he used you to hurt me, to teach me a lesson. He has been sabotaging our relationship this entire time. I couldn't let it go on."

"Your wrong." Confusion warring on Abraxas's face.

"I'm telling you the truth. We are brothers, and when the world left us with nothing, we had each other. Remember how we would steal food together in Merkabah and sneak onto the roofs to eat it, imagining ourselves in one of those towers?"

The dagger in Abraxas's hand shook slightly. "You got your tower in the end." His face twitched, and a mean scowl returned to his lips. "You dragged us to Panthea when I begged you not to. Mundas told us to never go there."

"I brought us there so we would have a chance to heal and figure out our lives. Where would you be without the training you received here? Who would have fed and sheltered us all those years without Panthea? This place has supported us. It gave us what Mundas could not."

"You never gave us that chance. We could have gone anywhere, but you forced us here and I hated it."

"Is that why you came to Panthea now? To teach me a lesson?"

Abraxas sneered. "Of a sort. As much as I despise your position as gatekeeper, it has been rather useful for my plans."

Anger roiled in Aldwin's gut, numbing his shoulder. "You will never use me or Panthea ever again."

"We shall see. What happens to Panthea when you're no longer gatekeeper? No one will let you stay in charge after this. They will whisper that you let it happen because I'm your brother. No one will believe you when you tell them you tried to stop me."

"If you go through that portal, you will never return to Chrysanthos."

His words were a promise. A curse.

"So you think. I grow weary of this conversation, and you have wasted enough of my time." Abraxas took a step backwards.

"Wait!" Aldwin lurched forward. To his great shock, Abraxas froze. "What do you mean?"

Abraxas laughed wickedly. "The doors between worlds will not remain closed forever. Not now that Dyadralite has been found and awoken."

"You will not be able to return to Chrysanthos without Incandesite or Dyadralite, neither of which you have."

"Huh," Abraxas said in mock worry. "Good thing this wasn't the only trap set today."

"Vaylin," Marshall said weakly behind Aldwin. "What have you done to her?"

"*I* haven't done anything," Abraxas said coolly. "Although I can't speak for other creatures that must now be infiltrating Panthea Central and destroying your precious capital. You see, the true reason I needed Panthea was to create a portal at both ends of the line. While I distracted you down here, the real threat could move against Panthea."

Aldwin was rooted to the spot. "No."

"Traps within traps, brother." Abraxas tapped his temple. "We knew it was only a matter of time until Incandesite showed up at

Panthea, especially after your wanderer acquired the sphere. I'm sure Mundas is making quick work of your guardians now."

"How could you?" Aldwin asked. The monster that had haunted him for years was alive, and he didn't have the luxury of waking up from this nightmare.

"The kindhearted are easy to manipulate. I knew you'd do anything for a chance of redemption with me. You are very predictable, Aldwin. I'd work on that if I were you."

The sensation of magick rushed in the pit of Aldwin's stomach. It overflowed into his heart and throat, gutted with anger, regret, and sorrow.

He let it all go—his frustration, his humiliation, his grief—and hurled yellow-white fire at Abraxas with both arms. The pain in his shoulder was nonexistent as he emptied all of his emotions into the blast.

It never touched Abraxas, who disappeared with a single step through the silver veil of the archway. Aldwin's attack hit the portal and ricocheted off the metal into the sky. The night around him was all encompassing, a suffocating shadow smothered him, and he was stranded alone in the darkness.

No more Abraxas. He was in shock.

"Hearthfire!"

He'd lost his brother and who knew how many more at Panthea.

"Aldwin, get a grip on yourself man." Someone shook his uninjured arm.

His brother was gone, and Mundas had won in the end.

"This isn't over yet, Al. I need your help."

Help. *Help.*

The word triggered him, and he blinked rapidly.

The portal archway sent red sparks in all directions. The buzzing that permeated the air increased in volume, like a swarm of bees inside his skull.

"Aldwin, how do we stop the portal?" Marshall pressed. "If we don't do anything now, we better start running, or we're done for."

"I—" Aldwin started, unsure of himself. "I don't know."

"That's not good enough," Marshall shouted. "Come on. I think I know which lever it is, but I can't operate it. I got blasted last time I tried."

He helped Aldwin to the control boxes. The pain in Aldwin's shoulder was back and worse than ever. All the buttons and dials swirled. The screen on the monitor flashed "danger," and underneath, a timer counted down to implosion.

"Which one was it?" Aldwin asked blearily.

"This one." Marshall pointed at the red-stained handle.

Aldwin observed it for a moment before reaching with his good arm to try for himself.

"I wouldn't do that if I—"

Aldwin received the same shock as Marshall had, only ten times worse with his right shoulder mangled by Abraxas's psychic lightning. It felt as though hot coals had dropped onto his burn, the heat of it unbearable.

He cried out, and fresh blood welled from his wounds. His vision was slightly obscured by blackness, and it was all he could do to breath.

"I told you not to do that." Marshall pulled Aldwin to his feet as though he weighed nothing and held him steady. The world was a spinning mess of sparks and silver, swimming in shadows and starlight.

Aldwin's good hand gripped Marshall's shoulder.

"I know you're in pain, but we've got to hurry," Marshall said.

"The dagger." Aldwin's tongue felt like a piece of dried bark. "We need Br—" He couldn't say his name. Not now. "We need his dagger. There was a spell on it."

Marshall looked wildly around. "Where is it? I heard it fall when I tackled that golem."

Aldwin focused his mind's eye on the object and called it to him. What little magick he had left summoned the dagger out of the darkness and into his hand. He looked down the blade of the dagger. It was ugly to him, black and cruel, full of hateful intent. This would work, because if he had learned anything tonight, it was that his brother would want to prolong Aldwin's guilt and pain.

If the portal could be stopped, only Aldwin would be able to do it.

The final act to prove his brother was a traitor—sealing Abraxas off from Chrysanthos.

There would be no coming back from this.

With a shaking left hand, Aldwin ran the blade across his right palm. The dagger's bite was sharp, parting his skin like butter as the spell work gnawed its way into his flesh. Blood magick.

It was brutal, and Aldwin felt like he was being branded a traitor.

He gripped the handle and pulled.

The buzzing decreased. The portal sounded like a giant machine coming to rest as it groaned and clunked. Pieces of the metal brace surrounding the stone arch broke apart and hung at odd angles, several lengths of wire were steadily smoking, and the silver veil to Nimrothag faded away to nothing. Aldwin watched the empty space, holding his breath.

The golden veil did not return.

Pieces of the sphere at the zenith of the arch cracked like eggshells and tumbled away. A black stone fell from its remains, landing in the dirt like a sword plunged into the ground.

Aldwin was in a trance as he walked forward.

The aches in his body were nothing compared to Abraxas's betrayal. These last few years were nothing but lies. His own and his brother's. He deserved this pain, and it seared through him.

He knelt over Ebenosite like a child over an anthill.

The stone was the exact same size and shape as Incandesite. It was translucent black, like smoky quartz, but infinitely darker and with silver rutilations. The thin strands spread within the stone like a network, all intersecting and colliding with another.

It was mesmerizing, calling to him like a siren's song.

Aldwin reached forward and claimed Ebenosite for himself.

41

RISK

VAYLIN

DENSE SWIRLS OF GRAY MIST WOVE AROUND VAYLIN'S FEET AND LEGS AS she stepped further into Nimrothag. She stood in the middle of an amphitheater-like hollow, shallow ridges cut into its sides like the layers of a rice field. The crumbling archway was stone and stood at the center point of four intersecting paths. The air was stale, and the sky glowed opaquely yellow tinged with shades of gray. There was little in the way of shrubbery, only twisting roots, withered trees, and dead grasses. It reminded her of the jungles near Mingalla and how the world there was sucked of its life.

Vaylin glanced down at Incandesite. It looked different here than in Chrysanthos. It emitted a phosphorescent white glow, and the red stones looked like drops of liquid gold sprayed across the crystal's surface. It shimmered in the pale light, glinting as she rotated it. It was like peering through a window that captured fractals of light and froze them in time. Pure starlike and comet power made physical.

She could've sworn the stone was whispering and strained her ears to hear. It was telling her something, a warning.

A rock shifted, and Vaylin snapped her head up out of the trance.

She blinked, realizing her feet had carried her away from the portal.

Closing her fingers around Incandesite, she backtracked, keeping eyes on the surroundings. All she had to do was create a shield around the arch in this place, and she could return to Panthea. Nothing but Ebenosite would have the capability of destroying the shield and even if it remained open, they would all be safe.

If possible, it seemed to get quieter the longer she was here, which didn't make sense.

Where were all the creatures they had fought? Wouldn't they be nearby, or did the guardians destroy them all?

Trying not to panic, she gently pried Incandesite from its metal cage, removed her trusted opal, and fitted the stone into the end of her staff. The phosphorescence bloomed brighter, and the stone's power coursed through her staff and up her arm. It was not the same feeling as when she'd used it on the mountaintop or just now at Panthea. This time, she was elated, not drained. Energy rushed into her exhausted limbs, and her heart felt like it was infinitely expanding and collapsing in on itself.

Emboldened, she envisioned the spell, centered her magick, and called on the power of Incandesite.

Vaylin walked in a slow circle around the arch, imagining a dome of light comprised of the five elements, the building blocks of all magick and matter held together with psychic force and laced with the cosmic power of Incandesite. Her whispered spell sounded like a soft melody, rising and falling gently like waves along the shore. There was a constant push and pull with Incandesite. She was learning her limits with the stone, intuiting the movements of its energy like a dance. The magick flowed through her and into the golden bubble forming around the stone archway. It was divine, and she had never witnessed anything so pure. She needed to anchor twelve points of the spell into the ground. Only three more to go and she could return to Panthea. To Oberion.

The portal could close at any moment if she didn't hurry.

Two more points left. She was so close.

"This is fascinating," an empty voice said behind her.

Vaylin halted her spell casting and turned.

The shape of a man loomed from the gray mist, which had formed thick walls of white around her. She couldn't see anything but the man and her shield. The hum of her spell died slowly, and the light seemed to drop a little after she stepped into the dome of light. He looked solid, but an odd transparency flickered around and throughout his body every few seconds. Like he was blinking in and out of existence.

"Who are you?" Vaylin reacted instinctively and pointed Incandesite at the unknown figure.

The scraping, raking sound of claws came from the fog, and here and there, limbs of beasts and spiked tails of monsters came in and out of sight.

"Someone who has been waiting a *very* long time for your arrival," he replied.

This did nothing to ease her feeling of imminent death.

She kept her voice full of bravado she did not feel. "My arrival?" she said in mock confusion. "How could anyone know I would arrive here, on this day, at this exact moment?"

The peculiar man took steady, assured steps toward her, fog closing behind him, making her feel trapped. A different type of claustrophobia. The details of his face were hard to make out as the shadows around him moved constantly, always keeping him slightly obscured.

"Yes, your arrival. See, I knew it was only a matter of time before someone from Panthea ended up here. There are only seven jump points, and this one connects to all of them. The doorway opening caused quite the disturbance these last few hours, as I'm sure you can tell. I see you have enjoyed my welcoming gifts." He eyed her.

For the first time, she was aware of how much blood and gore covered her. She didn't care. She just wanted to leave. Her apprehension grew as the power of Incandesite slipped from her, leaving her weakened.

"As soon as I saw that beautiful burst of energy pulse through the world, I knew it was time." His voice was a slither across her skin.

"Sorry to disappoint, but I don't plan on being here much longer," Vaylin said with a bit of impatience. She had two more anchors to complete, and then she could leave this dreadful place. How could she do it without turning her back on this thing? There was no way it would let her continue casting.

"Good, let's skip the niceties. I've waited far too long for this opportunity, and I don't plan on letting it slip from my fingers." He took another step toward her and came into the dim radiance of her golden shield. His face was gaunt with large, shining eyes that were ghostly white.

The small hairs on her arms rose pin straight. Whatever this thing was, it was pure evil.

He looked at her hungrily, yellow-black teeth showing behind skin like parchment. "I want that lovely stone you have brought here." His eyes flicked to the staff then back to her face. "You will give it to me, or you will regret denying me with your dying breath."

Vaylin knew he would kill her like any other foul thing that lived in this world without hesitation. Could this monster even touch Incandesite, the crystal of light and goodness?

"Why do you want the stone?" She didn't know what made her ask. She was protective of Incandesite and was appalled to consider it in someone else's hands. It was her duty to keep the stone safe. It was their only weapon against the ruptures, and Panthea needed it.

She needed it.

"I thought you wanted to make this short," the man replied.

The shadows around him moved faster, covering him as he took another step, nearly at the edge of her dome. The effect caused him to blend into the background, becoming nearly invisible.

"It has been an age since I conversed with someone who wasn't begging for their lives at my feet," he continued imperiously. "Seeing how I have infinite time here and you do not, I have no objection getting to know one another." He grinned wickedly. "I want the stone for plans your tiny mind cannot understand. The complexities of magick and the energy that exists between this world and Chrysanthos are far too intricate to explain, but let's just say, to those who know how to wield the mighty power of Dyadralite, the world is theirs to control and change as they desire."

Vaylin listened, captivated by the strange man, knowing he spoke true.

She had little time, while he did not. If she were stuck here, how long could she hold out in this bubble? Without escape, it was inevitable that she would be trapped.

That left her with two choices: fight or flight.

The part of her that was flooded with Incandesite's magick wanted to stay and fight, to burn this thing into nothingness. The other part was her dwindling magick, strength, and time to finish what she came here to do. The light of the shield dimmed with the passing seconds, and one of her anchor points had come undone, leaving three points to be completed.

Why wasn't the spell holding?

"Aww, your magick is struggling," he said with mocking sadness. "First lesson about this place, girl, is that the magick you have and channel in Panthea doesn't work here. This is another world. The same elements exist here but with a different base structure, thus manifesting in a similar but opposite principle of composition of the elements in Chrysanthos. Let me demonstrate for you."

He didn't move, but all around Vaylin, a creeping cold leaked into her shield. Poking, and investigating her defenses. Shadows pressed into her magick, encasing her own shield with its own. She reacted instinctively and pointed her staff up, the brightness of the shield was blinding as it filled with fire and light.

The shadows whisked away like curls of steam but remained to hover several feet over it. They solidified in the air above and laid across her shield like a blanket. The shadows ate away at it like a thousand ants. Her knees felt weak, and she had to steady herself with the staff as the shadows weighed her down.

Incandesite pulled on her magick, to use more, to fight.

But she couldn't. There was a subtle pain in her chest, tightening with every passing second, just like in the mountain pass.

Her magick was waning, draining away from her second by second.

Incandesite was trying to consume her. She had asked for too much, and now she was going to pay for it with her life.

Her mind flashed to Oberion. The power she was pulling wasn't just her own but his too. It was the bond. Had she taken too much?

Was he still alive? She stepped back, trying to get closer to home, to freedom.

The demon was closer now, laughing at her feeble attempts to work magick. "You were never fit to use Incandesite. It is a stone created by the cosmos, and one has to understand the magick of both realities to truly wield Dyadralite. All others are unworthy."

A crackling noise came from behind her. Vaylin glanced over her shoulder. The edges of the portal were deteriorating.

Time was up, she had to leave or be trapped here.

Oberion came to mind, those blue-gray eyes flaring into her heart.

Vaylin yelled her frustration to the darkness and pointed the staff at the demon. A beam of light shot directly for the center of its chest.

It never reached him. Shadows coalesced in front of him to block the attack, swallowing the light Vaylin had conjured. Pain racked her body, Incandesite as pulling the last dregs of her magick out of her.

She had to stop this. Incandesite would steal Oberion's magick if the bond was still intact. It is what Skyminer had warned them of. She couldn't allow that to happen. Couldn't allow Oberion to be the cost of her choice to come here.

The portal inched closed, and the demon laughed.

Vaylin made an all-out sprint for the archway.

"You're not going anywhere." He shuddered and blinked out of sight.

She was yards away from the portal and threw her staff like a javelin at the closing archway. If she could get Incandesite away from this demon, it would be enough. Even if she didn't make it.

A black mass flashed in front of her, and the wooden staff exploded, sending splinters of wood everywhere and knocking her off balance. Incandesite soared through the air like a shooting star, away from the portal. The demon shuddered again, reappearing in the trajectory of Incandesite. He reached up and caught the stone effortlessly, triumph in his eyes as he turned to deal with Vaylin. Incandesite flashed brilliantly in his hand, and pain pierced her heart like an arrow.

She tripped, still running towards the portal, and the momentum of her fall carried her through the silver veil.

It was too late to do anything else. She was out of time and had failed, leaving Incandesite in Nimrothag with its new keeper—a demon who knew about Dyadralite's true power and now had access to Panthea.

42

BINDING

VAYLIN

VAYLIN ROSE TO CONSCIOUSNESS BLEARILY. EVERYTHING WAS SORE, AND her mind was murky. It was dim and quiet where she lay. The familiar scents of herbs and other medicinal ingredients soothed her. It brought memories of easier times spent in the apothecary, mixing healing tonics with Jessamine Solance and working with familiar plants and flowers. Those memories were detached and far away, like someone else had experienced them.

Flashes of that night came to her hard and fast. The golden shield, the demonic man, and Incandesite soaring into its hands. The absence of its weight around her neck caused her heart to ache.

Curling onto one side, she buried her face into the pillow and let the tears fall, body racked with sobs. They were warm against her cheeks, leaving salty trails down her nose before absorbing into the pillowcase. She had failed everyone when she'd lost Incandesite. The demon had known Dyadralite's secrets and used his knowledge against her in those final moments, taking his prize.

Vaylin shuddered as she held on to her pillow and relived that moment again and again, the consequences of her actions unbearable.

Disappointment. Regret.

What did this mean for her? Would Aldwin strip her title as an

Elite? Had she singlehandedly created a bigger problem than the one they were already in? Would anyone forgive her for being so reckless? Would Oberion?

She knew the real reason why she'd gone into Nimrothag that night. It had come to her when she'd seen Oberion broken after the hell hound attack. Bond or no bond, she couldn't bear to see Oberion broken and injured.

Her feelings for him had grown strong these last few weeks. He had been there for her, comforted her when she was lost, and fought with her and for her. It was his voice that pulled her back on that mountain pass, and the thought of never seeing him again drove her desperation to save them all.

Vaylin was willing to risk her life to keep him safe, and the power of that decision, that emotion, frightened her. She couldn't remember the last time she'd felt this way about someone. Her choices and movements were always by the book and safe. Made with her in mind and no one else. That was how she'd become an Elite Guardian. Examining her most recent behavior made her feel like a fool in love, taking pointless risks for what? Losing the best weapon they had to stop this demon and these ruptures in their world.

It was stupidity at its finest.

There was a tap on her doorway, accompanied by the aroma of crisp winds and petrichor. Oberion's presence was so familiar that she could tell it was him without looking. She sensed his energy getting closer and she pulled herself together and began to face him.

Vaylin wiped her face inconspicuously on the corner of the sheet and rolled over to face him. Her face felt puffy, and her red-rimmed eyes stung as she tried to clear them.

"Hello," she croaked, wiping her nose on her sleeve.

Her head spun as she sat up and tried not to squirm under his penetrating stare.

Oberion looked bad but he was alive. The bruise around his temple was yellowish purple, and his body was speckled with scabs and scrapes. His once injured arm was whole and unblemished once more. He would have been much worse without Incandesite. At least she did one thing right that night.

Another pang of guilt twisted in her stomach at the thought.

"That hell hound did quite a number on me. I would have lost the arm if you weren't there to save me." He tried to make light of what had happened.

Vaylin didn't react. She was a stone in deep water, lying in clouds of mud and filth, detached from herself. The fact that he was alive and talking to her was too much to handle as gratitude filled her heart. Tears threatened again, and she looked to the ceiling, trying to stop them from falling.

It didn't work.

"I thought you were gone," she said in a small, cracked voice. "I thought you were gone, and I just reacted. I used Incandesite to heal you. Once it did, I thought... I thought it could save all of us. I thought I could give you time to get away. I don't know if that decision was mine or Incandesite's, but I did it and now everything is lost because of me."

Oberion pulled a chair over and scooted it right next to the bed, reaching for her hand and holding it gently. She squeezed his fingers, relishing how solid he felt, the pulse that beat beneath the skin proof that he was real.

"It's all right," he said. "I thought I was done for there too. I would've been if you hadn't saved me. I could feel your rage and pain through all of it. Even when you were in Nimrothag."

"That wasn't me. It was Incandesite," she said glumly.

"You were the one who wielded it. It was your energy I felt, not the stone's."

"If I hadn't used it, it would still be here in Panthea. When I saw you get hurt, I don't know what happened to me. Incandesite took over. The only thought in my head was to save you, to protect you. I thought I could shield everyone from within Nimrothag. I was convinced it would work. We didn't have Ebenosite, and I had to try something."

Oberion looked as if he were struggling between shouting and at a complete loss of words. He hung his head, and pulled his hand free of hers to cover his eyes. "Is that why you went through the portal? I wondered what could have driven you there. You were the one who begged me not to go into it when it appeared, and then you went yourself so willingly. I didn't understand." His voice sounded restrained, as if he kept a tight leash on his emotions. But he couldn't hide the anger and hurt in his voice from Vaylin. "What if you had gotten stuck? No one would have known where you were or how to help you. You could have been lost—or killed! What happened to our promise?"

"I never promised you anything," Vaylin said solemnly and felt wretched for it.

Oberion recoiled. The hurt in his expression plain, and she flinched, scared for the first time at the true depths of Incandesite's power. Scared of Oberion and what was between them. The khans cold voice echoed in her mind. *You cannot trust those with Elder blood.* Guess he was right about her after all. Acid burned in her chest at the very thought.

"Oberion, I–I thought I had control. I almost finished creating this shield to protect us and come back, but then this demon came and stopped me—"

Oberion paled. "Demon? What demon? Tell me everything that happened once you crossed over."

She explained everything. He listened, not saying a word the entire time. Vaylin thought he was either incredibly angry or incredibly shocked. Or both. He contemplated her with those blue-gray eyes, full of stormy emotions.

Vaylin held his gaze, waiting for him to speak or to react. He didn't. He only let the silence spiral on.

"Say something," she pleaded.

"What is there to say? What's done is done, and we can't go back and change it."

"I'm sorry. I didn't think that was going to happen."

Oberion rolled his eyes, visibility exacerbated. "That's exactly the point. You didn't think. You never do! You told me Incandesite wasn't influencing you. You lied. And you broke your promise to me. Now that I think about it, you technically never answered me, did you? Then, without a single hesitation, you jumped a world away, risking our lives, Panthea, and the stone. When I was unconscious after the attack, I had dreams that you were in trouble. And I could do anything about it. Do you know what that felt like?"

The world closed in around her, darkness edged her vision. Yes, she did know. It was exactly what she experienced when he was bleeding out before her.

"Did it ever occur to you what *I* would have gone with you. To wake up and find out you were gone was awful. No closure, no anything. All because you felt my life was worth more than yours. Well, here's some news for you, Vaylin. It's not."

"Why is my life more important than yours?" Her heart was on fire.

"Because I can't live in a world that you're not part of," he shouted, face anguished as the truth of the statement settled over the pair of them. "Because I would rather go down fighting with you, as an Elite Guardian, than attend your funeral and lament the fact that I wasn't next to you in the end."

Vaylin wanted to believe these words were real. Not fabrications of Incandesite. How could she be sure?

Incandesite wasn't here.

Their bond was broken. Wasn't it?

Did that make this genuine? His words rang in her own soul, feeling and understanding exactly what he was going through.

"That is precisely why I made my choice," she said. "Something snapped in me when I saw you half-dead and mangled. Leaving didn't matter anymore. If I died in the attempt, I would have been just another Elite Guardian doing her duty."

"I'd care," he said fiercely.

She glared at him. "Don't you get it? We are all in worse danger now than ever before. If I had achieved what I meant to, the portals would have been cut off from Nimrothag forever. Panthea Central and all of Chrysanthos would be have protected with both stones residing in this world."

"But you didn't." His words stung. "You didn't actually know if that would have helped at all. You took a risk, and we lost Incandesite because of it. If anything, we're in as dangerous of a position as we were when this all started."

"How so?" Her guilt was heavy, and she didn't understand what he was trying to say. Whether she deserved to be forgiven after all that had transpired.

"We knew something had happened to Incandesite when we couldn't find it on your person. Aldwin acquired Ebenosite in the Terra Nation and brought it back. If things had gone according to plan, we would have had both halves of Dyadralite and been forced to decide what to do with it. The fact that a demon in Nimrothag now possesses Incandesite is less frightening to me than knowing the stones are worlds apart."

"They are keys, Oberion. The demon can use the stone to gain access to Panthea! The stones have the power to connect our worlds. Incandesite connects to Chrysanthos and Ebenosite connects to Nimrothag. If he creates another portal, then we are right back to square one."

"We have no idea the type of technology or magick that Nimrothag has." he said calmly.

"That demon sent those creatures after us to get Incandesite. We have Ebenosite. Don't you think he will come after Ebenosite once he has the power of Incandesite under control?"

"Vaylin, we can't say, all right? As far as we know, it was only ever Incandesite that he wanted. The stone is an ancient and powerful object. All artifacts of this nature are desired by many throughout the ages."

"That demon knows about Dyadralite and what it's capable of when both halves of the stone are united."

"But everything in that world is 'of darkness'. How could there ever be a *good* caretaker for the stone by that standard? Besides, it's the stone of light. Maybe creatures there can't even use it because the power is opposite to their own."

"You're wrong. That demon will come back for us. Mark my words. It wants Ebenosite, and it won't stop until it unites the stones."

"Why though? To what end?" He searched her face for answers.

"I— It's just...a feeling."

"A feeling?" Oberion raised an eyebrow. "Say this demon comes back to Panthea, what's it going to do? If your magick was struggling there, by the same logic wouldn't this demon's magick struggle here?"

"If he has both halves of Dyadralite, it won't matter." She refused to give up on the idea.

"Say this demon creates a portal to Panthea, of all places, he is dropping his entrance point to this world into a stronghold of magick filled with elementors, paladins, and us. We would be there instantly to stop him."

"Then we are still in danger, which is ultimately proving my point."

"That's life, Vaylin! There is always going to be *something*, and you can never stop it. I think the real reason you are holding on to this is because you are determined to punish yourself for making a mistake."

"I did make a mistake, Oberion, and it cost us the one tool we had against the ruptures. Whatever happens going forward, we need Incandesite back and we need to hide Ebenosite at all costs. It's the only way to truly stop this from happening again." She was exhausted in mind, body, and soul.

"There is no proof of *this* happening again. The source causing the ruptures was Aldwin's brother in the Terra Embassy, and he's gone."

Vaylin pointed at the floor below them. "Nimrothag has been connected to Panthea from the beginning of time, and it was shut down for a reason. It still exists and will open up again."

"Be that as it may, it doesn't change that we are here and we need to move forward."

"You're only happy because the stone is finally gone. Well, guess what? That also means our bond is too." She was wretched for saying it. It was the truth however, and unless it was acknowledged, how could she ever be sure what was real between them?

Oberion drew back, visibly caught off guard. He never liked that she had found Incandesite. He was afraid of the stone and always has been.

"So. What if I am? Does that make me a monster because the woman I love is less likely to kill herself with it now that it's gone?" They both seemed to register what came from his lips and looked at each other with apprehension.

"Love," she repeated, almost like a question.

He continued to stare at her before answering boldly, "Yes."

Vaylin didn't know what to do with herself. She wanted to flee from the room, to never see this man again because he made her so damn crazy…and yet she wanted to hold on to him. To fight off every darkness and fowl thing in this world side by side.

The pain of the last few days was fresh. Incandesite was gone, and she questioned her position at Panthea, her every thought and action, unsure of anything. Oberion seemed to be holding his breath, waiting for her.

She couldn't meet his eyes. All the air seemed to vanish from the room, her lungs, as she forced herself to say what she had to. "Perhaps we shouldn't."

"Shouldn't what?"

"Shouldn't love each other. Our lives are at risk, and countless others hang in the balance at Panthea while Dyadralite in play. I don't know what is right anymore. I need time to sort myself out. We both know Incandesite has influenced our behaviors and created this bond. I don't know what is real. If what's between us is real." She hated the words, but she had to say them. He had to know where she was coming from.

"I felt these feelings for you long before we ever reached the Strom Peaks and that bond was formed. You are my equal in every way, and we have given each other strength to fight these fights and survive this. What you did in Nimrothag was because of your love for me and Panthea. Incandesite fed on that love. That was the bravest thing I have ever seen. That power was your own strength came and from your heart, not Incandesite."

"And yet here we are, hurt and broken because of it."

"There's always risk, Vaylin. I think to truly love someone means you have to accept the pain that comes along with it. You have to be vulnerable to truly know who is worthy of your love."

His words unraveled her. Couldn't he see her falling apart because of all this? She had nothing to give him and needed time to piece herself back together.

"You have your answer. We do it together, like we have been this whole time. I promise I care about you and you can be sure of this. Of us. We won't let any harm come to the others at Panthea so long as we can help it."

She looked directly at him. "You can't make a promise like that."

"That's it, then? Everything we have gone through is out the window because you are scared. Our kiss was real, Vaylin. I have never been kissed like how you did in that corridor. No stone or crystal could have made up what I felt, what you felt. I can't forget it, and I don't want to."

She didn't know what to say. She thought her resolve was solid. Now it wavered. If this was the right choice, why did it hurt so much?

"You're wrong. And you know you're wrong." Oberion stood from his chair, which toppled backward onto the floor. "I'll be here for you when you're ready to admit that."

Vaylin's heart broke a little further at the tears sparkling in his eyes and the temperature in the room dropped several degrees.

Oberion walked away, leaving her more alone and desperate than ever before.

FROM THE ASHES

MARSHALL

MARSHALL WALKED THROUGH THE CARNAGE ON THE PORTAL DAIS WHEN they returned to Panthea Central the day after everything happened. He was astounded by the gore and number of massacred dark creatures. Thankfully, many of their own had not suffered any long-term injuries and no one had died. It had been a close call, and Marshall was grateful that he and Avon had made it out of the Terra Embassy alive. Avon thoroughly admonished him for wasting an entire bottle of Telrithian on him, but seeing as it saved his life, he dropped the matter quickly. Marshall didn't care.

In the week that passed, Oberion, Aldwin, and Neko made full recoveries. Neko was finally released from Abraxas's enchantment after months of captivity. Aldwin confessed his brother's betrayal to the politicians and senators of Chrysanthos and that he was the cause of all these distressing events. Aldwin Hearthfire now faced a formal inquiry into his actions as gatekeeper and would have to stand trial to be proven innocent and keep his position.

Word spread of this scandal, but luckily Dyadralite remained a mystery to the public. The official story was that a magickal disturbance glitched the portals' power source and the Elite Guardians were able to stabilize the premises—which was mostly true. The Terra portal, however, remained offline, and that was the biggest news everyone was discussing.

Vaylin recovered and had private words with Aldwin. He did not blame her for what happened with Incandesite. On the contrary, he commended her for risking her own life to try to save Panthea and that even the strongest hearts could fall victim to the power of such objects. Marshall could hardly imagine what she was going through right now. Entering Nimrothag was enough to make anyone's head spin. She was going back to the Aqua Realm to follow up on the ruptures and see for herself if they had disappeared now that Abraxas's portal was destroyed. Marshall privately thought it would be good for her to go back and be in the jungle for a while. Nothing was as good for the soul as returning home after a long journey.

Aldwin called another council once they all were relatively healed and told them all their top priority to keep the knowledge of Dyadralite secret. Vaylin and Neko were the most affected by what happened the night the portals collapsed. Both had dark circles under their eyes and were reluctant to talk much. Marshall knew they both felt some level of guilt about the roles they had played in this outcome. Aldwin did his best to comfort them, saying, "We cannot blame ourselves for what has happened. We acted as best we could with the knowledge we had and now must work to rebuild."

Oberion seemed down too and didn't speak that entire meeting. Perhaps they all needed some time to let the dust settle.

It was after this meeting that Marshall had finally caught up with Aldwin for a private word. He wanted to discuss what would happen with Avon and the southern elves in the aftermath of everything.

"Do you think this will change much here?" Marshall asked.

"It's hard to say." Aldwin fingered Ebenosite, a new habit of his, which hung on a chain around his neck. "The portal network appears stable for now, but we will need to come up with a solution with the Terra portal and proceed cautiously. No one can know we have Ebenosite or the significant role it played in these events. We cannot ignore the position it puts Panthea in either."

"Vaylin seems to think danger is inevitable and that something like this will happen again in the future."

He nodded gravely. "I think she's right. But as long as we have Ebenosite, time is on our side. We are also aware of the threat, which makes it easier to prepare for. We need to conduct further research into the stones and see if these claims about Nimrothag and the difference in magick between our worlds are true. The more we can learn with the time given to us, the better we will be."

Marshall's eyes flicked to the chain around Aldwin's neck. *Like calls to like, Ebenosite will call on the darkness within.*

He hesitated, not sure if he wanted to give voice to the warning in his heart. How much darkness had now seeded itself in Aldwin?

Aldwin looked miserable, and Marshall asked tentatively, "How are you doing? I know with Abraxas… It must be hard to process."

Aldwin couldn't cover his brother's actions and had to bear the punishment of it. It took him a long moment before responding, head bowed, the chain of Ebenosite glinting darkly between the folds of his robes. "My adopted father passed on his obsession with portals and grandeur to my little brother. He made us believe that Nimrothag was a place where we could be kings, to start our lives over. It was all a lie of course, but Brax could never see that. I have always despised them for their beliefs. I have felt isolated and ashamed of them my whole life. I came to Panthea for a fresh start, and I swear I will never betray this place. The fact that it was my brother who did this pains me deeply. I always knew this existed within him, and I thought he would be strong enough to withstand its lure. I thought I taught him to be more, to be better. I was wrong."

Marshall put his hand on Aldwin's back, and the gatekeeper slackened his shoulders at the touch. "We aren't always born into the family we want. It's about finding your soul family, the people who aren't blood that care enough about you to make them family. It doesn't make you a bad person for wanting to be rid of Mundas's oppression and abuse. No sane person would. By the sounds of it, he put you through what no child should ever go through. Your brother made his choice, and you've made yours. Look at who you have become because of your trials and tribulations. You are stronger than your brother and father combined and have done everything within your capability to help them. It's time to let that burden go."

"Abraxas... He jumped through the portal to escape me. I don't know if he survived, but if Vaylin did, then so did he, right? He made it so the only way to destroy the portal was with my blood, *our* blood. I was the one who banished him from Panthea, and now he's trapped in Nimrothag. Doesn't that make me as bad as he said I was?" Aldwin's face was a mask of pain and confusion.

Marshall's heart went out to him. "Only you can say what defines you. Abraxas may or may not be alive. If he survived the jump, there is still a whole world of darkness he needs to face. I think the veils between our worlds are thinner than we realize, and with Dyadralite in play, who knows what can happen. Put it from your mind for now. If your brother returns, he might not be the person you knew when he crossed over."

Aldwin brought a hand to his face and wiped away the tears that had come. Marshall stopped walking and pulled the gatekeeper into a tight hug. He was almost a foot taller than Aldwin, who grasped Marshall tightly as he cried. All he could do was hold on to his friend, his gatekeeper, as he wept.

They stood like that for a long moment before Marshall spoke again.

"What you did, you had to do for everyone here. Abraxas forced you to make that choice, and it does not make you a terrible person," Marshall said. "I, for one, appreciate that you are our gatekeeper. You've given your life to Panthea, and no one can deny you that. The right choices are never the easy ones. It's hard to accept that now, but you will in time."

"You think so?" Aldwin asked hesitantly, face pressed against Marshall's chest.

"Yes. If you ever need someone to talk to, I'm always here for you."

"Thanks, Marshall. You're a good man."

They broke apart, and Marshall rubbed Aldwin's shoulder gruffly as he cleaned his face.

"Speaking of me being such a good man," Marshall said, changing the topic, "I have a proposal to run past you—if you'd be willing to listen."

His face went hot, and he focused on his composure. It was a simple request. For the first time in a long time, Marshall was going to ask for what he wanted.

"Go on." Amusement flashed on Aldwin's features.

"I, er—Avon and I have formed a...well, I don't know what you'd call it technically, but it's a"—he cleared his throat—"sort of companionship. He saved my life more than once lately, and in light of recent events I think it might be safer, and best for Panthea really, if I had someone with me during my reconnaissance missions. I can't find it anywhere in our code that forbids the wanderer from having aid, and I thought he would be right for the job."

He crossed his fingers in his pockets and kept his posture relaxed as he waited for Aldwin's response. He didn't want to seem too eager but couldn't pretend it wasn't important.

"I think that would be quite amendable." Aldwin smiled.

"You mean it?" A flash of heat washed through Marshall's body, and he tried unsuccessfully to suppress a grin.

"Yes. These are dangerous times, and I think we could all use someone we trust by our side."

"I couldn't agree more." Marshall positively beamed. He felt like he was floating inches above the ground and couldn't wait to tell Avon the good news.

"I have one condition though." Aldwin held up a finger.

Marshall's face stiffened as he came back down to earth with a bump. "And what might that be?"

"Ask him if he would consider being the official Elven Liaison for Panthea," Aldwin said coolly. "We need to contact the northern elves and strengthen our relationships with them. They might have knowledge we need regarding Dyadralite and Nimrothag. With Avon helping us, they may be more persuadable to relinquish that information. The elven kings and queens must be made privy to this information and the truth behind the attack here if we are to gain their support. I believe the elves could be tremendous allies for Panthea. I'm entrusting this top-secret mission to the pair of you."

Marshall mulled over his words. Aldwin had a point. It wasn't what he was expecting, but he could see nothing wrong with the proposal. In fact, he was excited at the prospect of visiting the northern elves. It had been some time since he'd seen their forest citadel. But he had to be sure about one tiny, little detail. "So, it would just be the two of us going there together then, correct?"

"Yes. You two will go together and learn what you can. I'd like for you both to set off within the week, if possible. Time is of the essence." Aldwin's eyes twinkled.

A rush of gratitude swept through Marshall. "I couldn't agree more. I'll find Avon straight away if we need to start planning a trip north."

The friends walked together until they reached the dining hall, and Marshall held out his hand to shake Aldwin's before setting off to find Avon.

Avon was in the stables, brushing down one of the southern horses that he had dragged all the way up here after the attack on the Terra Embassy. He spoke to it in elvish. The horse whinnied and pushed its large body into Avon, who laughed.

He looked up to see Marshall coming and waved. "How did the council go?"

"Some good news, some bad news," Marshall said evasively. "Aldwin faces an inquiry about the events in the Terra Embassy. Hopefully, he will be cleared of all charges."

"Aldwin has enough to deal with now that the Terra portal is down. Once the news gets out that it was his brother who caused all these atrocities, he'll have a hard time proving his innocence."

"I think he will be okay. He is doing all he can to defend Panthea even as we speak, and his choices in the Terra Embassy saved us from a worse fate. He actually gave me my next assignment already."

"Yeah? And where are you off too now?" Avon said, unamused.

"Somewhere up north."

"I bet you'll be happy to leave here and get away from everyone."

"Sure am. He's also approved my request for an official companion during my missions too." Marshall grinned.

"Really?" Avon did not look up from brushing the horse. "I suppose it will be you and another Elite Guardian?"

"No, actually. It's you."

Avon's eyes went wide as he stopped brushing the horse and turned to Marshall. His gold dermal piercings glinted against his dark skin, and the memory of their kiss seared Marshall like fire.

"He is offering you an official position at Panthea as our Elven Liaison. You will be in direct contact between the northern and southern elven kingdoms to help us strengthen our relationships with them. Think you can handle it?"

"Oh," Avon said, a blank expression on his face. "But I-I don't...I'm not."

Marshall spoke over Avon's stammering. "If you accept, this means you get to join me on my mission to the Northern Citadel and other unknown and dangerous adventures I have yet to be assigned."

Avon's jaw dropped as he realized what Marshall was saying.

After a few speechless moments, his shock subsided, and he stared at Marshall in total disbelief. "You asked for someone to follow you?"

"I did." Marshall smirked at the look on Avon's face. "I take that as a yes?"

Avon lit up with an inner radiance. His beautiful yellow eyes reflected the flashes of gold from his skin, and the effect was stunning.

Marshall reached across the horse to hold Avon's hand. His slim, dark fingers dropped the brush and wove between Marshall's tanned ones.

In that moment, Marshall felt like he discovered his truest self and was finally aligned with his heart.

Avon grinned. "Then we mustn't wait."

ACKNOWLEDGMENTS

This book has been such a tremendous effort of love and dedication over the years. There are so many people to give thanks too.

Firstly, I'd like thank Melissa Koberlein for her loyalty to publishing and the genuine knowledge that she teaches her students. Your advice and opinions have been instrumental to my success, and I can't wait to see what our future in publishing looks like.

To my classmates, Laurel and Anna, and fellow authors who have inspired me over the years to keep working on my manuscript until the end. Holding this book for the first time brought so much joy to my heart and I couldn't have done it without you.

To my wonderful editor, Jeni Chappelle, who knows exactly what a story needs and how to deliver the most meaningful and inclusive message for readers. You're the best.

A big thank you to Emily's World of Design for creating such a beautiful cover for me. You were infinitely patient and I can't wait to see future book designs in this series.

To my coworkers, especially Justin Rupert, who has always believed in me and listened to my endless chatter about this book. Thank you for never making me feel bad for pursuing my dreams.

And lastly, to my family, partner, and friends. Thank you for all the love and support you have ever given me. I hope this book makes you smile.

ABOUT THE AUTHOR

Sarah Neville is an adult fantasy writer and lifelong artist from Bethlehem, Pennsylvania. From slinging cocktails to crafting manuscripts, her strongest skill set resides in the act of creating. She passionately believes there is nothing more magical than seeing one's artistic vision become a reality.

Her roots as an artist taught her how to bring her imagination to life through pen, paper, and ink. This evolution has led her work into the vast wilderness of the publishing world, and what it means to be a writer and creator in the 21st century. She started Panthea Publications in 2020 and is releasing her debut novel *"The Breaking"* in October 2021.

MAP MAKING

BY PANTHEA PUBLICATIONS

Panthea Publications specializes in creating and printing maps for authors. We offer clients the opportunity to customize every aspect of their design. This includes stylistic choices, level of details, decorative borders, illustrated icons, compass layout, and much more. All of our maps are hand-drawn digitally and completely unique to each individual.

Scan QR code for more information